Kat Richardson i⁣s ⁣⁣⁣⁣⁣⁣⁣⁣⁣⁣⁣⁣⁣⁣⁣⁣⁣⁣⁣⁣⁣⁣⁣⁣⁣⁣⁣⁣ed Los Angeles in the 90s. She curre⁣⁣⁣⁣⁣⁣⁣⁣⁣⁣⁣⁣⁣⁣⁣⁣⁣⁣⁣ houseboat in Seattle with her husband, and a crotchety old cat and two ferrets. She rides a motorcycle, shoots target pistol and does not own a TV.

her website at www.katrichardson.com.

Also by Kat Richardson:

Greywalker

PIATKUS

First published in Great Britain in 2007 by Piatkus Books
First published in the United States in 2007 by ROC,
A division of Penguin Group (USA) Inc., New York, USA

A CIP catalogue record for this book
is available from the British Library

ISBN 978-0-7499-3895-6

Papers used by Piatkus are natural, recyclable products made from
wood grown in sustainable forests and certified in accordance with
the rules of the Forest Stewardship Council

Data manipulation by Phoenix Photosetting, Chatham, Kent
www.phoenixphotosetting.co.uk

Printed and bound by Mackays of Chatham, Chatham, Kent

Piatkus Books
An imprint of
Little, Brown Book Group
100 Victoria Embankment
London EC4Y 0DY

An Hachette Livre UK Company

www.piatkus.co.uk

POLTERGEIST

Kat Richardson

THIS IS FOR ALL THE PEOPLE WORKING TO
LEGALIZE FERRETS IN CALIFORNIA.

ACKNOWLEDGMENTS

Many thanks to all the usual suspects for their support and patience: my husband; my mother-in-law, Sandy, the guerrilla bookmark distributor; my family in California, who forbore to slap me silly when I deserved it; my fabulous agents, Steve and Joshua, and all their associates; the stellar team at Penguin/Roc—Anne, Ginjer, Cherilyn, Sarah, and the talented production team too numerous to list; the lovely lunatics at Bouchercon, RAM, and Crimespree; friends and family in person and those online; all the wonderful writers who've helped me along the way and put up with my whinging about this book; and the readers who pestered me to "write *faster*!" And a shout-out to the Seattle bookstore folks who let me run rampant through their shops in this novel.

Special thanks to: Richard Kaufman of the Genii Forums for help with table-tapping techniques; Detective Nathan Janes for information about SPD criminal and homicide investigations (I fudged a bit here and there to make things more dramatic); and to the friends who let me borrow their names for characters in this book (Ken George, Ana Choi, Rey and Karen Solis)—any resemblance to their real selves or lives is strictly imaginary.

If I've forgotten someone—and I'm sure I've forgotten many someones—I hope they will forgive me my Swiss-cheese memory. I'm indebted for everyone's assistance, and where I've gotten things wrong, it's entirely my own fault.

POLTERGEIST

PROLOGUE

L iving, lambent fog overlay the living room around me. Vague shapes and eddies moved through the gleaming mist trailing subtle colors while the bright gold of the house's protective spell coiled around the structure like a friendly vine. It was almost restful in that place and company, though I doubted I'd ever come to like it. Though Mara Danziger was safely in the normal world while I was in the Grey, I was able to see the sleeping child in her lap as a white shape, and my friend had been shrouded in a blur of blue light and gold sparks. I was even able to hear her, though the sound had a slight underwater quality to it.

"You know, you don't go slipping accidentally anymore," Mara said in her tumbling Irish voice. "That's good. Are you still seeing things the same way?"

"Yes, and no," I murmured, sitting on the couch—the shadowy shape of a couch on my side—and closing my eyes. "When I'm in here, it's not much different. When I'm outside, I can look at it without having to go all the way into the Grey, but I see layers now, and colors—people and things have ... colors, like threads, tangles, glows. I can slide down below the fog if I want to and look at the power lines "

"Can you, indeed?"

"Yeah. The deep part of the Grey is like ... It's all bright lines, like computer drawings." Then I shut up because I didn't want to say that the lines weren't just lines or conduits or paths; they were somehow alive and I felt compelled to conceal that.

Mara was quiet a moment. "I think that's the grid itself—the network I've told you of, through which raw magic flows."

"What are the colors? What do they mean?" I asked.

"I'm sorry to say you'll know more than I on that score. I don't see magic as you do. The glows are auras, but the others ... I'd guess they're connections, like electric cords that connect related things in the Grey to each other or plug the things into the power grid, but I'm not sure. Y'could ask Ben, if he can stay awake long enough. Between the class schedules and keeping after the child, we've neither of us enough free time to spit."

The Danzigers were both instructors at the University of Washington—Mara taught geology and Ben languages and linguistics—but they each had personal interests in the paranormal and they'd helped me out with this Grey business from the very beginning. Ben was the theoretician and scholar. Mara, being a witch, was a bit more practical.

Mara continued. "Still, you're doing much, much better than a few months ago. Feeling better about it?"

I drew a deep breath, pushing the Grey away, and opened my eyes as I exhaled. "I don't feel sick all the time," I replied. "And I don't have to live in it, most of the time. Sometimes it still gets the better of me and I fall in, but mostly I have control of it more than it has of me."

Mara grinned at me from her couch, her green eyes sparkling, and said, "Don't go getting too cocky, now, Harper. There's still a vast trickiness to the Grey."

I snorted. That was not news to me, even then.

*　　*　　*

That was a couple of months ago. We'd been sitting on the matching couches in the Danzigers' living room, a sunny, comfortable spot and a far cry from the slippery mist-world of the Grey—the here/not here place that lies like a fringe of shadow between the normal and the paranormal. It's the world of ghosts, vampires, and magic, and I am one of its few dual citizens. There are people like Mara—witches and so on—who can touch the Grey in some way and draw power or information from it, but as far as I know, only ghosts and monsters truly live there. I, however, seem to be half in and half out all the time. I can't do magic, or exorcise spirits, or anything flashy like that: I'm a Greywalker—a human who can enter the Grey and move through it as if it were the normal world. Apparently I got this way when I died for a couple of minutes.

So far, no one had been able to explain why me and not everyone else medical technology pulls back from clinical death, but I seemed to be the only Greywalker around the Pacific Northwest. There didn't appear to be a cure or even a way to quit, but Mara and Ben had been teaching me how to keep it under control and how to stay out of trouble, insofar as I could stay out of trouble. My work and the Grey seemed to intersect more often than I'd have liked and it hadn't been pleasant. As a private investigator, I usually carried a pretty dull case-load, but once the ghosts and vampires found me, things got weird fast.

In October, months after the calm on the couch, I wished that the meeting I was driving to would be normal, even boring, but since I'd been recommended by Ben, the self-proclaimed "ghost guy," I wasn't holding out a lot of hope. Within a few minutes of my arrival, even that bit of hope was totally dashed.

ONE

I sat in a boxlike office for twenty-three minutes as Professor Gartner Tuckman told me that he and a motley group of strangers had made a ghost. Not in the film noir, bang-bang sense but in the creepy, woo-woo sense. Frankly, I found Tuckman creepier than some of the ghosts I've met. He was thin and intense with a hectoring, arrogant manner, a sharp voice, and the cultivated piercing gaze of a silent film villain. He was also a liar—at least by omission.

I held up a finger to stem the battering wash of his words. "Let me see if I understand this, Dr. Tuckman. You put together a group of people who made up a ghost and haunted *themselves*?"

"No. They did not 'haunt' anything. There is no ghost. It's an artificial entity powered by their own belief and expectation. The parapsychologists would call it a group thought-form—"

"I thought you were a parapsychologist."

He scoffed. "I'm a psychologist. I study the minds of people, not spooks. The point of this project is observing how rational individuals become irrational in groups and how that is reinforced by the group itself. In re-creating the Philip experiments, I gave them an acceptable focus for their irrationality."

"The group in the Philip experiments claimed to have created an artificial poltergeist, right? Psychokinetic phenomena and all."

He rolled his eyes. "Overly simplified, but yes."

"So you told your group to make up a ghost, believe in it, hold these séances, and they'd get phenomena. Did they?"

Tuckman tossed his head. "Of course they did. Regardless of anything else questionable about the Philip experiments, they did, undeniably, manifest minor instances of psychokinesis—PK. Once my group had that information, they became open to the idea that it could be done. Then I supported their belief in the phenomena so they produced PK effects on their own."

"You're sure this isn't a real poltergeist?" I asked.

"Poltergeists don't exist. They're the conflation of simple events, suggestion, coincidence, and minor stress-induced PK activity by the operator. There is no 'ghost' involved. Just people. By reinforcing their expectations and subconscious irrational beliefs, I hope to see how far they'll suspend rationality before they rein themselves in."

"Your group produces measurable, reproducible PK phenomena?"

"Yes. But suddenly the phenomena are off the scale. We've had a massive jump in the number and strength of the phenomena, as well as the kind. I think one of the participants is faking additional phenomena. I want you to find out who is doing this and stop them, help me get them out of the group before they ruin the experiment."

"If the faked phenomena are helping the group believe in ghosts, how is that bad for you?"

Tuckman glowered. "Because those phenomena aren't under my control and are too far outside probability to be legitimate responses."

I sat back in my slick chair and let Tuckman stew in his angry silence. His request—and his anger—didn't make sense. He wanted to see how far his group would go, but when they went farther than he expected, he assumed he was being scammed. He didn't seem to believe in the paranormal himself, but he'd accepted PK—or had he? I tilted a glance at Tuckman through the Grey and watched green tendrils dart out from around him like tiny snakes striking at flies. I hadn't seen anything quite like that before, but I could make a good guess what it meant.

"Why do I have the feeling you're not telling me something, Dr. Tuckman?"

"Nothing you need to know."

Fat chance. I stood up and slung my bag over my shoulder. "Dr. Tuckman, I doubt Ben Danziger told you I was an idiot when he recommended me, so why you're treating me like one I don't know. But I don't need the money enough—or the aggravation—to work for a client who lies to me or hires me under false pretenses. If you want a serious investigation, you'll have to level with me about your ringer, because I'd find him or her eventually. But if what you really want is a patsy to go through the motions and take the blame for something, you need to look elsewhere."

"I don't know what you mean."

I gave him the tired face. "Bullshit. You said you reinforced the group's expectations. The easiest way to do that is to create apparent PK phenomena yourself—or have a confederate do it for you. I've seen plenty of con games and this is pretty much the same thing—get someone or a group of someones to believe they're special, then you see how much you can get from them before they figure out they're being conned. Now, I don't care about the particulars of your experimental technique, but if you want me to find your problem—assuming you really have one—you have to disclose the truth. What you tell me is confidential, but I don't work well in the dark and I get a bit testy when I feel like I'm being had—or set up."

I stood and stared at him a moment. He gave me the villain eyes again. I rolled mine in response. "Fine," I said and turned to go.

Tuckman leapt up. "No, wait." I felt his hand close on my upper arm. The cold of his personality licked my skin like the little green snakes I'd glanced in his aura.

I spun back, yanking my arm loose, and gave him a glare that burned up from the very depths of the dead through the network of Grey that limned my bones—the "gift" of a meddlesome vampire that tied me into the grid at the deepest level of the Grey. Tuckman pulled his hand back to his side with a sharp inhalation.

"I'm—I apologize, Ms. Blaine. I need to find the individual who's undermining my project and I cannot do it myself. I do have a … confederate in the séance group who helps reinforce the phenomena. Please sit down and we can discuss it further."

I sighed and gave the chair a sour look. It was bowl-shaped and upholstered in repulsive green vinyl. I threw my bag into it and pulled out my notebook, again. Still on my feet, I turned back to Tuckman as he returned to his desk chair.

I can't like every client—economics doesn't let me be that choosy—but I disliked and distrusted Tuckman and was sure I'd regret staying on. I comforted myself with the petty pleasure that at five foot ten I towered over him.

I summarized his recent recitations and asked for a list of project participants. "Be sure to include all of your assistants, including the ones running the magic tricks—they're the most likely to be involved. I'd also like to see exactly what phenomena you're getting. I'll need to see recordings, but I can tell a lot more if I can observe the whole setup in person, in real time." If Tuckman was getting any legit paranormal activity, I probably wouldn't be able to see most of it on a recording, but in person was a different situation. Even glass and sound baffles wouldn't filter it all from my Grey-adapted eyes.

For a moment, I thought Tuckman would object, but he swallowed it. He had to. Spoilers at work wasn't the only possible answer to Tuckman's problem, but he wouldn't consider any that couldn't be seen or recorded. I, on the other hand, had firsthand knowledge that ghosts and poltergeists did exist and weren't just conflations of ordinary events by stressed minds. Few people get smacked as hard by them as I'd been, though. OK, so call me prejudiced, but I did wonder what he was really getting.

"All right," Tuckman conceded, looking sour. "There's a session tomorrow afternoon. I'll arrange for you to observe from the booth—"

"I'd prefer to be in the room."

"Impossible. Disruption of the setting may cause the legitimate phenomena to fail. The experiment must remain clean—that's why I need you. Everything is monitored. Everything is documented. I have an early session video here and I'll get my assistant to sort out some more representative recordings for you to study. But unless there is no other way, you cannot be in the séance room during the session."

It was frustrating, but I had to give him the point for now. "All right. Now, you said that your group did produce some actual PK activity on their own, yes?"

"Yes. They do produce some verifiable and reproducible table raps, movements, light flickers—that sort of thing." He let his mouth curl into a smug little smile. "They've demonstrated remarkable skill at it, especially considering the short time they've been working together."

"Then it's possible your group is actually producing all these phenomena themselves."

"It is *not* possible."

So speaks a mouth attached to a closed mind—and here I'd had such hope for science when I was younger. "What makes you think so?"

"The phenomena are too large, too powerful. It's beyond the ability of simple human minds to exert such physical force without physical contact. You'll understand when you see the sessions."

I suspected I'd understand a lot more than Tuckman did. "How big is the group?" I asked.

"Eight. Seven study participants and one assistant—I'll count Mark Lupoldi as a participant, though he's my ... special assistant."

"The one who fakes phenomena."

"Yes."

"OK. Make sure he's noted on the list that way. Can you take me to see your experiment space now?"

"No. I have a lecture to give in fifteen minutes."

"I can go by myself if you'll give me the key and directions. Unless there's something in the room you don't want me to see …"

"If you want to start digging into it right away, I won't object." He took a ring of keys from a tray on his obsessively neat desk and removed two. He held the large, brassy keys out to me. "Here. It's room twelve in St. John Hall. The building is unlocked this time of day, but you'll need the key to the rooms, including the observation booth. The room numbers are stamped on the keys. Sign in and out with the front desk and leave the keys with the proctor when you leave."

He unlocked the file drawer in his desk and pulled out a pristine manila folder with a typed label that read CELIA.

"Who's Celia?" I asked.

"Our 'ghost' is named Celia Falwell. It took quite a while to find a name for which there was little or no information on the Internet."

"Why did it matter?"

Tuckman shook his head with impatience. "Because I didn't want them Googling the name and dragging information in, subconsciously, about whoever they found. The personality had to be consistently their own creation." He looked at his watch. "I don't have time for this." He drew a computer disc and a sheaf of paper from the folder and stood up. "I have to get to my lecture." He picked up an expensive, soft-sided leather satchel and pocketed the rest of his keys.

He waved me out and locked up his office before handing the pages and disc to the department secretary. "Please make a copy of these for Ms. Blaine and put the originals in my box, Denise."

Denise frowned at him. "OK." She was over thirty, but wore her hair, clothes, and makeup like a twenty-year-old. As soon as Tuckman turned away from her, she puckered her face into a disgusted expression.

"I'll see you tomorrow at the session. You can call me this evening if you have questions," Tuckman said, giving a little nod before he left me alone with the secretary and her sour silence.

Once Denise had finished making copies for me, I headed for St. John Hall.

Pacific Northwest University was founded by fire-breathing Calvinists in 1890. I guess they figured that the visitation of more literal hellfire in 1889, when the downtown core of the city burned to the ground, proved that Seattle needed some salvation through education—since neither temperance nor politics seemed to have had much effect in that direction. Its religiosity didn't take very strong root, however—the school is pretty secular now, and not as large or prestigious as the nearby University of Washington. A lot of people mistake the small campus of PNU for a private high school. Its apparent size is deceptive; quite a few of the large houses nearby are actually school property, in use as dorms, labs, and offices.

I strode west through the quad, raising flurries of new-fallen leaves before me and a scurry of phantoms in the edges of my vision. Places people frequent tend to build up a layer or two of ghosts and lingering Grey things after a while and the campus of PNU had collected its share. So long as I kept my eyes straight ahead, I could keep the vague, uncanny figure that flowed along beside me in my peripheral vision. If I turned my head, it seemed to vanish, though I knew that was just the treacherous nature of the Grey. I held it at bay for now. The ghost turned and faded through me as I stopped in front of my destination. I shuddered from the rough cold of the phantom's passage.

St. John Hall was a squat Art Deco building of yellow brick and odd-sized windows. I suppose the intent of the architect was a warm, golden building with glinting windows that filled the interior with light. Time and use had made the building look grubby and half blind where the windows had been covered up inside. I peered at it, letting the chill and the cloudy light of the Grey well up around me. The building didn't look a lot different in the Grey than it did in the normal, except for the usual flickers of history and a bright, hot spot of yellow that seemed to penetrate one of the upper windows like an arrow shaft through a target.

I was reluctant to step all the way into the Grey and take a clear look at that yellow shaft of energy. Bad enough that I was standing out in public looking at it, without risking going all translucent and slippy myself. I had no idea what anyone else would see if I let myself go through to the deep Grey. I knew what I would see, though: black emptiness and a blazing grid of lines that describes the world in hot colors of energy and potential magic—this was the inexplicably alive thing I could not describe to Mara or anyone else. That gleaming yellow shaft looked like part of the grid and I was willing to bet it ran through room twelve.

I pushed the Grey back to a controlled flicker and entered St. John Hall. Although there was a small reception desk in the entryway, no one was manning it. I could hear a couple of people talking and giggling nearby, but I didn't disturb them. I just signed the guest ledger and took myself upstairs.

Room twelve was at the front of the third floor, right across from the stairs. The door labeled 12 was intersected by the hot yellow shaft, as I'd expected. Beside it was another room marked 0-12. The keys in my hand matched the numbers on the doors. The lair of Tuckman's merry band of ghost-makers was hardwired directly to the Grey via that bright piece of the grid. They wouldn't be able to avoid tapping or touching it in some way if they had any psychic or magical ability at all—and it, in its way, would touch them, too. I wondered if the power line had started in that position or if it had been pulled there by the activities of the group. Either could explain the sudden elevation in phenomena, though I didn't think Tuckman would buy that.

Still, grid or no grid, something had triggered the change, and finding that trigger was what I was being paid for, not proving my client to be an ass. And the intrusion of the grid could be a coincidence. In spite of my unusual knowledge, I couldn't assume the problem was strictly paranormal any more than Tuckman could assume the opposite. People are more likely to do bad things than ghosts are: people have volition and imagination; most ghosts or paranormal constructs have neither.

I let myself into room twelve and closed the door behind me. The space had been converted into a sitting room complete with bookshelf, end tables, and bric-a-brac. A pillow-strewn sofa sat against the wall that faced the control room mirror and a large round wooden table standing on a flower-figured Oriental rug in the middle of the room. A small brass chandelier hung from the ceiling above the table. The corner nearest the door had a tall white-painted board with Christmas lights sticking out of it in disciplined rows sorted by color. A few wooden chairs stood against the walls. A potted plant and a stuffed toy cat sat on the sill below the window that was transected by the Grey energy shaft.

Someone had put up a few pictures and posters on the walls. I walked around and studied them. Several were publicity photos or movie posters from the 1930s and '40s. One of the pictures was a modern computer art portrait of a pretty young woman with her hair rolled back in a style from the 1940s. She looked a bit like a blond Loretta Young and had a wistful look as she stared out of the page that had been framed and hung on the wall. Next to it was a ragged photo of a man in the uniform and patches of a World War II pilot—or that's what I guessed the winged patches meant, since the picture looked about right for the era.

I spotted a few bits of obvious recording and sensing equipment set around the room, but not as much as I'd expected. I got down on my knees and rolled up the edges of the rug. There were several black objects with wires running out of them attached to the bottom of the rug. Some of the wires poked up into the tufting and wound their way around in the design on the top side. Most likely these were part of Tuckman's equipment for creating phenomena. I'd have to get someone more tech-savvy to take a look at them and tell me what they did and how. I didn't want to be in the dark about what Tuckman's team could manifest without aid and what was mere trickery. If the elevated phenomena were the real thing, I would have to prove to Tuckman that they could not be anything else. But, if Tuckman was right about additional faked phenomena, I'd also have to know how the machines could be interfered with—if they could be at all. I laid the rug back down as it had been and sat on the floor.

With the door closed, I thought I was safe enough to drop my guard and step into the Grey to take a different look around. I got comfortable, closed my eyes, and took a deep breath—this part still weirded me out and I needed to brace myself before full immersion in the Grey.

Even sitting, I had a moment of vertigo as I pushed across the barrier into the Grey, feeling the sudden burden of exertion and an unusual sensation of weight. I opened my eyes to the cold and the foggy light of the Grey, filled with the shapes and shadows of things long gone hanging in an endless mist-world. I could hear the mutterings of Grey things and the thrum of the grid. Room twelve was still there, dim under the swirl of the Grey and as shadowy as if it were the ghost world, instead. The table in front of me was hung with a drapery of overlapping shapes so various and complicated I couldn't make them out. Among them a few swirls in the fog glowed with red, blue, and green traceries, and a crowd of half-formed human shapes seemed to press toward the table. They were unrecognizable, having no faces or details, only fog creatures that had no gleam of life. They weren't ghosts, but the habit-worn impressions left in the Grey by live people doing the same thing in the same spot over and over.

A harsh yellow glow emanated from under the table. I looked, then crawled forward, pressing between the chilly shapes. A globe of pale yellow energy pulsed brighter and dimmer in a slow breathing rhythm. The thing was beneath the exact center of the table, about the size of a basketball hovering over the floor. It was difficult to keep in focus as I crept near. I was panting a bit as I worked to hold my equilibrium against the two worlds—normal and paranormal—that pulled on me.

Closer, the ball of energy wasn't an even glow, but a jumble of gleaming threads like a living scribble made by a giant child. I staggered a little on my hands and knees, tossed off balance by the writhing view. Bits of history, mist-things passing through me, and shifting layers of Grey made me dizzy for a moment and I tumbled forward, getting a shock of ice and fire as my head and shoulder punched into the loose knot of Grey light and energy. I pulled myself back from the cold/hot sensation that had whipped through me and rested on my haunches, unsettled by the eerie feel of the thing in front of me. I wiped at my face, trying to remove the cobwebby sensation of it.

I peered at the ball of energy, narrowing my concentration further. The mist thinned, leaving more of the grid exposed as I burrowed deeper into the Grey. I could see that gleaming threads spun out of the yellow ball and crawled away over the room, like creepers gone wild across an old brick wall. The room was thick with them; they twisted together, finally, into the energy shaft from the grid that stabbed through the window. Even the mirror wall was scrawled with them, though less thickly than the rest of the room. I turned my head with care, the worlds slipping over each other like half a dozen old black-and-white films projected at the same time on a stained screen, but I couldn't see any reason for the energy vines. They were static, not growing or moving, yet they were throbbing with some imminent coil, producing a nerve-scraping whine.

I yanked myself back from the Grey, feeling the jerk and twist of the transition throughout my chest and spine. I kept my head down and gulped in air that tasted of dirt and dust until the sensations of nausea and pressure passed. I crawled from beneath the table and got back to my feet, my arms and legs a little shaky as I did so. I hadn't expected to feel so worn out. I checked my watch and thought I'd lost some time, somehow. Working in the Grey is tiring and takes concentration, but this was disproportionate for the duration I'd been in there, even though I wasn't sure how long that was. I'd left Tuckman's office almost an hour earlier and the walk to St. John Hall had taken no more than ten minutes. Time passed oddly in the Grey, but I'd never just lost so much while I was fully immersed in it before. I'd have to ask Mara what was going on, when I had the chance.

I leaned against the doorframe, getting my equilibrium back and letting my breathing return to normal. I peered through the corner of my eye into the Grey and took one last glance around. The glowing vines, the knotted ball of energy all had the air of something poised, waiting. I disliked it and felt a ripple of disquiet run down my back.

I left the séance room and went into the observation room. It was even less enlightening. Through the glass, one corner of the main room near the door was a bit obscured, but the rest of the room was in view—only the room itself, however. I could barely see any sign of the Grey from inside the booth—just some of the strongest concentrations of light as dim gleams, nothing of the ghostly shapes or finer energy strands. In the booth, monitors, recorders of various kinds, switches, and black boxes with mysterious acronyms stenciled on the cases were arrayed neatly on or under the counters. There was no sign of wires or other rigging I would have expected, although there were controls for the room lights and for "ambient sound." I would have loved to have a baseline reading of the room, but I didn't dare touch the switches. I'd get it from Tuckman, later.

I wondered why the Grey was all but invisible from inside the booth and if the double-thick panes of mirrored glass were somehow filtering it out. I'd noticed before that glass sometimes held the Grey at bay, or made it harder to see at least, but this seemed more filtered than usual. I was getting curious about the number of Grey oddities in this set of rooms. In the absence of a greater authority, I was the expert on the scene, but I didn't know enough to guess why things seemed … off.

I checked and double-checked, but there was nothing more to find. At least not at that moment. I gave it up and headed for my office to go through the files Tuckman had given me. I wanted some idea of their contents before the session on Wednesday.

TWO

I n my tiny office in Pioneer Square, I stretched out in my chair and skimmed through Tuckman's files. I didn't have the time to dig into the details—I just wanted an overview of the project and the people involved in it.

File information indicated the group had been working together since January and having remarkable success. There were two layers to the experiment: the official goal of creating and controlling a "poltergeist" through the power of the human mind, which the participants were made aware of; and the deeper goal—which Tuckman kept between himself, his assistant, and Mark Lupoldi—of studying the group's reactions, interactions, and evolution when their increasingly outrageous goals met with success. They had followed the protocols, such as they were, of the Philip experiments conducted by the Canadian group New Horizons in the 1970s. Tuckman's group at PNU jumped past the Canadian experiments' mis-starts and improved upon the techniques a bit with modern technology, mechanical and objective observation and recording, and the help of specialists in illusion and misdirection. An appendix explained the function parameters of the equipment in technical terms I couldn't decipher: leverage, nanometers per second, air resistance, impedance, induction, and so on.

As in the original experiment, the PNU group had created a deliberately flawed and error-ridden biography, history, and even a portrait of their "ghost," whom they'd named Celia Falwell. Naturally, Celia's was a tragic story. Born in 1920, she had been a student at PNU in 1939 when World War II broke out in Europe. She was then nineteen years old, frivolous, headstrong, and engaged to a "wild" young man named James Baker Jansen—also entirely fictional—who was a civil aviation pilot. Desperate to get in on combat action, "Jimmy" had volunteered and gone to China to join up with Chennault's Flying Tigers—even though a quick check of info on the Internet proved that the American Volunteer Group had included no nonmilitary pilots. He later transferred to the Army Air Corps and moved on to fight the Japanese in the air war over the Pacific.

Idealistic and romantic, Celia—who had often flown with Jimmy—earned her own civil aviation license and left school altogether in May 1941 to volunteer with the Air Corps Ferrying Command, flying planes from the factories to the training fields and transshipment points. When the Ferrying Command became the WASPs, she stayed on, in spite of Jimmy's objections. Celia never saw Jimmy again. She was killed in 1943 when the B-26 Marauder she was ferrying crashed on landing at MacDill Army Air Base in Tampa, Florida. The notorious "Widowmaker" bomber had claimed another victim, while, ironically, Jimmy—the combat fighter pilot—survived the war unscathed.

Tuckman's group had committed this story—flaws and all—to memory and concentrated on making Celia a real person in their minds. With the Philip experiments as a guide, the group made Celia the focus of their thoughts and attempted to create the right mental and emotional atmosphere to foster poltergeist phenomena they could attribute to her. They'd been successful from a very early stage—with the help of Mark and special equipment installed in the room. Now they were just trying to see how powerful the unaided phenomena could get. At least that's what they thought.

I glanced through the participant and staff dossiers—Tuckman had not included one for himself—trying to get an idea of what the group members were like, but they seemed very dry and bland on paper. I thought I might have better luck with the video, so I gathered the files and the disc and hauled them home where I could watch the disc while eating dinner.

Chaos, my ferret, kept me company while I ate. She clambered around trying to find a way to snatch a mouthful of whatever I had and doing her war dance, hopping and chuckling and waving her bared teeth around, whenever she was thwarted—which was more often than not. She managed to dump my water glass twice and get halfway across the table towing a slice of bread backward by humps and jumps before I gave her something else to do.

"OK, goofus," I said, scooping her up and touching my nose to hers. "Enough of that. Jar time for you." I'd discovered that she liked to crawl into a large mayonnaise jar I'd tried to put in the recycling bin. Putting the jar on the floor with one of her balls inside was guaranteed to keep her occupied for ten or fifteen minutes—an eternity in ferret terms—as she squirmed about, in and out, trying to catch the ball as the jar turned and rolled around the kitchen linoleum. If the ball escaped out the open end, she skittered after it, slipping and hopping across the slick floor until she caught the ball and returned it to the jar, wriggling her way inside and starting the whole show again. I smiled at her antics and finished my dinner while the first séance videos flickered across my TV screen.

As I watched, occasional Grey blobs streaked through my living room and small objects fell off the bookshelves with or without the assistance of Chaos. I let the things lie and smacked the floaters aside with a mild irritation at the unusual level of activity. I put it down to the fact that since I was paying more attention to the Grey than usual, it was paying more attention to me.

The first segment on the video was unremarkable. Eight people sat around the table in the séance room I'd seen earlier, chatting and discussing "Celia." They were self-conscious and, except for some false-positives, nothing much happened. By session three, Tuckman's group had managed to make some knocks and the table had rocked a bit from side to side and scooted a short distance across the floor. The lights flickered on the colored light board and the overhead lamp swung. Nothing seemed out of the realm of mechanical fakery or very simple PK and I wondered how much the phenomena had changed since the early sessions. But, as I'd expected, I couldn't see any Grey indicators on the video, so I couldn't tell if they hadn't had any Grey activity or if the recording just hadn't been able to show it. The video wasn't very good quality—hastily copied for me on the secretary's computer from what was obviously not an original master to begin with. I'd have to judge their real ability by tomorrow's session.

I sighed, shook my head, and reached for the phone. I was going to need some help to understand the room's mechanics. I paged Quinton and waited for him to call me back. He was a renaissance man of technology, though he didn't seem to own a phone or a computer of his own. He could hack, kludge, or wing anything. He'd once installed an alarm system in a vampire's car for me. No matter how bizarre Tuckman's setup turned out to be, I doubted it would ever beat running a panic button into the spare tire well of a classic Camaro that sported two inches of dirt in the trunk.

THREE

It drizzled on Wednesday, the sky that homogeneous Seattle gray from horizon to horizon that lasts from mid-October through the first of May. This is the weather some people claim induces suicide—difficult to credit when you consider Seattle's death rate is lower than most US cities its size and its homicide rate equally small. I suspect it does contribute to our large number of bars, though.

I'd decided to pack the ferret along for the investigation of the séance room since she was curiosity personified most of the time and good at finding small openings and hidden things—usually when I didn't want her to—which could be useful.

I spotted Quinton outside St. John Hall. He was standing under a tree near the doorway, wearing a full-length waxed drover's coat and hat against the rain, though some had managed to get into his close-trimmed beard, somehow. His long brown hair was pulled back and tucked into his collar. He kept his coat on as we collected the keys and went upstairs.

"What's the setup?" he asked.

"This group is trying to create psychokinetic phenomena in a series of monitored séances with a fake ghost. Some of what they get is caused by the sitters, but some of it is caused by the technicians in the booth and a ringer in the room. What I need to know is what equipment are they using, what does it do, and has any of this stuff been tampered with or added to."

"OK," he replied, opening the door to room twelve.

"Is it always like this?" Quinton asked, looking at the small room and its overload of furniture.

"I'd assume so. It was this way yesterday." Well, physically, at least.

Quinton hung his coat up by the door while I put the ferret on her leash. Once harnessed, she scampered around, digging at the floor and looking for holes. I glanced around and noted that the ball of energy threads was hot and bright under the table—even hotter than the day before and grown to the size of a beach ball with an unpleasant, beach-wrack stink and streaks of red. The sound was now a buzzing howl. I pushed the Grey away and used a trick Mara had taught me, pulling the edge of the Grey around me and Chaos to make a shield between us and the pulsing thing under the table.

Quinton walked around for a while, then stopped.

"I'm going into the observation room for a minute. I'll be right back," he said.

I could hear nothing but some creaking of the floorboards once he'd left the room, closing the door behind him. I guessed the room was pretty well soundproofed. I shouldn't have been surprised, but I was. Tuckman had gone to a lot of trouble with this room.

Quinton returned and put a sensor wand against one of the walls. "Thought so—power switch for all of this is in the other room. Now that it's on, I should be able to find the toys." He lay down on his back under the table, waving various devices at the furniture and rug, then began crawling around the rug itself, following some kind of invisible electronic spoor. I cut a glance into the Grey and saw that the ball of energy almost seemed to shy from him. He didn't notice.

Chaos discovered a shallow pit in the wall near the floorboards, obscured by the dark molding, and dug her claws into it, scrabbling and trying to make the hole big enough to crawl into. I went to see what she'd found.

A series of holes had been made in the walls near the floor and hidden behind fine-mesh screen the same color as the dark molding. Chaos had managed to find a small tear in one bit of screen and rip it open. Behind the screen was a small speaker cone. Chaos and I crawled around the room's perimeter and found a total of eight hidden speakers of several sizes. After a while, we ran into Quinton, who was now moving along the walls as well, waving his various sensors up and down the heavily plastered surfaces.

"What have you got?" he asked.

"Speakers. There's a whole bunch of them at floor level." I showed them to him as Chaos lost interest and attacked the rug, darting at the edge of the Grey, like a dog challenging the surf.

"Don't let her bite that rug too much," he cautioned. "It's got a lot of live wiring in it and she could get a shock." That wasn't all she'd get, but Chaos had had her run-ins with the Grey, too, and knew better than I when to head for cover.

"There are a bunch of plates and things on the bottom and on the floor under it, too," I said, moving my pet farther from the table.

"I figured there would be. I'll get to that in a minute."

We looked at all of the speakers and Quinton ran some more tests of the walls before getting me to help him move the table and rug for another inspection. The ball of energy rolled around when we moved the table.

I followed the ferret around the room, though it appeared she was just taking a general tour now. Quinton stopped near the observation room mirror and looked around to catch my eye.

"Make some noise and move around. I'll be right back."

I picked up Chaos and tried out a few old dance steps, muttering the words to "You Are My Lucky Star" to the ferret as I did.

Quinton returned, looking bemused, and grinned at me. "Keep that up for a while," he instructed as he repeated his crawling and waving, stopping a few times to take a spot reading of something in the walls or floor.

I'd faked my way through the first two numbers of *42nd Street* when Quinton called out again. "OK, you can stop." He was chuckling, but I didn't mind. I knew I was out of practice—and I never could sing worth a damn—but if you ask me to make frivolous noise and motion, Busby Berkeley dance numbers are the first thing that comes to my mind. I'd been dancing since I was eight due to my mother's ambition—pro since eleven—and the happily goofy routines were as natural to me as English.

At last, we sat down at the table. Chaos ran around on the tabletop, snuffing the surface and chuckling to herself. I gave her a couple of treats to keep her busy.

"What have we got?" I asked.

"The room's pretty wired, but it all comes back into the booth. There's nothing here that's either run by a remote location or sending information to one. There's a lot of passive sensing that I couldn't pick up until there was something to send—that's why I needed you to move around and make noise. About half the monitoring equipment uses passive sensors so, in theory, they ought to be unobtrusive and largely immune to most interference. Most of it's built into the walls or furniture so it's out of the way and safe from knocks and rough handling. It's a nice setup—and pricey, 'cause the antenna and power technology on those subminiature units is pretty cutting-edge. Some of the stuff under the table is passive and remote sensing equipment, too, with slightly bigger antennas.

"Beyond all that, there's the active systems. This is the interesting part. Those speakers you found have a sister set of speakers in the crown molding. Now, I'm just guessing, because audio isn't really my thing and I haven't run numbers or made diagrams, but the positioning and type of speakers suggests to me that the room is one big sound cabinet. The speakers at the floor level don't put out much sound per speaker, but their cumulative wattage, aimed as it is, would make the whole wooden floor one giant subwoofer—not a very well-tuned one, but sufficient for subaudible frequencies. When it's firing and properly timed, the effect would be very disturbing, but you wouldn't perceive it as sound. The people in the room might think it was an earthquake or they might just experience unexplained disquiet."

"That would probably be controlled by that console marked 'ambient sound,' " I suggested.

"Yeah. With the upper range speakers in the crown molding, the combined sound effects could be used to manipulate mood very effectively, or even to cause vibrations and knocking sounds in the floor and walls. Basically, they can 'haunt' the room with sound waves. Even at a low level, it would make people very suggestible. That's just the walls and floor. Most of the furniture in the room is normal, but this table isn't."

"I figured. Tell me about the table."

"It's not as heavy as it seems. It's only heavy enough to be awkward for a single person to lift. Now, one of the large black pads you found in the floor is an electrical induction feed hardwired directly into the booth through a cable that's hidden under the boards—there's a little panel of wood covering the channel cut in the floor for it. The rest are induction or magnetic plates. It's nicely done, very neat. But the feet of the table are metallic and the rug has enough electrical coil in it to induce a very mild magnetic field that would make the table seem to get lighter or heavier—and would also make it easier or harder to shove around. Selective activation of the coil in the rug and the magnetic plates in the floor could also make the table bounce up and down or rock side to side a little—it wouldn't be dramatic, but to someone who's already suggestible and wants to believe, it would be a pretty convincing poltergeist.

"I'd guess they keep the table 'heavy' most of the time to make movement seem more dramatic when it happens. The table is also wired through the legs, picking up electricity through the induction plates and feeding a grid of tiny electromagnets embedded in the tabletop from below. This is all concealed by a wood veneer thin enough to allow someone with a control to move a metallic object around on the surface without touching either the table or the object—it would be a little hard on people's electric watches, but who'd notice? Now, you couldn't make the table jump or become heavier or lighter while you did that, but it would be a pretty cool effect and would distract almost anyone from noticing that the table was a little lighter than usual. It's a nice setup for making a ghost. Most people couldn't afford it and it wouldn't be worthwhile to most stage magicians, since it requires control of the room. But it works great in a setting like this one."

I scooped the ferret off the table as she attempted to jump down and stuffed her into my purse. She began digging around. "Just how much movement or noise could you get out of this equipment?" I asked.

"Nothing flashy—this is a subtle setup and it's supposed to create subtle effects. It's all based on the suggestibility of the people in the room," Quinton replied. "You could get some dramatic effects with some kind of mechanical rig, I imagine, but that's not my field. You'd need to talk to a stagehand or a magician for that. I'm not sure you could hide the mechanism, though. You want to take a look in the other room with me?"

"Sure." I stood up and followed him out of the séance room and into the observation room.

Quinton identified which monitors recorded what and identified the location of recording cameras and microphones; then he sat down and made the chandelier and side lamps in the other room flicker and the table jump and turn. The table was wobbly and jerky and moved very little, though it still moved enough to see and measure on the equipment. He ran through some sound combinations that made me cringe, hearing them through the speakers in the booth. If I hadn't known the source of it, I would have been squirming around in restless discomfort. I could see an occasional flare of red or yellow in the other room, but it didn't seem to be connected to the sound Quinton made. It woke the ferret, who abandoned my purse for Quinton's pocket.

He shut down the effects and reached into his pocket to pet Chaos. "Hey, stinky." He looked up at me, then cocked his head toward the room. "Tricky, huh?"

"Yeah," I replied. "Very tricky. What about the board of Christmas lights?"

"That's what it is—Christmas lights. It's plugged in, but there's no separate control for the board or the plug. It doesn't have any switch or controls on it, either. As far as I can see, it's there just to be there—maybe it's a control unit. I don't know."

"So some of this stuff is here for legit purposes."

"A lot of it. It happens that you can also manipulate some of it, but the recording and monitoring equipment is on the level and there are good reasons to have the sound and light manipulation capability. Now, the modifications to the table I can't see any purpose for except demonstrating fake table movements and sliding objects around, but the rest are solid."

"Then, except for the table, this stuff is mostly meant to create a conducive mood for belief, not to fake phenomena."

"Yeah. And to record the phenomena and associated conditions with a high degree of reliability. It's a good arrangement and the distances are so short there'd be little chance for signal loss or interference with the antennas from outside the room. It's a decent old brick building without a lot of iron framing to interfere electrically, but built solid enough to block a lot of outside sound and vibration."

I sat and thought about that for a moment, until we were interrupted by a knock on the observation room door.

We looked at each other before I opened the door to find a young
black man standing in the hall with a large manila envelope in his
hand.

I looked at him. "Hi. Can I help you? Dr. Tuckman told me we'd
be undisturbed here."

His face was as unrevealing as an ebony mask and his tone was dismissive. "I don't intend to disturb you. Tuck told me to deliver these—
assuming you're Harper Blaine—and since he knew you'd be here, I
thought I'd come over early."

This was not helpful and neither was his lofty attitude. "Yes, I'm
Harper. Do you work for Tuckman?" I asked.

He rolled his eyes. "Yeah, I do. I'm his graduate assistant on the
poltergeist project. Terril Dornier. Terry." He didn't offer me his hand
or a smile, just held out the envelope.

According to his dossier file, Terry Dornier had an undergraduate
degree in psychology and was continuing on to a specialization in
abnormal behaviors. His cold outward reserve bordered on disdain. I
wondered if that was usual or if he just didn't like me for some reason.

"Hi, Terry. What have you brought?"

"Recordings of the séances and the recent monitoring and notes."

Quinton stepped into the doorway. "Which codec did you use to
encrypt the video?"

Dornier looked startled. "Nothing special. The school can't afford
the licensing fees for proprietary software. It's all open source 'nix."

Quinton grinned. "Great."

"Terry," I interrupted. "Has anyone been in these rooms since the
last session?"

Dornier gave me a flat look. "No. Frankie was going to check the
room today, but Tuck told us to leave it be until you were done. He
told everyone to stay out until three."

It was hard to resist grinding my teeth at how thoughtless Tuckman had been about securing the room. I couldn't be certain no one had nipped in to change anything before Quinton and I arrived—the security of the front desk being what it was. Damn Tuckman for complicating the investigation.

"Who's Frankie?" I asked.

"Denise Francisco," Dornier said, "the department secretary. She used to work for the project, but she quit. She volunteered to reset the room after the sessions since she helped set it up in the first place."

"Why would she make extra work for herself?" I asked.

Dornier gave me a sideways stare and a frown. "What extra work? She does it all the time. I think she just likes to keep some kind of tabs on the place, feel like she's still involved." Then he closed up as suddenly as an anemone catching a fish. "You should ask her yourself."

I held out my hand for the envelope. "Thanks, Terry, I'll do that."

He handed over the envelope without enthusiasm and stared at me a moment before he turned away and headed down the stairs. I stayed in the doorway until he left.

Once we were alone in the booth again, Quinton looked at me with raised eyebrows. I shrugged. "No idea what that was about," I said.

"Are we done here? I don't think there's anything more I can tell you."

"I wish I knew how long Dornier'd been out there and if he heard or saw anything."

"Wouldn't matter how long he was in the hall, he couldn't see or hear anything from there and"—he pointed to a red light on the monitoring console—"there're indicators for the door and both windows that show if they're open or closed."

"Why would they monitor that?" I asked.

"Control. To confirm the condition of the room at all times, make sure no one was sneaking in or out or throwing something through the window, I'd guess. There's a bit of a blind spot near the mirror and in that corner near the door."

I nodded and looked down at the envelope full of discs. "What was all that business about codecs and 'nix?"

Quinton chuckled. "Just geek-speak. Basically, PNU is too cheap or too broke to use Microsoft or Apple or some other licensed computer system, so all the discs were encoded using free software systems. To be honest, I'm surprised they've sunk so much money into this room if they're running that close to the bone, but there's nothing wrong with the systems they're using—it's pro stuff, even if it's free or cheap."

"So, am I going to need some kind of special machine to watch the rest of this video?"

He shook his head. "Nah, the video format is about as basic and universal as it gets. You just need a computer with a DVD drive or a decent DVD player. The files are in really basic formats—that's the easiest way to be sure your information's compatible with as many other systems as possible, and it sounds like the school is using whatever systems they can get. It isn't fancy, but it's reliable."

"All right. Are you free later to look at some of these DVDs with me? I want to be sure I understand what I'm seeing."

That earned a huge grin from Quinton. "I'm so free I float."

I snorted at him, then caught a look at the clock in the hall. "Damn. It's later than I thought. The session's going to start in a little over an hour." Chaos stuck her head out of Quinton's pocket and tried to escape to the floor. I grabbed her as she made a leap for the lino. "Oh, no, bandit queen. No wild rampages for you."

She thrashed around and slipped out of my hand, doing her punk-ferret pogo and chittering in annoyance.

Quinton scooped her up. "What's the matter, tube rat? Past your nap time?" He stuffed the ferret into his sweater. She wriggled about for a moment, then calmed down and poked her head out of his collar, resting her body in the sagging knit. She flipped open her head and yawned.

"Great, now I have to get her to come out of your clothes, then drive back to West Seattle to drop her off, and get back here before three," I groaned.

"I can keep her."

I peered at him. "What?"

"No problem. I like ferrets. If you give me those treats—and if you trust me—she can hang out with me until you're done, then we can hook up and look at those DVDs."

I wasn't certain it was a good idea. "I'm not sure how long this is going to take," I said.

Quinton shrugged. "I can keep her all night, if I have to—if you're OK with that. I know what ferrets eat and I can put her on her leash if she's too crazy. I have plenty of warm pockets for her to sleep in. I don't mind if you don't."

I thought about it. I liked Quinton and I'd trusted him to do some pretty strange jobs for me—including one that could still get us both arrested. I'd trusted him with my life and my freedom—I guessed I could trust him with my pet. I took a deep breath, feeling a little nervous.

"Well. All right. Don't let her eat anything sugary—it's like speed—or anything rubber—"

He grinned and patted the air between us. "OK, OK. Atkins ferret diet: no carbs, no rubber. Really—I've kept ferrets before. She'll be fine with me."

I laughed. "OK. I'll page you when I'm done." Quinton took the ferret's stuff and we went downstairs. I caught the furry little traitor nuzzling him as we headed out to get some food before I had to return to observe the séance.

FOUR

even people were gathered around the heavy table. They didn't sit, but stood with their fingertips resting lightly on the ash wood surface and their heads bowed to look at a vase of flowers in the center. A portable stereo in the room was playing the Glenn Miller version of "Imagination" at a low volume.

Earlier, the people in the room had been joking around as they waited to see if the eighth member of their group would show up. They were an interesting mix: two apparent couples—one college-age and racially mixed, the other middle-aged and Nordic—plus one more woman who looked like a harried housewife, one vaguely Middle Eastern young man with a sly grin, and one more man who seemed to be a military retiree. I hadn't yet linked names to faces, since there'd been no photos in the files. After some chatter, greetings, and clowning around, they'd decided the eighth wasn't coming and had gone to stand around the table.

The military man looked at the flowers and said, "Good evening, Celia. Are you standing by?"

Two quick raps came from the table. I raised an eyebrow. When I'd been under that table, there had been nothing there that could have made that sharp, hollow noise and I was certain nothing had been placed there since. At least nothing official or large enough to see from the observation booth.

Tuckman leaned his head close to mine without turning his eyes away from the scene on the other side of the observation room glass. "Two raps for yes—that's the code."

I gave half a nod. "That's the usual thing." I tried to look into the Grey and see what was going on in the overlap between the normal and the paranormal, but the two layers of glass between me and the séance room baffled my unnatural vision and all I saw were vague blurs and wisps of colored light writhing around the members of the project and painting occasional squiggles on the floor and walls. Whatever had made the rap didn't seem to be normal and I wished I could stand up and walk into the other room to see for myself.

"Was that one of yours?" I asked.

"No. That's a phenomenon they caused." I noticed from the corner of my eye that Tuckman smiled smugly as he said it.

The rest of the group in the room greeted the poltergeist. A flurry of taps sounded all over the table and in a few locations in the walls. The board full of Christmas lights flashed a complex sequence of colors. Tuckman was frowning.

"You're in a feisty mood, Celia," observed the military man. "Are you happy to see us?"

The table seemed to quiver. Its wooden feet rucked the carpet and then it gave a distinct hop, coming back down with a thump. I wasn't sure that movement was within the limits Quinton had explained, but it didn't seem that way to me.

The sitters looked at one another. "Is that 'yes'?" the military man asked.

A single loud crack sounded through the room, coming from the tabletop and sending out a sudden flare of red I could see even through the glass.

Someone murmured, "No?" Then the table flattened, bucked, and began a rapid jigging from one leg to another. The people gathered around it had to watch their toes and dance a bit to avoid having their feet crushed by the capering table.

In the observation room, I glanced at Tuckman. He was staring into the séance room in confusion.

"Is your ringer doing this, Tuckman?" I asked.

"No, Mark's the one who didn't show up."

Dornier cleared his throat. "There's some really odd electrical activity in there. There've been several small spikes on the meters and whatever it is seems to be affecting the thermometers, too."

"What?" I asked.

He started making notes on a pad beside the meters, not looking at me as he responded. "Usually the temperature in the room goes up as things get more lively and the subjects get more excited. They can work up quite a sweat if Celia is active. Sometimes we have to leave the window open. But it's getting a little colder in there today. That's anomalous."

That was when the table broke loose from the group and careened around the room. I could see it trailing red and yellow streamers in the Grey—they would have blazed like fire if I'd been able to see them without the glass in the way. The table slid wildly back and forth, then seemed to scurry around, dodging the sitters who chased after it. It ran faster and faster, galloping with pounding thuds around the wooden floor, scattering the lighter furniture, overturning a bookshelf to send books and pads of paper fluttering everywhere.

"Electrical readings are spiking again," Dornier said. "Continuing upward ..."

Tuckman glowered. "What the hell ... ?"

"This isn't normal, I take it?" I asked.

"No," he replied. "It's damned stranger. They shouldn't be able to move it that much by themselves. Damn it, when I find out which one of them is manipulating this, I'll ..."

"Hire him?" I supplied.

Tuckman gave me a black glare. I would have laughed if I hadn't been so unnerved by the table's motion. I've been glared at by scarier things than Gartner Tuckman.

The séance participants chased the table into a corner by the window. The table reared up onto one leg. First it tried to climb the wall; then it pirouetted on its single leg and began to menace the people gathered around it by waggling back and forth. It hopped forward. They fell back. It spun. Faster. Faster. A wisp of smoke rose from the wooden floor where the twirling table leg rubbed against it.

The table lurched forward, twisting a little, flaring red ...

And collapsed onto the floor, top down, with a crash that shook the room.

Then it lay there, still and inert and dim. Everyone seemed frozen a moment, catching their breath. Watching them, I seemed to have caught their enervation and felt a little dazed by the sudden change.

"Electrical readings back to normal. Temperature returning to normal."

"OK," I said. "That was kind of weird."

Tuckman turned to me. "That is what I was talking about. It's not within possibility."

I glanced toward Dornier. "Yeah. Do they do that all the time?"

"That's the wildest one yet," he replied in a cool tone. "They don't usually approach that sort of show without Mark in the room. They've had some good days without him. Nothing like that, though."

Tuckman gave me a significant look. "You see what I mean?"

I bit my lower lip. Without doubt someone was contributing more than their fair share to that performance—there was something going on in the thin fold of reality between the normal and the paranormal—

but whether I believed it was sabotage or not was another matter. But I wished I could have seen it better. The flashes and glimpses I'd caught had been indistinct and intermittent, but there was something Grey going on.

I looked into the other room. The participants buzzed around the séance room like an agitated swarm. The table didn't show any further sign of life. It just lay where it had fallen in the debris under the swinging shadows thrown by the brass chandelier.

"Can I get a copy of the readings from this session?" I asked.

Tuckman was almost out the door, and he threw a glance back at me and his assistant. "All right. Mark those up and get Ms. Blaine a copy before she goes. I have to talk to the group in the lounge."

Dornier started scooping up his pads and pens and followed Tuckman out of the booth, not quite closing the door. I heard them talking in the hall as I lingered, watching the other room for signs of any further Grey activity. Through the glass, I couldn't see any if it was there, and the people wandering through the space gave no indication that anything new disturbed them—they seemed excited the way some people do after an accident, but not as if they were still experiencing anything surreal.

Tuckman reappeared on the other side of the glass in a few minutes, rounding up the participants and urging them downstairs. I went out into the hallway once it was clear of study participants. There was an odd scent to the air from the séance room: a whiff of something sharp and burned, a hint of iodine—the lighter perfume of its earlier, uncanny stench. I went in, but I couldn't see anything much. The ball of energy had disappeared and the vines and power line were dim, no matter how hard I looked. There was nothing else in the room—if anyone had brought something with them to stimulate the phenomena, it was gone now. I turned and left.

Dornier met me in the hallway with a fistful of yellow paper.

"I had to transcribe these," he said, thrusting out the notes to me.

"Thanks, Terry." Now I was glad he'd introduced himself before, since Tuckman had just waved at him as if graduate assistants were as interchangeable as Shakespeare's Rosencrantz and Guildenstern. "Can I call you if I have any questions about these readings?"

He shrugged. "I guess. You're working for Tuck."

"Terry," I started, uncomfortable, but needing to ask, "do you believe that's all … real? That they couldn't actually be raising something paranormal in there?"

He snorted. "If you think it's really some ghost or spook or something, you had better be prepared to back yourself up—all the way to the wall Tuck'll shove you into if you come up with crap like that. Hard proof. Whatever you think it is … you better have stone-hard proof it can't be anything else."

I frowned at him but said nothing before I excused myself and headed out with the papers in hand and a list of questions already tabulating in my head. Dornier had quite the sandpaper personality and I suspected he wasn't the only one. The tone of the byplay in the séance had been more tense than I'd expected for a group that supposedly worked together to create a ghost—their clowning had an edge to it. It was an odd group and I needed some immediate information about what I'd just witnessed.

As Tuckman's ringer, Mark Lupoldi was supposedly vital to the production of high-level PK phenomena, yet we'd all seen something that was beyond the group's normal activity in spite of Mark's absence. I was more convinced now that Tuckman's problem wasn't attributable only to normal, human activity. The recordings and monitor readings might help me figure out what had happened, since I'd been unable to see into the Grey much through the mirror—another thing I'd have to bring up with Mara and Ben Danziger. But first, I needed to find out why Lupoldi hadn't shown up for the séance session. And I hoped he'd be able—and willing—to tell me how the system worked and how one of the participants could have boosted it without anyone else knowing. It looked paranormal to me, from what I'd seen and from Tuckman's reaction. But as Dornier had said, I'd have to prove it couldn't be anything else.

I paged Quinton and left a message that I couldn't pick up Chaos yet. He might be stuck with her furry company for a while longer. I had to pin down Lupoldi.

FIVE

I drove over to Lupoldi's apartment in the Fremont district. Autumn twilight was already falling with a scent of impending rain. I knew the address was near the troll under the Aurora Bridge—a cement sculpture of a life-sized monster crawling from beneath the structure to snatch an ancient VW. Along with the amusement rocket mounted to a building and the heroic bronze of Lenin that stood in the patio of a fast-food restaurant, it was typical of the neighborhood the locals had dubbed the Center of the Universe and others called the Haight-Ashbury of Seattle, in spite of a recent spate of yuppification. Parking is always bad in that funky little neighborhood and worse so close to quitting time, so I didn't even try to get close. I left my old Land Rover in a pay lot near the supermarket on Fremont Boulevard and started hiking up the hill.

The street was choked with cop cars. An unpleasant cold trickled down my spine at the sight. I paused outside the building and looked it over; a grim black and yellow haze wrapped it. I narrowed my eyes, searching the Grey shroud for anything that might be lurking, but all I spotted were confused or fragmented shapes and shadows.

My study was interrupted by a voice near my ear. "You have business in this building, Ms. Blaine?"

I shook myself and refocused my vision on the man in front of me. Detective Rey Solis: a wiry, dark-haired Colombian émigré with a face like the surface of Mars. I hadn't seen him since we'd both been looking for the same hit-and-run witness over a year ago. His sloe-eyed calm was as impenetrable as ever but the uncharacteristic red-orange gleam around him made me wary. This aura thing might be useful once I figured it out, but that particular color didn't reassure me.

"I thought I did," I replied.

"Now not so much?"

I tried to shrug, but it didn't come off so well. "Don't know. What about you?"

"Homicide."

I felt sick. Solis watched me. He glanced at the building, then back to me.

"I wanted to talk to the tenant of apartment seven on business."

"Client?"

"No, just information-gathering for a case."

Solis made a tiny tilt of his head. "Come up."

I followed him into the old brick building and up to the second floor. The dim hallway smelled of musty carpet and resonated with conversations and TV noises from the open doorways of curious neighbors. The closer we got to apartment seven, the colder and queasier I felt.

The door was open, bright light flooding out, and the crime lab crew was still crawling over everything. The photographer was done and heading out the door as we stopped just outside. Solis stood with his back to the room. Looking at him, I could also study the room beyond without entering the crime scene.

It was a small no-bedroom apartment with a Murphy bed folded up into the hallway wall and a long counter that served as a kitchenette to the left of the door. A bicycle with a U-shaped lock leaned against the far wall under the window. The closet and bathroom shared the wall on the right with a blood-spattered dent about the size and shape of a man. The room was hazy with layers of memory and Grey shapes left by past occupants and, to my eyes, thick with a swirling miasma of red and black. The reek of the fumed cyanoacrylate used to pick up fingerprints carried an uncanny undertone of gunsmoke and iodine that made me shiver and cough on a sudden sour taste in my mouth and a tightness in my chest.

Solis noticed my gagging shudder. "We don't have a positive ID yet, but I'm assuming the victim was the tenant. Can you identify him?"

I shook my head. "I never met him. He was supposed to show up for a lab demonstration at PNU, but he didn't. I came to find out why."

The coroner's crew was preparing to bag the body, which lay crumpled and facedown on the ragged carpet by the dented wall. As they rolled it into the bag, the weirdly limp form flopped and the misshapen head lolled, turning its staring face my way for an instant.

The silent force of an unreleased scream crashed into me. I jolted backward a step, squeezing my eyes shut and pressing my hand over my own mouth. The shock of the blow drained away. Solis put his hand on my shoulder and I shook him off. "What did that?" I demanded. I thought, if he'd been dead a few hours, shouldn't the body be stiffer?

Solis thought a moment, casting his gaze over me and around the hall as if there were an answer there somewhere. He watched the men carry the corpse away. Then he motioned me to follow him back outside.

We watched them load the black bag into a discreet blue van and drive off. We both took a few deep breaths of the cool, moist air and didn't look at each other. A small crowd had gathered at the end of the street, but they kept their distance and we were left alone.

At last, Solis spoke up. "Not sure yet. Looks like he was thrown against the wall. Maybe an accident." He didn't sound convinced. "We're working on it. You have any ideas? Anything like that demo he missed?"

"When did this happen?" I asked, dismissing momentary visions of dancing tables.

"A couple of hours ago, possibly three. I'll know more when the autopsy is done. What do you know?"

I stared at Solis, my mind racing. Lupoldi had died before the séance started, while I'd been eating lunch with Quinton. The scene gave me an unsettled feeling. What I'd witnessed at St. John Hall stuck in my mind and, though I'd been thinking Tuckman was wrong about it, I suddenly didn't like the thought that a poltergeist—real or artificial—could have the energy to do something like this. It was ludicrous, but I knew better than to assume Solis wouldn't be interested in at least some of the possible connections; someone who could fake PK phenomena might be able to fling a man across a room as well as a table. Fake ghost he wouldn't buy, but killer acquaintance he might.

Reluctantly, I started. "The demo is part of a psychological study at PNU. The researcher hired me to find out who in his group might be sabotaging his results, and today's demo went a bit wild. I came to see why Lupoldi—Mark Lupoldi is the name I was given with this address—why he hadn't shown up and if he knew anything about the demo going bad."

Solis regarded me in silence.

"And I do recognize him," I conceded.

He blinked slowly and gave half a nod. "From where?"

"He worked in the used bookstore a couple of blocks from here— Old Possum's. I only knew him as Mark, and I didn't make the connection until I saw his face." I shivered again, harder and nothing to do with the sharp tingle of tiny raindrops that had begun falling. Now Lupoldi wasn't just a name on a list, just someone who was horribly dead; he was someone I knew, however fleetingly, who was horribly dead. The situation didn't feel like an accident to me any more than it did to Solis.

He must have seen the speculation on my face. "Ms. Blaine, I don't need to warn you against obstructing an active felony investigation."

"The two cases might not be related," I suggested. "But I won't get in your way. I can't just drop my investigation on the chance that it might parallel yours, but I'll share any information I get that might be relevant. OK?"

"What if it's your client who did this?"

"Then he probably won't pay me and I won't feel too bad about ratting on him," I answered.

Solis almost smiled. "OK."

I started to go, then stopped and looked back. "I'm going to head down to Old Possum's—I know the owner and I can ask her some background questions on Lupoldi. Do you want me to break the news or leave that to you and your partner?"

"I'll do it. I want to talk to the staff later."

I nodded and walked back down the hill. I hadn't put Mark's death out of my mind, or the possibility of some paranormal involvement in it—the look and feel of the Grey in Mark's apartment was too abnormal to ignore. The idea of a killer thought-entity didn't sit well with me, but I wasn't sure which way Occam's razor would cut this time: person or poltergeist?

SIX

Old Possum's Books 'n' Beans was one of the first businesses I'd patronized when I moved to Seattle: it was cluttered, overstuffed, and as full of odd objects and comfortable, shabby chairs as it was full of interesting old books and the smell of fresh coffee. I'd run in to get out of one of Seattle's fifteen-minute downpours while apartment hunting. Two hours later I'd still been curled up in a chair with my rental listings, a pile of books, and a cup of coffee, the rain by then long gone. The shop cats had dropped by to vet me—some of them literally dropping from the cat highways over the tops of the towering shelves. Wearing their fuzzy badge of approval all over my jeans and jacket and carting a stack of books for which I didn't even have bookcases yet, I'd been adopted into the shop's ragtag family. The fact that I loved weird old stuff hadn't hurt, either.

The owner, Phoebe Mason, still seemed to see herself as a bit of a surrogate mother to me, though she wasn't much older than I was. Phoebe was working at the front counter when I arrived much as I had the first time, dashing in from a sudden delivery on the promise of rain. I stood in the doorway shaking off the water as she laughed at me.

"Hey, girl!" she shouted, the dim childhood memory of Jamaica lengthening her vowels. "Where you been? And when are you going to buy a proper coat?" She beckoned to the nearest employee to take over while she exited the cash desk island to chivy me. She grabbed my jacket and hung it up on the rack by the door. A sign over the pegs read HE WHO STEALS MY COAT GETS TRASHED.

"Hi, Phoebe. I wanted to ask you some questions. Do you have time?"

"Sure! Let's go back by the espresso machine. The minions can run the store for a while."

I can't remember when they'd picked up the collective nickname "Phoebe and the minions," but it had become universal among the regular customers and the staff. It made the ensemble sound like a punk band, which seemed to please everyone.

I followed Phoebe to the back, where she evicted the minion from the espresso stand and sent her out to police the shelves. We were alone in the coffee alcove with its fake fireplace and grand mantel of papier-mâché stone guarded by cat-faced gargoyles. One of the gargoyles looked a bit dyspeptic, leaning at an angle on a recently chipped base. A traffic mirror hung from the ceiling to give a view of the alcove from the cash desk.

I kept on my feet and toyed with some of the books and knick-knacks on the shelves in the alcove. I needed information, but now that I was here, I wasn't sure how to start—especially in light of Solis's desire to interview the staff without their having prior knowledge of Mark's death. It would have been easier to ask someone I didn't know or like about someone I'd never met.

Behind me the steam valve on the espresso machine roared. In a minute, Phoebe nudged me and handed me a large cup of coffee. "Sit down and drink that. You're all cold and fidgety." I let her push me toward one of the scruffy armchairs near the cardboard hearth and sipped the drink.

"Hey ... what is this?" I asked, looking up. The hot drink was much richer than I was used to.

"That's a breve—like a latte with cream instead of milk. And don't you make that face at me," Phoebe added, flipping her hand. "You need a little padding on those bones of yours. You look like a bundle of brooms."

"You've been hanging out at your dad's place, haven't you?" I asked. Phoebe's restaurant-owning family chided me for being underweight every time I saw any of them, which was a refreshing change from my own mother's insistence that I was in danger of running to pudge at all times and must be ever-vigilant against rogue calories that might stick unbecomingly to my hips or thighs.

She laughed. "Hugh and Davy convinced Poppy to put an espresso machine in at the restaurant—though I say what's espresso got to do with Jamaican food? So I went up to show them how it works. They already got bored with steaming milk and so I said I'd show them some fancy drinks next time." "Them" came out sounding like "dem"—Phoebe had definitely been spending a lot of time with the older members of the family. She gave me a toothy leer. "You're my guinea pig. So drink up, cavy."

I gave a good-natured shake of the head. "Squee squee," I said.

While I tried to sneak up on the hot cream and coffee, Phoebe made her own drink and joined me in the comfy chairs. "So," she started, "what did you want to ask me about?"

I looked away as I put down my cup. "Mark."

Phoebe sighed. "That boy is bad luck lately. Whenever he's around, things get broken, books fall off the shelves, the power goes out—you'd think we'd angered a duppy."

"What's a duppy?"

"In Jamaica that's what we call a bad ghost—or what Poppy calls it—I can hardly remember the place now, but I remember Poppy telling me how the duppies'd get me if I threw dishwater out the window without calling out first. Or how he said I shouldn't throw rocks at night or sit in the doorway, 'cause the duppies'd come over and smack me."

"Why would they do that?"

Phoebe scowled. "They're just evil old things. They got no heart to tell them right from wrong, so they just get mean and spiteful." She stopped and laughed. "But that's just old wives' tales. You asked me about Mark, didn't you? And why d'you want to talk about Mark, anyway? You finally giving up on that boyfriend who's never around?"

I shook my head with a moment's stifled pang. "Phoebe, I'm not man-shopping. I'm working. Mark was part of a research project at PNU that's got some problems, so I'm looking into the participants to see who might be causing the trouble."

"You think it's Mark?"

"No, but I have to know more about him. Seeing someone a few times a month doesn't mean you know him."

Phoebe snorted. "That's what I've been saying about that man of yours."

I turned a quelling look on her. "Phoebe."

"All right, all right. What d'you want to know?"

"How long had he worked here? What was he like? What did you know about his life outside of the shop?" I caught myself using the past tense and was relieved Phoebe didn't seem to notice.

"I think Mark's been working for me for … about three years. Always been reliable, though he's a big flirt and a joker. He's always making people laugh or playing pranks on them, but people like it—he's not mean about it. He's a nice guy. He's good with the stock and the customers, smart, reads a lot, of course—you know I don't take on people who don't love to read. Everybody likes him, women especially—those big, dark eyes and that wild hair look kind of Byronic or something. Heck, men probably like that, too, but he isn't interested, not so I ever noticed."

"Does he have a girlfriend?"

"Not right now. He was going out with Manda for a while, but that cooled off. Good thing, too—I don't like workplace romances. He doesn't seem to have another girl lately—too busy, I guess."

"What was he doing—aside from working here?"

"I think he's trying to get some kind of apprenticeship or something."

"For what sort of work?"

"Oh, he got his degree in theater lighting and set design last year. I think he wanted to work with the opera, but they weren't looking for a junior designer, so he's looking for smaller stuff. I think he wants to stay on the coast, but the only offers he's been getting are in the Midwest or back east."

"And what's been going on recently? You said he was bad luck."

Phoebe laughed. "I don't mean it. About a month ago the shop was being vandalized—just petty stuff, things thrown around, messes in the stockroom and office, alarm going off, stupid electrical problems. Then we had the poltergeist."

"What?" I started.

"I don't know what else to call it. And you know I'm not all spooky and like that, but what else you gonna call it when books go flying around the room with no people holding them and things moving around and turning up places they shouldn't be? And the cats hiding under the furniture." She waved her hands around. "You see any cats out here?"

I looked around and up into the mirror. "I see Mobius on the cash desk."

"Moby's just a stomach with legs who thinks he can get a piece of Manda's sandwich if he looks at her long enough. It never worked before, but he still thinks it will someday. That cat's brain-damaged. But what I'm telling you is the cats hide whenever Mark is in the shop. They're just now coming out after his shift."

"The cats don't like Mark?"

"Hell, no, girl. They used to love Mark. They're scared of the things that happen when he's around, these days—they may be animals, but they're not stupid. Mark comes in, things get kind of weird—like poor stupid Moby got his tail under a volume of the *Oxford English Dictionary* last week and that dinosaur head come right off the wall during happy hour once." She pointed up at a three-quarter-scale reproduction of a tyrannosaur skull that presided over the espresso bar. "I tell you, this has got to end, or I may have to let Mark go."

I looked down into my cup and discovered I'd finished the drink. "So Mark worked today?"

"Yeah. He's splitting a shift today. He had a half-shift to open and he'll be back for the late-night shift at ten."

"What time did he leave?"

"Noon. Came in at eight. He has some class or something on Wednesdays—oh, that's the project you're working for, right?"

"Yeah, they have a regular meeting on Wednesdays."

"Well, now I know."

"Phoebe … who's working with Mark tonight?"

"Just me. Wednesdays aren't too busy—sell more coffee than books."

"What do you do if someone doesn't show up?"

"Just work through it."

"What about the minions?"

"I usually cover for missing minions and then I chew them out later." She narrowed her eyes at me. "Why?"

"You might want to have someone stay late, in case Mark doesn't show."

"And why wouldn't he come to work?"

"Just a feeling. Things didn't go well at the project today."

Phoebe gave me a speculative look.

"I'm just suggesting." I stood up. "Phoebe, I know I'm going to have more questions, but I can't think of them right now."

"You aren't the only one with questions, Harper. I'll want an explanation if Mark doesn't show up."

I glanced away. "You'll get one."

I collected my jacket and left the shop. It was now a quarter of eight and still raining.

I walked a block in the rain to the statue of Lenin and used the pay phone on the side of the building behind him. The zigzag metal awning of a shop called Deluxe Junk kept me from getting soaked as I called Tuckman.

"Dr. Tuckman, Harper Blaine. Have you received any information about Mark Lupoldi yet?"

"No. Why? Didn't you speak to him?"

"He wasn't available." Chances were good Solis was still looking for next of kin to notify and wouldn't catch up to Tuckman for a while, so I'd keep my knowledge to myself for now. "Look, Dr. Tuckman, I'm not sure that what you're getting is normal activity you can—"

He cut me off. "There is nothing normal about what happened this afternoon. That table was not acting 'normally.' "

"What's normal about a table running around the room and climbing the walls?"

"Exactly. Exactly," he emphasized. "It shouldn't have that much energy."

"I understand that, but what I meant is that I think there's a bit more going on here than someone faking phenomena."

"What are you suggesting? That there's a real ghost?" He scoffed. "Before I'd consider that, you'd have to prove it couldn't be anything else—which you won't be able to do. Don't go chasing ghosts, Ms. Blaine. All I require is that you take the usual steps and follow the usual protocols, nothing more. Leave the ghost stories to my subjects.

And when you catch up to Mark, make sure he knows I need to speak to him."

I could feel myself frowning and was glad of the darkness that concealed my sour expression from passersby. "If I catch up to Mr. Lupoldi, I'll be sure to let him know," I replied. And I hoped I wouldn't ever see him again. I'd had as much contact with his shock and pain as I wanted. I didn't know what the medical examiner would find, but whatever had caused Mark's death had surprised him as much as anyone and left some freakish traces—or a lack of them.

"Good. I'll be very upset with Mr. Lupoldi if he doesn't show up on Sunday," Tuckman continued. "The group may waver if he misses two sessions in a row." Then he hung up on me.

I doubted the group would have much enthusiasm for Sunday's séance once they learned Mark was dead, but that revelation would have to wait on Solis. While I was convinced they could go further unaided than Tuckman believed they could, I wasn't sure they could go far enough to harm someone. The table had been damned frisky. What else could they do? And, as Tuckman had put it, how far would they go?

I hoped I wouldn't have to convince Tuckman of the existence of things that go bump in the night. If it was more than a physical saboteur, I'd have to exhaust all the prosaic options before there was any chance Tuckman would agree that his phenomena were real, and he would resist that to the end. I'd have to know how it all worked and who might have the motive as well as the ability—or not—before I could prove to him it wasn't faked. There were days my life would have been easier if more people believed in ghosts.

I had a strange feeling about this case. I still didn't think Tuckman was being straight with me and that pissed me off. And I didn't like what had happened to Mark. I tried not to make assumptions, but Solis was just as bothered as I was, and though Mark's death wasn't my case, it didn't seem entirely unconnected.

I stuffed down my misgivings and paged Quinton. I waited for him to call me back, listening to the rain play music on the metal awning. When he called, I arranged to pick up the ferret on my way home, then headed back to my truck.

About eleven o'clock, I was stretched out on my sofa at home with Chaos snoozing in the crook of my arm while I pretended to care what was on TV. The phone rang, interrupting a commercial that featured dancing clams. I smiled, remembering Phoebe's jibe about my absent paramour, and picked up the phone.

"Hello," I said.

"Hello, Harper." The warmth in his voice was almost a caress, speeding my breath and raising heat beneath my skin all the way from England.

"Good morning, Mr. Novak."

"Should I say 'Good evening, Miss Blaine'?"

"Do you want to sound like a Cary Grant movie?"

"Only if it's one of the films where he gets the girl."

"Wasn't that most of them?"

"Probably. He even got the girl in *Suspicion*, though he wasn't supposed to."

"Yeah, I know," I said. "I read the book."

"So … which ending do you prefer?"

"I'd have liked to see the book ending. Even charming, handsome guys can be coldhearted killers—but that's probably my cynical occupation talking."

"How is your cynical occupation at the moment?"

There was a slight chill in his sigh and my rush of happiness crashed. I frowned and was glad phones didn't have video feed. I sometimes thought his absence kept our on-again, off-again relationship from foundering completely on the rocks of my occulted life, but even fondness-engendering distance didn't seem to be working now. "Nothing special," I answered, "though I ran into Detective Solis today."

"I remember him. I recall he's pretty fierce for a quiet guy."

"I wouldn't care to be on his bad side."

"I hope nothing you're doing is tangled up with any of his cases."

"No," I lied. I did not want to talk about Solis or my job. "How's Sotheby's?"

"I'm almost at the end of this contract."

He fell silent. I waited.

"An independent valuation firm is chatting me up, though. It's mostly insurance work, but it's interesting, and I guess I'm getting a bit of a reputation in the right circles."

Another stumbling silence. "So, are you thinking of taking the offer if they make one?" I asked.

"Maybe. I'd still have to come home for a while to satisfy the alien worker requirements. But I could be home for Christmas. I wouldn't want to disrupt Michael's school schedule here, but we could work it out." Michael was Will's much-younger brother, still in school, though studying for British college exams now—when he wasn't cutting class to work on vintage motorcycles. "I could always look for something in the US…"

"If you're thinking of doing that for me, Will, then you know I'll tell you not to. If you want to come back, you have to come for yourself."

That was the crux of our problem: Will wanted a stable, honest relationship and the best I could offer was a catch-as-catch-can string of interrupted dates, creepy clients, and mysterious disappearances— which had almost brought our romance to an end on the first date. I wasn't very good at separating my work from my life—especially since the Grey and its denizens didn't respect office hours—and that was something I doubted I could break Will to, even if I'd wanted to.

I'm not the sort of woman who wants to remodel "her man" and I wouldn't care to be in the opposite position, either. We'd set off sparks from the moment we'd met, but Will and I didn't have compatible lives and I could never tell him the reason and he wouldn't believe it if I did. Which was why I was in Seattle and Will was in London. I may have fallen into bed with him the first time for all the wrong reasons— and I didn't regret it one bit—but neither of us could live our life for the other no matter how great the sex was when we managed to have it.

Will sighed. "You're still impossible."

My heart dropped and I felt cold with a childish desire to cry. I swallowed it back down, like I always have. "Yup," I replied in a bright voice. "That's me: Impossible Girl."

"Sounds like a cartoon."

"The kind the Korean studios make for Japanese audiences and then dub with American voices: seriously messed up."

He laughed. "All right, Impossible Girl. I—I have to cut this short. Maybe I'll make it for Christmas. But now I have to go. The bloody tube's on strike again, so I'm walking to work."

My turn to laugh. "You sound so British. Next you'll be complaining about the wretched Americans, voting Labor, and insisting that 'tire' is spelled with a Y."

"Can't vote: I'm one of the wretched Americans. OK, I'm off. I'll call again Friday, OK?"

"I'll look forward to it."

"Me, too." He hung up and I shivered, still holding the phone and conscious of being alone but for the ferret.

SEVEN

Thursday I chased down other cases and read files until three, when Quinton showed up to help me install a DVD drive on my office computer. I had a DVD player on my TV at home, but I didn't want to have to drag all the files and notes back and forth every day. Once the device was up and running, we sat down to watch a few of the discs together. I hoped Quinton would be able to point out the ghost-making machinery in action. We huddled in front of the monitor like a couple of kids watching scary movies on Halloween. All we needed was some popcorn and blankets.

The first session hadn't been very interesting and they didn't improve for a while. The group had sat stiffly around the table in reduced light, meditating for a while, then just sitting and talking about Celia and getting nothing, though they did seem to establish some rapport. Eventually, they'd tried to replicate the Philip group's technique by singing a song Celia might like—an off-key version of "Don't Sit Under the Apple Tree."

"They sing as badly as you," Quinton said. I dug a sharp elbow into his ribs and snorted.

After quite a while, they got a single distinct rap, which we both suspected was caused by one the participants—possibly by accident.

But even though it was plain to us that the rap wasn't a legit phenomenon, the group seemed to be pleased with it and gave themselves credit. No one was upset by the knocking, though the Asian woman and the man in the business suit both frowned a bit. Other reactions ranged from surprise to delight, though I thought the young tawny-skinned man looked just a touch smug about it.

It was strange to see Mark alive and well and sitting at the table with the group. He seemed a touch more solemn than the rest—more serious than I'd ever seen him at Old Possum's. Except for Mark's demeanor, nothing seemed odd about the early sessions.

I made a couple of notes and we worked through more of the early recordings. The group got more relaxed with one another and their methods over time. They chatted a bit before each session. I noticed that the middle-aged couple kept their backs to each other most of the time and that the housewife tended to scowl unless she was in conversation with the young, single men—then she got coquettish. In one session, the group talked about the recent start of baseball season. One of the young men asked if Celia liked baseball and they began discussing it, elaborating on their ghost.

The middle-aged woman—striking, blond, and buff even in a suit—broke in, impatiently: "Why don't we just ask her? Celia, did you enjoy baseball?"

The table jiggled side to side; then one loud rap was followed by a quieter second knock. Mark's eyes got very big.

We both leaned forward and peered at the screen. "Can you pause that?" I asked.

Quinton tapped the computer keyboard and the image froze.

"Back it up. I want to see what happened."

The event ran backward for an instant, then began crawling forward, frame by frame. The table rocked the same way Quinton had made it move on Wednesday. "That's the booth controls moving the table, isn't it?" I asked.

"Yeah. You can see the feet of the table rising the same way they did in the lab, and the infrared camera recorded the slight rise in temperature in the rug's coils," he confirmed. He advanced the frame a bit farther and we could see Mark's elbow flex off the edge of the table a little just as the first knock came. "The guy with the long hair did that."

I nodded. He advanced the picture. The group remained still. The second knock came. "But he didn't do that," I said.

Quinton studied the frame. "No, he didn't. I don't see anyone else moving, so the sound wasn't made by anyone at the table. And it sounds different. Let me take a look at that…"

He began typing and poking about in the files, using the mouse to select something from the recording's timeline. He dragged several jagged waveform bits off to the side of the screen and enlarged them. He typed a quick tag for each one.

"All right. Look at these and listen." He poked the machine and it began playing the knocks while it ran a red line over the waveforms.

"This is the knock the Indian guy made in the previous session." It had a large lump in front and a short tail and sounded sharp, deep, and wooden.

I glanced at Quinton. "Indian?"

"Well, he looks Indian to me—Asian Indian, not Native American Indian—though I guess he could be Arabic or Asian…"

I considered it and logged the identification in my mind. For some reason "Indian" hadn't even occurred to me as a tag for the bronze-skinned man with the puckish smile. No one on Tuckman's list had a name that sounded Indian, though.

Quinton drew me back to the knocks, pointing at the next waveform on the screen. "This is the one the long-haired guy just made—the first knock." It was blunter in front than the first one, but otherwise very similar in shape and tone.

"Now, this is the second knock." The waveform was shaped like a porpoise with a long, shallow slope before a bulging round shape that tailed off slowly to a sudden, short spike. It had a more hollow sound than the others and ended with a pop almost too short to notice.

Quinton moved the cursor down to another waveform on the screen. "This one I got from the comparison report file. It's labeled 'Celia'—which is the name of their 'ghost,' right?"

"Yes."

Quinton made the last two waveforms larger. "They're not identical, but they're very similar. The length of the slope on the front is shorter in the comparison notes version and the decay at the end is a little shorter, too, but the basic shapes of the main waveforms are the same, right down to the sharp snap at the end."

"So that knock came from Celia."

Quinton nodded. "Yeah, I'd say that whatever Celia is, it made that noise."

I nibbled on my lower lip for a moment before asking, "Why are the two knocks different?"

"I'd guess that's caused by experience. The slope at the front is some kind of windup that you can't hear at normal volumes, but the mics picked it up under the table. And I'd guess that pop at the end is, basically, the shutdown—kind of like pulling the plug. As they got better at making the noise, they didn't need to wind up so long, or wait as long to pull the plug."

I considered that and agreed with Quinton's analysis, though I wasn't thinking in terms of switches and household wiring. "But what is the noise?" I thought aloud. "It's not some object hitting the table…"

Quinton nodded. "Yeah, it's not. Something hitting the table would have a similar waveform to the other two. In those two, the hard peak at the front is the actual impact of a fist or something on the wood and the rest of the envelope is the resonance and decay through the wood surface. The Celia knocks have that subaudible component in front of the impact on the wood, and their resonance and decay are different, more like they're happening in the wood rather than on or under it."

I cocked my head to the side and looked at him. "What could do that?"

He shrugged. "I don't know."

"Do you think … it actually could be a ghost?"

He looked hard at me and frowned. "You're serious."

"Yeah. What do you think?"

"I've seen enough weird stuff in this town that I wouldn't say it couldn't be a ghost, but I don't know."

I looked at the screen again and pointed at Mark. "The guy using the table tricks—the one with the long, dark hair—he died yesterday in a very nasty way."

Quinton looked at Mark's image, then back at me. "What are you getting at?"

"I'm not sure. This thing is giving me a bad feeling."

"Well, the guy's dead, so … yeah, I can understand that."

"Tuckman thinks someone is faking more phenomena than they're actually getting, but if that knock is real, then maybe they aren't. And if they aren't faking, what *is* going on? The stuff they did yesterday was a lot more impressive than this."

"You think it's real? Or do you think they faked it?"

"I just don't know."

"Well, let's see what else they can do, on camera, before you make up your mind." He resumed the session replay.

On the screen, Mark Lupoldi still looked surprised. The rest of the group just nodded. The female executive continued to question the ghost. "Did you go to the games with Jimmy?"

There was a long pause before a pair of hesitant knocks sounded.

I glanced at Quinton. He paused the replay and opened the sound window again. Expanded to a large size, the waveforms were easy to spot. Two porpoise shapes, closely connected nose to tail with only a single pop at the end of the pair.

"That's interesting," Quinton noted. "These are connected and the slope on the second one is shorter, even though there's a pause in the sound. Maybe it needs less energy to create another noise once it's started."

"And the pop comes only at the end of the whole message," I added.

"Can't be sure with such a small sample, but that looks like the case." He peered at the computer's status bar. "Damn. I have to go—I have to meet someone at eight."

"It's only six thirty," I protested.

"Yeah, but I have to do some prep and pick up some stuff first. But you know how to do this now. And I shouldn't be hanging around, compromising your client confidentiality any further."

He seemed a little uncomfortable, but I was reluctant to see him go. It was nice to talk to someone I didn't have to lie to or be wary of. My social life had never been exhausting, but since my fall into the Grey, it had become minuscule. I don't mind most of the time—being the prickly sort I am—but I go through fits of noticing the vacuum of social contact and regretting it. No surprise that this often coincided with phone calls from Will.

I made a face. "You're right. I shouldn't keep you. And these clips aren't exactly Oscar-quality material."

Quinton grinned. "I'd love to know how they make that noise, though. When you find out, tell me."

"OK," I said, and watched him snatch up his backpack and coat as he headed out the office door.

I returned to the séance recordings and notes, though I had to concentrate harder now that Quinton had left. The group continued to ask Celia about baseball for a while. The knocks got more firm as they went on and the table rocked several more times, though

I suspected that was still under the control of Tuckman, Terry, and Mark. There wasn't much more to that session, since the members grew tired and ended the séance early. During the review session afterward they'd been elated by the knocks, and most hoped the phenomena would get bigger soon. Mark, I noticed, had said very little once the knocks started and not much more after the session. Mark's statement in the file confirmed he'd made none of the knocks after the first one. In spite of the participants' hopes, Tuckman had worried that additional table manipulations might be too much reinforcement too soon and requested that Mark and Terry not escalate the effects until further notice.

They'd done as he asked. In the following six sessions, the knocks had become common but the table continued to move only under the secret manipulations of Tuckman and his cohort.

One month after the first Celia knocks, however, the table got into the act on its own, making a dramatic jump straight up that knocked some of the sitters out of their chairs. The jump had exceeded the height available from the magnetic pulses by several inches and left a clear gap between the table and floor on the infrared recording. Neither Mark nor Terry had claimed any responsibility for the movement. After that, the group stood at the table. As I watched the recordings, I began to put names and dossiers with faces and make note of interactions.

The phenomena became more pronounced as the sessions progressed and the group began to think of the table as Celia's primary manifestation. Celia developed a distinct personality in the knocks and table movements. She liked swing music and would sometimes cause the table to "dance" around the room in a clumsy, teetering way by lifting three legs a little and pivoting on the fourth, or hopping it with all four legs off the floor at once. She learned to flicker the Christmas lights in patterns to match the music, if she was in the mood. She liked movies and was a fan of Tyrone Power, though she liked modern films, too. The young Caucasian man—his name was Ian—who always sat with the Asian woman, Ana, suggested that Celia snuck into movie houses since she didn't need a ticket and everyone had laughed. Celia had rattled on the tabletop for several seconds, which the group interpreted as laughter. What they agreed upon was like law.

Celia's taste in films and music would change a little depending on which members of the group were present. She also had a bit of a magpie streak and often dumped the women's purses or played with their jewelry. Several times Ana's hair got caught in her swinging earrings and had to be disentangled by Ian while Ana winced.

One of the most interesting sessions occurred when Ken, the young Indian man, brought in a portrait of Celia he'd made on his computer. It was very similar to the picture of the woman I'd seen on the wall of the séance room, except that her hair was darker and the picture showed her from the hips up—her outfit was a rather provocative black dress. The table had roiled with excited knocking and teetered about on the rug as though impatient when he offered to show it off.

Ken had pulled a page from his bag and put it down on the table. The table became quiet and heavy, sinking against the floor as if the magnets had pulled it down, though the infrared indicated no such activity.

Ken hadn't noticed. He looked around at the group, then down at the table. "What do you think? Do you like it?"

Nothing.

"You don't like it."

The table thumped with two loud bangs neither Mark nor Terry had made.

Ken frowned and nibbled his lower lip, his brows pinching and quirking. "Yes, you don't like it?"

Two more loud thumps.

"OK. What don't you like about it? The hair?"

The group had taken turns asking questions about her looks as Ken tried to use his pens to adjust the picture to Celia's satisfaction. There had been no hesitancy in the answering raps. Even though the group wasn't sure what Celia looked like, Celia was. The hair was too dark, the dress was too sexy, and she objected to the generosity of curves Ken had given her—they were just a bit outrageous. By the end of the session, the group had become convinced of Celia's existence and they left the room both happier and more thoughtful than usual.

When Ken had returned with the new portrait in a week, the table capered and bounced in approval. The artist was pleased—even relieved—at the response. From that date on, the table had become more and more active and had a particular fondness for Ken, sometimes chasing him like a friendly dog in a way the booth controls could not have caused. Ken seemed to be taking the whole thing a bit more seriously as well, concentrating on the table and biting his lower lip.

Tuckman had tried isolating Ken to see if he was causing the changed phenomena. The table would still perform if he didn't come to a session, but it wasn't quite so demonstrative. If the group was smaller than four, Celia would not manifest at all—not even a knock or a flicker of the lights—no matter which members were in the room. Tuckman tried every combination of participants, even putting Terry and Denise, the department secretary, in the room—but no matter the combination, the table remained inert and the lights static until there were four or more members of the séance team in the room with it, when the movement, knocking, light-flickering, and noises would occur with varying intensity. The level of the phenomena seemed to be incidental to how many participants more than four—or which ones—were present, but the table's actions toward Ken continued with odd partiality for quite a while. Terry and Denise were ignored.

After several more hours, I still hadn't finished the whole set of discs and notes, but I had lost my ability to concentrate and it was growing late. I threw in the towel and headed home.

On the drive to West Seattle, I thought about the project. I could see how Tuckman would be upset by the unusual levels of PK activity the team was currently recording. It was a lot to swallow, since it takes a pretty powerful ghost to move objects at all, much less cause thirty-pound tables to dance. Quinton had shown me that the systems in place didn't have the power or the leverage to move the furniture as I'd seen it move, either in person or on some of the recordings. But unless someone else could show me how it was done mechanically, I'd have to assume the table was moving by itself—or by the power of the group, at least.

I was also bothered by the apparent movement of the Grey power line out of its alignment with the rest of the grid. Normally lines of that size lay near the ground, and I couldn't see any reason for it to be where it was. It seemed likely that the grid link was providing additional power to the phenomena. If the group had moved it, that, of itself, was extraordinary, though I doubted I could explain that to Tuckman.

None of this had shed any light on Mark Lupoldi's death. It wasn't my case and Solis wouldn't appreciate me poking around in it, but I couldn't help wondering about the connection. Mark was deeply involved in Tuckman's project and it seemed from what Phoebe had said that the project had begun to affect his life outside the lab, too— he'd been the focus of the paranormal, duppy or poltergeist, before his death. The manner of that death, from what I had seen, was weird enough to disconcert even Solis—who had seen much worse before he left Colombia than Seattle's criminals could dish out.

I trudged up the stairs to my condo, still thinking and frowning, and opened the door on an epic wreck. Every book had been tipped off the shelves, the fluffy innards of a disemboweled pillow had been strewn to the four corners of the living room, and most of my shoes had been dragged out of the bedroom and left anywhere the culprit pleased. One blue running shoe—much chewed around the padded ankle bit—had become a nifty cot for the perpetrator, who was uttering little ferrety snores from within it. I just stared into the room with my mouth open, amazed at the destruction two pounds of frustrated mustelid could make.

I didn't have the energy to swear. I just plucked Chaos out of the shoe and tucked her into her cage. Either I hadn't latched it right or she'd grown thumbs while I was out. She snuffled and went back to sleep, leaving me to clean up. It was my own fault, but it still took a couple of hours to put the place back together. I was too tired to face the mound of laundry that had collected all week, and threw myself into bed thinking it could wait for morning—or at least later in the morning.

EIGHT

The phone rang at five a.m. and kept on ringing until I groped around in the autumnal predawn darkness and answered it.

"What?" My civility doesn't function well before nine.

"Harper?"

I knew the voice but couldn't connect it to a name in my half-asleep state. I grunted. "Who's this?"

"It's Cameron. Cameron Shadley."

That woke me. Cameron had been my first vampire client, and I thought we'd solved his problems, but he sounded scared. "Cam? What's wrong?"

"I am in big trouble and I need some help. Carlos thought you'd be the best person to call." Carlos was helping Cameron learn the ropes of vampirism after a rather bad start and he was one of the few vampires I respected for something more than their ability to kill. He was a scary bastard even as vampires went and not particularly friendly to "daylighters," though he seemed to find me interesting. I wasn't sure what sort of interest he had, however.

I turned on the bedside lamp and snatched a shirt off the floor and yanked it on. Even with a phone line between us, I felt vulnerable and nervous talking to a vampire while undressed.

"What's wrong?" I asked when I had my shirt on. I clamped the phone between my shoulder and cheek as I struggled into the nearest pair of pants.

"I don't have a lot of time to explain. The sun's coming up soon."

"Then talk fast."

"Someone died and I need you to go to the morgue and make sure he's truly dead."

"What kind of someone? Your kind of someone or my kind?"

"It was an old man. Just an ordinary old guy. He wasn't supposed to die, but I made a mistake and—"

"You killed him?" My voice had gone cold with disgust. I'd liked Cameron, even when I realized the nature and necessities of a vampire's existence. I'd hoped he wasn't going to be like the rest, somehow, though that wasn't possible.

"No!" Cam protested. His voice swooped with emotions—at least he still had that bit of humanity. "He just died. He had a heart condition. I didn't know. Carlos was trying to teach me ... something. I miscalculated and the guy was too weak and he died. I didn't know what to do and while I was trying to figure it out, someone found the body and the cops took it to the morgue. I can't get to him before the sun comes up. I need you to go and find out if the guy's going to rise or not."

"What?"

"Rise. You know—come back as a vampire. Or something ... else. Carlos is furious with me about this."

"Why are you asking me to do this? I know Carlos must have someone he can send."

"I made the mistake. I have to fix it. I can't let my mistake cause Carlos problems with Edward. If Carlos sends someone to fix it, the word will get out and things could get pretty nasty."

"I thought Carlos and Edward were getting along these days." Edward was top dog in the local vampire pack. He and Carlos had reconciled some of the bitterness that had simmered for over a century between them when I had stepped in to help Cameron with his problems.

"It's more like detente, really," Cameron said. "Man, Harper, I'm running out of time here. Please say yes. I'll pay you whatever you want and I'll owe you a favor—we both will. All you have to do is go to the morgue this morning, look at the guy and see if he's dead. Then call me first thing tomorrow night and let me know. Please."

I sighed. "How am I supposed to tell?"

"You know what a vampire looks like in the Grey. He might look dead to the ME, but he won't to you. If he's dead—true death, that is—he'll just be cold, like any other dead body."

"Any chance he's still alive?"

Cameron went quiet a moment. "Trust me, Harper. He's dead. The only question is if he's going to sit up and scare the hell out of someone or not."

Oh, goody. I sighed again and got a description of the man. I hoped that he was dead and staying that way. I had no idea how to put a vampire down for good and I doubted the pathologists would be enthusiastic about experimenting. I said good-bye to Cameron and figured I might as well go to the morgue before the day got too much further advanced. I wanted to arrive at the end of the night shift, when the small staff was least likely to be on the ball.

I looked down and realized the clothes I was wearing were filthy and I didn't have time to wash anything. I couldn't find a clean pair of jeans in the place.

Muttering, I rushed through a shower, then dragged from my closet a pair of wool slacks I'd bought in a fit of incomplete wardrobe overhaul and put them on with a cashmere sweater foisted upon me by my mother one Christmas. It was a nice outfit, but I always cringed at the dry-cleaning bill. I prayed the corpse was clean and not inclined to get up and lead me on a merry chase into filth-laden alleys. It would be just my luck to get covered in gore or garbage the one day I wore something that couldn't take the strain. Well, at least I looked good.

Chaos yawned at me and stretched luxuriously when I checked the cage latch on my way out. She didn't even protest the lack of playtime, still sated with her condo-wrecking exertions of the night before.

Traffic was light when I got onto the West Seattle bridge, and the sun hadn't yet risen high enough to pierce the cloud cover and stab into my eyes as I headed east.

Harborview Medical Center perched on the edge of First Hill—Pill Hill to the locals—and loomed over the freeway like a stone vulture waiting for something to die. It seemed appropriate that the county morgue was located in the basement of this Topsy-like maze of extensions, wings, annexes, and walkways that had "just growed" from the original core over seven decades. I parked on the administrative side of the hospital to avoid the busy trauma center and made my way down.

I walked through dim images of the buildings that had once flanked the hospital and crossed through the memories of sickness and health, birth and death. Ghostly accident victims lined the halls, lying on misty gurneys. The odors of illness and the sounds of newborn babies pushed on my attention and I moved aside without thinking for the shades of long-ago nurses bustling past me. The boring elevator was a small relief, though even it had a few lingering shadows that defied the lights. The doors opened on a throng of ghosts.

The morgue had been in the basement for a long time, collecting Grey, dead things. I'd been down there before—missing persons, insurance, and pretrial investigations sometimes led to the deceased— but I'd never before been able to see what everyone always imagines: the spirits that never leave the place. There were plenty of them, though as I stared, I realized there were fewer than I would have thought. Most were oblivious to me, but some had gathered around the elevator door, making the apparent crowd. Two or three looked at me as if they expected something.

"I don't have time for you right now," I muttered. "Go away."

A few of them backed away or faded as I stepped out of the lift. Something whispered, "We don't know the way." I wondered if that was literal truth or something more spiritual in nature.

I thought I might regret it, but I murmured, "You can follow me out when I leave. But after that, you're on your own." The rest of the ghosts that could, moved aside and let me through, though I still had to step through a couple to get to the desk. Each phantom I touched had a different icy feel as they slid through me. I shivered and was glad of the cashmere sweater.

The sleepy clerk at the desk wasn't someone I knew, but she was a type I was familiar with—college student working an undemanding job late at night so she could make money and do homework at the same time. Since Harborview was the county hospital and administered by the University of Washington's medical center, the chances were good the clerk was a UW med student doing work study. She didn't even close her textbook when she looked up at me, a little puzzled by my natty appearance in such a place.

"Can I help you?"

"I hope so." I showed her my license. "I'm checking for a missing person and I wondered if you had any unidentified males who matched his description." I rattled off the information Cameron had given me, and tried to ignore the cold presence of the dead around me. It occurred to me that Mark Lupoldi's body was somewhere nearby, but I didn't want to see it again and didn't mention it.

It took some scuffling with papers and phones first, but I was escorted back to the cooler by a young man who called himself Fish and looked like a badger in blue scrubs. A small cortege followed me down the narrow hall. Most visitors saw the deceased on a monitor in a viewing room, but there wasn't time or personnel to set that up before the shift changed and everyone just wanted to get this over with, which I had counted on. I saw the body in person, my retinue of ghosts spreading around to look at him, maybe wondering why he was so important.

He didn't look like much lying on his metal tray. Just an old man, white-haired, dressed in ragged clothes, and dead. Just plain dead. I peered at him from several angles, but couldn't see anything, not even a mark of whatever Cameron had done to him. I sank as far into the Grey as I dared, but he had no gleam of living power to him at all and certainly nothing like the dark red coronas I'd seen around most of the vampires I'd met. I closed my eyes and thanked every god who might have an interest that he was only a cold husk of empty flesh with nothing Grey to him, not even a ghost.

I shook my head. "Not my guy."

"You sure?" Fish asked. "You were looking pretty hard..."

"He's similar. The beard threw me a bit. But it's not him. I'm sorry for the trouble."

He shrugged. "No biggie. At least someone's looking for someone. Makes me hope someone'll come looking for him, too."

I glanced at Fish as he pushed the corpse back into the chilled drawer. "You care about these guys?"

He nodded. "Yeah. No one should have to stay in a drawer forever. Couple of these bodies have been unidentified for more than ten years. That's just wrong."

I nodded, disturbed by the thoughts he'd started in my head, and took my leave. I was followed by a macabre parade, like the Pied Piper of the dead.

The ghosts trailed me all the way out the parking lot door, where they dispersed with a sigh. I looked back over my shoulder, but couldn't see a single one. They'd just wanted out of the morgue, I guessed, out of the hospital where some of them must have died. They had escaped at last. My good deed for the day, like the Girl Scout I'd never been. I wondered about the bodies that had lain so long unidentified and hoped the old man wouldn't be joining them.

NINE

I drove down the hill to Pioneer Square and buried myself in work. I made phone calls, managing the usual cases that paid the rent and bills and hoped to forget about ghosts trapped in the morgue and unnamed corpses in cold steel drawers. I turned my mind to other problems and called the Danzigers.

The phone rang twice and Mara answered.

"And how are you, Harper?" she asked, her Irish accent tumbling over the words like brook water on smooth stones. "We've not seen you in a while."

"I've been pretty busy," I hedged. I'd found their child a little harder to take lately and had, I admit, avoided them as a result. "I wanted to talk to Ben about an old ghost project and a few other things. Is he free today?"

"I'll ask him, shall I." She muffled the phone for a few moments before returning. Something was making a thumping and growling sound in the background. I had to concentrate to hear her. "Ben'll be here all day, he says. He's taking this term off to manage Brian while I've got the unholy course schedule, though how he'll survive it, I'm sure I don't know. Will you be dropping by, then?"

"I will. When's good?"

She snorted. "As well ask the wind. Come by if you like and if you hear pounding and screaming, walk on by and return later. I swear some wag had the right of it when he said boys should be put into barrels at birth and fed through the bunghole."

My eyebrows went up. Voluntarily and adamantly childless, I'd always assumed that most parents were blissfully unaware of the horrors their little darlings could be. I would have to apologize to a few parents, though not my own—we'd burdened each other with enough mutual horror to call the deal even, by now.

"Okaaaaay ... ," I drawled.

Mara sighed. "Never mind me. Come when you can. You know you're always welcome and Ben'll relish a chance to chat up an adult who's not as shell-shocked as himself. I must fly—department meeting today with the head fossil, himself."

"Thanks, Mara. Good luck with the fossil."

She laughed her sudden whoop. "I'll need it!"

I'd put myself on the hook, but I'd manage. After all, I could leave anytime I wanted and not be arrested for child abandonment—Brian wasn't my kid.

Putting down the phone, I spent some time online trying to find information on faking a séance, but found little. I'd have to add that to my list of questions for Ben. I managed a few other details, then headed to the Danzigers' to get some background information on the Philip experiment that Tuckman had based his experiment on.

The Danzigers' house was in upper Queen Anne, just a short trip up the hill that looms over Seattle's famous Space Needle. In spite of the competition for parking spaces, there always seemed to be an empty one within twenty feet of the pale blue clapboard house. I wondered if Mara had put some kind of spell on the street or if it was just magic parking karma associated with the gentle glow of the Grey power nexus beneath the house. Whatever. I managed to park right in front.

I trotted up the steep stairs to the porch, where the door was flung open and a black-haired juggernaut ran full tilt into my knees, butting me with a head as hard as a meteorite while giggling and shrieking with glee.

"Whoa!" I staggered backward, hooking my elbow around a porch column so I wouldn't go cannoning off the platform and tumble into the rosebushes below. The grab converted my backward momentum to a turn and I pivoted against the stair rail as Brian Danziger tripped and flopped down onto his belly at the top of the steps.

I caught a glimmer of a ghost near the open door and jerked my head up. Albert. The resident specter had materialized in a thin, incomplete column just inside the house. One corner of his mouth twitched in what I took to be a smile; then he vanished as Brian began to howl. Having no siblings, Brian appeared to have found a substitute tormentor/punching bag in the incorporeal person of the dead guy in the attic.

Quick, heavy footfalls preceded the appearance of Ben Danziger. "Brian! *Mein Gott, was jetzt?*"

"Papa!" the little boy yodeled, rolling onto his back and holding out his arms.

Ben stopped on the porch and blinked at me. "Oh. Hi, Harper. Did Brian butt you?"

I steadied myself and dusted at my trouser legs. "Nothing so soft as a butt. Call it a full-on ram."

Ben folded his six-foot-plus frame, scooped up his son, and set him on his feet again. He held on to the collar of the two-year-old's shirt as Brian squirmed about and attempted to bolt off again. Ben fixed the boy with a blue stare that contained all the menace of a cotton ball.

"Brian, why did you butt Harper?"

"I's a rhinerosserous!" shouted Brian, bouncing up and down and clapping his hands. "Graaaah! Graaaaaah!"

Ben sighed. "Not 'I's,' Brian. 'I am.' 'I am a rhineross—' I mean, 'I am a rhinoceros.' "

Brian looked at his father with wide eyes and an open mouth; then he shouted again. "Yay, yay, yay! Daddy's a rhinerosserous, too!" Then he lowered his head and smacked it into Ben's shins.

Ben rolled his eyes. "Oh, Lord … No more Animal Planet for you. Now, let's go back inside."

Brian scowled. "Donwanna!"

"But it's feeding time. There's cheese sandwiches for the rhinos today."

The boy looked skeptical. "Wif pickles?"

"Yes, with pickles, and tomato soup."

" 'Mato soup!" Brian cried, and charged into the house.

Ben watched him go, then looked at me. His black hair was wilder than ever, his face wan and thin under his curly beard, and the sockets of his eyes were drilled deeper into his skull than I remembered. "Welcome to the zoo," Ben said, waving me inside.

I followed him toward the kitchen. "When did the rhino phase kick in?"

"About a month ago, right after 'jaggywahr' and 'doggie.' They each lasted about a week. The rhino, however, shows no signs of imminent extinction." He heaved another fifty-pound sigh.

"Maybe it's just the company he keeps. Albert seems to egg him on."

Ben frowned, shaking his head as he picked up a plate of sandwiches. "Albert. Sometimes I'm not so sure of Albert's benign nature. His impishness gets pretty mean-spirited once in a while."

I suspected that Albert wasn't as nice as Ben gave him credit for. Even when he seemed helpful, he caused trouble. It wasn't easy to tell much, though. Albert didn't have an aura of any kind—just a body of Greyness he exposed or not as he pleased.

While Ben fed the rhino-boy cheddar-and-pickle sandwiches,

which were devoured in snapping gulps more suited to a crocodile, I asked about the Philip project. The old didactic glow began to burn in Ben's eyes as he replied to me, while managing his offspring—so far as a normal human could manage the devil's own Energizer Bunny.

"Oh-ho-ho! The Philip experiments are the cold fusion of parapsychology," Ben stated. "Kind of the unholy grail of ghost enthusiasts. The group who did them said they were entirely scientific and reproducible. Other groups at the time claimed to have reproduced the effects, too. But the documentation has disappeared—newsletters, notes, even a sixteen-millimeter film documentary and a studio recording done by the CBC—and no one has been successful at re-creating the experiments since. Or at least not anyone respectable, with proper scientific processes and verification. But as you know, parapsychology isn't the respectable field it was in the 1970s."

I refrained from saying it wasn't all that respectable then, either, and had only gotten less respect ever since.

"This group made an artificial poltergeist of some kind, right?" I prompted.

"Broadly speaking, yes." He paused to wipe tomato soup off Brian. "They were a self-selected group, led by a respected professor from the University of Toronto who was interested in ghosts and psychic powers, but he was also pretty skeptical—A. R. G. Owen was one of the guys who demonstrated that Uri Geller's spoon-bending wasn't caused by any kind of magic. He believed that the powers of the human mind—whether delusion, imagination, or psychic—were the mechanism for most of what gets attributed to ghosts and hauntings. That was pretty new stuff at the time, though the ideas of self-fulfilling expectation and conflation are now standard concepts in psychology."

He waved one hand in the air as if clearing an invisible chalkboard. "Not the point, I know. Anyhow. So, the group started with the proposition that poltergeist activity was the result of the power of the human mind. They didn't believe in ghosts and they didn't set out to call one up. They were convinced that since physical poltergeist phenomena could be produced on a small scale by a single person, much bigger and more directed effects could be produced at will by a group who was focusing on producing them. They called it 'PK by committee'—essentially the idea that while the power of a single human mind might not be enough to move a heavy object alone, it should be easy for half a dozen minds together. They suggested that group expectation allowed them to work together toward the creation of phenomena that would otherwise be deemed impossible."

"So they pretended there was a ghost doing these impossible things?"

"Not exactly. The experiments were based on PK research by two English psychologists—Kenneth Batcheldor and Colin Brookes-Smith—who'd both noted that PK phenomena occurred most reliably when the parties involved expected that it could happen but weren't actively trying to make it happen, and phenomena grew in strength and frequency when there was a personality to attribute them to. The people producing the phenomena had relieved themselves of conscious responsibility and blamed the movement of objects, table-rapping, noises, writing, electrical effects, and so on, on a personality outside themselves—a 'ghost.' Basically, once there's a personality to attribute the incidents to, it's easier to accept that they might happen. Then the people begin to expect that they *can* happen and *will* happen. And, of course, more things happen. It's self-reinforcing behavior. The big difference between the observations of Batcheldor and Brookes-Smith and the Philip project was that the participants created their ghost in advance and consciously—purposely—placed responsibility for phenomena on that constructed personality."

Brian brandished his spoon, laughing and sending droplets of tomato soup flying. Then he belched, looked surprised, and laughed harder.

"OK, feeding time is over," Ben announced, standing up to remove Brian from the chair.

Brian tossed the spoon, splashed his hands into the dregs of the tomato soup, and smeared two wide orange streaks on his face. "Mud, mud, mud!" he chanted.

"You are one dirty rhino. You know what that means…" Ben slung the little boy under his arm like an oversized football. "Off to the watering hole with you!" He shot me an apologetic look as he carried the wiggling, giggling Brian off to the washroom.

While the sound of water running and splashing came from the bath, I carried Brian's plate and bowl to the sink, leaving Ben's untouched food where it was. The cozy country-style kitchen didn't display quite the gleam it used to have. Chasing after the rhino-boy seemed to be having a deep impact on the house as well as its occupants. They were all looking a bit more tired than usual—except for Brian.

The water cut off and a wet rhino-boy—his hair slicked up into a small horn over his forehead—charged past the kitchen door, followed by a large towel and Ben, thundering behind like the herd in pursuit. They were both laughing, although Ben was a bit out of breath.

Once Brian was netted in the towel and dried off, Ben tranquilized him with twenty minutes of TV and rolled the sleepy rhino-boy into bed for a nap. Ben gobbled down his sandwich as we headed up the stairs to his office in the attic.

He licked mustard off his thumb as he rooted through the stacks and boxes until he found a black, cloth-covered book. He handed it to me. The lime green print on the spine identified it as *Conjuring Up Philip: An Adventure in Psychokinesis,* by Iris M. Owen and Margaret Sparrow.

"That's the book about the experiments. Unfortunately, it was written for laymen and neither of the authors seems to have thought of including their original newsletter reports or any technical data in an appendix. That may be part of the reason there's been so little success re-creating the experiment."

Ben threw himself down in the chair behind the desk and sprawled there, limp. Albert drizzled into view in a corner behind him.

I turned the book over in my hands, but didn't open it. "I don't understand Tuckman's angle," I said. "He's not interested in ghosts and he doesn't believe in them. He claims to be looking at the group's behavior in reaction to 'impossible' phenomena—something about the effect of group stresses and internal factors, how far they would give themselves permission to go while they believe they can make these things happen."

Ben raised his eyebrows. "That's an interesting angle. The New Horizons group—the original experiment group—noted in passing that there were a lot of tensions among them, including some sexual tension. The group was very diverse—married and single, couples and non-couples, ages from twenty- to fifty-something. The more tension there was, the more phenomena they got. The book claims that the group was harmonious and happy most of the time, but Owen and Sparrow admit that things got more exciting when there were unresolved issues among the participants."

I frowned. If Tuckman's group had internal tensions—and I thought I might have glimpsed a few in the recorded sessions—maybe it wasn't so far-fetched to imagine a connection to Mark's death. I chided myself for getting sidetracked and tucked the thought away. I couldn't waste my time here; I needed to pick Ben's brain while Brian was still asleep.

"OK. What about this poltergeist personality? The file copies Tuckman gave me include a six-page biography of this ghost who doesn't exist and the participants seem to accept it as an actual ... person, I guess."

Ben perked up a bit. "Ahh, yes. That was where the Owen group was unique in the study of PK up to that time. They created the personality to which they would ascribe the poltergeist activity first, rather than attributing activity to a random personality only after it happened—which is what you see in classic poltergeist cases. Since their premise was that they controlled the entity, they gave it a distinct background, complete with mistakes, fictionalizations, and historical errors. Then, if the answers to their questions during the séances matched the flawed biography, they were obviously drawing on their own story only—not an actual ghost or collective psychic knowledge of a real person. Philip was a collective endeavor and only existed through the group and under their control. The most interesting side-light was that Philip's tastes and answers would change depending on which participants were in the séance circle at the time."

"But they all knew the bio," I objected, "so how could that happen?"

"There're always details you don't think of at first, like 'What's your favorite color?' or 'Do you like ice cream?' Philip's personality developed over time as those details were filled in and was colored by the preferences of the sitters. Those with the strongest opinions tended to have a stronger influence, but if one of those people was missing, Philip's preferences would change. For instance, one of them didn't like a certain song, so when she was there, Philip didn't like that song, either—but when she was gone, he liked it fine." I'd seen that with Tuckman's group a bit, too.

"So Philip could manifest even if the whole group wasn't present?" I asked, thinking of Celia's appearances without Ken or Mark.

"Oh, yes. They discovered that they could get Philip to perform with as few as four of the eight group members—and it could be any four." I was becoming disappointed in Tuckman's group for lack of originality. I wondered when I'd see them break Philip's mold, since I couldn't understand why Tuckman would be so sure someone was messing with him so long as his study continued on the same tracks.

Albert started to rove around the room, eyeing us both as if he found the conversation distasteful but couldn't quite tear himself away. Ben carried on without even noticing I'd started to glaze over. "Later, they noticed that they individually experienced incidents of minor PK when they were alone, too."

"What happened?" I prompted.

"Nothing spectacular—and this was all near the end of the experiment—just object movements, flickering lights that seemed to respond to questions, the sensation of being watched. It might have been suggestion and conflation, but the group attributed the incidents to Philip, even when they happened in multiple locations simultaneously. Unfortunately, none of the at-home incidents was recorded in any objective way.

"The other telling thing was that they couldn't get anything to happen collectively or individually if they were consciously trying. Phenomena only occurred when the members were expectant, but otherwise relaxed and making no effort to create phenomena. They thought that would change eventually. They said they had hoped to create a visible apparition or an apport, but the group broke up before any greater advances were recorded."

"Hang on—what's an apport?"

"Oh, sorry," Ben said, then cleared his throat and continued. "An apport is a real, extant object that appears from empty air. Usually it's something significant."

I leaned back in my seat on the book-laden sofa and looked at the volume in my hand. It wasn't very thick or heavy. Quite unimpressive. I thought of Tuckman's manipulations and fancy equipment. "Did the Philip group do this in a lab?"

"No, more's the pity. They did it in a house with very little recording equipment, no monitoring, and no control."

"Then how is anyone sure it wasn't a hoax?"

Ben squirmed around and found room to prop his feet on his cluttered desk, tipping the chair far back. Albert dimmed and vanished, giving up on the conversation at last.

"That's the million-dollar question," Ben said. "Most of what the group claimed they could do has been shown to be possible, but only on small scales and inconsistently. Recent psychological studies into false memory and expectation claim it's all conflation, but they've only addressed the traditional séance, not the Philip experiments themselves, which—for all their flaws—were at least held in a lighted room with an attempt at neutral scientific inquiry. As I said, no one's been able to reproduce the level of phenomena the Owen group got. Most who've tried get little or nothing. That tends to bolster the hoax idea—or self-delusion.

"But there are broadcast records of a TV episode and a short documentary film about the experiment. The tape and the film have since disappeared. But the book came out in 1976—the original paperback, that is." He pointed to the hardback in my hand. "That one, there, is a later version from 1978 with some additional chapters. A lot of people still remembered those TV episodes in '78. If the book were published in the last ten years and had the same lack of documentation for events that happened thirty years ago, I'd be skeptical, but it's contemporary with the events claimed and though it's been doubted, it's never been debunked. Even the psychological experiments into conflation and false memory don't disprove the events claimed by the Philip group. The fact that some members have since died or disappeared and the rest now refuse to discuss the experiment doesn't help to clear up any questions."

I sighed. This was a mess. Dicey experiment number one leading to dicey experiment number two. "Did anyone ever get hurt during the Philip experiments?"

Ben frowned. "No. Not unless you count a few bruises from the table getting frisky—at least I never heard of any injuries. Why?"

I shrugged. "It just seemed that if you could move a table around, you could also do some damage with it."

"I don't think they ever got anything so dramatic. It was only a folding card table."

The original group hadn't invested the time or equipment Tuckman had. That wasn't the only place they differed, but how significant were the differences? The fact that Tuckman's group worked in a lab under monitored conditions would make me expect fewer oddities, not more. I tried another tack. "Why did you recommend me to Tuckman?"

Ben blinked. "To be honest, I was surprised he asked—I hadn't heard from him since he moved from U-Dub to PNU—but my reputation as the 'freaky-things expert,' as he put it, had stuck in his head and he said he figured that if anyone knew an open-minded investigator, it would be me. I'm not sure it was a compliment..."

I looked askance. "Probably not."

Ben crooked his mouth into half a smile. He looked about six minutes from falling asleep and his mouth was operating on autopilot. "Yeah, he's a bit of a jerk."

"Y'think?"

Something thumped downstairs. Albert rushed into visibility. More thumps echoed up the stairs punctuated with a series of grunts and growls. Ben tried to twist in his chair and fell onto the floor in a tangle of limbs.

"Oh ... drat it! Rhino on the rampage." He dragged himself upright. "I'm sorry. He usually sleeps longer after lunch."

"When do you sleep?"

"When Mara's home—which is about four hours twice a week. Or that's what I remember. Brian will probably grow up thinking I have early Alzheimer's and that Mara is my caseworker."

"I thought your mother babysat on occasion to give you guys a break."

Ben shook his head as the thumps approached the attic door. "Not for a while. She fell and fractured her leg."

I stared at him in horror. "Not Brian ... ?"

Ben made it to the door. "No. She slipped walking up some steps in the rain. But she's a tough old lady with strong bones, so it's not too bad."

I heard Brian say "Graah!" on the other side of the door and then the door bulged inward with a cracking noise and a rattle. Ben snatched it open and Brian tumbled through into his legs.

"Graaaah!"

Ben tried to look stern, but only looked a little cross-eyed. *"Schreck-liches kind!"*

I wasn't sure what it meant but Brian rolled on the floor and giggled. I didn't think that was the effect Ben had wanted.

"You may need to switch to Russian," I suggested.

"Unfortunately, my mother's already got him started. German is my last recourse for emotional outbursts and my grammar goes all to hell—heck!—when I'm mad. Soon I'll have to switch to Finnish or learn a new language to stay ahead. How long do you think it will take to learn Urdu?"

I didn't know if he was serious.

"Maybe you should try pig Latin."

Ben hoisted Brian up. "How 'bout frog Latin? If transmogrification actually existed, I would ask Mara to turn him into a frog."

Brian laughed harder. "Ribbit!" he shouted, clapping his hands.

I followed them down the stairs, reserving judgment on the existence or nonexistence of anything. "Looks like you don't need a witch to do that."

Brian planted a loud kiss on his father's cheek, then wriggled out of Ben's arms at the foot of the stairs and charged across the hall toward the living room in full rhino-mode once again.

"Well. So much for froggy," Ben sighed. "I think I'm going to have to take him to the park, or he'll never run down. Do you want to come along, or would you prefer to cut short your visit to the wild animal park?"

I did feel a pinch of guilt, but I said, "I'd better get back to work. I've got another couple of quandaries for you, though."

Ben began stalking the wily rhino-boy as he called back over his shoulder, "What quandaries?"

"First, how come glass—especially mirrored glass—filters the Grey?"

"What do you mean?"

"I mean when I look through glass I see less detail in the Grey. If the glass is mirrored, the filtering is greater, and multiple layers of glass filter still more of the visual component. Why?" I called to him.

Ben tackled his son and carried him into the hall to put on his coat. He reached for what looked like a dog harness and leash hanging from the coat rack and picked it up while keeping one eye on Brian. "OK, you want to go out and run? Do you need a leash or will you let Papa keep up this time?"

Brian eyed the leash and pursed his tiny mouth. "Not doggie. Rhinerosserous."

Ben knelt down in front of Brian. "*Hören, mein kleiner* rhino—you need to hold Papa's hand till we get to the park or you'll have to wear the leash. I don't want you running into traffic again. OK?"

Brian looked grave. "OK."

"So, holding my hand all the way to the park, right?"

"Yes."

"OK." Ben stood back up and took Brian's hand; then he looked back at me as Brian tugged him toward the door. "What was it … ? Oh, yeah. Glass acts as a filter … There's a lot of folklore about the effects of mirrors and silver on spirits and monsters, but I don't know how that would relate—folklore's not a reliable source."

"Science hasn't been batting a thousand for me," I reminded him.

"True … I'll have to look into it. Brian, hang on. I need my coat first." He struggled into a jacket while trying to hold on to Brian's hand and talk to me. "Is this a general question or is it germane to the case at hand?"

"Both. Tuckman's observation room is separated from the experiment space by two layers of glass and I could barely see the Grey effects on the other side, most of the time. The energy concentrations had to be very large or very close to the window for me to see anything distinct. But it's happened before—I can see less Grey in my truck than out of it."

"The truck might be a special case, but I'll see what I can find out, in general. What else? Quick, before the rhino charges."

"I need to know how fake phenomena could be manufactured so it would fool the participants in Tuckman's séances."

"Do you mean that Tuckman is faking his results?" Ben was aghast.

"No. But I need to know how the effects could be faked so I can show him they aren't—I think."

"OK, you need to know the mechanics of fakery and how to spot them. I'm sure I've got some information about it, somewhere. I'll have to do some research."

"You don't mind?"

"Not if you don't mind waiting for me to find the time. And it's something to think about aside from playdates and chores."

Brian tugged harder and made his rhino roar—I wondered why he thought rhinos made that noise and wished he would stop. I shouted over it as we walked toward the porch. "Thanks. I'll give you a call another time, unless you call me first."

Ben frowned. "Sorry we were interrupted."

I waved him off and opened the door for us. "It's OK. You answered the most important questions I had." I held up the book. "I'll get this back to you as soon as I can."

"No rush." He was yanked out the doorway by the charging rhino-boy. The door clicked closed on its own and I heard the latch turn, though no one touched it. I assumed it was Albert, playing security guard.

As I followed the rhino and his dad down the front steps, Albert whispered along beside me.

I peered at him. "What?"

He just stopped and looked at me, blinked, and gave me a thin-lipped smile before fading away.

Carrying the book, I went to my truck to begin looking into the project members.

I'd left the files on my desk. I berated myself for it and headed back to Pioneer Square to get my paperwork.

In my office, the answering machine light was blinking. I poked its button.

"Harper," Phoebe's voice shouted, "you are so in trouble, girl! Is that why you're not answering my calls? I been calling you since yesterday. You don't call me back, I'm gonna find me an old obeah-woman and have her put a curse on your scrawny behind!"

Scowling, I pulled my pager off my belt and stared at it. The display was dark.

Rey Solis's voice curled out of the speaker. "I would like to discuss your interview list with you. Call me before three. Oh, yes—Phoebe Mason threatened to skin you. I assume she's not serious, but do I need to change my mind?"

Terrific. Phoebe was mad enough to threaten violence in front of a police officer. Hell hath no fury like a pissed-off Phoebe. I scrounged in the desk drawers and found spare batteries for the pager and swapped them in. The pager remained blank. Even the little green power indicator wouldn't light.

"Damn it." I knocked it on the tabletop. The case popped open and spilled bits onto the desk. I spat dirty words. How long had it been nonfunctional? It should have vibrated when I opened the office door, but I couldn't remember the last time I'd felt it buzz and I hadn't noticed when it had stopped.

I called the pager service, picked up messages, and told them to forward all calls to the office until further notice. Phoebe had called three times, among other business calls I hadn't gotten. While Phoebe might skin me, I needed to pay my bills long enough to survive to be skinned, so I put the business calls ahead of hers. One of my steady clients was a litigator with the heart of a demon from the inner rings, so it was in my best interest to pour oil on the permafrost as the first priority. It would be a positive joy to take the heat from Phoebe after that.

Phoebe didn't answer the phone at the shop. I got the answering machine that told me Old Possum's was closed due to a death in the family. As far as I knew, the shop had never been closed before—not even when Dyslexia, the ancient and addlepated queen of the cats, had died and Phoebe had cried for three days. I tried her apartment and her parents' restaurant with no result. Then I called the store's office number.

"Old Possum's," Phoebe snapped. "We're closed. Go away."

"It's Harper."

Phoebe growled. "Oh, you! You!" she sputtered.

I sighed. "I'm coming up there. I'll explain everything and you can yell at me all you want."

She was still trying to get a good harangue started when I hung up.

One more quick call to Solis to say I'd drop by at three, then I was back out the door with the Tuckman files under my arm and on my way to Fremont.

TEN

P hoebe had reacquired articulate fury by the time I arrived at the back door to Old Possum's. I knocked and was greeted with a storm of words as the door opened.

"Harper! You are mean and sneaky! You askin' me all those questions and already knowin' Mark was dead! You better have some good damn reason why you didn't tell me. You bring your sneaky-ass self in here and start talkin'." Phoebe waved into the dim interior of the back office with an emphatic gesture.

I held position on the stoop. Bright sparks of red and white fury leapt from her, stabbing the air and leaving a sour tang of grief. She glared at me until the sparks died down and her lower lip began to tremble.

"Aren't you comin' in?"

I leaned left and right, making a big show of looking around her. The big overhead fluorescent light was off and only a pair of green-shaded clerk's lamps threw pools of light onto the big messy desk in the room.

"OK," I said.

"What are you looking for?"

"I'm looking for Phoebe Mason."

"What d'you—"

"She said she was going to have an obeah-woman curse me and you don't seem to be doing a very good job, so I thought I'd have to tell her to get her money back."

She reached up and clouted me on the shoulder—Phoebe's not very tall and though her temper is just as short, so are her grudges. "Girl! Listen to the mouth on you. You get in here, now. But I'm not making you coffee this time. I'm still mad at you."

I blew out a sigh of relief. "OK. I can take my punishment without caffeine." Which was technically true, since I'd managed to miss both sleep and my morning coffee and it looked like I wouldn't get any lunch, but I'd have to carry on without my favorite crutch. At least until Phoebe relented.

I entered the dim office and went to tuck myself into a chair too ratty to be allowed on the shop floor. "I'm sorry, Phoebe," I started. "When did you find out about Mark?"

Phoebe sat behind the desk and squirmed the chair back so her face was hidden in shadow. I could still see the wavering colors of her distress casting her into Grey silhouette. "Yesterday afternoon. Some detective from the police came round."

"Hispanic?"

"Uh-huh." The chair creaked as she nodded and I could hear her sniffle in the dark. I couldn't see her expression, but I could imagine it well enough. "Why didn't you say anything Wednesday? Why'd you just let me find out from some stone-faced stranger?"

"Detective Solis asked me not to. And I didn't want you to feel you shouldn't say anything bad about Mark because he was dead. We both need to know what he was really like and what he was doing. And if anyone already knew what had happened."

"Well, we didn't."

"Who was here when Solis came in?"

"Jules and Amanda—poor thing—and me. I had to send Manda

home in a taxi. She started crying so hard her eyes all swelled up and I couldn't let her go home on a bus like that."

"What sort of questions did Solis ask you?"

"Pretty much the same as you—how long had he worked here, what was he like, was he upset or in trouble recently, who were his friends, and like that. I even told him about the poltergeist, but he didn't seem very interested, so I didn't tell him about the accident."

"What accident? You didn't tell me about any accident, either."

"I did! I told you things fell on people." She shrugged. "It wasn't such a big thing. Couple of days ago Mark was shelving books in the back near the espresso machine and there's a customer talking to him. Then one of the gargoyles come right up off the mantel and smacks into the shelf by Mark's head and the big book he's putting up falls and hits Mark in the chest. Mark fell down and the book fell down and hit the gargoyle and broke the base and the customer goes yelling out the front door."

"Who was the customer?"

"I don't know. I wasn't in on Monday—yeah, it was Monday. Manda saw it all in the mirror."

I bit my lip. "Amanda saw it. Was the customer male or female?"

Phoebe flipped her hands upward in impatient annoyance. "I don't know! Ask Manda!"

"Did anyone else see the accident?"

"Mark."

"Besides Mark and Amanda and the customer?"

"I don't think so. Monday's pretty slow. Why is this so important? That stupid gargoyle didn't kill Mark and the customer didn't throw it at him, anyhow. Manda said it just come after him all of its own."

I looked through the dimness toward Phoebe. A sad kind of gray green funk wrapped around her. The minions were as much family to Phoebe as her own huge clan of actual relatives, and angry as she was at me for not telling her about Mark, the sadness was worse. It

would be awful of me to tell her Amanda was now the prime suspect—
ex-girlfriend and the only witness to some kind of attack that couldn't
be proved would move her to the top of Solis's list. The chances of
finding the mysterious customer weren't good—if there had been
one at all—and Solis would think the same thing. It looked as if I
was stuck between deceiving Phoebe some more or hurting her
worse.

I sighed.

"Phoebe, you do know Solis is investigating this as a homicide?"

She flapped a hand at me. "Of course I do. Didn't he say so? Someone broke into the apartment and killed poor Mark."

"Is that what he told you?"

"Of course it is! That's what happened! Poor, poor Mark. Poor
Mark …" She began crying, her round, dark face dipping into the
light as she lowered it into her hands.

"Oh, Phoebe, I'm so sorry," I said, getting up to put my arm over
her shoulder. "So very, very sorry."

She shuddered and gulped air, heaving in a huge breath, then
howled a bellow of deep red agony. I clenched my eyes shut and shook
with it.

Phoebe cried like a hurricane for over an hour. I finally got her into
my Land Rover and took her to her parents' place. Most of the clan
was down in the restaurant, already prepping for Friday night rush,
but her brother Hugh was at the house, behind it. He took Phoebe
inside, asking me to stay a moment, until he got her settled.

He came back down a few minutes later and I told him what had
happened. He nodded, looking grave. "We'll look after her, don't
worry." Hugh had a soft voice for a man with a chest as broad as a
Buick. "She's got a big heart, my sister. It's got a little hole in it right
now, but we've got the love to patch it up with. She's gonna be OK.
Shop, too. Poppy and Mamma'll scare some of those no-account cous-
ins into helpin' out till Phoebe can't stand it. She'll be running back to

the shop in no time to save it from Germaine and his sisters, and once she's back to bustling about and bossing people, she'll be fine."

I gave him a smile. "You certainly know your sister's soft spots."

He laughed in warm billows. "I should—she was bossing me from way back. I had to learn to defend myself." He put a hand on my shoulder. "Now, you take care of yourself, Harper—and you know what I mean."

"Yes, Hugh," I replied with mock exasperation, grinning. "I'll go out and tie some steaks on my body so you can tell Poppy I put some meat on my bones, OK?"

He laughed again and waved me off and I smiled and laughed as I left.

Once I was back in the Rover, the grim feeling of trouble returned. It was a good thing I was already heading to Solis's office. The business of the accident couldn't wait.

The police department offices in the glass-and-granite tower of the new justice center were much nicer than the aging lino and fifty-year-old paint of the old public safety building, but Solis still did not have an office. Like most of the crime investigators, he had a large cubicle with walls high enough and thick enough to cut the noise down to an acceptable degree for phone conversations but not private enough to encourage isolation. As a result, he preferred to have meetings almost anywhere else. He met me in the lobby with a folder in his hand and we walked down the steep pitch of Cherry Street to the SBC coffeehouse above the Seattle Mystery Bookshop.

SBC was only a block from my office, and I wished he'd thought to tell me to meet him there in the first place. At least I'd be able to have a decent cup of coffee, at last. Solis chose a small table in the corner farthest from the door.

I spoke first. "I haven't had much chance to meet with the project members yet. So far the only person I've talked to you'd have any interest in is Phoebe from Old Possum's, and I understand you've already talked to her."

"Yes."

"Have you talked to Amanda Leaman yet?"

Solis cocked his head and raised an eyebrow a little. "For a short while, yes."

"Did she mention an accident on Monday?"

Solis said nothing.

"I was talking to Phoebe a little while ago and she said that there had been an accident in the shop on Monday when Mark and Amanda were alone with a single customer. Phoebe didn't witness this. She only reported the story she got from either Amanda or Mark, so this is hearsay, but might be important."

"Go on."

"According to Phoebe, Mark was shelving books near the coffee equipment in the back of the shop and talking to a customer while Amanda was at the cash desk. Supposedly, one of those cat-gargoyles on the mantel was flung against the bookshelf Mark was stocking and dislodged a very heavy book, which hit Mark in the chest and knocked him to the floor. The customer left the shop immediately. I've seen the gargoyle and it has been chipped on the base recently."

"So your conclusion is that the customer threw the gargoyle at Lupoldi?"

"Phoebe claims that the gargoyle levitated by itself—that's what she was told—and that the customer left in fear."

His mouth twitched with amusement. "Flying gargoyles? Not a very convincing story."

"No, it's not, is it? Did the medical examiner find any bruising on Mark's chest that might be consistent with the falling book?"

Solis tapped the folder in front of him thoughtfully. I stole a gulp of my coffee as he deliberated.

"Yes, he did. At first we thought it might indicate something about whatever mechanism was used to kill him, but it was several days older than the fatal injuries. Now I shall have to ask Miss Leaman about that accident."

"And go looking for the customer."

He gave half a nod and looked into his coffee cup. "If there is such a person."

"If there isn't, then you have two possibilities—Amanda threw the gargoyle at Mark, or the gargoyle threw itself."

Solis shook his head. "Or the book simply fell."

"Then why make up the story about the gargoyle?"

Solis considered. "It is an interesting question. Would you consider Amanda Leaman capable of such a cold-blooded murder?"

I squinted, trying to remember the exact conditions of Mark's apartment. My instinct agreed, but I wanted to know Solis's reasoning. "Why murder?" I asked. "Why not an accident? Mark was notorious for playing elaborate jokes on people. If it was Amanda, maybe she was paying him back."

Solis was quiet for a while and I noticed that he had no bright corona around him this time, only a sort of cold blankness—an absence more than a presence—that constrained his emotions. Then he picked up the folder and looked into it. He closed it again and put it down on the table. He was very still as he spoke. "Mark Lupoldi was lifted and flung about five feet with enough force to crush the back of his skull and fracture his spine and most of his ribs. But there is no sign of a fight with an attacker. He was surprised and killed very quickly. He was in excellent health and condition and it would take a lot of force to pick up a young man of his size and throw him. It's what you expect in an explosion. But there was no explosion. Amanda Leaman could not have the strength to throw him like that—a single very large man perhaps could, but only perhaps. If she were responsible, she would have had to use some kind of machine. To assemble the machine and disassemble it afterward, leaving no discernible trace, would take nerve. If Amanda Leaman harbored such malice toward Lupoldi after their relationship was over, her facade of friendship for so many months while she plotted his murder would require very cold blood.

"This is a thing that bothers me. A well-liked young man is found dead in his apartment. If it were an explosion in the steam pipes or an overdose, it would be an accident. Had it been a gang killing or a quarrel, it would be a tragedy, but quickly resolved. There is nothing to account for the force it would take to kill him like this, and yet he's dead. It's a mystery. I don't like mysteries. They belong in books and TV shows. We had thirty-four murders in Seattle last year—a bad year. Half of them were cleared within a few days by the simplest police work, the rest within months—perpetrators bragged, confessed, or were ratted on by friends. None of them were mysteries. Now I have this." He glared at the folder and tapped it with his fingertips.

"You don't usually share information, so … what do you want from me for this?"

"I want your list of the participants in that project you're investigating."

"Why don't you just ask Tuckman?"

"Because, until now, you hadn't told me who your client was."

I gave myself a mental kick in the head. "Ah. I'm still not sure the cases are related…"

"It doesn't matter what you're sure of, Ms. Blaine." His voice was still calm and low, but he was starting to show that angry orange glow again. "I need to talk to everyone who might know the victim well enough to want to kill him. This is a crime of motive, not of a moment's anger or opportunity."

I bit my lip. There was no reason to withhold the list, but I hadn't gotten well started on my own investigation yet, and I didn't want to deal with the complication of frightened subjects.

"I'd like to have a few days to interview them myself, before you start on this list. They don't know that Mark's dead yet—or they shouldn't—and I'd like to get in a few questions first."

He studied me. "Monday. I'll give you until Monday."

I shook my head. "Tuesday morning. Today is Friday and it's already half shot. You can chase down the rest of the employees and the family over the weekend while I chase down these guys."

"I've got my own family to see."

"Come on. I've never known you to take a weekend off during an investigation like this, Solis."

He growled a sigh. "All right. Tuesday morning."

I pulled the list from my own folder, but hesitated to give it to him. "This is my only copy."

"I'll write it down."

I put it on the table between us and snatched his folder as he was copying the information. Solis didn't even look up. "I don't know why you want that. Preliminary autopsy report's got nothing to do with your case."

"Hey, I'm a snoop. Sue me."

"Don't tempt me."

I leafed through the report, but there was little I hadn't already gotten from Solis or my own impressions. They'd done some experiments to see if Mark had been flung from the Murphy bed, but the angle was wrong. The long, rectangular bruise on his chest was noted, as was a smaller one about the same age on his left shoulder and some kind of old marks on his forearms. A photo showed what looked like shallow dents running all the way around his arms about four inches above his wrists. There were no defensive wounds and nothing under his fingernails but the usual dirt. Residue in the bedsheets indicated a woman had been there very recently and very intimately, but little else of interest. The long catalog of items found in the apartment ranged from the bicycle, with its lock intact, to the contents of the bathroom cabinets and dresser drawers, and I skimmed over it all without much interest.

I handed the report back to Solis as he returned my list of project participants.

"I've got a freebie for you, Solis."

"You are too generous. I wonder what you'll expect in repayment later."

I smiled. "That's for later. Now, you should know that Mark's job on the project was to fake poltergeist phenomena during séance sessions. The rest of the participants didn't know, but the research team did."

He looked thoughtful and the orange glimmer receded a little. "That's interesting."

"Yeah. I thought so, too." I finished my coffee and stood up. "Now that you've got what you wanted, I have a request."

He glanced up and waited.

"I've been yelled at once for not saying Mark was dead. I'd like to earn that myself, rather than by keeping secrets for you. Is it OK if I say Mark's dead now?"

He gave a shrugging nod. "Sure."

"Thanks. I have to get back to work. I imagine I'll be seeing you around."

"Probably."

I left Solis studying his file with his eyes narrowed to thoughtful slits.

I walked back to my office through a traffic jam of ghosts. Pioneer Square seemed to be gearing up for Halloween in a couple of weeks and the spooks seemed to know it. I'd gotten to the point of recognizing some of the ghosts, though I didn't know who they'd been when alive and I didn't care to. Most were just loops of memory going through some repetitive routine of their lives for as long as they persisted. A few others were more autonomous and aware. If I'd ever been curious about them I'd too often come to regret my curiosity to indulge in it anymore. If they wanted anything from me, they would let me know. In the meantime, I preferred to avoid them the same way most people avoid too-talkative or nosy neighbors and relatives who expect favors.

I let myself into my tiny office not quite overlooking the historically unattractive parking structure and noticed the flashing of my answering machine. All of the messages were numbers forwarded from my pager service. I reminded myself I'd have to do something about that soon, then sat down and called Tuckman's cell phone.

He was in a bad mood when he answered.

"What is it?"

I got perky just to irritate him. "Hi, Dr. Tuckman. Sorry to disturb you, but I just got finished talking to the police about Mark Lupoldi."

"Oh, for heaven's sake! Is he in jail? Is that why he didn't come to the session? Thoughtless son of a—"

I dropped perky. "No, Tuckman. Lupoldi is not in jail. He's dead."

I could hear Tuckman breathing and the noise of students echoing around him. He took his time replying. "When did this happen?"

"Wednesday afternoon."

"So this would have been before the session he missed?"

"Yes. The report says he died about two o'clock. About an hour before the session."

His voice was still tense. "What happened? Is there any connection to the project?"

I wasn't inclined to give too much information to Tuckman—who was showing no concern for Mark's death except as it affected him— since he hadn't proven himself to be discreet and thoughtful in the recent past and I doubted he'd suddenly changed. "I don't know if there's a connection. He was killed in his apartment and it wasn't pretty. I arrived as the cops were collecting evidence, but there isn't much I can tell you. Besides, you'll be talking to the police yourself, soon enough."

"What? Why?"

"Because that's standard operating procedure for homicide investigations. They'll want to talk to anyone who might know why Lupoldi was killed or who killed him. Since the project was a major part of his life recently, they'll be interested in everyone else who was involved. Don't get paranoid about this—they'll talk to everyone he knew, from his family and co-workers to the bums he gave handouts to. It's a cop thing. They're kind of like me—when they want information they ask for it and they don't like to be lied to." I paused to let that sink in. "If I were you, I'd cancel Sunday's session."

"Absolutely not!"

"Why?"

He explained as if I had not been paying attention in class. "If we're to expect disruption, it's all the more important to get as much done as possible before the group can be distracted. It's just as important that you complete your assignment in good order, so this is no excuse to let your investigations slide. The group will be less interested in you so long as the project is moving ahead. The moment it stalls, they'll start to fragment and focus on you or on Mark rather than the work. I can't allow that. The session must go on as planned and you must not tell the subjects about Lupoldi's death until I can break it to them in a way that causes minimal disruption. Now, do you understand?"

"Oh, I understand, but I don't think you do. You're about to be involved in a murder investigation and the detective you drew isn't very forgiving or easily distracted. He is very smart, though, and he has a glacier where his heart ought to be and will tolerate no bullshit. If he thinks you deliberately concealed the fact of Lupoldi's death from your program participants and staff, he will wonder why and he will dig relentlessly to find out. And unlike me, he has no interest in protecting you from any fallout. If you're not going to cancel the session and if you don't tell the group what happened to Lupoldi, you had better be prepared to answer the questions *that* will raise. I'm working for you, so if you insist that I say nothing I'll have to do that, but I would advise you to consider what that will look like to the police."

"Ms. Blaine, you persistently lecture me, and I find it extremely annoying."

"Dr. Tuckman, I suspect you'd be annoyed by anyone who didn't let you trample over them. I am trying to do my job and keep you from being hampered in doing yours. If you choose not to take my advice, that's up to you."

I could hear him simmering. "I will brief the group on Sunday. Meanwhile, work on finding my saboteur."

I started to tell him off on that point, too, but he'd hung up.

I made more phone calls to his project team, but only managed to catch up to two of them: Dale Stahlqvist and Ken George. From the voices, I recognized George as the artist who'd made the picture of Celia, and Stahlqvist as the middle-aged, blond businessman. George was on his way out, but said he could spare me some time on Saturday morning. Stahlqvist granted me the last hour of his day, if I could be at his office in ten minutes. The swanky Columbia Center wasn't any farther away from the dirt-crusted charm of Pioneer Square than the justice center, though it required another hike up the hill. I said I'd be there and rushed back out.

ELEVEN

Columbia Center is the tallest building in Seattle. It rears up from Fifth Avenue like three obsidian tors melded into one jutting prominence by some weird volcanic fit. In defiance of the prevailing winds, curved surfaces face Puget Sound like black sails. It is the bastion of billion-dollar corporations and millionaire executives. Someone called it the most obscene erection of ego on the Pacific Coast and I don't think he was too far wrong. Occupying the top two floors is the most expensive businessman's club in the city—the Columbia Tower Club—out-Babbitting even the venerable Washington Athletic Club. Dale Stahlqvist came down to the soaring red stone lobby to meet me.

Stahlqvist was one of those tall, pale blond men Hollywood likes to cast as Nazi Übermenschen or Viking raiders. In spite of my natural height plus the heels on my dress boots, he was still taller than me and he was inclined to look down his narrow beak as he assayed me.

"Well," he rumbled as he stopped in front of me and shook my hand, "we should go upstairs. A little more privacy in the CTC."

"All right," I agreed, and I hoped he was paying.

"So," he said as we rode up in the elevator, "you're what, another of Tuckman's graduate students?"

"No, Mr. Stahlqvist. I'm a private investigator."

"Really? I didn't think they actually existed. How interesting. You're not what comes to mind when I think of private eyes."

"Yeah, I'm taller than Bogie."

He laughed. "And much prettier."

While I suppose I am prettier than Humphrey Bogart, I'm no standout beauty and I know when I'm being buttered up, if not why. I imagined that Stahlqvist would have continued trying to turn my head a while longer if we hadn't arrived at the seventy-fourth floor just as he opened his mouth.

"Oh. We're here. Please," he added, gesturing me ahead, into the hushed modern opulence of the Columbia Tower Club's lobby. Stahlqvist paused at the big mahogany reception desk to sign in and asked me to do the same; then he whisked me into the lounge, but not before I noticed the small sign thanking guests for adhering to the dress code and eschewing denim. It appeared that my lack of laundry time had brought me more than a dry-cleaning bill.

All right, so the view was breathtaking—even with the drizzle. The lounge faced Puget Sound through the only flat wall in the building. The dark glass stretched uninterrupted across the whole width and height of the wall and around the exterior corner until necessity required a less transparent segment for the service area. Cold water, painted pink and orange with sunset, spread at the foot of Seattle's hills and, to the west, the sudden, white-peaked serration of the Olympic Mountains cut into the clouds above the peninsula. In spite of the tinted glass, it seemed as if I were a mere step from floating out over the view, weightless and free. This was not a room for those who suffer vertigo.

Since it was four o'clock, the lounge was a little crowded and I was relieved there were no free stools at the bar, facing that distracting panorama. We were forced to take a table, though both seats still commanded the view with the merest turn of the head. I chose the seat with the poorer aspect and Stahlqvist, acting the gentleman, couldn't argue with me when the declining sun was in his face instead of mine. Though I can see a great deal that Stahlqvist couldn't in any light, I still like the old-fashioned advantages, too.

He tried to order me an impressive drink, but I insisted on soda water with lime. "I'm working. I shouldn't drink."

"Oh, yes. But I am not, so I'll have the Balvenie Fifteen on the rocks, thanks."

The waiter nodded, smiled, and left us. Stahlqvist turned his attention back to me. "So. What can I do for you, Harper?"

"I'm doing some additional checking on Dr. Tuckman's project and I wanted to ask you a few question about it."

"On whose behalf are you asking?"

I smiled, even though he couldn't see it. "I'm not able to tell you that. Will that be a problem?"

"No. I can't see that it would. I have nothing to hide."

"You'll pardon me for saying, but this project doesn't seem like your sort of thing at all, Dale."

The waiter returned with our drinks as a frown flickered across Stahlqvist's face—he didn't like my using his first name. He sipped his scotch before answering. "It's not, really. My wife's thing—friend of Tuck's from the university days." And Stahlqvist didn't approve of that friendship. He rambled on for a while about his college days and his climb to economic power in the local community, dropping names and numbers. His only interest was money. It was obvious he didn't have any background that would enable him to fake any phenomena, nor would he care to.

I nodded for a while, then nudged him back on track. "You've been with the project since the beginning, so what's your general impression of the progress? And how do you feel about Tuckman's premise—that the human mind is the force at work?" I asked.

"I was skeptical at first, I admit it—I don't have any patience for mystical crap. Tuckman's completely right—this magic mumbo jumbo is just that. It's people who make the world what it is. It's people who really have the power to move—well, to move mountains! It's quite satisfying."

I'd just bet it was. Peeking at him through the Grey, I could see that Stahlqvist glowed with excitement. He loved justifying his power and position. As he blithered on about what he felt they could do, I noticed that he had a thin yellow thread of energy encircling his head. It trailed away to the north, dimming in the sunlight and distance until I couldn't see it without taking a big step into the Grey—which I wasn't going to do then and there. There was something familiar about the thread… As I tried to bring it to mind, I lost track of his words. Until he put his hand on my knee and bent a suggestive look at me.

I glanced at his hand, then back into his face. "I doubt your wife would approve of that offer."

"Cara's her own woman. I'm my own man."

My bullshit meter pegged to the redline. Even in the Grey he had a smarmy shiftiness to him that only reinforced that feeling. I let my inner bitch chill the stare I locked onto his. "My leg doesn't belong to either of you."

Stahlqvist looked surprised and pulled his hand back, making the movement into a glance at his Rolex. "It is getting a bit late. What else did you need to know?"

I asked him for his impressions of the other participants and watched his aura flicker and shift colors as he replied, flushing through oranges and reds and into sickly green spikes. He said they were all great friends, though it was obvious he disdained them. He was jealous of Celia's fondness for Ken—the artist—and of the older military man's ability to assume control of the group. Dale Stahlqvist felt he merited more consideration from both ghosts and humans—including his wife. Something between them caused Stahlqvist distress, but he slapped a lid on it.

The only time I was sure he was telling the truth as he saw it was when I asked him if anyone was faking the phenomena.

He shook his head, laughing. "Not possible. Tuckman's made sure of that. What we get is real." He'd convinced himself, in spite of his own disbelief in "mumbo jumbo." Tuckman seemed to be right on track there.

I stood up and offered Stahlqvist my hand. "Well, that's all I needed to know. Thank you. I appreciate your time. May I call you if I have any additional questions?" I noticed that the little yellow thread hadn't wavered once and I was still wondering what it was.

He stood up, too. "Certainly, Harper. It was a pleasure to meet you." He shook my hand, leaving an odd cold spot on my palm, and watched me go.

I exited onto Fifth Avenue in the long, dark shadow of the black tower behind me as the streetlights came on. The road ahead was choked with cars trying to turn left onto I-5 southbound. I was glad to be on foot. I turned and started up Fifth toward Westlake Mall, thinking about that thin yellow thread that looked so much like the strands of energy I'd seen wadded into a ball under the séance table.

The Pager Cart had gone out of business. I scouted around and found a kiosk selling mobile phone service, but not pagers. After two other stops, I emerged from a shop in the lower level of the Pacific Place Mall with a cell phone I'd been assured could accept my pages and receive forwarded calls from my office number, too. I was a little nonplussed about the two-year contract I'd had to accept to get the plastic marvel of miniaturization and modern convenience, but I'd been impressed by the fact that it got a signal at all two floors below street level.

I poked the phone, amazed to see that it was already working. I realized that the sun was well down now, so I tried calling Cameron. He sounded anxious when he heard it was me.

"So?" he asked.

"Your dead guy is just a dead guy. Nothing to see."

"Good. Great. Thank you, Harper. I owe you."

"Yeah. OK. But I'd like not to do that ever again."

"Never on my account."

I hoped not on anyone's account. I finished up my business with Cameron and made another call. It was two a.m. in London, but I was expected.

Will sounded tired when he answered.

"Hi, Will," I started.

"Hi, Harper. You sound far away. Usually, you sound close enough to touch. And I miss touching you."

A mild flush heated my face. "I'm on a cell phone—that's why I sound odd. In the basement at Pacific Place. If I move I'll lose you."

"Oh." His pause stretched as he shifted conversational gears and we talked about nothing much for a few minutes. Then he said, "Now I'm lying in bed, thinking I need to get up in four hours..."

"I shouldn't have called."

"You always call on Fridays."

"Maybe I shouldn't. Maybe—"

"Maybe you shouldn't call from the mall."

"What?"

"I just mean we can't have much of a conversation when you're in a public place with bad reception. There are things I want to say to you that I can't say in those conditions. I want ..."

"What?"

I imagined him shaking his head, some stray light from the street glinting off his pale hair in the early-morning gloom. "Never mind. Good night, Harper."

My own good-bye was made to a dead phone. I felt tired, frustrated, and sad. I wandered into the bookstore in the opposite corner, hoping to raise my mood. My feet hurt and I hadn't eaten all day, so I bought food and collapsed into a corner of the bookstore's café with a Michael Connelly novel.

One of the most pleasant aspects of that bookstore to me was its location so deep in the earth of the Denny Regrade that no ghost stalked there. Pacific Place lay at the southern edge of what was once Denny Hill until R. H. Thomson got his hydraulic mining equipment turned on the offending bluff. He'd watered it down to size to make the north end of downtown hospitable to the wide, gently sloping avenues he preferred over the vertical insanity that defined the original shape of the city. The current street level at the corner of Pine and Seventh lay more than a hundred feet below the hill that once towered over it, and the basement bookstore snuggled down into the glacial silt that lay undisturbed until the foundations of the current building were laid in 1998. I reveled in the paranormal quiet with Harry Bosch and a cup of soup until I had the energy to head home.

Chaos and I sorted laundry that had developed the sudden urge to levitate and move around the room, which amused the ferret, but just turned my dissatisfaction into irritation. I yelled at the moving clothes and swore at my purse, which spilled its contents all over the kitchen floor, sending coins and small objects everywhere, to the ferret's delight. I fell into bed late and in a mood so bad I had disjointed, angry dreams, and woke up swaddled as tight as a medieval baby.

TWELVE

Later Saturday morning I was finishing my breakfast when Ken George arrived at the Alki Café. I already knew what he looked like, so I had no difficulty spotting him when he paused at the hostess's desk. She pointed him toward the back and I put up my hand to wave him over. Since the weather was lousy, the restaurant was half empty and no one had tried to rush me out as they often did on weekend mornings—a good thing considering I'd only just managed to kick my bad mood of the previous night by indulging in ridiculous amounts of coffee.

Ken was about my height, slim, and had a loping, slope-shouldered gait that made his leather jacket swing as he came toward me. I now knew from the file that Quinton had guessed right: he'd been born in India, and while his coloring was classic Indian—black hair, bronze skin, brown eyes—the presentation was Western and unconsciously hip—as if other people copied him—right down to the wire-frame glasses and the soft mustache with close-trimmed goatee.

He stopped at the table. "Hi. Are you ... Harper?" His voice reminded me of Sean Connery without having a discernible accent—low and broad as if it came up through a trapdoor behind his teeth rather than his throat. His smile was bright white and I'd have taken him for a vampire if I were going by incisors.

I nodded. "You're Ken George."

He grinned and ducked his head. "Yeah. Sorry I'm late. I can't seem to get the hang of the buses." He sprawled opposite me, swinging a black courier bag under the table. He kept his chin tucked down and looked up at me with a self-deprecating smile. His long fingers toyed with the silverware roll. "So. What did you want to talk about?"

The waitress passed by and he caught her eye with the same little-boy grin. "Hey, could I get a cup of coffee, please?"

She smiled back. "Sure."

As he turned away from me, I peeped at him through the Grey and found myself stymied. There was a sort of glassy, shifting emptiness between us, giving only brief glimpses of color through its moving surface. It reminded me of my own Grey shield. Ken's barrier was incomplete and unstable and he didn't seem conscious of my probing. Like Solis's blank walls, it was turned to the world, not to the Grey, and had the worn ease of a habit. This piqued my curiosity and raised my mental hackles a little.

He returned his gaze to me, raising his eyebrows, and I reverted to a more normal view, smiling.

"I'm doing some additional background on Dr. Tuckman's project. I just wanted to ask a few questions."

"Shoot."

"How did you get involved in the project?"

He smiled and ducked his head, taking the silverware roll apart; then he looked me in the eye again. "I'm in love." Then he gave a short laugh. "No, that's not true—I exaggerate. I wasn't in love when I started."

He went quiet, thinking and plucking at the edge of the napkin. Then he sat up, leaning forward, staring into my eyes without blinking.

"How did I get involved … I was bored. Let me tell you, Harper, a couple of years ago I thought I was a real badass." His voice was low and soft, coming slowly and with a subtle rhythm. "I drove everybody crazy, I got into trouble, got thrown in jail, messed with people, just did mean, stupid things because I could. And my friends thought I was damn cool for it—or they just really loved seeing me screw up. What a bunch of jerks. I figured out how dumb it was—eventually. And I've been trying to get my life together since then. But sometimes it's … well, it's boring. So this guy I know says this ghost study sounds like a trip, and I thought it could be … fun. And Tuck thought I was cool, so I was in." He sat back and let the waitress put down a mug of coffee. He thanked her with a sincere look straight in the eyes as if coffee from her was a blessing. He started tinkering with the drink as soon as she left, dropping his gaze and keeping it from mine.

"Fun," I repeated, dismissing the odd mood he'd created. "Is that why you knocked on the table at the first séance?"

He jerked his head up and stared at me, his eyes wide. "What?" he squeaked. "Me?"

I nodded. "I studied the recording. It was you."

He laughed and seemed very ordinary, the hard walls around him momentarily dropping, and I saw a thin yellow thread of energy looped around his head. "All right, all right. Yeah, I did it. It was all just so … goofy. Here we're all taking this thing so seriously and trying to be cool with it and in my head I'm laughing my ass off. So I smacked the table with my knee. And they're all so excited and I'm trying not to bust up. God, it was funny! But it was … an icebreaker or something and after that things started to happen." His voice dropped a bit and his demeanor flickered toward serious, the blankness covering him again.

"What do you think of Tuckman's premise?"

"Tuckman's premise." He thought a bit. "Seems plausible. See, I don't really believe in this ghost thing—all that spooky howling around the windows stuff—I figure what's the point? But … I think I met one once. There was something there, at least. This was back when I was about thirteen, back when I started smoking, and I was outside at night, having a smoke, and there was a shadow where there couldn't be a shadow. And me, being a stubborn bastard, I went and I stood in it. Just stood. And it was cold there. I mean, it was the middle of the summer and this one spot is just freakin' cold. Then it moved away and disappeared. And I want to know what the hell it was. This project hasn't answered that question, but it's making me think and that's something. Challenging."

He gave a sudden laugh. "Most of what I do in class or even at work is boring—I'm always putting things off until the last minute and then pulling something out of the air the night before and everyone goes nuts about it and I know it's just some half-assed junk I whipped up. But this is not something I can fake. It's not just me. It's kind of cool making stuff happen. And, yeah, it's fun."

"Same kind of fun?"

"Same kind of fun … What do you mean?"

I noticed his habit of repeating phrases to buy himself time, of thinking and gauging his answers before he gave them. "I mean have you faked anything else since then?"

Ken chuckled. "I don't have to. Stuff happens by itself and it's a lot funnier than what I could fake. Wednesday, the table was galloping around like a horse. That was a laugh."

"Do you think anyone else could be faking any of the things that have been happening?"

"I know they could, but I don't think they are. That's not the point."

"What is the point?" His clever evasions and cold shield irritated me. I was reminded of the abusive boyfriend I'd run away from in college. He had also been charming and attractive, slipping out of hard questions and dealing damage for them later while he seemed unscathed by anything I did. I tried to shove the feeling aside, but it pricked me as I watched Ken.

He toyed with his coffee mug and built his reply. "The point? The group, I guess. Power of the mind. Self-control. We're all working together, but we're still alone, still ourselves, controlling this thing we made." He paused and played with the mug, then drank from it before continuing. He lowered his eyebrows and shifted his gaze to the side, and his wall was solid and slick as glass. "Maybe I'm not so sure, after all. I need to think about it."

"OK. What do you think about the rest of the group?"

"The rest of the group." There was a sudden flare of brightness around him before subsiding and he looked at me again with a smile lighting his eyes. "About half of 'em are dicks in one way or another. The rest are OK."

"Who's OK?"

"Mark's all right. He's funny, you can hang with him, have a beer, that sort of thing. Wayne's good—"

I stopped him. "I'm not sure who's who yet, give me a clue."

"OK. Mark's the guy with the long hair. Wayne—he's the old guy with the crewcut—sometimes he acts like he's still in the army, but he's a good guy. Cara's the blonde married to Dale Stahlqvist, very rich, beautiful. She"—his tone grew cold and bitter—"no ... I take it back. I can find her attractive—I can want her—but I think she'd cut my throat and keep my scalp when she was done with me. Ana—Chinese woman—she's ... she's magic." He shrugged and looked down. His skin was too dusky to blush well. He peered back up at me from under his brow. "The rest—they're just there."

"Just there?" I echoed.

He chuckled, catching on to me. "OK, they're dicks."

"I've got one more question for you."

"Fire away."

"When did you start to take it more seriously?"

"I'm not sure. Maybe when I started talking to Ana."

"And why'd you do the portrait of Celia?"

"You said only one more question."

I shrugged. "I lied. Why the portrait?"

He returned my shrug. "It's just what I do. It's one of my tricks—people get all impressed that I can use Illustrator and Photoshop—like it's hard. I'm not even that good at it. But I get an obsession and then I want to do something about it. So I do. I wanted to know what Celia looked like. I couldn't think of her as real until I knew and I had to know, had to dig in. So I painted her." He glowered and seemed both more human and more dangerous, exposed in sudden, bright red ire. "She didn't even like the damned picture. I had to work it over for days. Man! You know how hard it is to draw a person when you can't even see them? It's not like there's even a photo of her to work from. We had to do this sort of Twenty Questions thing to get it right. I wanted to smash something before we were done. It was frustrating."

"Do you think of Celia as a real person?"

He blinked at me, his Grey shutters sliding back into place. "A real person? No. A real personality, yes." He frowned and sucked in his lower lip. "Does it matter?"

I shrugged. "I don't know. What does Tuckman say?"

"Huh. He'd probably say the reality of the personality is the only thing that matters."

We both sat back and I watched the glassy emptiness around him. I wondered just what the hell he was trying to hide. He wasn't very good at keeping his shield in place and I couldn't tell if he did it on purpose or not. When it faltered, something bright and passionate showed through, but he always hid it again. Some vulnerability, in spite of the tough-guy pose? Or something else?

My silence made him uncomfortable. Ken looked at his watch. "Wow. I have to get going."

"Thanks for talking with me."

"Hey, it was a pleasure. Seriously."

"Can I call you if I think of anything else?"

"Sure. No problem. Gotta go."

I watched him grab his bag and stride out. I wasn't sure if I'd learned much from Ken except that he was hiding something I wanted to discover. He'd answered my questions—not saying he'd been a theater major before switching to art. His obsession about Celia's portrait seemed a bit unusual and I knew I'd missed something through my own annoyance. I didn't think he knew how he affected the Grey—if he'd known I could see it, he would never have let his shield slip. Something had caused that psychic wall to rise, but I had no clue what, no matter how much it bothered me.

I put down money for my breakfast—the waitress had forgotten to charge for Ken's coffee—and picked up my still-strange cell phone. I thought I might be able to catch a few more of Tuckman's group at home now and I was pleased I didn't have to waste time going back to my office. Eventually I'd have to get in some background research on this lot—Stahlqvist and Ken both left me wanting to dig, and who knew what I'd get from the others?—but since all offices were closed, I'd do better spending the small grace period Solis had given me interviewing the principals than grubbing Internet records.

I made calls and was able to catch up to most of the rest of the group and schedule time to talk before Tuesday. I wondered why I hadn't gotten a cell phone long ago.

Patricia Railsback—the harried and unhappy housewife at the séance sessions—met me at the Harbor Steps play yard under a sky that threatened rain, but hadn't yet produced any. Her hair was pulled back into a hasty ponytail that left her made-up face strangely naked and let too much light fall onto the stains of sleeplessness under her eyes. No amount of makeup could hide her expression of pinched dissatisfaction and frustration. She hunched her shoulders under her fashionable wool jacket and stared into the small play yard wedged between two of the complex's four towers.

Three children rollicked over the climbing equipment and kicked clouds of cedar bark into restless wakes whenever they touched ground. Greenery dripped from overhead galleries and orange beams running between the residential towers. Patricia put herself sideways to the yard, leaning her hip against the rubberized rail so she could talk to me and watch the kids at the same time.

I looked over the shrieking, giggling mayhem. The kids were playing some elaborate game of climbing and jumping. "Which one's yours?" I asked.

She sighed. "All of them—Ethan, Hannah, and Dylan," she added, pointing at them in age order. "Demolition experts in training." A large bit of beauty bark winged Patricia on the temple. "Ow!" she shouted, brushing it aside. "You brats stop that! You know better than to throw things at people!"

Hannah and Ethan stopped and stared at her. "It wasn't us! It was the ghost!" Hannah yelled.

Patricia rolled her eyes. "Damn it," she muttered under her breath. "OK, I'm sorry," she called back. "You guys just play carefully, now, OK? Ghosts can fly but you can't, so no jumping around. And no throwing and blaming it on the ghost."

A careless "OK, Mom" came back, but the kids were already back in motion.

I gave her a sideways look and spotted a bright yellow gleam around her head. "Your kids know about the project?"

"Oh, God ... yeah. Sort of." Her mouth turned down as she spoke and her vowels seemed to spill out the corners. "It's not like you can miss the stupid thing with their dad gone all the time. It's their best little playmate—most kids have imaginary invisible friends, mine have an honest-to-goodness poltergeist to play with."

"Are you certain this is Celia at work?"

She rolled her eyes and shook her head. "What else would it be? It's not like I have any other life outside my home, my kids, and this project."

Bitterness spilled out with every flooding word. She felt abused by life—although I thought that for a woman with no college degree and no apparent skills or charm, she hadn't done too badly in a socioeconomic sense. I wondered if her whining was bred from her husband's constant absence or the other way around. Half a life led in the shadows of a successful man to whom she no longer felt more than a mechanical duty might lead to many things. Yet she would not break from him, except to join this insane project. She was on the fence about the whole thing—life, family, project.

She'd been a drama major in high school—a bit of a drama queen to my mind—and that seemed to have been the high point of her life. I got the idea she resented the children who kept her tied to her gilded cage and that she wanted attention from someone, anyone—preferably male—and the project had seemed like a place to get it. But it wasn't working out so well. She didn't fit in with the younger members or the older members, and the only person she'd ever had a reasonable conversation with was Mark, whom she'd driven home once when his bike had a flat tire. She didn't really like any of the rest of them, though she wouldn't say so. But she did believe that their poltergeist was real, that they'd made things move and caused the knocks and light flickers through their own power of the mind. She didn't see any contradiction in the idea that everyone else was hateful, yet they somehow worked together.

As she babbled on, bemoaning her life, I glanced at the three kids who had sat down on the ground with a pile of cedar chips and leaves and were tossing them up one at a time. Once in a while, one of the leaves or chips would make a sudden shift to the side and the kids giggled. What were they doing? I peered at them through the Grey and could see a scribbled yellow shape, continuously shifting, stabbed randomly with silvery shards, hovering around them and moving the wood and leaves. Patricia noticed I'd stopped listening and looked at the children also, her yellow thread stretching toward the uncanny shape of the same color.

"What are they doing?" I asked.

She threw her hands into the air. "Who knows? They're kids!" She balled her fists on her hips and shouted. "Hey, stop that! You're getting dirty!"

I took a step closer to the kids and their Grey companion, but as they turned to look at Patricia, they saw me moving toward them. The kids jumped up, dusting at their clothes, and the yellow shape imploded with a muffled bang that sounded a lot like the table raps from the recordings and left a weird ringing in my head. I frowned and peered harder at the kids, but there was only the thinnest yellow strand now, looping around them from a source in Patricia's body, and the thread which had tied her to the shape now pointed only to the empty space where it had been.

I looked back at her. She was making a big-eyed face at her kids, oblivious to what had just happened in the Grey. "Well? You have another fifteen minutes before we have to go upstairs and get cleaned up to see Daddy. Better make the most of it."

The children jumped up and scurried back to the business of playing on the jungle gym. We went back to talking.

Patricia didn't believe the phenomena were being faked. She became defensive when I asked if she'd ever experienced anything like it before and I had the strong impression she was lying. Pecking at her a bit, I got her to admit she'd had some "odd experiences" as a teenager, but she wouldn't go into detail. I wouldn't have been surprised to learn she'd been the focus of a classic poltergeist haunting—emotional whirlwinds leading to increasingly bizarre events in a bid for attention, a self-justifying sense of persecution. Before I could broach the subject, though, she looked at her watch and turned away from me with her shoulders hunched.

"I have to go." She called out, "C'mon, you three! Time's up! Gotta get cleaned up for Daddy!"

The kids sent up a collective whine, but they dragged themselves toward their mother. She began to herd them toward the nearest tower and its elevator, dismissing me with an absent flap of her hand.

I watched her go, then started to make my own way out to the sprawling hillside staircase for which the complex is named, past the brushed steel sculpture of pi and the tiers of waterfalls. I shook my head as I went down the steps toward Western.

I'd only gotten the bare bones of information out of her and never had a chance to ask if she'd had any further contact with Mark. Annoying as she was, I'd have to find another time to talk to her.

While she might not be causing any of the phenomena herself—legitimately or not—it was possible she was putting in a bit of extra energy and boosting the effect of the rest of the group. She was the only one of the participants I'd seen so far who seemed to have daily contact with Celia—if the thing I'd glimpsed was, indeed, the group's construct, which seemed likely. It bred an odd feeling in me on sight and sent a flash of frost over my bones. The sudden lassitude that had fallen on me when it left bothered me and I wondered why it had happened. This ghost unsettled me more than most.

THIRTEEN

A rich man might enter the gates of heaven more easily than a 1972 Land Rover can find a parking space on Capitol Hill on a Saturday afternoon. Especially if it wants to be within walking distance of Broadway. I finally gave in and paid to put it in a tiny surface lot at the north end of the main strip. Any other day I'd have taken a bus up from my office in Pioneer Square, but I had too many people to see to do without the Rover.

As I parked, I heard some kind of J-Pop bubblegum music of bleats and tweets with a mechanical drumbeat issue from my purse. It took me a moment to realize it was my cell phone. I didn't yet connect the silly little song with a phone call—I'd have to change it, when I could figure out how. I dug into my bag and answered the phone.

"Oh. Hi, Harper. I thought I was calling your pager…"

"It's OK, Ben. I got a cell phone and the number is being forwarded for a while. What can I do for you?"

"Well, it's more what I can do for you. I found some information about the table-tapping business and I was hoping you'd have some time later today to see it. Mara's chasing rhino-boy for a while, so I can show you exactly what the books describe, if you want."

"That would be great. When and where?"

"Uh ... four? At the Five Spot up here on Queen Anne?"

"Happy hour? OK."

Ben let out a sigh. "Yeah, happy hour—well, quiet hour by comparison, at least."

I laughed. "I understand. I'll see you there. Thanks, Ben."

I shut the phone off and tucked it into my jacket pocket.

By the time I reached the Harvard Exit Theatre, the first shows were more than halfway through—a film from Poland and an American independent film I'd never heard of. I asked for Ian Markine at the ticket window—which really was a window in the side of the building—and was told to go right in and wait until he came down from the third floor.

The theater was a large, bland brick building in a sort of mock Georgian style. Over the door the words "Women's Century Club" were preserved on the decorative cement surround. Inside, the lobby was freshly renovated and more like a posh living room from the flapper era than a theater. It was a long, narrow room with a patterned wall-to-wall carpet, a fireplace, cozy chairs, bronze Art Deco lamps, and a glossy black grand piano. There was a constant flicker of silvery ghosts—tracks of memory worn into the room—and a few squiggles of Grey energy rippling around the lobby.

Seeing no sign of anyone, I ducked into the washroom.

As I was standing over the sink with a handful of foamed soap, I glanced up into the mirror and blinked in surprise. There was someone standing behind me, but I hadn't heard anyone. I turned my head and the worlds slid over each other. The woman standing behind me was a ghost, without a doubt. Well, she could wait.

I rinsed my hands and turned to look at her. She was a plump woman with an intense gaze. Her dark hair was dressed back into a bun at the nape of her neck and her clothes were those of a fashionable matron of the Jazz Age. She frowned at me.

"I imagine you're a woman of sense, even if you stir up hornets by profession," she said. Her voice was firm, but quiet.

"Pardon me?"

"I have always believed women were the equal of men, but they must both come by their rewards honestly. Dishonesty repels me. That brooch is an outright fake. Like her claims to my family. Were it in my power, I'd throw it in her face, the jumped-up hussy. I hope you will tell her so."

She turned and strode from the room, fading into the mist of Grey time before she reached the door.

"Flabbergasted" seemed an appropriate word at that moment. I looked around for the ghost in the immediate Grey, but she'd moved too far away and I couldn't find her nearby in the living mist of the space between worlds. "Who are you?" I called out, but she didn't answer. Nor did anyone else. I didn't have time to go searching through the Grey for her and wondering whom the ghost was so angry about.

I left, shaking my head and wondering whom or what I'd just met. I returned to the comfortably opulent lobby preoccupied.

"Nice, but stodgy. Sort of the anti-Gatsby, don't you think?"

I turned sharply and came under the beam of a toothpaste-ad smile. Blue eyes twinkled at me with well-schooled charm above that glittering white expanse of dentition. A yellow thread seemed to ring around his head and shoulders like a halo.

I nodded with a reflected smile. "Yes, it is. Very East Egg." I watched his smile broaden—he even had dimples. "I assume you're Ian Markine." He was the handsome white guy dating the Asian woman from the project. I'd watched him untangle her black hair from her earrings.

His eyes sparkled a bit at his name. "Yes, I am. You must be Harper Blaine, then."

I just nodded. He was about my own height but where my brown hair was straight, his was wavy. He had remarkable good looks that he seemed well aware of, though he made a show of the opposite. His hair was just a little mussed, his spotless white shirt a touch too large, tie carelessly knotted, but still smooth. It looked like being young and sexy took a lot of work and I was glad I didn't have to do it, myself.

"You wanted to talk about Tuckman's project, right?"

"Yeah. Do you have time?"

"Oh, yeah. The audience won't be coming out for a while and nothing's had a chance to get messy yet. Why don't we sit by the fire? No one will mind."

I agreed and Ian led me to one of the armchairs in front of the fireplace. He sat down near me, rather than across the hearth, and leaned over the chair's arm to look me in the eye.

"So, what do you want to know?" His eyes were lit from within by some amusement.

"When did you join the project and why?"

He chuckled and there was an odd glimmer around him, like color fragments reflected in a warped mirror. I'd never seen anything like that before. "Back in December I was feeling ... stagnant. You know—you keep on doing the same thing, seeing the same people, and it gets dull. So I thought I'd find something outside of the sociology department—that's my major—that would give me some new people to get to know. I admit I'm"—he broke off to laugh at himself—"well, I'm always kind of studying any group I'm in, and sociologists are just not fun to watch. They're never disarmed. And there's not much that's further away from functionalism than making your own ghost, you have to admit. It does start to smack of collective behavior, of course, but I just try to enjoy it, instead of analyzing all the time."

"So this is a mental break?"

"Yes. And they're a good bunch of people."

"Interesting?"

He laughed again. "Yes, they're great people. We get along well. Ana and I have been out a few times for drinks with Mark and Ken—good times. Well ... I have to admit that Terry's an ass, but I don't have to deal with him, so it's no issue. Most of the time it's fun. It's certainly been rewarding."

I raised my eyebrows. "In what way?"

He smiled crookedly, looking down. "It's not good of me, I know. I just find it difficult, sometimes, to be everything to Ana. She's the center of my universe but ... it's been good to have a few other people in it, to make some other friends. That's very selfish of me, very thoughtless of Ana."

"That's Ana Choi, correct? She's also on the project."

He looked up. "Yes. Please, don't rat on me. I don't want Ana to think I like them better than her. We can both be a little jealous and I assumed this was confidential," he rushed on, his blue eyes begging, but there was a flicker of dimple as he gabbled and that sparkle of strange color.

"Of course it's confidential, Mr. Markine." I wondered why he'd brought it up so fast.

He sighed and sat back. "Harper, you don't know how much that relieves me. This experience—with the project—has been so remarkable and I don't want to ruin it."

"And how do you think the project is going?"

"Terrific! It's great! Sometimes it's very exciting. Wednesday, for instance, we really had something going." He gave a low whistle. "It was impressive, but, you know it's pretty tiring. We were all completely blown out afterward. Wow."

"Have you ever thought that the phenomena were faked? Even just once in a while?"

He blinked and lowered his head to stare at me. "Faked? No. I mean, that's just—well, why bother? We do so well without anybody faking anything. And wouldn't we notice if it was? It's not as if you can hide something that can move a table around like that. I've been working in this place a long time and I've seen some of the equipment you'd need to do that—there's still a ton of the old stuff in the storage attic. It would be far too obvious."

I didn't bother to tell him that modern stage rigs had come a long way since this had last been a live theater. Even as a mere chorus dancer, I'd seen my share of flying wire rigs and trapdoors that post-dated anything in storage here. But I had to admit I wouldn't know anything about the equipment needed to fly a table with a roomful of people less than a foot away.

"One last thing and I'll let you get back to work. What would you think if I told you someone on the team had been faking phenomena?"

"I'd say you were mistaken."

"But if it were true, who would you suspect?"

Ian frowned. "I don't like to point fingers ... but I'd have to guess Ken. He's got a tricky sense of humor."

And eyes for your girlfriend, I thought, and wondered if he'd noticed. But since it was Mark who was dead and not Ken George, I presumed Ian hadn't noticed. He didn't seem bothered by it if he knew and his ego didn't seem to have taken any dings as a result. He seemed like a typical, self-involved young man who wanted to look more knowledgeable and impressive than he was. I couldn't have cared less.

I got to my feet. "Oh, one more thing. Do you ever experience anything strange away from the group?"

"Well, not really," he confided. "A lot of people claim this place is haunted by several ghosts, including the ghost of Seattle's lady mayor, Bertha Knight Landes, but I've never seen anything like that. No apparitions, no mysteriously moving objects. Our ghost is PK by committee, remember? It doesn't work outside its own little room." Ian winked at me.

"I see. I think that's all I needed to know. Thanks for your time, Ian."

He stood up and offered me his hand to shake. "It was no trouble," he said as I accepted the handshake. He closed his other hand over mine. I found his grip cold and just a touch too intimate as he smiled at me. "If you think of anything else, you have my number."

"Yes, I do," I replied, stifling a sudden spike of anxiety and the same chilly sensation I'd felt when I saw the poltergeist with Patricia's kids. The thing seemed to be knitted to the members of the séance group, present even when invisible. I dreaded the next handshake from one of them if this feeling was going to be repeated.

In spite of his practiced charm, I was glad to remove myself from Ian's presence and head for my next interview.

Looking up at the woman on the wall, I had to squint against the sudden sunshine pouring through a tear in the cloud cover. I wondered why she'd chosen the outside climbing wall when Stone Gardens offered walls inside, protected from the weather.

"Mrs. Stahlqvist," I called up. "I'm Harper Blaine, you agreed to talk with me about Dr. Tuckman's project."

"Yes. Go ahead." She glanced up and scanned for her next handhold.

The gravel I stood on below her was damp and dark from the persistent sprinkling of rain that had started as I drove between Capitol Hill and Ballard—rain now turned to visual white noise by the shaft of sun. Even the Grey was hard to see and I couldn't tell much about her from this angle, other than the fact that she had no need to fear spandex. I knew healthy twenty-year-olds who didn't have the muscle definition of Carolyn Knight-Stahlqvist at forty. Her blond hair— nearly the same pale shade as her husband's—was woven into a smooth braid that hung like a pendulum as she moved up into the first overhang.

The hoots of boat horns from the canal locks nearby and the swish of car traffic on the street beside us forced me to yell. "This would be easier if you came down."

Her snort echoed off the wall. "I said I could give you some time. I didn't say it would be exclusive."

I shrugged. "When did you join the project?"

"January. Dale told you that."

"Yes, but husbands and wives often have differing memories of events."

"I've no doubt of that. Dale sees the world by his own light."

"What about you?"

"Of course I do. Women in business have to make opportunities as much as seize them. I seized Dale when I had the chance and I'll hold on so long as I need him. We both get what we want and we don't interfere with the other's life otherwise." She dug a foot into an artificial crevice and pushed the other foot free, planted it against a knob and stood higher on the wall.

"Sounds a little cold-blooded."

"It's business. Hot blood is for other endeavors—which is not what I married Dale for. Younger men whose ambition doesn't rise above the bedsheets are much better for that, anyway."

"Is that why you joined the project—to find someone to rumple your sheets?"

She laughed a precise and modulated derision. "Plato was right about women being like library books—he just had the sexes wrong. I can check a man out of anywhere and put him back when I'm done. And it's what they want, so they don't complain. I really don't need a stalking ground. Most women don't, they're just too sure it's wrong to help themselves."

She pulled herself up and braced against the hard corner of the wall. White sunlight shimmered on her wet skin and clothes and threw a moment of butterfly illumination onto her face, leaving a flashbulb impression of film goddess perfection before she shifted slightly and the light slid away.

"I joined the project because Tuck asked me to. I took some classes from him at the U as an undergrad and we understand each other. He thought I'd enjoy it. And I do. I enjoy the creation of Celia. There's a challenge in reaching a successful consensus of minds and moving forward from there. It's an exhilarating change from leading the corporate pack for a while."

"How successful is the project?"

"Very. We are able to accomplish extraordinary things. There were some early hitches and recently I lost a piece of jewelry that I'm annoyed over—but other than that it's very smooth now."

"Do you think one of the participants stole your jewelry?"

"No. It was a Knight family heirloom—it belonged to my great-aunt Bertha, who was mayor of Seattle, and it has great sentimental value—but I'm sure it's just misplaced. Our poltergeist sometimes hides things from us and she's fascinated with jewelry."

I nodded, remembering Celia's interest in Ana's earrings in the recordings—but I also recalled the ghost in the theater who'd said a certain brooch was a fake. Same brooch? If she was the ghost of Bertha Knight Landes, it might well be. "Do you believe in it?" I asked.

"You'll need to rephrase that question. I don't know what you're asking." She slipped a little on the wet grips and grunted as she dipped her hands one by one into the chalk bag at her back, then dug her hands and feet into new positions.

"Do you believe the phenomena are genuine?"

"Yes. I was doubtful initially, but I've been convinced. There truly is more to the world than we can see."

"Do you think that any of the phenomena are faked, sweetened, or manipulated, now or ever in the past?"

She laughed again. "I know the early days were faked. Seeded, you could say. We no longer need that crutch. We control Celia through our committee of the mind now. No one's faking anything." She chuckled. "Anything."

"How do you know?"

"Mark told me how it's done. Once I knew what to look for, I could spot it. Now I never see it. We're clean." She sounded rather smug as she wedged herself into another chink in the overhanging surface. She checked her position. "What time is it?" she asked.

I looked at my watch. "Three twenty," I called back.

"Good. Almost done here. If you have any other questions, you'd better ask quickly."

I asked her what she thought of the rest of the group. She replied they were pleasant enough but, like her husband, she found the college students a bit silly and not of her social class. She also didn't like Patricia and called Wayne, the retired military man, "a likable sot." The only people she seemed to truly like aside from herself were Tuckman and Mark. I kept speculation to myself on why she liked Tuckman, and I wondered why Mark had told her about the faked effects and how she'd react when she found out he was dead.

By the time she'd finished answering my question, she had come to the apex of the climb. She hooked onto the rappelling rope and glided down, chalk-streaked, her thin shoes crunching into the gravel in front of me.

Carolyn didn't look the least chilled or uncomfortable. I held in a shiver, realizing how damp I'd gotten standing in the drizzle while she clambered above me. She was breathing a little fast, but not much, and she glowed through the sheen of sweat and rain with more than exertion and health. She fixed me with brilliant blue eyes and looked me over, nodding. Then she gave a very small smile. "You can call me Cara. Any other questions?"

"Not right now," I replied. It was strange to feel my height was, for once, no advantage. Cara radiated assurance beyond physical stature, though she certainly wasn't short. I was irritated at my small pleasure in her evident approval. I squashed it with quick self-reproof. Cara Stahlqvist was a first-order opportunist, driven by ambition. There was nothing soft to her, inside or out. She didn't like people, she used them and thrived on competition.

"Are you satisfied with your investigation thus far?"

"It's about what I expected." I looked at my watch again and snuck a peek at her through the Grey now that the sun was no longer obscuring my view. Like the others, Cara had a thin yellow thread mantling her head and shoulders, but nothing like the shifty aura that had surrounded Ken or the strange colors around Ian.

She glanced down at her left hand and frowned at a bleeding scrape. She had removed her wedding ring, but I noticed there was no band of untanned flesh to mark it. "What time is it?"

"Three thirty."

"Then your time is up." She looked back into my face. "If there's anything else, call me."

I let my eyes narrow. I didn't like her and she didn't have to like me. "I'll be in touch."

She gave me a cooler smile and strode away into the building. I gave her time to get into the locker room before I followed through the building and back out.

I headed for Queen Anne, thinking that there was something wrong. None of the participants so far seemed to have any unusual ability in the Grey that could account for the power of the poltergeist. Unlike a vampire or a witch, they had no inherent power and no apparent tie to the power grid except the thin yellow tether to Celia. But they also seemed to have no knowledge or opportunity to manipulate anything physically to create the effects Tuckman was recording. I was still convinced that what Tuckman was getting was real phenomena, but I wasn't sure how they'd jumped the barriers that had stumped the Philip group. And if the poltergeist was involved in

Mark's death, I couldn't figure out how without the whole group to support it, which seemed unlikely.

But before I could argue with Tuckman about the poltergeist's power, I'd have to prove to him that none of his people could have faked the phenomena physically. And I still needed to know how that could—or couldn't—be done.

FOURTEEN

B en sat at a small wooden table in the Five Spot's bar with a canvas book bag beside him. The seasonal menu looked to be Hell's Kitchen Italian, to judge from the collection of American tin advertising signs and picturesque laundry arrayed overhead while the Bobby Rydell version of "Volare" played in the background. Excess is the Five Spot's stock-in-trade, though they'd forgone the red-and-white-checked tablecloths in the bar. I slid into the bench opposite Ben's chair.

"Hi. I thought I'd be ahead of you. It's not four yet."

"Mara shooed me out of the house early. I tried to call you a little while ago, but I just got your voice mail."

I snatched the cell phone from my pocket and saw I'd never turned it back on after leaving the theater. "Damn," I muttered. "This thing has the worst ringer—some kind of annoying pop song. I shut it off and forgot to turn it back on. I miss my pager."

"I'm sure it's got a vibrate mode."

"Yeah, I just can't find it."

"Can I take a look at it?" Ben asked, holding out his hand.

I shrugged and handed it over.

Ben poked at it and the phone made several aborted yelps and squawks before giving forth a rich purr. "There. That should do it."

I peered at him. "How did you do that?"

"It's the buttons on the side. You press the top one to unlock the mode, then poke the bottom one until the screen says 'vibrate' and then lock it again."

"Now I feel stupid."

"Don't. I had to get one of my students to show me three or four times." He handed the phone back to me and I tucked it back into my jacket pocket. "Do you want a drink?" Ben asked, putting his hands flat on the table.

"Not yet. What are you going to show me about séance tables and knocks?"

"Well, not a lot. My technique is pretty rough."

The table lurched toward Ben, kicking its feet up at me and sending the candle on the tabletop clattering to the floor. I yelped and slid back in my seat.

"Oops," said Ben as the table settled back onto all fours.

I ducked down and retrieved the candle, replacing it on someone else's table.

"What do you think?" he asked. "Did that look familiar?"

"Sort of. How did you do it?"

Ben's smile split his dark beard. "It's almost too easy. This technique was very popular with spiritualists and phony mediums at the beginning of the twentieth century when the Spiritist movement was at its height. A lot of people do it without knowing that they've done anything and then take it as evidence of spirits. That's called 'ideomotor'—the idea becomes motion—and Tuckman, as a psychologist, is certainly aware of it. The technique is the same whether it's deliberate or accidental and it takes very little pressure or strength to do it. You can use a pretty heavy table, but the lighter it is, the more dramatic the effect."

"OK, I think I get this, but what's the difference between a Spiritist and a spiritualist?" I asked.

"Oh, Spiritism was the movement, and people who adhered to the Spiritist Church or beliefs called themselves Spiritists—so did a lot of frauds. Spiritualist was and is a much looser term."

"OK. So, yeah, what about this technique?"

"It's all just friction and leverage. See how my hands are flat on the table? So long as I have friction on the surface and can exert force outside the fulcrum point of the legs, I can tilt the table just by pulling my hands toward myself while not allowing them to slide across the surface. See?"

The table lurched again and I noticed that it leaned down toward Ben. I looked under the table. It was resting on the two feet closest to Ben with the other two feet in the air about an inch. Ben eased the table back down until it hit the floor with a bang.

"Sorry. I lost my grip. But that wouldn't matter. In the conditions of belief created in most séance circles, the sitters will be as impressed with the sudden thump as with a smooth return, if not more."

"Drama," I agreed.

"Exactly. And you can do more with a few simple modifications of this same technique. It's easiest with a table like this that has the legs set a bit inside of the edge of the tabletop. The farther the legs are from the edge, the easier it is, and a table with a central pedestal—even a heavy one—is shockingly easy to tilt. Now, watch this."

He placed his hands flat again and the table immediately slid a bit to the left and eased up onto one leg so the other three were off the floor. It wasn't much, but enough for most people to be impressed with. Once more I looked under the table and this time took a glance into the Grey. Nothing paranormal was acting on the table, even though the restaurant had the usual share of ghosts and memory.

As Ben continued speaking, he demonstrated. "You see that if I pull, the table leans down toward me. If I push, it'll rise on my side instead. Angular change changes the direction of tilt. With a confederate at the table, a phony medium can make the table tilt or even 'walk' in any direction. And if I push forward with even pressure and no tilt, the table will scoot in the direction of push, instead of rising. With a confederate to create or maintain the tilt, the phony medium can remove his or her hands from the table and still get phenomena. The other sitters will join in without recognizing it because of the suggestive quality of ideomotor. Takes a little practice to be smooth about it, but it's not hard. Try it."

He settled the small table back down. I put my hands down and pushed a little. The table scooted toward Ben.

"Put your hands a little farther out and push down as you push forward."

This time the table rose slowly about half an inch.

"Congratulations, you're a spirit communicator."

I gave him a sour look. "What else can you do with this?"

Ben grinned and demonstrated how to make the little table turn and several techniques for making it rise off the floor, including one he called "the human clamp," which involved holding the table between his hand and the edge of his shoe, the same way most of us would hold an object between our thumb and finger, and moving it around without touching the floor. It was a full levitation with only a foot and a hand as tools.

Next, Ben reached into the canvas bag on the floor and brought out a large, stiff loop of heavy wire, which he strapped onto his forearm so the closed end was cupped under his hand like a gigantic hollow spoon. He slid his hands back onto the tabletop so the loop went under the lip. "This is called a crook and the operator uses it to lift the table. There are several kinds and they require a lot of discretion to use, but …"

The table leapt, the legs on my end flipping upward so fast I had to squeeze backward into the bench to get out of the way. Ben waved

the table side to side and up and down. It was sloppy, but a little practice would have solved that. He waggled the table so it rotated around
the axis of the loop and then put it back down.

By this time, the happy hour crowd was staring at us with varying
degrees of boldness. "It's just a trick," I said to the nearest table full of
gawkers. One of the men nodded and slurped his beer, but didn't stop
looking at the table with suspicion.

I found myself shaking my head and stifling laughter. "Wow. How
does anyone blame that on a ghost?"

"They don't get caught. If they do, they say they only did it to
encourage the spirits. A stage magician does the same thing, priming
the audience with little revelations and ideas that encourage them to
suspend their disbelief and buy into the bigger illusions. Quite a bit of
psychology goes into a successful magic act." Then he added with a
growl, "Or a faked séance."

I cast a speculative look on Ben. "Is this upsetting you?"

"Only because I suddenly realize how easy it is to fake these things
and how many people—including me—have probably been taken in
by willful fakes and sincere 'assistance' by well-meaning believers who
make fools of the lot of us."

I sat back and regarded him in silence a while.

He avoided my gaze and stared at the table.

"Disillusion's a bitch, isn't it?"

He snorted. "Yes, it is. And now I really want something to
drink."

We caught the eye of the waiter, who sidled up with a dubious
glance at us as if he wasn't sure what would happen next. I ordered
coffee. Ben asked for a dark beer.

He'd stripped off the crook and was rolling his sleeves back down
when I noticed red dents on his forearms. I pointed at them.

"What caused those marks?"

"The crook. Pressure from lifting the table. I imagine that if you use a crook a lot, you probably build up some kind of callus or marks."

I nodded as the waiter returned with our drinks. Mark had had very similar dents on his forearms, according to the autopsy. I'd bet that a closer examination of the recordings would show that he had used a crook a lot in the early days of the sessions. Now I understood why Tuckman thought the heightened phenomena could be faked— the crook *was* impressive—but I was more sure than ever that they hadn't been. I hadn't seen the same movements from anyone else, but I'd seen Mark make the same hand slides and elbow dips I'd just seen from Ben.

Ben licked foam from his mustache and sighed. "This reminds me of university in Germany. I think the amount of beer I drank then is probably why I still don't speak German as well as I read and write it. I suspect the other guys in the program liked to get me drunk just to hear me butcher the language. I didn't mind at the time—I got a lot of free beer out of it. Damn good beer." He shook his head. "I haven't done anything that stupid in years."

"There must be something stupid in your more recent past. There's plenty in mine."

Ben laughed. "I prefer to pretend it's all the folly of youth and not endemic foolishness."

"I don't have that excuse."

"Don't be so hard on yourself, Harper."

I frowned into my coffee and changed the subject.

"Ben, how would someone make a knocking sound?"

Ben picked up the crook again and rapped it on the underside of the table, making a sharp noise. "Like that?"

The rap sounded very much like Mark's first efforts. "Exactly like that. Is that how all knocks are made?" I asked.

"Oh, no. You can use your feet, hands, knees, or a hard object concealed in your hand or clothes. A character in a book once used a tin box strapped to her knee. When she pressed it against her other knee, it deformed and made a cracking sound."

That rang a bell and I wondered which book I'd read it in but couldn't bring to mind.

Ben gulped some more beer and continued. "The Fox sisters—they started the whole Spiritist movement by accident—used to crack the joints of their toes or rap their toenails against the floor to create raps, and even though people caught them at it and they even admitted it, people wanted to believe. So they did. Investigations of people like the Fox sisters and their imitators led to modern parapsychology."

"They chose to believe ... ," I repeated, thinking. "So parapsychology grew out of fakery?"

"The search for truth in the face of fakery," Ben corrected me, frowning. "A lot of the early investigators were magicians and scientists—Houdini was famous for debunking phony mediums. In fact," he added, reaching again into his bag, "one of the big names in modern skeptical investigation is another magician—James Randi. I brought you one of his books as well as one of Houdini's books. Neither of these guys is shy about showing how the trick is done. And they're both pretty blunt about what they think of the whole field. Although I think they're both wrong in condemning the whole without adequate proof."

Ben was a bit defensive about it, but I reserved judgment. While I had more personal experience of ghosts and the paranormal, I wouldn't care to step forward and make any claims or attempt to prove any such thing to professional skeptics of the Houdini grade. As I'd already noted in Tuckman, the blindness of belief and desire isn't restricted to the oddball side of the discussion.

I put the books into my own bag as Ben finished his beer.

"Ben, could any of these techniques make a table break away from its sitters and run around the room?"

Ben chuckled. "Not without being about as obvious as a rhino in a bathtub. Some things can't be concealed at that proximity, no matter how good a psychological manipulator the magician or spiritualist is. And speaking of rhinos, Brian and Mara will be waiting dinner on me and we'd all like it if you would come, too. It's roast beef, and Mara might have some answers for you about glass and spirits. She did ask me to ask you…"

I hesitated, but Ben looked puppy-eyes at me. I gave in. Mara was a great cook—even without any witchcraft to help—and they were my friends as well as the closest thing I had to professional advisors in the Greywalker line. I smiled. "Dinner would be really nice. Thanks."

"Great!"

We paid up and left, catching a few more stares from the patrons as we went. I wondered how many tables would be tilted tonight and how outrageous the beer-fueled stories would grow by Sunday morning. If they, too, wanted to believe, then I expected that by next Thursday it would be common gossip that the Five Spot was haunted by a fictional ghost of someone killed by the old counterbalance trolley, whose long-gone upper terminus the Five Spot now occupied.

When we walked into the Danzigers' house, the scent of savory meat and bread wafted to us along with a despairing cry of "Brian!"

Ben and I exchanged a look. He sighed, heaved his shoulders, and went ahead of me into the kitchen.

Brian sat in the middle of the kitchen floor in a pile of vegetables and lettuce, staring at the kitchen table and rubbing the top of his head. Mara, her new-penny-copper hair sweeping over her face, crouched beside him, holding a large bowl.

"Now, wasn't I after telling you you'd regret that? Hm? Smarts a bit, doesn't it?" she chided him.

"Owww … ," her son replied, patting his head with a lettuce leaf. Mara snatched it from him and put it into the bowl.

"None of that, y'wild animal. That's for eating, not for wearing."

Brian stuffed the nearest chunk of vegetable into his mouth, then made a face and started to spit it out. Mara clapped a hand over his pursed lips. "Oh, no, you don't. It shan't kill you, so you'll go ahead and swallow it. Polite people don't go spitting out their food."

Brian forced the lump down his throat. "I's not a people. I's a rhinerosserous!" he objected as Mara pulled her hand away.

"Well, polite rhinos don't spit, either. And they clean up their own messes or they have to go outside and eat thorny bushes in the garden."

"Noooooooo ... ," Brian wailed.

Mara shoved the bowl into his arms. "Then you'll clean up the mess, won't you? And you'll pick up every piece or you'll be eating the ones you miss later."

Brian's lip stuck out in a very rhinolike fashion. He put his hands on top of his head and said, "Head hurts."

"Yes, darling, I imagine it does." She kissed him on the forehead and stood up.

Ben gave her an inquisitive look. "What happened?"

"Rhino versus table," Mara answered, brushing off her skirts. "The table won, and the bowl of salad got jostled off and onto the rhino-boy's head."

"Jostled?"

"Of course. Y'don't think I'd go pitchin' salad on his head, now, do ya?" She grinned a little, radiating good humor in spite of the mess. "Hi, Harper. I see Ben cajoled you into dinner at the wild animal park."

"How could I miss it?"

Brian was now crawling about on the floor, picking up the salad and beginning to enjoy himself. I hoped Mara wasn't planning on serving the salvaged salad, as Brian's idea of fun seemed to be to toss handfuls of greens and vegetable chunks in the general direction of the bowl while making various noises. If the pieces missed the bowl, he kept on trying until they made it in, by which time the salad looked quite grubby. Albert appeared behind Brian and seemed to be whispering into the boy's ear.

Mara relieved my anxiety by turning toward the fridge and announcing, "Meat's almost ready, so I suppose I'd better start a replacement salad. Why don't you stay with me while Ben sets the table and keeps an eye on the rhino-boy."

That was fine by me.

"Now then," Mara began as she brought fresh produce from the refrigerator, "you wanted to know about mirrors and glass and their effect on the Grey."

I nodded. "Yeah. There's some kind of filtering effect..."

"Hm. I'm not so sure about why the glass does as it does, but the mirror is probably acting in much the same way as silver does. It's reflective, of course, but it's also conductive—whether it's silver, or mercury, or mylar, it still conducts—and I've often suspected that the power lines that run through the Grey energize the metal in a mirror such that it becomes a mild barrier—literally reflecting the ghost from passing through—and most things either can't or won't push past."

"Why don't they know it's a mirror when they see themselves?"

"Most ghosts are stone stupid. Unless it's been enchanted," Mara said, "most mirrors reflect what is, not what the ghost sees. Most ghosts see things as they were in their life, not as they are now. They certainly don't see themselves as wraiths. I imagine it's a bit confounding to come upon a reflection that doesn't answer your idea of yourself."

"I suppose ... but what about the glass, then?" I asked.

"I've been thinking about that," Ben piped up from behind us.

I swung around so I could see both of them by just turning my head.

"You see," Ben started, brandishing a handful of silverware, "I think what you're seeing there is a sort of material resistance. The energy state of the Grey is extremely high and fast—we've discussed this before, you recall—"

"Yes, I remember."

Brian made motorboat noises under the table as he pushed the bowl merrily around the floor, trailed by Albert, who stuck half through the table as if it weren't there. I found myself watching the ghost, rather than Ben.

"OK, so the particles of energy that make up the Grey travel much more slowly through the dense material of something like glass or brick or stone, but we only see them in glass because when they are slowed down to a certain degree, we experience a sort of persistence-of-vision illusion. That's why you can see a ghost in a photograph when there was none visible at the time—"

I interrupted him, refocusing on Ben. "You can? I thought those 'spirit photos' were all exposed as fakes."

"Oh, the ones taken by charlatans in the same era as the Spiritist Church were mostly fakes, but you can spot those easily. Others seem to be legit. Odd images of people or things where no one was at the time, but they fit in the picture. They don't have to be old photos. They could be anything from any time, taken with any camera."

I'd seen photos like that—some snapshots taken by my mother or friends from college—and found some of them disturbing beyond reason. They never seemed to merit that disquiet, but I'd never shaken it. "OK, assume I buy the idea. What's your theory?" I asked.

"I think the ghost's reflection on the surface of the glass lens persists long enough for the camera to capture it. If you could see through rocks or bricks, you could see the ghost reflected in the side of a building, too, but since most materials aren't transparent, you can't see the reflection of the ghost."

"That doesn't explain why I see *less* Grey when I look through a window."

"You actually see *into* the Grey, not just the reflections of a few stray ghosts. The energy of the Grey just doesn't move through the glass fast enough for you, so the glass acts like a filter, holding back a percentage of the Grey from your sight," Ben explained.

"Mirrored glass seen from the back would reflect much of the initial energy," Mara added, "and you'd see even less."

"So ... are you guys saying that this high-energy stuff simply gets ... trapped?"

Ben nodded. "Much of it, yes."

I shook that idea aside. "But if they can't move through something dense, how can ghosts walk through walls? We know they do that."

Brian popped up from under the table with the bowl of dirty salad clutched to his chest. Albert shooed him toward Mara and me and the boy trotted across the floor, giggling.

"We assume that's what we see," Ben said, "but I'm thinking that there's more to it."

Brian stumbled to a halt against my legs and looked up at me with a huge grin as he offered me the bowl. "Harpa." He gurgled with excitement and glanced back to Albert, then up at me again.

I gave Ben only half my attention as he said, "I've been thinking about this a lot since you asked and it seems to me that the Grey must have a property of time that's different than ours. You know that a lot of ghosts are nothing but the persistent memory of something or loops of time and action. Most repeating specters, for instance, have no consciousness or personality—they're just like loops of film that keep on running on, doing the same thing they've always done until they finally wear out completely and fade away."

"Yes, OK. So?" I shrugged, taking the bowl from Brian and wondering why Albert seemed to have sent the boy to me with it. I handed it off to his mother as Brian threw his arms around my legs and hugged them, pressing his face against my knees.

"Well, they're an instance of time," Ben continued. "An isolated, persistent shard of time that's suspended in the Grey. And I think that there must be layers on layers of time like that scattered throughout the Grey. When we see a ghost walk through a wall, what we're actually seeing is the ghost moving through an opening that exists in his own plane of time within the Grey."

Mara spoke out of the corner of her mouth as she dumped the filthy greens into a bin by the sink. "Say thank you."

I looked at Brian as he clutched me in unexpected affection. "Um ... thank you, Brian."

Brian shrieked in delight and let go of me to run back and "help" Ben at the table.

"Very nice, Harper   I think Brian has a crush on you. And I agree with Ben about time," Mara said, tearing up freshly washed lettuce. "If there are instances of frozen time, they must exist all over the Grey, or time itself must be sort of stacked up in the Grey in some way. And that's how most ghosts—which are just memories, time-shapes, so to speak—can move about through what appear to be solid objects. The object doesn't exist for them, since they don't really interact with the present."

"Exactly," added Ben, bending to pick up Brian and secure him in a high chair by the table. "Ghosts with sufficient personality retention and volition can move through any layer of time they are familiar with, but ghosts with less volition and the simple repeaters are stuck on the time plane they lived in."

Albert had vanished by the time we sat down to eat, leaving only the corporeal people at the table. Without him nearby, Brian was a little more subdued and ate his dinner with more giggling than rhino roars. I supposed this sort of behavior was the positive reinforcement that allowed most children to survive to the next stage of parental stress: adolescence. Between considering Brian's sweetened temper and mulling ideas about glass and mirrors, I didn't talk much during the meal and the conversation turned to academic power struggles at the U over upcoming funding and tenure issues. I nodded and ate in comfortable ignorance.

FIFTEEN

I rang the security buzzer outside the Fujisaka building Sunday afternoon and was answered by a birdlike voice speaking Chinese. I knew I'd pressed the right code, so I replied, "Ana Choi, please."

I overheard snatches of a rapid, singing exchange of Chinese; then another voice spoke out of the speaker. "Hi, hi! I'll be right down."

The speaker clicked off and I turned around to look out at the cloud-shadowed length of Sixth Avenue South. This was the brittle edge of the International District—the real heart of Chinatown being a block north and east on King. This street was the true international mixture the city trumpeted with pride—and which had sometimes been decried as mere racism in pretty words. Across the street was the old Uwajimaya department store building with its blue-tiled roofs and upturned eaves—still partially empty since the new Uwajimaya Village complex had risen to the immediate south. Farther south was one of the enclaves of Nihonmachi—Japantown—and around any corner you could find a feast of Chinese bakeries, Filipino groceries, Vietnamese noodle houses, and Tokyo-style coffeehouses.

The Fujisaka was the only modern condo building in the ID—the rest of the International District's housing was apartments or hotel rooms. Expensive and glossy, it snuggled in with its older, smaller neighbors, no longer the strange, shiny interloper since the arrival of the towering Uwajimaya Village.

The door behind me opened and an Asian woman stepped out wearing a fluffy white jacket against the chill. She had a round face with a pointed chin, high cheekbones, and a slightly reserved expression. Any claim to Oriental mystery vanished when she grinned, making her face sweet and sunny. She looked up at me.

"You're ... Harper, aren't you?" Her speech pattern wasn't so much an accent as a vague tint over her English.

"Yes," I replied. "Ana Choi?" I recognized her from the recordings, but I asked anyhow.

She nodded. "Sorry I made you wait. My parents were having an argument. If I just walk out, they think I'm being disrespectful, so I had to wait for them to quiet long enough to say I was leaving."

"You live with your parents," I said, making a mental note.

"Yeah. We moved from Macao twelve years ago and they're still very old-fashioned. I'm not a traditional Chinese girl, but I try to make them happy when I can. Sometimes it's hard." She looked around the damp street. "Let's go, huh? We can talk while we go."

"Sure," I agreed. I'd parked across the street in the sparsely used lot of the blue-tiled building.

"I'm grateful for the ride," Ana said. "Usually I take transit, but it's a long ride on Sundays—one of my buses runs once an hour on weekends."

I shrugged. "It works out for both of us. When did you start with the project?"

"Back in January. Ian wanted me to. He said it would be fun."

"Is it?"

Her turn to shrug. "Yeah, I guess it is. It was kind of stupid at first, but it got better. I like it."

We stopped to get into the Rover. Ana smiled. "This is neat. Very tough."

"Yeah, it's pretty good. Except for the gas mileage—then it's a bit of a hog."

She nodded, settling herself in the seat. "OK. So. What do you want to ask me?"

"How do you feel about the group?"

"I said I liked it."

"I mean the people. Do you like them?" I asked, starting the engine and heading the truck toward PNU.

"Yeah, mostly."

I watched her reflection in the windshield glass. I didn't see any yellow line of Grey energy around her from that angle. "Anyone you don't get along with or feel uncomfortable with?"

She laughed. "You know, I don't care one way or the other. I like most of them pretty well, but I don't feel like I know them enough to care a lot. They're nice, but ... they're just nice and nothing special to me."

"Even Ian?"

She made a face and rolled her eyes. "Oh, Ian. Sometimes I think I don't even like him anymore. Sometimes he's mean and so selfish. He never spends any time with me anymore. He's always busy and we don't even— Our sex life doesn't exist except when it's bad. I only joined the project because he wanted me to and I thought we could see more of each other, and now he sometimes acts like he doesn't even want me to come to the group."

This didn't jibe with Ian's version, but I wasn't surprised by that sort of thing anymore. And I remembered how Ana had flinched in the recordings as Ian pulled her hair from her earrings.

"Why wouldn't he want you to come?" I asked.

"So he can flirt with Cara Stahlqvist. He's such a dick."

"If he's a dick, then why do you go?"

She scowled. "It's my project, too. Why should Ian get to scare me off? Besides … he's not the only person there who matters."

"You just said none of them meant anything to you."

She looked at the side window. "I lied."

"You're seeing someone else from the group?"

"No! Not outside the group, really. Sometimes we go out for drinks after … And I like talking to him. He likes to talk to me, too."

"Who?"

She blushed. "Ken." She kept looking out the window.

I nodded. "Does Ian know?"

"I don't know. I don't think so. Ken teases Ian sometimes and I know he's doing it because of me, but Ian just laughs it off. I think he'd be nasty to Ken if he knew, but he seems OK."

"Do you plan to do anything about this?"

She sighed. "I don't know. I can't just leave Ian and start going with Ken right now. It would be bad. For the group. Ian's not the sort of guy who takes a breakup well. And besides … it's hard, you know. Sometimes I just want to keep the peace. I don't want a big deal over everything."

I shook my head, but kept my mouth closed. They'd cooked up a rotten little triangle. Misery not only loves company, it makes its own. The whole group was full of sexual tensions and power plays, so far, and this seemed about par for the course.

"I just don't seem to pick the best men," Ana said. "But at least Ian was OK with my parents. If I started dating Ken, they'd be furious."

"Why?"

"My father would say he's not good enough. And my mother always sides with my father—it's part of her role, you know. Traditional Chinese wife."

"I'm still not getting it. Why is Ian—who's mean to you—OK, but Ken's not?"

She turned and blinked at me. "Because Ken's brown."

"What?"

"Brown. He's not white."

"You're not white, either."

"I know that. But my father's racist. He thinks there's something ... dirty or bad about being colored if you're not Chinese—or at least Asian."

"He doesn't know India is part of Asia?"

"It's not the right part. If the people are darker than he is, they're dirtier than he is. It's OK for me to date a white man or an Asian like us, but someone who's brown? No. It would be even worse if I wanted to date a black man. He'd never speak to me again. My sister went out with a black guy once and he's still angry at her. He'd go insane if he knew they slept together."

"That's a bit over the top."

"My dad." She looked grim. "So ... you know ... that's why I don't want to stop going to the group, although it would be the best thing. I wish I could just make it all change. Why can't we all be happy? If we can make a ghost, why can't we make ourselves happy?"

I grabbed the chance to get back on topic. "Are you certain that you're making a ghost?"

"Yes." She gave a hard, decisive nod. "I'm Chinese—we know about ghosts. They're all over the place. They live through us, so our ghost is real, too, even though we made it up."

"What do you mean 'they live through us'?"

"I mean we give them strength—energy. We remember them and they continue. That's why it's important to remember ancestors and family, or they fade away. Or they become angry and then you're in trouble. We made up our ghost and we keep her alive by our thoughts, so if we stop believing in her, she'll go away."

"How do you know it's not just a fake? That someone in the group isn't making it seem real when it's not?"

"That would make Celia very angry. It can't all be fake—there's no way for everything to be made by one person fooling us—so the part that's real would know when someone was faking. How would you feel if someone was pretending to be you? That's how Celia would feel and she would get even."

"What about you?" I asked, turning the truck into PNU's west parking lot.

Ana looked surprised, her narrowly plucked brows arching upward. "What about me?"

"If you found out someone was faking anything, would you be angry?"

"Yes. Sure I would."

"And would you want to get even with them for it?"

She gave me a bemused look. "No. I would tell them to stop, but Celia would be the one who would punish them, if they needed it."

"Do you think she could?"

A deep frown took over her face. "I don't know. I really don't." She looked up again. "We're here. Good. Thanks for the ride," she added, opening the door and swinging out. "I hope I was some help."

"Quite a bit."

"Cool, cool. See you later." She closed the door and walked toward St. John Hall. In the dismal sunlight I could see the bright yellow thread around her, pointing toward the hot yellow spot on the window of room twelve like a compass toward north.

I stayed in the truck a while longer, thinking and waiting for the group to be assembled so I could sneak into the observation room unnoticed.

I saw Gartner Tuckman heading for the building with his briefcase in his hand. He was playing villain again, wearing black and glaring. I followed him into the building, keeping far enough behind to give him a chance to round up any séance members loitering in the hall.

At the head of the stairs, an uncanny fog shot with light lay across the floor. Strange traceries swirled in the Grey remnants. I peered at it, but couldn't understand it any better than the last time I'd been near this room. Odd colors roiled through the puddle of Grey like lightning leaping cloud to cloud, and then the colors seeped toward the closed door to room twelve and oozed away. I felt it tug like a tidal race and then move away. I didn't see the yellow wad of tangled lines.

Frowning, I let myself into the observation room. Terry ignored me. I stayed on my feet and looked out through the double-paned glass.

Tuckman was in the séance room, standing near the observation mirror with his back to us. Some of the participants had taken seats at the table, but others had chosen to sit on the sofa. Ana was seated at the table in one of the hard chairs, along with the only séance member I hadn't interviewed yet—Wayne Hopke, the elderly military man. Ian, I noticed, was standing near the sofa, which put him in position to both look down Cara's blouse and hover over Ken like some mythic avenger—so he wasn't oblivious after all. All attention was turned to Tuckman, as he spoke in a mellow, soothing tone I'd never heard from him before.

"... begin today's session," he said. "Our friend Mark Lupoldi has died in an accident. This is ... a tragedy, and since I know we were all very fond of Mark it is a blow both to our project and to our feelings."

Tuckman must have had a bit of theater training himself, to judge from his posture and delivery as he counterfeited sorrow. His shoulders were slumped a little forward and bunched as if he anticipated a blow. The angle of his arms indicated he was clasping his hands together and I imagined his knuckles were white. He probably had a convincingly sad mask arranged on his face.

I looked at the rest of them. Each wore some expression of surprise, startlement, or shock. Cara closed her eyes. Even through the double filter of the glass, I could see Grey sparks and flickers of yellow, red, and the unhealthy green I was beginning to associate with illness and distress. But I still could not see clearly enough to know which coil of energy belonged to whom. I ground my teeth with frustration; the thorough protocols that protected the project—and which I'd normally have cheered—were making my job difficult and there was nothing I could do about that.

"Although this sad event was in no way connected to our project," Tuckman continued, "it's entirely understandable if any of you feel you cannot go through with today's session or even if you want to withdraw completely from further participation. Mark was so enthusiastic about and devoted to the experiments that it is difficult to imagine them going forward without him. He has, of course, left an impression on all of us, colored our sense of the world and our work with his easy friendship and generous nature. We will all miss him.

"I know this seems abrupt, but in deference to everyone's feelings at this time, I think that we should postpone this session and consider if we wish to proceed at all—"

Dale Stahlqvist glowered. "What? Are you suggesting that we quit?"

Cara's eyes flashed open as all other heads turned to stare at her husband.

"Not 'quit,' " Tuckman said, raising his hands. "Consider—"

"Consider quitting," Dale snapped. "Just throw the whole thing out because we can't go on without Mark? That would put the lie to everything we've done—make the group meaningless—and I simply do not believe that's true. Mark worked as hard as any of us and I think he'd be appalled at such a suggestion. You mean well, Doctor, but it's the wrong thing to do."

Tuckman sighed as the others began to ring a cacophony of rejection. They would see it through and they would start right now—for Mark's sake. Cara was the only one who remained silent, keeping her eyes down and her face impassive.

Tuckman deserved an Oscar for his performance. He didn't look smug or pleased when he gave in to their demands to continue as planned. He looked resigned and tired. He excused himself and told them to begin as soon as they felt comfortable.

Patricia was availing herself of a tissue as Tuckman entered the observation room. I wondered what had taken him nearly a minute in the hall. He brushed his hands over his hair and sat down. Now he did look a bit pleased.

"Terry," he said, "make a note of the fact that the group chose to go ahead and there are no plans at this time to replace Mr. Lupoldi." He shot me a smug look, then returned his attention to Terry. "How's the monitoring looking?"

"Everything is pretty normal so far, though there was a small spike in EMR activity when you made the announcement. It's returning to normal now."

Tuckman nodded to himself. "Good. Now let's see what they do..."

For the first ten minutes or so they sat around the table and talked about Mark; then they started swapping stories about Mark and the séances and the whole thing took on the aspect of a wake.

Patricia suddenly giggled. "I'll bet Mark's with Celia," she said.

"Don't be stupid," muttered Cara.

The table gave a loud cracking noise and thumped up and down.

"Is that you, Celia?" Wayne Hopke asked, as usual assuming control of the questions.

The table thumped and skittered side to side, knocking Wayne and Cara out of their chairs. A hail of knocks roared on the tabletop. The rest of the group stood up to avoid the table's sudden agitation. A small bookshelf crashed over, spilling decks of cards and stacks of magazines onto the floor.

"Temperature's dropping. Electromagnetic activity is rising quickly." Terry glanced over his shoulder to catch Tuckman's eye. "I'm getting subaudibles."

"What is it?" Tuckman demanded. "Is it from outside?"

"No, it's in the room. Can't tell what it is yet."

"Mark it and analyze it later." Tuckman's gaze was intent on the scene in the other room.

The table was zooming back and forth with the séance group chasing after it and having difficulty keeping it under their fingers at all. The activity was nothing like the motion of the clamped tables that Ben had shown me. The table was almost writhing and making a horrible clatter as it warped the rug into folds and corrugations.

"Celia, are you there?" Wayne called again.

The table let out a bang.

"Is this Mark?" Patricia yelled.

Another sharp bang and then the table lurched against the fallen bookshelf. The stereo in the room blared a random segment of modern noise as the table stopped and trembled. Through the distorted music there came a loud pop.

Something hovered over the table in a flare of red light, spinning. Panting, the group drew around the table again. The light dimmed a bit and I could make out a flat, translucent shield shape about half the size of my palm, turning in empty air over the center of the table. Whatever was holding it there was strong enough for me to detect right through the double glass and I didn't like the feeling I got looking at that carmine glow, or the sudden sense of being tied to it.

Cara gasped and started to put out her hand. "That's mine!"

The thing flung itself into her face. She let out a short, sharp shriek and flinched, clapping her hand over her left cheek as she turned away from the impact of the thing. She crouched over and scuttled for the door. The table thumped one last time onto the floor, the eerie light dissipating.

"I think it's over," Terry had been saying as I bolted out of the observation room.

In the hall, I saw the door open and flaring red and yellow energy flooded across the floor as Cara stumbled out, clutching her bleeding cheek. I went toward her, tripping in the sudden flood tide of the paranormal pouring out after her. The worlds heaved and laid a shattering weight over me, pressing me down as I tumbled into the boiling Grey wave. I staggered, concentrating on getting to Cara Stahlqvist across the knife-edge of the Grey between us.

"Cara," I said, reaching to catch her arm. This storm of power didn't feel like the outraged ghost of Bertha Knight Landes lashing at Cara for impersonating her niece. It was sickening and brutal. My limbs weighed too much to move, and I felt I was mired in knee-deep muck and tendrils of avaricious horror as I shuddered and forced my arm to move.

Cara shoved me aside and hurried past. I stumbled back as if she'd swung on me with a two-by-four and gasped for breath I had not known I was missing. I choked on a taste of ice and scorched earth and put my shoulder against the wall, pushing myself away from the flashing, roiling edge of the Grey, at last. It had swamped me for mere seconds, yet it felt like I'd fought against a raging sea for fatal minutes. I felt dizzy.

The force that had flooded out the door drained away in eddies of color, drawing away like an outgoing tide. The remains of the poltergeist had a repulsive, sickly feeling, like a vine that had learned to thrive on poison and grown huge and virulent. It didn't have any distinctive shape this time, but I was sure that's what I'd felt brush past, dragging the edge of the Grey. It was much worse than it had been the day before at Patricia's. Something was wrong with Tuckman's ghost. It was far too strong. The cause might be the power line through the séance room—the power line that shouldn't have been where it was—but even that wouldn't account for the sensation of foulness. Even with it gone, I felt it.

As I leaned against the wall, head down, catching my breath, several other participants ran into the hall and milled about in confusion until Tuckman emerged from the booth with his assistant trailing behind.

I headed for Terry as Tuckman went to calm his flock.

"I need those recordings," I told Terry. He narrowed his eyes at me and looked truculent.

"What do you think I am? Your personal Mr. Step'n Fetchit?"

That took me aback. I'd seen two sides of the racism die in a single afternoon—it was no simple two-sided coin. What were the odds? "You think that my asking for the recordings is demeaning?"

"I notice you didn't ask Tuck," he hissed.

"Tuck's not the systems monitor. You are. But if you can't see past that chip on your shoulder to do your job, maybe I *should* get them from Tuckman."

Terry glared at me. In the furious pause we heard the conversation behind us.

"We shouldn't have been thinking about Mark," Patricia cried. "We must have attracted his ghost and now he's upset with us."

I glanced over my shoulder to see Tuckman's lips tighten in suppressed anger. "Don't jump to conclusions, Patricia. I assure you it was no such thing. Monitor readings were as they always are," he lied. "It was all your own doing. All of you. Not the spirit of our dead friend. It's just your own creation."

Cara was walking back to the group with a moist paper towel pressed to her bloodied cheek. She stopped and listened, glowering at everyone.

"Maybe we shouldn't have been talking about Mark," Ana suggested. "Maybe we were too upset."

"It must be Mark's ghost—it didn't act like Celia," Patricia insisted.

Cara barked a derisive laugh. "Bull! It acted just like Celia has been lately—mean. There's no damned ghost of Mark! There's no such thing!" She glared at them.

Tuckman shook his head. "I think you're a little upset…"

Dale turned and tried to put his arms around Cara. "Cara … you're bleeding. Let me take you to the hospital."

She shoved him back. "Leave me alone, Dale. I can take myself." She turned and stalked down the stairs. Her husband stared after her, a moment's bleak hurt on his face.

"She won't go very far," Ian said. "She left her purse."

"Oh, God," Dale muttered, shivering back to himself. "I'd better take it to her." He darted into the séance room.

I turned to Terry. "I'll be back for the recordings in fifteen minutes. I am not above siccing your boss on you, but I'd rather you chose to do this yourself. Don't force me to knock that chip off your shoulder—you'll look pretty stupid if you get your butt handed to you by a skinny white chick."

I brushed past the milling group of project members, past Tuckman—who glanced at me with curiosity—and down the stairs to find Cara.

She was standing in the building lobby, staring at something in her hand, when I caught up to her. I peered over her shoulder and caught a glimpse of a creamy stone streaked with amber and brown set in some kind of dark yellow metal. I'm no jewelry expert, so I couldn't tell if it was a real Edwardian brooch or a fake.

"What's that?"

She caught her breath and snapped a cold stare at me. "It's none of your business."

"Maybe not. Unless it's a brooch you lost that might have been stolen by someone here."

Her eyebrows knitted together. "All right. It's my brooch."

"It doesn't seem like something to make much fuss over."

"It was my great-aunt's! Bertha Knight—oh, damn it, have a little respect. I thought I'd—I thought I'd left it at Mark's."

Her usual cool reserve had cracked for a moment, but it wouldn't last long. I'd have to pry into her before it froze back over. We locked eyes and I cocked my head a little, inquisitive. "How did you happen to leave it at Mark's?"

She wavered.

I didn't. "I'll keep on asking until you tell me, but since your husband is on his way down here, you might want to talk fast."

"Oh, God … All right. I left the brooch at Mark's place on Wednesday. We were having an affair and I didn't want anyone to know, so I said I'd lost it. Happy now?"

"No. Why didn't you go back for it?"

"I was *going* to go back for it, but I didn't have the chance and Mark didn't return my calls. One of *them* must have gotten it from Mark … or stolen it from him," she spat.

"Why do you think it's one of them?"

"It has to be one of them. Celia threw it, but it was one of them that made her do it. She's not like she used to be. She's not like the Philip poltergeist Tuck told us about. She's become cruel and spiteful. We used to have such fun…"

"Why couldn't it be Mark's ghost? Maybe you pissed him off."

"There's no such thing as ghosts," she spat. "We made Celia up. We control her. Or one of us does. You saw how the session went, didn't you? One of them threw it."

We heard quick footsteps on the stairs behind us. Cara broke off and turned to look at her husband, trotting down to the lobby holding her purse and jacket over his right arm. He beamed at her, then looked crushed and angry when he saw the oozing red wound on her cheek.

"Come along, dear," Dale said, draping her jacket over her shoulders. "Don't want your lovely face to scar, Cara." He kissed her on the forehead and helped her out the door.

Cara. It means "beloved."

I stood and watched them until the door swung shut. I almost felt sorry for Dale Stahlqvist. He'd married a trophy—a goddess of quick-silver and steel—and now he had fallen in love with it. He'd forgotten that both quicksilver and goddesses can kill you.

Someone here was just as lethal. Someone had picked up the brooch from Mark's or caused Celia to pick it up, and it had to be one of those who'd been in the séance room. Now they had shown off their cleverness by throwing it back in Cara's face in front of everyone. It wasn't much of a stretch to imagine that someone who thought him-self that clever also thought he could get away with murder, bringing the poltergeist along for the ride. It could have been any of them, including Dale or even Cara herself, lying through her perfect teeth about the brooch, though I doubted that. Her distress seemed too genuine to be an act—a much better act than her impersonation of Bertha Knight Landes's great-niece.

I trudged back up the stairs to get the recordings, bracing for battle with Terry and Tuckman.

SIXTEEN

Tuckman was still snake-oiling the rest of the séance sitters at the top of the stairs. Terry had disappeared. I walked back and spotted him in the observation room. The Nebraska-sized chip on his shoulder left me wondering what he had to be defensive about, since it now seemed unlikely that Tuckman had a saboteur.

I whispered to Tuckman's back, "Keep the remaining sitters here while I review the video with Terry. I want to get a better look at what happened. Cara thinks one of the others threw that thing at her and if so, we need to find out who, right away."

He made a twitch of one shoulder and I hoped that was agreement, not dismissal.

I ducked into the observation room.

Terry was poking buttons on the video recording equipment. He didn't look up.

"Now what do you want?" he demanded.

I closed the door and pulled a chair around to sit in. Terry was a little in front of me and to the side, so I could see most of his profile as well as the tense set of his shoulders and back. "I want to know what your problem is."

"You."

"Don't think so," I said. "You don't even know me and I haven't done anything or said more than a dozen words to you since this ridiculous investigation began."

"Ridiculous is right." He kept his head forward, but he pulled his hands away from the controls, balling them into fists and resting his wrists on the console.

"Ah. Now we're getting somewhere. This investigation bugs you?"

"Damn straight it does."

"Why? It makes you angry. Do you think it's critical of you? Or are you afraid of it? You have something to hide?" I didn't think so; he didn't have any Grey connection to the poltergeist that I could see or to anything else. But he did have a big, angry red aura, shot through with white sparks.

He spun his chair to glare at me, thumping his fists onto his thighs. "No! If Tuck thinks I'm padding his results, he should come out and say so! I'm not a cheat! I earned everything I ever got—I worked my ass off for it! I got no reason to undermine this project. If this goes down in flames, I go, too. And there's Tuck saying the results are too good. Too good! He says he's going to bring in an independent investigator to check the group. And here comes you—you snooping, sneaky nobody, poking into our stuff, into our records and methods like you know any damn thing. Which you don't. You had to bring someone with you just to understand the machines."

"I admit to being lost on certain subjects. I rely on experts to tell me what I don't know, like I'm relying on you to help me with that video."

He stared at me, his fury slackening into surprise, the furious light around him dimming.

"Terry, it's true that you're in a good position to sweeten or skew the results. But so is Denise Francisco or almost any of the people sitting in that room every Sunday and Wednesday—even Tuckman himself. I have to know what can be done before I can tell if it has been done."

"Are you saying you don't think it's me?"

"Yes and no. I'm saying I'm not sure that Tuckman's right about the problem. What happened today was so spectacular it should make or break Tuckman's belief in a saboteur. So what I want is to find out if what I saw through that benighted glass is the same thing the camera saw. I'm trusting that you haven't been up here doctoring that recording."

He scoffed. "It would take a lot more than fifteen minutes and the equipment we have in here to do that."

"Then show me the recording."

Terry chewed on the idea for a while, then scooted his chair to the side and let me sit next to him while he cued the video. "I've got three angles, but this one's the best."

"Three? The recordings you gave me before were only one angle."

He shrugged and didn't look at me. "You didn't really need the other stuff, anyway, just general records—that's what Tuck said."

I sighed. I didn't think Terry's spite was going to make any difference and I supposed I should be glad I hadn't waded through three times as much video to end up in the same place.

We watched the short session from every angle twice. By the end, we were both shaking our heads in amazement.

"That thing just popped in from nowhere and hung there in the air," Terry marveled, pointing at the close-up. "That ... that's just ..."

"That's an apport," I supplied.

"It's cool. The certifiable, real, live thing. The Philip group thought they could get one, but Tuck said he didn't think it was possible."

"Tuck seems to be wrong." I stood up and looked at him. "Thanks, Terry."

He gave me an embarrassed nod.

In the séance room, most of the remaining project members had regathered with Tuckman. Wayne Hopke, Ana, and Ian were lined up on the couch. Ian had his arm over Ana's shoulders, but she was looking away from him—at the floor or at Tuckman, who was sitting at the table with Ken and Patricia. Ken was frowning, his jaw tight, and listening intently to Tuckman while Patricia clutched his nearest hand and continued to sniffle. Wayne seemed oddly outside it all, just sitting beside Ana, nodding. Looking through the glass, I couldn't tell what might be happening in the Grey. There was no indication at all now—not even the wisps and lights I'd seen the last time.

Terry turned up the volume from the audio monitors.

"... sure it's not true. Cara was overwrought—momentary hysteria at having been hit. It's natural to feel stunned or shocked."

"We'd better tell him they can go home," I said. "None of them threw that brooch."

Terry stood up, stretching his back and legs with a series of small pops. "I'll do it."

In a few moments, he walked into the séance room and whispered to Tuckman, who nodded and put his hands together in his sincere salesman pose and smiled. "They've finished looking at the tape and everything's fine. No one threw anything at anyone. I'll speak to Cara and for now we can assume that the project is going ahead. Thank you for being so patient. I know this has been a very difficult day."

The sitters began stirring, sluggishly. Tuckman removed himself a little faster. A few seconds later, he strode into the booth.

"What's going on now?" he demanded.

"Nothing you shouldn't be spectacularly happy about," I replied. I nodded at the image on the monitor screen. "Looks like a legitimate apport."

He narrowed his eyes and looked at the screen. He shook his head. "How are they doing that?"

I shrugged, though I still felt a little dizzy from my brush with Celia. "Power of the mind? Terry's been running it through everything he can think of and there's no sign of wires or strings or that it's just been tossed there. You can run it back and forth from every angle and it just appears there. It's the real thing."

Tuckman stared at the image, his face blank.

"Tuckman?"

He scowled and flipped a dismissive hand at me. "Just finish it up." Then he turned and stalked out.

I put a hand through my hair, rubbing the impending headache developing in the top of my head. I was tired and feeling somewhat queasy and irritable. I hoped the hollow ache in my skull wasn't going to be a migraine, though Tuckman's attitude seemed good enough reason to feel irritated and worn-out all on its own.

"Do you want this one?" Terry asked.

"No. I think I can remember this. Besides, I'm almost done and that recording doesn't prove anything Tuckman wants to acknowledge."

"You got that right."

"Terry, why are you on this project? This seems like a waste of your time."

"Abnormal psych doesn't get more juicy than the prisoner/guard experiment."

" 'Scuse me?"

"There's this classic experiment in behavioral and abnormal psychology in which you give a group of people permission to do whatever they want to another group of people—even though you tell them they are supposed to take care of the other group. You let them know that their actions have no repercussions in the outside world. Pretty soon they're doing some horrible things to each other. This is an interesting variation, because this group has no prisoners, only guards, and they've been told that what they do has power in the world, but only if the group as a whole does it. I'm writing my thesis on permission, self-justification, and psychosis based on some of this."

"I see." I didn't, but I didn't want a deeper explanation at that point. It was ugly enough without going off on research tangents. "I'll get the monitoring information from you on Monday."

"All right. If you want any more of these recordings you let me know." He looked aside. "I'm—uh … I'm sorry I've been …"

I waved him off. "Don't worry about it. I'm used to it."

I let myself out, lingering long enough to miss the séance group as they left.

I couldn't just write off the idea that Terry had tweaked the information, but the apport pretty well put a bullet in the idea of faked effects; there's very little in the realm of paranormal research more convincing than a documented apport under proper scientific conditions—because there'd never been one. Even a professional skeptic of the class of a Houdini or a Randi would have to pause over this. I needed to clear off the last interview with Wayne Hopke and catch up to "Frankie" before I'd feel I'd completed the job, but I was convinced that Tuckman's phenomena—however impossible they seemed—were the real thing. Why they were so strong I couldn't be sure. He hadn't asked me to find that out, but I wanted to know, even if he didn't.

I wondered about the phenomena as I headed home, feeling the throbbing in my head ebb and flow with every pulse. It seemed as if the apported brooch had picked out Cara before flying into her face. It would have taken a considerable amount of power to apport the brooch in the first place, then hold it in place long enough to change its direction. Most apports just drop straight down out of the air—and according to Randi and Houdini they're faked by sleight-of-hand artists tossing things over their own shoulder behind their backs. This one had appeared, hung in one place, then twitched aside with enough force to hit a woman more than a foot away and cut her deep enough to need stitches. It seemed not only a show of power, but also a little vicious.

Cara's remark about Celia becoming cruel ran through my head. Maybe the group had somehow made their very own duppy—not just a simple poltergeist, neutral and playful like Philip, but a malicious ghost. Terry had said they'd been given permission. They'd been told they had power and perhaps somehow every piece of pettiness and bad temper had become manifest in their ghost. I was half convinced by my own argument, since most people will do more out of anger or spite than they will out of compassion or good feeling—there are always more people willing to complain than to praise, after all—but I didn't let myself buy it just yet. I needed to finish up before I could draw a conclusion. I didn't want to be like Tuckman and predetermine the solution before I'd got all the evidence.

I had to pause my maundering while I negotiated the last of the drive home. I continued my train of thought after I'd closed and locked the condo door behind myself.

I didn't like the fact that I was running parallel to a murder investigation. I imagined Solis wasn't too thrilled about my presence nearby, either. Odd bits of conversation kept pulling me closer to Mark's murder without solving anything. It annoyed me to have those few broken threads of information I could do nothing about. I wished I could just pass them all to Solis and call this thing closed. I wondered if I ought to tell him about the brooch. It was Cara's, and by her admission she'd left it at Mark's the day he'd been killed. That pretty well made her the woman who'd been in his bed, even without her confession to me, and that would interest Solis. He'd get the basic information when he interviewed the séance group—someone would mention such a startling event—but I wondered if I should mention it sooner. It might lead him to an arrest all the faster and then I wouldn't have to keep on thinking about this case.

Except that I'd seen the brooch apport and that meant Celia had taken it into the Grey. Had she taken it from Mark's apartment or from somewhere else? The uncomfortable thought stirred in my mind that a ghost so mean-tempered it would cut someone and strong enough to make a table run around a room and menace people might be able to do much worse. I had to know what the ghost's involvement with Mark's death was.

I didn't think I could get the answers from Celia and I didn't like the alternative route. I hated to ask vampires for favors, even when I was owed a few. I had no desire to mix with that bunch if I could avoid it, but I might be forced to ask Carlos for help if I was to discover how Celia was involved in Mark's death.

I didn't feel up to negotiating with anything tougher than a tub of yogurt that evening. My headache was not improving and all I wanted was to lie down for a while. I fed the ferret and watched her destroy my bookshelf while I lay on the couch gulping down aspirin with pints of water until we were both ready to sleep.

SEVENTEEN

Monday morning my headache had abated but I woke up feeling tired nonetheless and wished I had been drinking to justify feeling so hungover—at least then I'd have felt I deserved it. My morning run seemed to be uphill all the way and the air was thick and unpleasant. The ferret demonstrated a degree of ire at being returned to her cage that is more commonly seen in goofy Japanese cartoons, so at least I went on my way chuckling at her expense.

I hung out in the PNU Psychology Department office until Denise Francisco showed up for work. She took a look at me as she ducked into her desk and dropped a large, black canvas purse on the floor with a thump.

She avoided eye contact. "Tuck isn't in yet," she said. She snatched a lumpy blue coffee mug the size of a walrus off the desktop and headed back out the door. I followed her.

"I've seen all of Dr. Tuckman that I care to for a while," I said. "I came to talk to you."

Still thirty going on nineteen, she was wearing a short, flippy skirt over her pudgy hips with several layers of too-tight tank tops under a black denim jacket. If she hadn't been wearing cherry red Dr. Martens she would have scurried, but no one scurries in midcalf mosh boots. She whisked into another doorway that turned out to be a break room. She snatched the coffeepot off its warming plate and cursed loudly and creatively as the merest gloop of black, overboiled coffee oozed into her mug.

"Thirteen paralytic virgins and a partridge in a rutting pear tree! Who drank all the coffee already! You people suck, do you hear me? You S-U-Q-Q, suck! You couldn't give a blow job in a wind tunnel! If manners were makeup, you'd need plastic surgery first! Homeless winos put their hands on their wallets and cross to the opposite side of the street when they see you people coming!"

A voice floated out from somewhere deeper in the warren of offices: "Keep goin', Frankie. My abs need the workout."

She bent over—almost exposing more than the stiff black net of her trendy petticoat—and scrabbled through a cabinet beneath the coffeemaker. "Goddamn it," she muttered. "They got the hazelnut." She straightened and glared at me. "Do you drink coffee?"

I blinked at her. "Yes."

Her eyes narrowed. "Starbucks?"

"Only when desperate."

"What did you want to talk to me about?"

"The project. Terry said you worked on it for a while. I need to know more."

She shoved her massive mug at me. "Get this filled with hazelnut coffee that doesn't taste like crude oil and I'll tell you anything."

I looked at the cup, then looked back up at Frankie. "No."

She pouted. "No? Why should I tell you anything if you won't do something for me first?"

"Because I can just sit and watch you have a coffee jones until you give in and it costs me nothing, whereas filling that portable black hole of a mug will cost me twenty dollars and a half hour of time I won't enjoy in the least."

She stared at me and poked the tip of her tongue out to flicker over her top lip like a snake tasting the air. Then she huffed and turned away, saying, "I'll be right back."

She marched off into the warren and I heard the laughing voice yell briefly before she returned with the mug half full.

"OK," she announced. "I can stand to shackle myself to this job for about half an hour now. Or until Tuck gets in." She rolled her eyes. "Whichever. C'mon. Back to the pillory."

Frankie slurped some coffee and headed to the Psych office with me in tow.

"You don't seem too … pleased with this job," I hazarded.

"Oh, God, no," she replied, sliding back behind her desk. "I only came because of Tuckman. I used to be one of his grad students at the University of Washington—I thought he glided across water like eiderdown. Tells you what a big dope I was, huh?" She slurped coffee at every conversational turn.

"Anyhow, so, when Tuck got the chop at the U, I was still trying to finish up my thesis, so I transferred here to follow him and the project. I helped him set up the room and the protocols, and I'm still typing up his project reports, but …"

"I heard that coming. But what?" I asked, leaning on the counter.

"I have learned to my sorrow that Dr. Gartner Tuckman is a particular variety of dickweed that grows in the slimiest of swamps composed of rotten, overinflated ego. He is—to be delicate about it—a manipulative, unethical jerk who slants his protocol to get the result he wants. He only got the offer here because PNU was too starry-eyed about him to see he thinks this school is a second—no—a third-rate babysitting service for spoiled brats too stupid to get into a 'real' college. And he's got too big an ego to realize how lucky he is that no one spilled the beans about why he left U-Dub in the first place."

"And why did he?" I prompted, not because I had to, but because it was obvious she wanted me to and I didn't mind playing along a little, so long as she was talking.

"Technically it was a cutback, but really they were looking for a reason to get rid of him without looking like big idiots. His last couple of projects were major money pits. He's got a magic touch for making money go places it shouldn't and getting away with it, but his last projects at U-Dub didn't clean up so well and they both got buried because Tuckman's favorite thing is manipulating his subjects—and his assistants—into going way too far for safety or good sense. He likes to push people and he sets up experiments that push them to push others. People got hurt, but Tuck was able to blame some of the assistants and the participants and get away with it—mostly. Everybody on the review board must have known he'd been playing fast and loose with the cash and messing up his subjects, but they didn't have enough proof to do anything but unload him at the first opportunity. Which they did."

"And he took up where he left off when he got here?"

Frankie nodded. "Pretty much. He always wanted to try this ghost thing. At first I was all for it—I thought it would be kind of neat—but it's not. It's crap. And he's not being straight with anybody. He's doing the same bad things."

"How so?"

"OK, you understand this experiment is a really dangerous idea. Tuck's got this bunch of kind of wacky people thinking they can levitate stuff and make things appear out of thin air. This was supposed to be PK by committee, remember, but Tuck's stopped emphasizing that little detail. He's letting them think they have the power individually as well as collectively. Can you imagine what's going to happen to them when this project breaks up? He's got these guys thinking they can do anything—like they're all Superman or something—that the rules of the normal world don't apply to them. You know what we call people who think like that? We call 'em psychopaths. The whole thing's just creepy and I don't know what he thinks he's going to show, but I'm betting it'll be nasty—'cause with Tuck it always is."

"Then why are you still here?"

"Because I now owe PNU for my graduate program. So I took this job and—naturally—they put me in the Psych Department, where I have to see Mr. Ego every day except Friday. I'm trying to get a different job, but there isn't anything available midterm. Unless someone dies."

"You know, Tuck thinks someone is sabotaging his project…"

She giggled and drained the coffee mug. "Well, it's not me. I'm trying to make sure no one gets hurt if I can help it. That's why I volunteer to clean up the room for him—so I can see if he's changed anything. I wouldn't put it past him to electrify the chairs or something like that if he thought it would get him a novel reaction or push his subjects just a bit further. So I check for stuff every time I do the room. So far, so good. Although, you know, I heard he's got a theft problem."

"Really?"

"Yup. His poltergeist is a magpie. Likes shiny things. Steals people's keys and loots the women's purses. Always has, from day one. I was kind of surprised he just let you have those keys since he'd be in six feet of deep-fried trouble if they got lost."

"How much trouble would he be in if he lost an assistant?"

"Depends on how he lost him," she chortled. "You mean, like, quit—no problem. You mean, like, dead—not so good."

She didn't know. "Do you read the paper or watch the news?"

"As infrequently as possible—I don't need any more nightmares than I got out of Tuck the past few years. Why?"

"Did you know Mark Lupoldi?"

"Tuck's special effects guy? Sure."

"He was killed last Wednesday. He didn't make it to the session."

Frankie's jaw dropped open. "You're kidding. Right?"

"No. The cops are looking into it."

"Holy ... shrimp basket. For real?"

"Real as it gets."

Frankie gaped and started shaking her head. Then she stopped and stared into her coffee cup. She didn't look up when someone entered the office, but I did. A lanky gray-haired man in a sweater stood in the doorway holding a coffee mug almost as large as hers.

"Oh. Sorry. Didn't mean to interrupt. I was bringing Madam Frankie coffee. Before she decides to have my head boiled in it. Is she in here? I thought I heard her..."

I pointed over the counter. "She's a little upset."

He gave me a cockeyed smile. "She can't be too upset—she's not swearing." He looked over the counter. "Oh. Oh, no. That looks bad."

"A friend of hers died."

"Oh." He went behind the counter and crouched down next to Frankie, pouring the coffee into her mug with care. "Brought you coffee, Frankie. Hello. Earth to Frankie. Time for verbal abuse—it's Starbucks."

"You brought me Starbucks ... ?" she muttered.

"I know how you love to complain. So. I hear you're feeling like crap..."

"I don't feel like crap. I feel like the lowest trilobite fossil ever ground up and dumped on a roadbed in Tumwater under half a ton of tar."

"That good, huh?" He glanced up at me. "I've got her. She'll be all right."

Frankie exploded in tears and crammed her face against the man's shoulder. He looked startled, but waved me away.

I felt strange about leaving. It was my fault she was upset. But she wouldn't have felt any better about it tomorrow when it came from Solis. At least tomorrow she would see it coming.

I found a dry place to stop and make a phone call to the Danzigers. I wanted to double-check Frankie's story about Tuckman's exit from UW with Ben. As amusing as her version was, she had an axe to grind and that tends to color people's statements. But the Danzigers didn't answer their phones and I had to leave messages.

I didn't like the odd sensation in my gut. Maybe I was starting to get premonitions or something, though that seemed unlikely. Still, what I knew about Greywalking I'd come by largely through the worst kind of bumbling firsthand experience, so I might be wrong. I hoped not.

I had an appointment to talk to Wayne Hopke at one thirty and plenty to keep busy with until then.

Wayne Hopke lived on an old forty-foot powerboat that smelled of cigarettes, beer, and citrus-based organic cleaner. The boat was moored on the canal near the Ballard locks and Hopke had come out to greet me on arrival with a big grin on his face and a brew in his hand. He was, as Cara had said, a likable old sot who felt the loneliness of retirement and chased it off with conversation and cold ones as often as possible. Though he'd been fully retired from the army for a while and was approaching seventy, he was still sinewy and wore his white hair in a military buzz cut. The rest of his appearance had gone civilian—blue jeans, deck shoes, and a loose sweatshirt.

He launched into his background and his reason for joining the project with gusto—he'd been bored—and rambled on for quite a while about life in and after the army, draining several beers as he did. But the alcohol didn't seem to dull his wits any. He knew to the exact minute when he'd joined the project, what he thought of it all, and who'd done what when. He was the least judgmental and the most relaxed of the whole group. He seemed to have no discomforts or rancor with anyone and he believed in the project wholeheartedly.

He didn't quaver or qualify anything and he liked it all just fine, thank you.

Whenever he finished off a beer, he crushed the can flat and tossed it toward a box of empties before opening the fridge for a fresh one. A minuscule yellow thread seemed to unreel from him behind each flung can and tangle in a pale haze over the box.

One of the crushed cans made an abrupt veer and flew toward me. I ducked and knocked it aside.

Hopke glanced up. "I am so sorry. That's been happening more and more lately."

I waved it off, though I tried to keep an eye on the thin haze of Grey energy that floated peripatetically about the cabin, sending tiny tendrils toward us like test probes. "I'm getting used to it."

The boat heeled and pulled at the mooring lines with a creak. The sudden motion and the smell in the cabin forced me to swallow hard and dig my feet into the floor. Several books from the built-in shelves arced lazily into the air, defying gravity, and tumbled past my head.

Hopke scrambled to pick them up and stack them on a table. "Damn. Celia's getting frisky lately."

"Is this unusual?"

"Not entirely, but it's more frequent since last week or so. Celia's always been a bit of a troublemaker. I think she took my keys this morning—it's a good thing I'm not planning to go anywhere, because I haven't found them yet. I hope she didn't toss them overboard."

"That would be inconvenient."

"It surely would."

"All right," I said, resettling myself. "As long as we're on the subject, let's go back to yesterday, OK?"

"Sure."

"Why was yesterday's session so much different than the others?"

"Well, it's Mark."

"Excuse me," I said, putting up a hand to forestall him. "Are you saying that you think Mark's death is related to the events of yesterday?"

"Yes, I am. I think Mark's with us. Or at least the energy came from Mark in some way. Maybe because we were thinking of him or something like that, but whatever it is, you can't deny that yesterday's session was different and the only thing that had changed was that Mark was dead."

"How do you explain the rise in phenomena before Mark's death, then?"

"Natural progression. We've been working on it, getting better at it. Putting in all our effort."

"The change was very sudden, though. Do you think you're all contributing equally to the phenomena or is there something else going on?"

"If you mean fakery, I'd have to say no. We're all on the level. But I suppose it's possible that one or two people might be just better at it than others, or working just a touch harder. All teams have their work-horses—someone who leads the way or pulls a little harder to encourage others."

"Who would that be, in your estimation?"

Hopke laughed. "Oh, that I don't know. Celia's mighty fond of Ken, but that doesn't mean he's got anything special to do with it. She used to have a bit of a soft spot for Cara, too. I must say, I was surprised Cara got hurt. She's a bit chilly at first, but she's not a bad gal. I suppose it was just an accident because we were all upset—Mark was a good guy and we all liked him, and if he's with Celia, he wouldn't hurt Cara deliberately."

He paused to think, then went on, frowning. "All our sessions have been very pleasant up till now. But I know there's some hard feelings here and there—Dale's a jealous one and Patty's easily upset—so maybe we did it to ourselves. ? Huh. Makes you wonder, doesn't it?"

"Yeah, it does. Aside from Dale and Patricia, are there other ... hard feelings in the group?"

"Well, the kids are kind of funny. I'm sure they don't think an old fart like me knows what they're up to—your average twenty-year-olds think they invented sex themselves—but I've seen that sort of thing before. It's been the cause of more sorrow and stupidity than drinking and driving."

"What about Mark?"

"I'm not following you."

"Did any of the group have a problem with Mark or a reason to hurt him? You suggested Mark might be 'with' Celia. Would he have reason to be resentful or angry?" I was pretty sure it wasn't the ghost of Mark Lupoldi who'd thrown the brooch, but Hopke's ideas might point in an interesting direction.

"Mark was the easiest guy you ever saw. If he had a problem with you, he'd say something, maybe make a joke about it, but he wasn't the resentful type or mean. If anyone had a problem with Mark, why would they take it out on Cara? Unless you think Celia killed Mark, which is ridiculous."

"Is it?"

"Celia's made up of a bit of all of us, and since none of us would hurt Mark, why would Celia?"

Another can lofted and smacked into my skull.

"You OK there?" Hopke asked, leaning toward me.

I rubbed my head. "Yeah. It wasn't much."

"Good thing the can was empty."

I nodded and wanted to wrap this interview up and get out before Celia got any more "frisky."

"I've just got one more question. You said you wanted something to do, but why choose this particular project?"

"Well, I've lost plenty of friends over the years and I still wonder if there's more to all of this than just struggling in the mud and the blood and the—the poop. You should pardon my language."

"I've heard worse."

Hopke nodded and went on. "See, I just want to know what's out there after this, if there is anything at all."

"You're a braver man than I," I commented in all truth.

"I doubt that. You seem like a pretty gutsy gal."

"Maybe, but I'm not sure I want to know what happens after this."

He finished another beer. "You may change your mind when you're my age."

I doubted it, but, then, Hopke didn't know what I knew.

"Are you satisfied with what you've learned so far?" I asked.

"So far, I guess I am. I still want to know more, but I feel a little better having some idea that we're not entirely powerless in this world and maybe not in the next."

I stood up. "Thank you, Mr. Hopke. You've answered all my questions."

"Already?" he asked, standing himself. "That hardly took any time at all." He gave me a hopeful smile. "Are you sure you wouldn't like to stay for a beer?"

I shook my head, smiling back. "I can't. Thank you for the offer, though."

He walked with me to the edge of the boat and handed me over the side. As I started to turn, something shiny whizzed past my head and plopped into the water. Its passage made my head throb again.

"Oh, damn," Hopke groaned. "Those were my keys. Well, I guess I'll be fishing for them."

I stared down into the murky green water of the marina. "How deep is it? Can you get them back?"

"Probably. The canal's shallow right here, 'cause this bit used to be the bay." He looked back into the water and picked up another can of beer from a cooler on the aft deck. "Well, better get started with the fishing. And you know how beer and fishing go together."

I wished him good luck with the key-fishing and left him trolling a heavy magnet for the steel key ring and sipping beer. I kind of liked Wayne Hopke and I thought it was too bad that he probably wouldn't learn much about life after death from this experience. He'd have to pick it up when he got there, and I hoped that wouldn't be soon.

EIGHTEEN

ost people lie. They lie in little ways all the time—to themselves, to others, to the government, to their bosses and spouses and kids. Tuckman's project members had lied to me—it pretty well went with the territory and with their peculiar glib willingness to answer the questions of a stranger. What mattered was not the existence or the blackness of those lies, but the relevance. So I spent the remainder of Monday and all of Tuesday checking and double-checking biographies and backgrounds, looking for lies that mattered, for the cracks in the stories that might point to someone who could have moved the power line, boosted the poltergeist's input, or skewed it in a murderous direction. Tuckman was wrong about a mechanical saboteur and I wasn't convinced he'd been straight with me about why he wanted me on the case. The pieces didn't make a picture; they just made another puzzle and I had a bad feeling about it. Besides, running backgrounds would keep me out of the way of Solis, who would be starting to interview the same people I'd just finished with as well as Tuckman himself.

Tuesday morning I hiked up the hill to the county records office and requested files. I made phone calls. I stared at microfiche cards and paid for photocopies. I listened to people grouse and gave them money, and I looked through every scrap of paper Tuckman had supplied and everything I'd picked up since I'd started. The pile of oddities was smaller than I'd expected, though it was interesting.

Quite a few of the group turned out to have skeletons in their closets. Patricia had been under a doctor's care for depression and other psychological problems off and on since the birth of her last child—what kind of problems weren't given. She'd also filed for divorce once, but withdrawn the paperwork a few days later with no explanation.

Ken and Ian both had short arrest records with the SPD. Ian's SPD record was juvenile and therefore sealed now—except for a sexual harassment complaint lodged with PNU by one of the women in the dorms. That was being handled internally, and no one at the school would discuss it. The charge didn't surprise me, now that I had Ana's perspective on him. There was a rather odd note from the Humane Society in his file—a letter about a cruelty to animals complaint which seemed to have no follow-up. His project profile showed that his family had moved around a lot when he was a child—that might explain the lack of follow-up on the cruelty note—and I'd had no luck finding anyone who'd known him before college. His parents had moved to Idaho. When I tracked them down on the phone, they seemed vague and uncomfortable, rambling about their dog and the squirrel population and how they'd had to have the poor dog put to sleep when it ate a poisoned squirrel and how horribly the creatures had suffered. Their only comment on Ian was that they didn't get along with their son and they didn't seem to miss him. They would not discuss his juvenile record or the harassment charge with me. His mother seemed a little hysterical about it all and slammed the phone down at that point.

Ken's record was a little worse: minor possession, minor violence, lots of stupidity, an assault charge that had been dismissed, and note of a sealed psychiatric evaluation that didn't seem to be related to any-thing—I was guessing some more serious charge had been expunged from his sheet. I couldn't find a record of whatever it had been, even in our notoriously nosy newspapers, though it had been embarrassing enough to someone to rate a cleanup. His family also had no comment, though they waved it away, saying it was in the past and best forgotten.

Dale and Cara Stahlqvist both got rave reviews as backstabbing hard-asses, though most of their associates found Dale the sneakier of the two and referred to Cara as "honest" in her ambitions and intentions—they preferred to know who had the knives and where they meant to stick them. But Cara had not been honest in her application to the Rainier Club. She'd made her claim of relation to Bertha Landes—one of their earliest female members—but the membership secretary had discovered a flaw in her story. Cara's application to the venerable business club had been refused. As amusing as I found it, the fact led me nowhere relevant. Neither Stahlqvist seemed to have any history of paranormal contact or abnormal behavior, however.

Wayne Hopke yielded no surprises. An occasional overindulgence in drink since his retirement seemed to be the worst of his sins. Nothing strange or uncanny had ever been noted on his records.

Ana Choi was also not shaping up as paranormal femme fatale material. She was finishing her degree in graphics and working both freelance and part-time in the field as well as helping her parents. She didn't have time or energy for skullduggery—I doubted she slept more than five hours a night and generally not that much. What free time she had was spent with friends from work or school and a procession of manipulative boyfriends. She'd given the previous one the boot in Harborview ER after he'd broken her wrist—she sure couldn't pick 'em.

Which left Terry Dornier and Denise Francisco, both of whom seemed to have no Grey connection to the poltergeist at all.

The glaring blank in Ken's record reminded me of his weird isolation in the Grey. I didn't know if it was relevant, but I wanted that hole filled in, especially if it would shed any light on why he had those shifting Grey walls around him. That phenomenon might make him less likely to have access to power in the Grey, but I couldn't be sure and it was the only real lead I seemed to have.

Sitting at my desk, playing with a pencil and pushing paper around on the blotter, I decided I'd have to bite the bullet. I called Solis.

He sounded wary and tired. I was still feeling a bit worn-down myself, but I knew he wouldn't appreciate sympathy or offer any. I came straight to my request.

"There are a couple of sealed police files related to two of the project members. I'd like to see them."

"No."

"I haven't told you whose files."

"I know whose."

"Can you at least give me an idea what the files were about?"

"No."

"Not even broadly? Markine's is a juvenile record, so I suppose that's standard procedure. What about the George file? What was that about?"

He paused before answering, sounding irritated. "It was an unfortunate circumstance that is none of your business. Foolishness and bad attitudes made everyone wish it had never happened. Mr. George overpaid for his part in it. It should be allowed to die quietly."

I was as baffled as ever about what had happened, but if it had been so embarrassing that the SPD and the county court wanted to make it go away, maybe Ken had reason to hide himself in some psychic way. "All right. I'll assume it's of no interest to me."

"Assume so. What's of interest to me is your impressions of these people."

My automatic urge was to stonewall—he hadn't been of much

help to me in return for my information so far—but as a cop investigating a homicide, he had legal recourse to pressure me and he wasn't asking for the files, only for my impressions—which weren't my client's property. And I'd said I would tell him what I knew. I'd have to edit a bit, though. I sucked in a breath and let it out in a gust, tapping my pencil on the blotter.

"Where do you want to start?" I asked. "This is a messed-up bunch of people."

"Are they?"

"Have you interviewed any of them yet?" I asked.

"I have."

"Who?"

"I won't tell you that."

"All right," I conceded. "They seem like pretty normal people individually but as a group they have a lot of sexual tension and control conflicts, weird instabilities. I'm not sure that Tuckman didn't engineer that into the group dynamic deliberately."

Solis grunted.

"None of them were completely honest with me," I continued, "but then, I'm not investigating a murder and that might make a difference."

"Possibly. Mrs. Stahlqvist claims to be related to Bertha Landes."

I found myself parroting the words of Bertha Landes when I'd met her in the theater. "It's not true. She's no relation."

"How are you sure?"

"Standard background check."

"I'd appreciate it if you could be specific as to why you are so certain."

Well, I wasn't going to say a ghost told me so. And I'd had adequate confirmation elsewhere. "The membership secretary of the Rainier Club told me the Knight family Carolyn Knight-Stahlqvist is descended from moved to Seattle before Bertha Landes came here from Indiana.

Carolyn didn't seem to know this when she made up her story or she'd actually have had a better claim. But because she lied, Mrs. Stahlqvist didn't pass muster and the secretary didn't mind telling me so."

Solis's quiet had a speculating quality. I could almost see the sleepy-eyed expression he got when the wheels were turning.

"Here's something you might like to chew on," I offered. "A few days ago Mrs. Stahlqvist told me she'd lost a brooch that belonged to Bertha Landes—an heirloom as spurious as her background. She eventually told me she thought she'd left it at Mark Lupoldi's the day he was killed. It turned up at a project session Sunday and Mrs. Stahlqvist accidentally cut her cheek on it."

"Then she had not left it? Why would she say she had?"

"It appeared rather dramatically and Mrs. Stahlqvist claimed one of the other project members must have thrown it at her, which implies one of them stole it from Lupoldi's apartment. If she really did leave it there. Since she's a liar about her past, maybe she lied about that, too. Maybe she never left it at all, but used the story to try and cover her own presence at the scene or to cast suspicion on one of the other members of the group."

"Hm. Very much like an Agatha Christie novel."

"Yeah, it is, isn't it?"

"If she had left it behind and it was picked up by someone else …"

I grinned at the phone. "Makes an interesting puzzle, doesn't it?"

Silence. I should have been embarrassed at the amusement I took in his annoyance, but I wasn't. If it had been a Sherlock Holmes story it would have been titled "The Case of the Curious Brooch" and that amused me even more. And reminded me of Celia's kleptomaniac habits.

"Solis, was anything missing from Lupoldi's apartment?"

"It is difficult to say, since we don't know what he owned."

"Would you even tell me?"

There was that down-draining silence again. Then he replied with great care, "If you asked after a specific item, I might have to say no."

My mind raced. Solis was offering a hell of a favor. The brooch information must have piqued his interest enough to feel he owed me something in return, but being Solis, he could only bend himself so far and he'd already bent a lot with the information about Ken—paltry as it was. I would have to ask the right question—Solis might not even know it was important himself. There was something ... I just knew it.

"Did you find his wallet?"

"We did."

"Did it seem to be intact? Money and credit cards still in it?"

"Yes."

"Car keys?"

"Mr. Lupoldi did not own or drive a car."

"Bicycle keys? I know he had one of those U-locks with the cylinder keys. Did you find a key like that?"

"No keys."

"Not even the apartment key?"

"No. I searched for them myself. Now that we're done with the scene, the landlord will have to use his master copy to lock up, since no apartment keys have been recovered."

"You're releasing the scene?"

"We've taken all we can from it. The lab continues to analyze samples and fingerprints and to compare against any new ones I can supply."

I had a feeling he'd be supplying more samples soon, but relying on few. A lot of the tests and analyses take a while, so most forensic evidence is more important at trial than during the investigation. Solis would proceed with the more readily available evidence of people and their tendency to talk. The case was already a week old and unsolved, so Solis would be under pressure soon to show some progress. I shouldn't have been surprised that he was picking my brain or willing to give up what might seem like worthless information in exchange.

Whoever had those keys was likely to be Mark's killer. Unless Celia had them. I'd have to find out if the poltergeist had been in Mark's apartment when he died.

I wished Solis luck and assured him I wouldn't mention the missing keys to anyone—by which I meant anyone who might be connected to the case—and broke the connection.

It wasn't quite dark yet. The overcast sky made it seem much later, but it would do me no good to go looking for Carlos until the sun was fully set.

I burned the last half hour of sunlight typing up a report for Tuckman. I planned to tell him there was no saboteur at the next day's séance, but I'd have to have documents to prove it.

When I was done, I drove up to Adult Fantasies—the twenty-four-hour "home of live girls" and a half acre of exotic fetish wear and sex toys—to ferret out Carlos, who besides being Cameron's mentor also owned the place. If I appeared in person, he'd find it much harder to refuse my request. I hoped.

For the most part, I despise and avoid vampires—when I'm not revolted and in terror of them. They rarely needed my help as much as they wanted to command my obedience, and I didn't go in for that. I'd been pulled into their byzantine politics and personal wars once and had no desire to be pulled in again. They were unpleasant, manipulative, arrogant, and selfish, and their presence often made me physically ill, even when on their best behavior. I also owed part of my strange, irremediable connection to the Grey to one and I consider that grudge-worthy.

The employees in the shop had changed since my last visit. The current crop had a kind of Stepford genericness to them—as if Carlos had decided it was better to hire people easy to forget to work in a place most people tried not to remember. A man wearing a T-shirt

with the words "I wasn't there and you can't prove it" on it told me
Carlos was out and hadn't been coming in much lately. I guessed the
new employees were also more trustworthy than the previous crop.

After I'd fenced with him for a while and given him my card, the
T-shirt man made a phone call. His eyebrows went up as he listened;
then he hung up and looked me over. Curiosity gleamed on his face
like sweat.

"He says to meet him at Green Lake on the south side of the community center. He said he'll smell you coming."

For a moment, I felt chilled. Carlos scared me more than most—
but not all—of his kind. A powerful bloodsucker, he was also a necromancer. He could see, touch, and taste the ghosts and Grey bits that
clung to me and was an intimate of death and dead things. I'd almost
gotten him killed for good and all once and I still wasn't sure how he
felt about that, no matter how many favors might be owed otherwise.
I supposed I was going to find out.

I drove north to the gemlike park around Green Lake, slowed by
the remaining tail of rush-hour traffic on Aurora.

The last time I'd seen him, he'd still been a cinder creature with
charred skin cracking on burned bones and clothed in the reek of
destruction. I wasn't sure what to expect in either looks or attitude
since then.

I was glad there were people on the streets. Joggers wearing head-
lights and reflective vests ran on the path around the lake and neighborhood people came and went through the doors of the restaurants
and bars across the street. I hoped I had nothing to fear, but even a
busy, human-rich environment couldn't protect me from Carlos if he
chose to kill me.

I felt him long before I laid eyes on him. A pitching, queasy sensation in my guts and a shiver of icicles up my spine alerted me. Light
from the windows of the community center picked out his silhouette
but didn't seem to penetrate the dark clot of bleeding Grey that

hunched around him. I could see his eyes spark as they met mine, but he stayed still and let me walk almost to the water to meet him.

Up close, I could see that his skin was patterned with scars in coiling loops and baroque twists. He'd regained his intimidating height and breadth, but his black beard and hair were thin. He held himself stiffer than I remembered, but he still had the posture of a poised tiger. His eyes remained black pits that burned with intimations of Hell, even more horrible among the scars.

He gave me half a nod before I could speak. "Blaine. Let's walk," he added, tipping his head toward the water. "I imagine your business with me won't bear the scrutiny of daylighters."

It seemed Carlos no longer considered me one of the daylight people. I knew I had moved a bit sideways of normal, but I wasn't one of his own. He wasn't causing me the sickening discomfort I would have expected if he were angry, but Carlos was tricky and mercurial in his temper, so I went beside him warily.

We turned together and began walking along the lakeside path. "What is it you want?"

"A young man was killed last week," I started. He cast me a sideways glance. "It seemed to be an accident, but it's mysterious and the cops are treating it as a murder. I … have an interest in the case and I need to know if a ghost was on the scene when it happened."

"Can you not tell?"

"No. I don't have that sort of skill. And it's not a normal type of ghost."

Carlos had developed a small unevenness in his stride. "And what do you want of me?"

"Is this some kind of ritual? That I have to be explicit with you or you won't help me?"

His mouth quirked in cruel amusement, which sent my stomach on a crash dive. "It is. So be explicit."

I swallowed before replying. "You owe me a favor for checking on

Cameron's … mistake. I need to know if the ghost in question was there and what it did. So I am asking you to come and see the scene and tell me what you can."

"Where?"

"It's an apartment in Fremont. The cops are done with it and the key is missing, so I think we should have no problem getting in, as long as we're discreet."

"Ah. 'We.' You still accept equal risk. That's good. You do this for yourself, none other?"

"If you mean is someone else controlling me, no. This is strictly my side of the daylight."

"Such as it is. Your daylight is darker than most."

"Yes." I made myself level my gaze and look without flinching into his hell-depth eyes. "Are you going to help me out or not?"

He chuckled a small earthquake through my bones. "When?"

"Tonight, I'd hoped."

His eyebrows quirked. "Tomorrow. I've already given you too much of my time tonight."

"Then why did you?" I blurted.

He cupped one giant hand over my left shoulder and drew something off me, flicking it away like lint—perhaps some remnant of Celia. I shuddered and felt a hot twisting thrum in my chest and down my arms. He crossed his own arms over his chest and looked down at me. "You continue to interest me, Blaine. And as you say, I owe you. I'll go with you tomorrow, though I don't guarantee that what I can tell you will be to your liking."

"It never has been."

"When it is, I shall be very surprised. Come here tomorrow night at the same time and we'll see what there is to dislike."

I was dismissed and I left him, feeling the hot/cold bore of his watching gaze as I walked away.

NINETEEN

I was roused out of bed early Wednesday by the wretched intrusion of the cell phone's happy burp. I remembered now why I had resisted them for so long. No one likes a chirpy morning person—especially an electronic one—when they've slept like Pinkerton. Carlos's touch on my shoulder had set off a buzzing, burning sensation in my body that had left me with bad dreams and restless sleep.

Snatching the phone from its charger I snapped at it, "Hello."

"Ms. Blaine, I'm concerned, in light of Sunday's events, to have outside confirmation of the monitoring equipment for today's session."

It took me a moment to put the voice and information into context. "Tuckman, it's seven a.m. Your session isn't until three thirty."

"Yes. I'm making a last-minute request. I thought you'd appreciate as much time as possible to accommodate it," Tuckman replied. His voice oozed condescension. "You appear to have an electronics expert you trust to vet this. I'd like you and your expert to reexamine the room and observe the session to confirm our procedure is as documented."

"Look, Dr. Tuckman, my expert doesn't work for free and may not even be available on such short notice." My brain was kicking into gcar and I wondered if I could get ahold of Quinton so early. He kept bandicoot's hours. "This is a bit of an intrusion and I suspect he'll charge extra for it, if I can get him at all."

"Immaterial. Whatever got past us last time mustn't happen again. I've spent a lot of time on the phone with the subjects to get them to try one more time. I even had to concede to this ridiculous idea that Mark Lupoldi is haunting them. I've put some additional safeguards in place and added some additional protocols and checks to document the session. But they have to be inspected and checked off by an independent expert before the session. We only have today."

I hesitated.

Tuckman lost his cool. "Damn it! I've been up all night to do this!" I didn't know if it was caused by exhaustion or fear, but the sudden whining snap to his voice got me raising my eyebrows.

"Calm down, Dr. Tuckman," I soothed. "I'll get it done."

"I have to have outside corroboration." I could hear him breathing fast.

"I understand. I'll set it up as quickly as I can. Make sure the room is locked and remains that way until we get there unless you're in it. No one else should enter that room, if possible. If they have to, you need to be with them and watching them every second, or you can't guarantee that the room is properly controlled. And the same goes for the observation room. No access to anyone but you until I get there."

Tuckman took a long, deep breath and let it out slowly. That reminded me of the relaxation breathing I'd been forgetting to practice myself. "All right. I'll make sure it's secure. I'll have Terry deliver my lecture so I can keep working on the room." Lucky break for Terry—I imagined Tuckman's ego didn't allow anyone else much time in his limelight.

"Good. I'll see you later."

I dragged myself through a short run and a shower, followed by an argument with the ferret over the ownership of a banana she had tried to stuff into her mayonnaise jar. I always won, but the look she gave me made me feel guilty. Yet another reason not to have kids: if a two-pound ferret had me wrapped around her tiny toes, I'd be a full-time hostage to a child.

I violated the law and used the cell phone while driving. The height of living dangerously, considering the merry oblivion practiced by most Seattle drivers. You can spot a coffee mug or briefcase riding on a car roof every morning commute.

I had to leave a message for Quinton getting him up to speed on the situation and asking him to call me back soon.

He returned the call a little after ten. He agreed to do it and estimated it would take two to three hours to complete the job and document it. I suggested we meet at the Merchants Cafe for lunch at eleven and go on from there.

"I hope he's prepared to pay well for all of this," Quinton said.

"He is."

"Good, 'cause I've never met the guy but I'm pretty sure I won't like him. Working for jerks costs extra and working for jerks on short notice is even more," he added, then yawned. "I'll see you at eleven."

Tuckman was grading papers on the séance table when we arrived. His condescending sneer came out when Quinton walked in, but it vanished once the work began. Quinton's odd but thorough, and I had to smile a little at Tuckman's surprise over the scruffy technician's abilities. Quinton found several flaws in the installation of Tuckman's new toys and deftly rewired them as the psychologist watched. He also produced a complicated form on a clipboard and asked a bunch of questions about the previous installation, nodding and frowning and making notes.

After a while, he handed me the clipboard and asked me to fill in some blanks as he called things out. Then he stalked around the room with his tools and meters, testing the repaired circuits and running through an extended version of the same baseline performance he'd done the last time. We were done at ten to three and Quinton took the clipboard back from me to add some more notes and his signature.

Tuckman handed him an additional form and pointed to a place for another signature, saying, "You'll need to stay for the session and confirm the operation of the equipment."

Quinton shrugged and signed without looking up. "It's your money." He handed the whole sheaf of forms to Tuckman.

Tuckman looked a bit pale when Quinton told him how much money, but he agreed. When he reached for his checkbook I said I'd add it to the bill—Quinton worked on a cash-only basis, which Tuckman found amusing.

The observation room was packed once Terry arrived. The close quarters and lack of sleep made me feel raw. In the séance room, the sitters seemed nervous and keyed up, too. Their chatter was more shrill than usual and the meters showed spikes of sound and energy as the participants moved and talked, settling themselves for whatever was going to happen. No one seemed to have any doubt that something would.

Patricia put a spray of dried flowers in the center of the table and fussed with them as the others walked around. Something Grey and powerful was visible to me in there, even though the glass made it fuzzy and ill defined. I could see the swirling yellow mass I associated with Celia and feel the surge of cold. I heard Dale Stahlqvist and Wayne Hopke on the audio monitor arguing about the possibility of Mark's ghost appearing.

"Does anything look odd to you guys?" I asked, half expecting that they could see the strong Grey activity, too.

Terry and Quinton looked down at the boards as the participants gathered around the table. "Some of these EM readings are higher than normal," Terry said. "The new room barometer is also indicating rising pressure. We'll have to compare it to the outside pressure later. Those guys are kind of wound up, though, so it could just be that."

I nodded and looked back into the room. My earlier fatigue had revved up to nervousness, though I thought I shouldn't care.

The group had distributed themselves around the table at equal distances so their fingertips, resting lightly on the surface, never touched one another's. Ian had ended up almost sideways to the mirror between Cara and Wayne with Ana on Wayne's other side. Ken was right in front of the mirror between Ana and Patricia, who had Dale Stahlqvist on her left looking straight into the booth. Cara—the cut on her cheek still covered in a gauze patch—had the spot between Dale and Ian. Someone had turned on the stereo and it let a smoky blues guitar bleed moodily into the room.

Wayne cleared his throat and started to speak, but Dale Stahlqvist cut him off. "Good afternoon, Celia," he started, giving Wayne a sharp glare. "Are you with us?"

The table bulged upward in the middle, deforming like a balloon filling with air. Its metal-shod feet dug at the carpet and the flowers slid off onto the rug. I felt my own knot of Grey tighten in my chest and the air in the booth tasted metallic.

Terry looked up from his display of monitoring instruments. He sounded worried. "I'm seeing a static charge building up. And the temperature in the séance room is dropping."

"What?" Tuckman demanded. "How much?"

"Five degrees in one minute," he said, shaking his head and staring back down at the panel. "Most of my electrical monitors are acting up. I'm guessing magnetic interference…"

"It was clear during the tests," Quinton stated. "It's not the new equipment—that's working fine."

A thunderclap cracked the air of the experiment room.

The participants looked nervous, shooting glances at one another from the corners of their eyes. I could see the hazy yellow wad of energy was now streaked with sudden jagged welts of red. As I stared, the haze seemed to pull into pieces and draw back together, then apart, drifting from the center of the table toward the participants. The largest clouds of energy moved toward Ken, Ana, Ian, and Cara, fired with red and yellow flashes. Smaller balls like heat lightning twitched in the direction of Wayne, Patricia, and Dale.

"Celia?" Dale asked in a nervous voice.

"Maybe it's Mark..." Patricia suggested.

The table quivered, as if gathering itself.

"Nonsense—" Cara snapped.

The table sprang upward and fell back, digging its feet into the carpet. It jerked and shuddered, writhing under their fingertips like an animal in pain. Patricia yipped as it trampled her foot.

Hot light flared over the table in pure white fury and I felt a sympathetic burn along my limbs. The table spun under its brilliant Grey canopy, rising on one leg and striking Cara and Ian hard in the ribs. Cara dropped to her knees as the table knocked into Ian a second time before coming back down. Ian staggered backward, holding his side as the rest stared around.

"The pressure—" Terry started.

The stereo erupted in a burst of uncoordinated noise as the table rushed toward the glass divider, rising off the floor with a sudden bump. Alarms squealed and pinged in the observation room.

"No!" Terry shouted at his instruments. "It can't do that!"

"There's nothing wrong with the device," Quinton said, poking the monitors with his meter, but his face was pale. "But it's getting awfully hot—"

The table crashed into the glass, gouging a hole as big as a beach ball. Icy air gushed through the breach, dragging a stink of smoke and acid into the booth. I gagged on it and bent my body around a sudden punch of discomfort as the table thudded back to the floor. Unobstructed by glass, I could now see the four large power masses hovering over Cara, Ian, Ana, and Ken. Ken's Grey walls and Ian's prismatic flashes had vanished as if burned away. The four miniature storms of energy tore at the table in pulses of red and yellow.

Shouts broke out in the séance room. The table, cloaked in throbbing, paranormal fire, lurched into Ken, ramming him against the wall below the shattered window. Ana shrieked as the table attacked him again and again. Ken flailed and disappeared below our view, the hot red and yellow energy still hovering over him like a carrion bird on the thermals.

A bright orange flash struck the stereo and it blared a jumbled cacophony of swing music, chopping up "Jumpin' at the Woodside" with "In the Mood" and "Sing, Sing, Sing."

"Stop it!" Tuckman demanded, jumping up and blocking all exit from the observation room. Terry and I stared over his shoulder toward the pandemonium, appalled.

"I'm not doing anything!" Terry shouted.

"The meters are flipping out. There's something really nasty in there," Quinton snapped. "Where's the damned fire extinguisher?"

I couldn't keep track of which angry knot of energy had done what anymore. The room was thick with the dizzying strobe and strain of Grey forces, a rising tsunami of fury and panic. A cataract of books rushed up from the bookshelves and pelted down on the people in the room. Something red snatched at Patricia's head and she shouted in pain. A spangle of blood and the bright shape of her earring arced to the floor.

Under the boiling storm of Grey, the table lurched again, scrabbling its feet against the floor like a bull and jerking toward the corner beside the door. Ana was in its path, half crouched on the floor, covering her head with her arms. Nearby, Dale had flattened himself over Cara. Ian, Ken, and Wayne had all vanished onto the floor near the broken observation room window.

On the video monitor, there was no violent storm of light, only the strange movement of shadows from the swinging chandelier. I could see Wayne patting at Ken's legs, his voice steaming in the room's uncanny cold, sound smothered in the screaming of the stereo, then turning his head to watch the table.

I looked back through the broken window. Trailing red and yellow streamers, the table charged toward Ana. She dodged, jumping over the Stahlqvists and Ian, and ran up onto the couch, still covering her head with her arms as if she were being bombarded by an invisible flight of ravens.

The table jerked forward, changing direction and tipping toward the sofa cushions. Ana bounded across the upholstery, her feet skimming over the back, to leap off the arm of the sofa nearest the door as the table crashed down onto the couch.

Wayne ran to catch her, scooping her from the air with a ropy arm. He wrenched at the door handle. It came away in his hand.

The table bounced and wheeled on its edge, sweeping toward the door.

Beside me, Quinton and Terry began beating at the monitor board with their jackets as smoke erupted from below. "Get out! The panel's catching fire!"

Dale Stahlqvist snatched at a leg of the rolling table, pulling it away from his wife and Ana. Red and yellow light strobed in the room, lending a disjointed, horror-film aspect to the scene. Patricia picked up a wooden chair and began to beat at the rogue table, screaming at it as blood ran down her neck.

I needed a closer look at Celia. In the confusion, I bolted toward the observation room door as the board full of Christmas lights in the séance room exploded, raining colored glass and sparks over Ana, Cara, and Wayne. The stereo let out a final tortured howl and fell silent as both rooms blacked out.

I heard the whoosh of a fire extinguisher behind me as I rushed into the hall. The séance room door crashed open, flooding the hall with Celia's hot glow and tangled lines. Wayne, Ana, and Cara rushed out as I skidded into the sudden fire and knives of the poltergeist.

A tornado of fury twisted around me, pulling and tearing at me with murderous power. Crystal planes, glittering like ice sheets, cut kaleidoscopic slices of time, flaying me with instants of memory— flashes of lives and shattered jumbles of faces … and the odor of gun- smoke and salt wrack. The sensation of foulness pushed against me and I reeled forward, desperate to escape it.

Then I was through it and the séance sitters were milling, hysteri- cal and gabbling, into the hall around me. Acrid smoke and the smell of the extinguisher's chemicals flooded from the rooms on a raft of chill. But I still had the other smell in my nose—the stink that had clung under the scent of superglue at Mark's apartment. The odor of the poltergeist.

Turning, I saw the hot swirl of Celia's shape collapse, spiraling away like water down a drain and leaving only dim, frayed threads like a spi- derweb spun between the participants. I shuddered. It was a force—an entity—capable of great destruction, and the feel and smell of it only confirmed the sickening idea that had been growing in my mind for a while. I had passed through the thing that had killed Mark Lupoldi.

It hadn't just been present and it wasn't a coincidence. One or some of these people had created a killer ghost. I had no doubt of it, but Solis wouldn't like it. He would require a more prosaic solution and I might have to be the one to point him to it. No one else would or could.

I stood in the hall, breath heaving, and looked them over. Ken was still missing. Tuckman and Terry had come into the hall with Quin- ton a smoke-wrapped step behind them. Cara had allowed Dale to comfort her and I could see thin blood trickling from beneath her bandage as she leaned against him. Wayne had vanished again, leaving Ana in the care of Ian.

I caught up to Wayne exiting the séance room. Glancing in, I could see Ken sitting up against the control room wall. He shook his head as if dazed or deafened. I looked at Wayne.

"Bruised, but not broken, I think," he said. "Just knocked silly. How 'bout you call the medics and I'll take a look at the rest?"

"We'll have to keep them calm and here and not let them go wandering off like Cara did last time."

"Check. Go tell Tuckman. He'll listen to you more than me."

"OK. Be back in a minute." I glanced in at Ken one more time, but he hadn't changed any—his shield of blankness was still missing, but there was nothing much else to see. I dug up my cell phone and called 911 as I headed for Tuckman.

Quinton buttonholed me. "I really don't like this."

"Join the club. What went wrong?"

He gave me a grave look. "I was going to ask you that. The machinery was all doing what it should have—right up until the electrical surge that fried most of it. What caused the surge seems to be your field, not mine."

"I'm afraid I don't know, either. Some kind of ghost energy, but—"

He waved my explanation aside. "I don't want to know. Magic just makes my head ache. What I do want to know is if this is going to attract cops."

I chewed my lip. "I think so. There's a murder investigation involved and I suspect the detective in charge has been watching at least a few of these people."

"Then I need to go, but I'll call you later. There's something I need to check out."

"Something wrong?"

"Maybe, but I want to be sure first. I've got your cell phone number. I'll call you when I know. Now, I'm out of here."

I reserved judgment on his mysterious habits and blew out a breath. "I'm stuck a while longer or I'd offer you a lift back to Pioneer Square. Will you be OK?"

He chuckled. "I'm great at getting around. But you be careful, Harper. This thing's a mess."

I gave him a sardonic look. "No duh."

He gave me a small smile, then shook his head and loped for the back stairs with his pack slung over one shoulder.

I caught up to Tuckman next, hearing the screech of a siren and the clatter of noise from in front of the building. "Hey," I said, catching his arm to turn his attention from the hysterical Patricia, who was still pinching her bleeding ear. "You're going to have cops all over you in a few minutes and you need to keep this bunch contained—"

The Medic One team hustled up the stairs with their kits. Wayne sent them to Ken first, then resumed his position blocking the main stairs.

Tuckman seemed a little dazed. "What? Why?"

"I suspect that Detective Solis has been keeping an eye on you and your group. Someone has surely called campus security about the noise and the smoke, and Solis's guys will be right behind them. Keep these people in order and under control and try to get them coherent. No detective is going to buy the idea that your pet ghost got loose and attacked a few people—especially not when one of your project assistants died in mysterious circumstances a week ago."

His respiration was a little fast, his eyes still a little glazed. I leaned in and peered into them. "Do you understand me, Tuckman? Hello?"

He blinked several times. "Yes. Yes, I think so." He shook himself back to normal. "I need to keep them together. Will you stay or have you other concerns elsewhere?"

I smiled at him. "I have other things I have to do. I need to talk to you about all of this, but it'll have to wait."

"All right." He nodded and stepped away from me, beginning to move through the small crowd, soothing them and organizing their thoughts for them.

I watched the ghost-makers wander for a moment, beginning to fall back under Tuckman's calm. They seemed frightened and confused—unaware of what power they wielded. Most of them. But at least one of them was acting.

I followed Quinton's lead and slid away before the cops arrived. I had an appointment I couldn't miss. Not even for Solis.

TWENTY

Carlos paused a moment outside the building to study it, as I had a week before. The Grey fog of yellow and black that had hung over the building the night of Mark Lupoldi's death had thinned and contracted to a single blazing spot on his window. The police cars and barricades were gone, but the building still had an air of violation and depression.

Carlos said nothing until we were upstairs and standing in front of Mark's door. The snap lock had been engaged but it was old, unsophisticated, and poorly installed—easily bypassed with a credit card.

"Corruption is rife when even the locks take bribes," he observed.

I raised an eyebrow. I'd never expected a joke out of Carlos. "It doesn't usually work," I replied. "This just happens to be a very cheap lock in a run-down building."

I closed the door behind us, locking us into the murder scene. The landlord had not cleaned the apartment yet and the bloodstains and print-kit residue still marked the walls. Carlos looked it over and nodded approval as he began pacing around the room. His tread made no sound in spite of his size. He put his hands out as if touching objects as yet invisible to me.

I sank down into the Grey, hoping to see something of what he saw. The cold silver mist swelled over me, shot with the phosphorescent glow of energized objects, heaving and flickering with the shapes of ghosts and memories. Layers of old tenants had built up a map of their daily routines, laying a path paved with ghost footprints around the bed, kitchen counter, and bath. A similar pearly patch floated near the windows, where generations of tenants had gazed out, watered their plants, or sat to read in the sunlight a while.

I pushed myself deeper, to the lines of the grid. Bright white, yellow, and blue dominated the vertiginous view through the blackness between the worlds. I felt dizzy at the apparent emptiness below my feet. Cars left a blur of displaced energy overhead on the black smear of the Aurora Bridge as the neon wire-frame world rolled down to the cold cut of the canal below.

A tangled stain of red and yellow—like strands of poisoned cottonwood fluff—lay upon the air a few feet from me. They didn't seem to hover, but to have become caught on some invisible hook in the air. A boiling shape of black and red moved around them. I started toward it, curious, then saw it reach out, beckon to me. The shape was Carlos's presence in the deepest levels of the Grey. It was heavier and more solid than I would have expected, though it had strange rents and holes.

I fixed my sight on the shape that was Carlos and eased back toward normal, watching the energy-shape change and clothe itself in layers of power, appearance, and memory as I surfaced. Jagged shards of glittering ice danced in his shape and clustered through him, reflecting sudden glimpses of history before he regained the dark, hulking cloak of shadow and blood I was familiar with.

I emerged with a shudder. Carlos watched me, one eyebrow raised. We were standing in front of the bloodstained wall, facing the cracked dent Mark's body had made in it. I could barely see the faded red and yellow threads, hanging at chest height. Carlos pulled a filament from it and brought it to his face.

"This is the trace of your ghost."

"So it was here."

"It was. A strange ghost, as you said. It is very difficult for me to read—it's not dead. It's alive. It is a living thing of this power, created by ignorant will, thriving on many power sources. One is not alive—a natural power source, but not that of a human life. It is not the life of the man who died here. He is not part of this ... entity."

"What is it, then? They call it a poltergeist, but it doesn't seem to be that."

"A thought-entity," he answered. "The accumulation of their will with this power source they stumbled on, displaced time, memory, things dragged from their proper place in the net of combined human desire. It should not be as powerful as it is, except for whatever power source they found. A strange creature ..."

He rubbed the strands between his fingers and breathed in whatever odor rose from it, frowning and casting his glance to me.

I looked at the bloodied wall. "Could it have caused that?"

"It did. I would not expect it of daylighters, usually. But the mind that guided it is unrestrained."

"It was controlled? By a single person?"

"Without doubt. The smell of this is strange, though." He plucked another thread of it and I shivered. "It has a scent of you, also, and has the tang of fury and madness, surprise ... desire? Odd." He crushed the strand in his hand and drizzled it out as dust on the floor. "Why does it smell of you?"

"I fell in it earlier today and got caught in it at least one other time at one of their séances," I replied. "I suppose that would account for the smell of it on me."

Carlos frowned cold ripples across the surface of the Grey. "I did not say you smelled of it—though it clings to you. It brought the odor of you with it here."

I stared at him and my mind spun through the chronology of

Mark's death. "Wait. When I first investigated the lab, some of the threads of it were gathered under a table—I didn't know what it was at the time. I slipped and my head and shoulders plunged into the knot of threads, like a large version of that little snag here. That was the day Mark was killed. Maybe an hour or two before he died."

Carlos closed his eyes and smiled.

A surge of despair swamped me. "Did I have something to do with this?"

"No. The trace of you is a mere shred and I wouldn't have recognized it without your presence now."

"But—" I started to object, unsure I hadn't somehow pushed this thing.

His glance cut through me. "You own nothing of this."

"Then what happened here?" I asked.

"I can't see the whole of it—the death was quick and the shock short. The man who died did not linger. This thing came as fury and struck him with its power unleashed. It flung him, crushed him, sweeping the room like flash fire, then was gone."

"Did it take anything?"

Carlos snorted. "If it did, I cannot see that. It has no story, only these near-extinguished remains of its rage. The power of it amazes me."

"I think I know where the extra power came from. The room the group picked to work in has a power line nearby."

"A ley line."

"It seems like a feeder line to a grid nexus, not a big source, but they seem to have dragged it from the position I'd expect."

He nodded, narrowing his eyes in thought. "Dangerous enough on its own and remarkable that they've moved the ley line—such things are not easily diverted."

He seemed less bothered by that than I was. I refocused the conversation on the events around Mark's death. "Do you know who controlled it or how? Is there any way to tell from what you can ... see?"

"No. It is a single mind, though, and not the caprice of the collective personality that usually animates the entity. A powerful mind, unfettered by artificial limits."

"They're all a little 'unfettered'—they've been encouraged to believe in what most people around here think is impossible."

"This one is less restrained than any of them—it must be, to embrace the form of this thing. More like one of my kind than yours."

"Psychopathic?"

Carlos rumbled amused gales of ice. "A matter of perspective."

I frowned. "Then whichever one of them sent Celia here killed Mark and they meant to do it."

"The details are unclear, but isn't it still murder to you if the killer has used this harmful thing knowingly even if they may not have meant to kill?"

"Yes."

"Then, yes, one of them murdered this man."

"How could he or she know they could do this?"

"There would have been a previous event in which the murderer realized the power—even if they did not understand it." He seemed to linger over the word "murderer," turning my spine cold.

"Would it have to be by the same person against the same person?" I asked.

"Not necessarily, but it would be most likely."

"Then I have one more thing for you to see."

Carlos growled. "This begins to tire me…"

I was surprised. "You're tired?"

"Bored."

I pretended a cavalier attitude I didn't feel—Carlos didn't respect quailing. "Indulge me a little longer. It's not far from here."

I could feel his annoyance as Carlos followed me out of the building and toward Old Possum's. He displayed a slight limp that evening which had become marked over the hours and added to his grim presence. I tried to distract him a little as we walked.

"I have a more general question."

He didn't ask.

"Are glass or mirrors special in some way? Magically, I mean."

He sent me a sideways glance of interest tinged with irritation. "Mirrors have an unusual quality of resonance and reflection. The glass slows the reflection of magical things. If it reaches the silvered surface, the energy that made the reflection is captured as a charge in the metal until it dissipates or is discharged at the edge of the glass."

"Like a battery?"

"The charge is not indefinite. It dissipates with time, bleeding slowly away through the glass. The scientific uses of glass also serve magic—when pure it reacts to nothing and collects nothing. But it is much denser than meets the eye and its common resonance is not that of magic. Energies much greater or less than that resonance have difficulty passing through it and will seek other paths or become slowed in their passage."

I mulled that over as we turned in at the bookshop door.

I didn't recognize the wild-haired man behind the cash desk, happily bopping to his iPod. Carlos ignored him and followed me into the coffee alcove at the back. He glanced around, casting a dark eye on the room.

"And what is this place to your problem?"

"I think the first incident happened here. Mark—the man who was killed—was standing ..." I looked around and went to a spot near the shelf marked "Biography," checking the mirror to see if the cash desk was visible as it should have been. "He must have been standing here, having an argument with someone when that gargoyle flew at him," I added, pointing to the listing figurine.

Carlos turned his head slowly, scanning the mantel until he came to the black cat-faced creature. He picked it up and peered at it, drawing a long breath.

"This." In the light of the shop, his face had become drawn and the network of scars was more obvious, looking like sharp ridges in a wind-scoured landscape.

"Yes. The autopsy showed a bruise on his shoulder from something and one on his chest from the book, and though I was told the gargoyle was only thrown *at* him, that was third-hand information. Supposedly no one touched the figure or threw it, but I think it did hit him and that a book also hit him. I think the person he was arguing with must have been the same one who sent the ... entity after him later. Can you tell if I'm right?"

Carlos glowered at me with impatience. "Very little remains—as I expected. No one—no murderer—has touched this, so there is no trace of death to it. Only the finest thread of the entity. It has the scent, but no more."

"You don't think this may have been the precipitating incident?"

"It is possible," he snapped. "Probable. But there is no more to find here. This is even older than the death site, useless for anything but rough confirmation. Mere trivia."

There was a hot spark to his glare and the annoyance rolled off him in waves with a strange, feral scent that made me dizzy. He put the object down and moved close to me, making my stomach heave. I turned my gaze away.

"It grows late and I grow hungry and tired of this. An interesting puzzle does not feed me. If you want more from me tonight, I will require payment—though you'd be a fool for it. There is nothing more I can see here."

I felt frozen in place, fighting to keep my eyes turned from his. A rumble vibrated the air and my body.

"I'm done," I answered from a dry mouth.

I felt him withdraw, but didn't try to watch him go. I only waited until I was sure he was gone.

I sat down in one of the armchairs and took several deep, slow breaths. I'd been concentrating too hard on the problem of Celia—and the revelation of my connection to it—and not paying enough attention to the native threat of vampires. Carlos had always been the most controlled of them. He'd never threatened to make a meal of me before. I considered the limp and the scars, the incompleteness of his presence in the Grey. It had not occurred to me until now that even a creature who heals with preternatural speed would take a while to recover from being burned to a crisp—and it might be worse for a necromancer, whose relationship with death was not like that of other vampires.

I picked myself up and went to the front of the shop.

I waved and smiled at the bopping man until he pulled the tiny plastic buds from his ears.

"What can I do for you, pretty lady?" he cooed in a broad Jamaican accent that was laid on with a trowel.

"You must be Germaine."

"That I am. How'd you know?"

"I know your cousin Phoebe."

He rolled his head and his eyes. "Oh, man. You're not spyin' for the woman, are you?"

"No," I replied, laughing. "I need to talk to Amanda—she works here."

He blew out a full-cheeked sigh of relief. "Well, thank God. But she's not in. Not in all week. Poor thing. She stayed at home since her man died. You try her home?"

"No. I was hoping you had the address."

"Me? Man, no way Phoebe'd let me get at the records. As it is, Hugh make me bring the money and the keys to him every night. I'm just take in the money and send the books out. You could try tomorrow morning when the regular employees be in."

Given Germaine's ditzy performance, I could understand Hugh's belief that Phoebe would get over her grief just to get him out of her store. I was ready to do a lot just to get him to drop the accent, but instead, Germaine was saved by my cell phone blatting.

I backed away from the desk to answer it, letting Germaine go back to his music.

"Hello?"

"Hey, it's Quinton."

"Hey. Did you figure out what was bothering you at the séance?"

"Yes." His answer was a little sharper than normal. "I thought some of the old equipment looked different, so I checked my memory and notes against some lists and catalogs. I don't know why he did it or what he's up to, but your client has swapped out about half the original equipment for much cheaper models. It's still decent stuff, not cheap enough to fail under normal use, so he'd still have good data and control, but not like he had—not topflight. It's a bit more in line with what I'd expect a college like PNU to be able to afford."

"Yeah, you mentioned the school seemed a little strapped."

"A lot strapped. If they didn't get a big annual endowment from the church, they'd be in serious trouble. So I'm thinking maybe he had to scrape up more money to pay for the extra equipment and so he swapped parts for credit, but I'm not comfortable with the forms he had me sign."

"What forms?"

"An inspection report. There was a prior inspection report by the school's electrician for the original installation, but none for the new installation. He had me sign a report for my inspection, but if he doesn't sign off on the installation, it may look like I signed off on the installation of the new parts."

"Sorry, I'm not sure I'm following this."

"It's sloppy paperwork, so there's no chain of responsibility between the original installation and the new one. It may appear I did the installation and swapped the parts without documenting them at the same time. If there's any discrepancy in the paperwork when—not if—the project gets audited, I will take the blame for it. I think I'm just as glad I didn't sign my real name on that form."

It was odd that Tuckman had swapped out parts at this point. "What do you think he's up to?" I asked.

Quinton huffed into the phone. "My gut says he's cooking the books. It could be legit, but without knowing his original funding and budget, I can't guess if he's just trying to stay In budget or if he's trying to skim the difference."

No wonder he'd been so pleased about Quinton preferring cash. I felt a little spurt of anger and suspected Tuckman was up to his old tricks.

"Write that up for me," I said. "All the details. And your notes about the malfunctions today. I may need to nail Dr. Tuckman to the wall."

"You got it. I'll drop it off when I'm done."

I thanked him too curtly and hung up. Germaine kept a nervous eye on me as I put my temper away. Tuckman wasn't my most immediate problem, no matter how irritated I was at that moment.

Plunging out into the wet night, I kept all my senses alert for vampires and things that stream along the corners of the eye to walk in nightmares later.

TWENTY-ONE

Thursday morning I went back to research. Carlos had put words to the niggling idea in my own head: controlling and using Celia as a weapon required a psychopathic mind, and according to Frankie and Terry, the project was ripe to breed some. Only one of the participants controlled Celia and that one had to be truly unhinged. Given what I had seen at Wednesday's séance—the way the energy had divided itself over Ian, Ana, Cara, and Ken—I was betting on one of them, but I had to figure out which one and I couldn't take it for granted that Wayne, Patricia, and Dale had nothing to do with it. Dale had the classic excuse of the cuckolded spouse. And I wanted to know more about what Tuckman was up to as well. He didn't have any apparent Grey connection to Celia, but he was up to something at PNU's expense.

The deeper I went, the more awful the whole picture looked. Wayne Hopke was the most stable of the lot and his tendency to assume command—and to drink—provided a point of irritation for others and a dice-throw chance of sudden instability. Dale Stahlqvist didn't care for it and the records showed a continuous, low-level battle between them for control of the sessions. I'd seen that in action at the most recent event. The rest—including Terry and Frankie—were in a constant boil of interpersonal tension: fears, desires, ambitions, and imagined slights.

Tuckman's notes indicated he'd picked the members himself. I could only conclude he'd put this group together because of the potential strife, not in spite of it. But the records were thin. They gave ideas and hints, records of psychological tests I didn't understand, and lists of the oddities of the subject's personality, but there was no deep psychological analysis of any of them—as if Tuckman hadn't wanted to bother digging any further once he'd found what he wanted. He'd wanted drama and now rejected the results. Tuckman didn't seem much more reasonable or stable than his subjects. It was only his lack of connection to Celia that ruled him out as the killer, from my perspective, though I imagined he didn't look so much of an outside chance to Solis, who would consider the possibility of Mark's exposing Tuckman's financial hijinks as more than adequate motive for murder.

Ben called while I was staring at the pile of inadequate files.

"Hi, Harper. Sorry I didn't call you back earlier—things have been a little crazy here."

"That's OK. I just wanted to ask you a couple of questions about Tuckman. His former grad assistant told me he'd been let go from UW during cutbacks to avoid having to fire him. Does that sound likely to you?"

"Yes, actually."

"What cause would they have had?"

"Didn't the assistant say?"

"Yes, but she has a grudge, so I'm interested in someone else's ideas about it. What do you think?"

He made thinking noises for a moment. "I told you I think Tuck's a bit of a jerk, didn't I? So I'm not the most objective person, either. But when I worked with him I thought he was rigging his financial reports. It was small and subtle—he'd find ways of getting things free or cheap but report them as if he'd had to pay for them. He was always doing better financially than the rest of us at the same salary grade, even without a family to support."

"OK. What about the projects themselves? Would they be cause to unload him, even if they were successful?"

Ben clicked his tongue. "Oh. You heard about that. Umm ... yeah. Tuckman has a documented bad habit of setting up his experiments to push his subjects to the limits. He doesn't just study, he manipulates. One of his subjects was hospitalized a couple of years ago, but it was another subject who caused the accident. Still, he's continued to do studies in stress reactions and justification that lead to some ugly territory."

"Would he be looking for that in this experiment? This group has a lot of sexual tension and control issues."

I could hear him shuffling papers. "I wouldn't have thought of it until you mentioned it last time, but, yeah. The original Philip experimenters mentioned that they got more phenomena when the group had some level of internal tension. I had wondered why Tuckman was interested in this, so I looked into it a bit more and I'm thinking that Tuck's real interest is in the stress reactions and how the subjects rationalize and justify their own behavior or the phenomena. If he's on his usual course, the subjects could justify all kinds of nasty things by blaming the poltergeist."

"What kind of nasty things?"

He blew out a breath, hesitating. "Well ... almost anything. Temper tantrums, assault, theft certainly—if they get high-level PK phenomena, they would claim the poltergeist took the objects, or hurt the person, or broke things, and no one person would bear any guilt for it. It's a collective phenomena, but they would soon reach the stage of separation—where they think of it as separate from them and therefore acting on its own. It's unconscious. So long as the subjects don't acknowledge their own desires as the poltergeist's motive, they let themselves off the hook. If any of them did recognize their motive, they would have to acknowledge control of the poltergeist and, in theory, the phenomena only works when it's an unconscious consensus, so the poltergeist would break down."

"I can't believe it's so fragile that if one person stops believing in it, it falls apart."

"No, that's not it. If the group itself stops believing in the collective quality of it, then it breaks down. If they all give up belief, it falls apart. Or if they believe it's no longer collective—that one person controls it."

"Do they all have to believe that? Or just one of them?"

"I'm not sure. The collective has to break down, though. That's the key."

"What if the poltergeist didn't break down?"

"Theoretically impossible. But you know more about the impossible than most people, so what do you think?"

"I think I shouldn't say. But I'm not a psychologist and I noticed this, so ... I can't imagine what Tuckman is thinking he can get away with here."

"Probably that's all he's thinking. It's almost grant-review time, so he may just be trying to cover himself. He never had a high opinion of PNU—I was surprised he took the job—so maybe he thinks he can get away with something if he has other things to distract the committee with. He's the kind of guy who doesn't do the right thing because it's the right thing. He does the right thing because he can't find a way to get away with not doing it. He's been skirting the edges of professional censure for a while and if he gets caught with his hands dirty, he'll be out on his butt this time."

"I see." I ground my teeth on my anger and cursed Tuckman in silence.

"Harper?"

"What?"

"Are you OK?"

"Yeah. Thanks, Ben. I have to go."

"Um ... all right. Hey. We really enjoyed having you to dinner."

"It was nice."

"Except for the flying pudding part, right at the end."

I laughed. "Well, he is just a kid."

"I blame the company he keeps. God knows he doesn't learn that stuff from us. I hope you won't stay away because of Albert and Brian's bad behavior."

"Don't worry. I'll be around, I'm sure. Now I really have to get back to work. Thanks for the help, Ben." I hung up before I lost my temper.

Damn Tuckman. I had to think that when he'd asked Ben for the name of an open-minded investigator, what he'd meant was someone gullible. I'd thought it when he hired me, but I'd let my own knowledge—and smugness—get in front of better judgment. I was as angry with myself as with him. He appeared to be setting me and Quinton up for his misdeeds and that made me furious. He'd abused my professional trust, lied to his committees, probably defrauded PNU of money on the equipment swap, and engineered an experiment that had gotten someone killed. That was far more important than my pride.

As attractive as ruining the arrogant shrink was, it wouldn't do anything to solve Mark Lupoldi's murder or stop Celia, no matter how much I'd like to see Tuckman hoisted by his own petard. But perhaps I could use all that as leverage... If he shut the project down, Celia might dissipate before more damage was done, though I didn't have much hope on that score; this poltergeist defied so many of the Philip experiment's conclusions and theories and I wasn't certain what would happen, but I was sure that the project had to end. Now I just had to find Tuckman and push him to do it.

I poked about some more, made more calls, and checked a lot of papers; then I went looking for Gartner Tuckman in earnest.

It took several hours to track Tuckman to a regional psychological association dinner in a downtown hotel. They were still in the cocktails and chitchat phase of the meal, so I had some chance of getting Tuckman—who had turned off his cell phone—into a discreet corner for our conversation. I had a little trouble with the dining room staff, but I raised a ruckus until one of the organizers deigned to take my card in to Tuckman and ask him to see me. I cooled my heels in the lobby for about fifteen minutes before Tuckman came out.

He was wearing a suit and looking spiffy and a little pissed off. I made him come to me. When he stopped and glared at me I flicked up the folder full of reports I'd typed, holding it between us where he couldn't ignore it. He gave it a disdainful glance, then transferred the look to me.

"What did you call me out here for?" he demanded.

I felt cold with my disgust. "The sooner I give you this, the sooner I'm shut of you," I replied. "You lied to me, Tuckman. I thought I'd been pretty clear about the fact that I don't like to be made a scapegoat or played for a sucker."

"I have no idea what—"

"Save it. You don't have a saboteur, you never did, and you know it. You used the heightened phenomena as an excuse to call me in and create cover for your financial misconduct and the way you've lied about your experimental goals."

"We do have a saboteur!"

I was very calm on the outside. If I bit off my words a little, it was only to stop myself from screaming at him. "No, you don't. The people with the opportunity don't have the skills or the motive. Those with the skills and motive don't have the opportunity. Your own protocols guaranteed that and your recordings prove it. I have checked and double-checked every physical possibility and there is none. Your phenomena are real. What's faked is your books, so you don't want the grant committee breathing down your neck and checking the financial statements too closely. Reviews are, what, next month?"

He tried to brazen it out. "Ms. Blaine, you seem to have a prejudice that is making you unable to complete your assignment as required. I'm afraid I'll have to fire you."

"Go ahead. I'll march in that room and tell your professional colleagues all about your current experiment, the manipulations, the inadequate screening of participants, the equipment swaps and sell-offs. Your reputation can't stand another hit and enough of your associates know about your previous experiments and your interesting bookkeeping to take the accusation seriously. I doubt there are many people in that room who don't know the real reasons you were laid off from the University of Washington. Tell me—what happens to a psychologist who falls from professional grace? Do they disbar you? Tar and feather you? Or do they send you to jail?"

I fixed his gaze in mine, unblinking, and let him stew. He was uncomfortable but tough and stared back at me.

"You pushed things too far this time, Tuckman. One of your incipient psychos bloomed into a full-blown killer."

"No," he answered, but his voice was soft and unsure, his eyes shifting.

"Yes. You've created a breeding ground for psychopaths with your permission and empowerment scenario—you selected them personally. You told them they could make ghosts and move things with the power of their minds and then you proved it to them and let them see what they could do. One of them made a ghost, all right. You never thought one of them was going to go that far, did you? Or maybe it was you. You came pretty close once before. A couple of years ago you put a subject in the hospital—"

"It wasn't me! It was one of them." The ghostly green snakes that seemed to dance around Tuckman's head in the Grey had turned inward, squeezing around him like tentacles and turning a sickening yellow green. Was that panic? I pushed on.

"So you said last time. And I suppose you'll say the same thing this time when one of your current subjects gets arrested for murder and says the ghost did it. You are an accomplice to that. You made a little pressure cooker with your handpicked group of unhappy, messed-up people, and one of them turned out to be a psychopath just waiting to happen. And you introduced him or her to a whole pool of potential victims with a handy excuse for whatever he or she wanted to do to them. I've been hip-deep in these people's lives for ten days—closer than you, I'd bet—and everything I see tells me one of them killed Mark Lupoldi. And used your damned poltergeist to do it."

Tuckman went white, his dark villain's eyes widening with shock.

"You gave them permission and you put the weapon in their hands. One of them used it. There's nothing else that could have done it. One of them used the same power that levitated that table through the observation room window to throw Mark against a wall hard enough to crush his skull—"

He shook his head. "No. No, no, no …"

I pulled him down into a chair and sat next to him, putting my face close to his and glaring at him until he met my eyes. I talked fast and low.

"Shut it down, Tuckman. Even if you don't believe Celia killed Mark, this damned thing is off the rails. I called around—Ken's lucky his legs weren't broken. Ian's got two cracked ribs and Cara one, plus the stitches from last week. It took a couple of sutures to put Patty's ear back together, too, and everyone else has cuts and burns from the lights that exploded. No one picked up that table and threw it. No one shorted the wires in the light board. No one made the temperature in the room drop and no one touched the stereo. You gave them permission and power to hurt one another and they did. But you have the power to pull the plug. So pull it."

"No. I won't do it. This won't happen again—it can't."

"It will! It will get worse as it's kept on getting worse. It started with petty theft and pinches and throwing things. Now you have broken windows and people in the hospital. Can't you see where this is headed? Are you going to wait until one of them is a red smear on the damned observation—"

"That's enough!" He stood up and stared down at me. He was breathing too fast, swaying, white-faced, and the people at the table outside the dining room turned to look at us. I got up and stood still in front of him, as still and quiet as I could manage, letting my face go neutral and my voice slide back to normal.

"It's a flawed experiment, Dr. Tuckman. It was a mistake. A miscalculation. If you shut it down now and clear off the paperwork that makes me and my contractor look like thieves, you can return some of the grant money and no one will look too hard at what you've done. So long as no one gives them a reason to."

He turned a hopeful frown on me, licking his dry lips. He sank back into the chair and I sat down beside him again. It gave me the chills to do it, but I put my hand on his nearest forearm. Glutinous chill oozed up my arm and I stifled a shudder.

"I won't give them a reason to look if you shut this down now. If you do what I'm telling you, I won't have to defend myself from charges of theft and I won't need to give these reports to the police or your department chair. Just shut it down. Say there was a flaw in the protocol—write one in if you have to. Say it was a mistake. I know it'll be embarrassing, but a little pride isn't worth someone's life. It's just a mistake."

I saw him swallow it. His posture straightened and the glaze of fear left his eyes. "It's flawed. I'll shut it down. I'll take care of it—the papers, the team. I'll call them and tell them we're done."

I took my first decent breath in hours. Nodding, I said, "Good." I stood up one more time and put the envelope of reports in his hand.

"These are your reports—they're confidential and no one else has seen them. Just write a check for my fee and we can call this done."

He looked at the bill, then glanced up, frowning as if he were confused. "I'm not going to pay this. You didn't do the job I hired you for."

My mouth fell open in sheer surprise. "You have the biggest brass ones... Tuckman—do you understand any of what I just told you? You're a thief and a liar and I can prove it. Do you think that's the only copy of my report? We have a contract for the investigation of a possible saboteur. I've proved there is no saboteur but you. Contract satisfied. If I need to call my lawyer, I'll have to tell her the whole truth about this—that's covered in the contract, too. You want to hear that in court?" I jerked my head back toward the dining room. "You want them to hear it?"

He glared. Old villain eyes again.

I sighed. "Don't even try, Tuckman. I have the cards. You don't. Shut it down, *now*."

He dropped his gaze and pulled his checkbook from his pocket.

I left with his check in my purse. Tuckman was still looking at the reports. "A flaw. An oversight ... ," he muttered, trying to convince himself it really was just a mistake.

TWENTY-TWO

Maybe it somehow knew I was working for its destruction, or maybe it was just in a bad mood, but I spent much of Thursday night under attack by the poltergeist. Small objects in the Rover pinged against my head and face as I drove home. Flinching almost put me into the rail on the viaduct and I got a moment's vertiginous view of the waterfront below before I corrected my path back into the lane.

At home, I had never regretted my collection of books and funky objects until now. A dining room chair rushed at me like an angry dog as soon as I walked into the condo. A pair of bronze bookends soared off the shelf and came for my head. I yanked a bit of the Grey around myself and dodged, taking most of the impact on my shoulders.

Chaos ran back and forth in her cage, agitated by the activity. As I moved toward her, a hardbound book winged past me and crashed into the wall nearby. She's a tough little creature, but I doubted she'd have much of a chance against flying books. I snatched her from her cage and shielded her with my body as I ran for the bedroom. The phenomena followed me from room to room.

I put Chaos in the bathtub and rushed back into the bedroom. I dodged missiles while I dragged every heavy, pointy, or hard object out of my bedroom. I piled most of them in the hall closet and closed it, wedging the door shut. The objects rattled against the door until I moved away. I hauled the most dangerous objects out of the living room and stuck them in my mostly empty kitchen cupboards, tying the doors closed before I returned Chaos to her cage. It appeared she'd be safe enough if I wasn't near her. Celia only had a connection to me, not my pet, but I still stacked pillows and cushions all around her cage before I ran back to my bedroom and closed the door. I slept in fits, roused by small objects throughout the night, but the ferret was fine in the morning and the poltergeist seemed to have wound down a little.

I called Solis first thing in the morning, and he insisted I meet him at Le Crepe—a business diner on Second—rather than discuss Tuckman's project over the phone. So, of course, once we were seated at the same table, he was silent and inscrutable. His narrowed eyes and blank expression might have been caused by exhaustion and insomnia as much as thoughts or judgments reserved to his own mind, but I couldn't tell. I was nursing coffee after my bad night and feeling no more sociable than he.

I glanced past his shoulder to the midmorning lull on the street outside. "How's the investigation going?" I asked.

"Still open. Tell me what happened on Wednesday."

"I can't tell much—I don't understand it myself—but Tuckman's shutting the project down."

"Why?"

"The protocols were flawed—that's why things went awry. People have been hurt and it's just too risky. The details don't make a lot of sense, but the end result is that Tuckman is shutting it down. I still have a little follow-up to do with the participants, though. I thought I'd better let you know I'm not quite out of your hair yet, but I'm on my way."

"I'd prefer that you left this to me."

I sighed and lied. "Solis, I'd love to, but I have a job to do, too. Whatever's wrong with Tuckman's project is probably a common thread between our investigations, but I'm not going to just assume that and put the baby in your lap. I've been cooperative with your investigation—a little more than I had to be—so you'll just have to bear with my presence in your view a little longer. Unless you have grounds to lock me up."

It was his turn to sigh. "All right. What do you think these cases have in common?"

"Well." I paused to put my thoughts into sanitized order, restraining an urge to say things I knew he would write off. "I've been looking at these people and at the situation Tuckman's created and I think he's either pulled in or precipitated a psycho. I think what happened to Mark Lupoldi was caused by something and someone in Tuckman's project. It appears that the incidents Tuckman considered sabotage are just other symptoms of this individual at work. He deliberately picked a group of people with slightly unstable personalities and lots of problems, bound to develop tension in an environment where he encouraged them to believe they could do some pretty strange things and get away with it. Psychology's not my field but I imagine that in that kind of environment, if you've got an individual who's on the edge of psychopathic or psychotic behavior, they might find the last step all too easy to take."

Solis looked down at his own cup and nodded slowly. "That may be true, but my concern is still only the discovery of the killer."

"Do you have a suspect? I have a few."

He grunted. "Evidence makes a case, not suspicion. I'd like to find those keys or the method ... I agree Dr. Tuckman's project is involved and I've looked very hard at his subjects and assistants. Tell me who you suspect."

I told him and he raised his eyebrows, but said nothing. He refused to give me any response in kind. So much for sharing information.

Returning to my office was a walk through the Grey without even trying. As I crossed Pioneer Square, ignoring phantom traffic and the tipped layers of time, something winged into the side of my head, brushing my temple and yanking out a strand of my hair.

I whirled, looking for the culprit, and spotted a dilapidated man in greasy, filthy clothes sitting on a bench nearby. He held his hands open, a crooked cigarette fallen to the wet ground in front of him, and stared at me with wide eyes. I bent, looked around, and spotted a cigarette lighter—a Zippo-type with a metal case—lying against the building beside me. As I crouched to pick it up, I glanced through the deeper Grey at the lighter. A thin filament of yellow energy was fast fading from it, drawing back like the tail of a snake vanishing into a bolt-hole.

I glanced around, catching sight of a fleeting yellow haze, glittering with flecks of red and slices of silvery time. I picked up the lighter and flicked it into flame. The bit of Celia peregrinated around the square as if it had no interest in me at all. And maybe it didn't this time, but its presence near me was worrisome. I'd spent too much of the previous night dodging books and household objects. They'd all had a small yellow thread of Grey energy reeling from them. Given the violence of Wednesday and the previous night, I was surprised at this minor display.

I took the lighter back to the bum on the bench.

"This yours?"

He stuttered and fumbled, fearful and uncertain how to answer. Then he blurted, "I dint trow it etcha! Hones'! It jus' kina …"

I nodded with a rueful smile. "I know. It just got away from you. They do that." I looked down at the crumpled cigarette in the gutter between us and shot another quick look for Celia, but the thing had moved away. "That yours, too?"

He looked down and his face fell to the verge of tears as he saw the mud-soaked cigarette. "Yeah," he moaned.

I dug into my pocket for the change from my coffee and handed it to him with his lighter. "Take care of this. Don't lose it, OK?"

His eyes glowed and he offered me a snaggle-toothed grin on a raft of fetid breath. "I will. I will! Tank you, Miss. God bless you!"

I backed away, starting for my office again with a shrug and a mumbled "thanks." Sliding on the mucky cobbles, I hurried on through the October thickness of ghosts.

I was going up the stairs when my cell phone jiggled on my hip. I snatched it and answered.

"You have to do something."

"What? Excuse me, Dr. Tuckman, but we closed this case last night," I answered, shoving the phone under my jaw as I unlocked my office door.

"Yes, I know. But something must be done. You seem to be the one who understands this thing—"

"No, Tuckman. You understand it. You just don't want responsibility for it."

"Ms. Blaine!"

I reminded myself that his check hadn't cleared yet and heaved a sigh. "What's the problem?"

"Celia is bedeviling the subjects."

" 'Bedeviling'? Just how badly are they being pestered?" Maybe the relative calm around me now was the reflection of Celia's action elsewhere. I threw my things on the floor behind the desk and sat down.

Without his villain act to bolster the impact, he just sounded peevish and unpleasant. "Considering the range of injuries they've all sustained recently, it takes very little 'pestering' to make someone miserable. They've all called—every one—with one story or another of the poltergeist doing unpleasant things."

"Great. Look, Tuckman, as I understand it, the poltergeist is a collective phenomenon, yes?"

"Yes," he snapped at me, impatient and annoyed.

"Well then, if it exists because they believe it exists, the obvious thing to do is get them to stop believing in it."

"And do you think that's likely when they are being pummeled and assaulted by this make-believe ghost?"

I laughed. "You put it there, Tuckman. I can't do anything to help you on that score. You taught them to believe, you'll have to teach them to be skeptical again. Why don't you tell them it was a hoax? That you had the room rigged and almost nothing that they experienced was real? That should shake a few of them up. If you can get them to stop giving it credence, maybe it will stop harassing them." I didn't say a damned thing about its harassing me, too. The entity had gone off on its own with its master and I doubted that the rest of the group could do much more than weaken it by any lack of faith, but I wouldn't say it wasn't worth a try.

Tuckman remained silent, brooding.

"Dr. Tuckman. Seriously. You need to convince them to stop giving it their support. You have to. It's taken on a life of its own, but if you can break down their belief, you may weaken it enough to stop its doing anything worse. Be brutal. You have to."

"You've been no help at all," he spat.

"Then I won't charge you. Good luck, Dr. Tuckman. Remember that this is no longer a game. Your ghost killed one of your assistants. This thing has to cease and it's up to you to break it. Not me."

I could almost hear the slow boil of his vexation. Then he hung up on me. I didn't mind. If I was lucky, I'd never hear from Gartner Tuckman again.

I worked for a while, periodically fending off the random attacks of random objects. At one o'clock, I went to catch Phoebe at her parents' restaurant. Hugh had told me she'd be there, and I needed Amanda's address. I could have just called, but that wouldn't help me mend any fences—Phoebe might take it as another attempt to dodge my rightful dose of her wrath and that wouldn't be good in the long run. Besides, I loved the Masons and needed some kind of break from the grinding horror of this case.

The lunch rush had thinned to a trickle by the time I arrived and the family was, once again, revving up for Friday night. I seemed to be spending all day in restaurants, but this I wouldn't mind. I loved the company of the Masons. Even when they were in their weekly uproar, they were a warm and welcoming crowd. They laughed at full volume and smiled with infectious ease.

As the patriarch, Phoebe's father had taken his usual seat at the family table in back, his arthritic hand clutching a glass of tepid water, which he used more for emphasis than hydration. "Poppy" was gnarled and weathered, as brown as hand-rubbed walnut, and still ran the whole family merrily ragged without lifting anything but the glass and his voice. The clan fluttered around the table, flying in and out the kitchen doors like giddy fruit bats, somehow managing not to careen into one another while acceding to Poppy's every command. He spotted me as I came in and waved me to his table.

"Harper! Come on back here, girl. Where you been? I thought maybe you finally gone wasted away t'nothin' and blew off on the wind." His accent was still as thick as breadfruit—full of "de" and "dem" and soft Rs, lilting and bouncing like reggae—though he'd now lived thirty years in Seattle.

I wound through the crowd of family and sat down next to him against the kitchen wall, which was deliciously warm after the exterior chill. "No, Poppy. I still stick to the ground most of the time."

He uncurled his index finger from the glass and poked me in the shoulder, scoffing. "Barely. I suppose them foolish white boys you date don' know better. Too bad t'see a nice girl like you goin' t'waste."

I made a mock sad face. "Well, I just have to make do—Hugh is taken."

His body shook as he roared laughter. He was loud for a little old man in his seventies. He wound down after a minute, chuckling, and wiped his eyes with the back of his hand.

"Girl, I knew you could."

That confused me. "Could what, Poppy?" I asked.

"Unfreeze yourself."

I gaped at him. "What?" I squeaked.

"Harper, ever since you come out the hospital, you been hard and chilly like steel in the freezer—I'm surprised you got a man a' all. You built up some icy walls like you 'spect someone goin' t'hurt you some more, but when you ain't lettin' nothin' in to hurt, you ain't lettin' nothing in to love you, neither. Then you be stayin' away from here, like you don't need your family no more—'cause you family, even if you are thin like an ol' broom."

I stared at him for a while, this old man with sharp black eyes. I hesitated to ask. "You … can see some kind of wall around me?" If I had erected such a thing, surely I had good reason to keep the world at a distance. And maybe it was the same for Ken—even tough guys can't take it forever.

Poppy laughed and poked me again. "That's a metaphor, little girl! But spiritual walls be just as hard and cold as the real thing. Why you go look so sad now?"

I jerked back, swamped with bleak memory. "My dad used to call me 'little girl.' "

"Harper, I'm sorry. I'm not presumin' on him. How long he's been gone?"

"A long time. I was twelve when he died. Now there's just me and Mom and we don't get along."

"That I know. So … that why you don't be comin' round? We're too clingy?" Then he sat back and winked at me. "Or maybe you don' like Miranda's cookin' no more?"

I snorted a laugh, relieved to be off the subject of me and my wretched family—even if it did mean dealing with the oddities of the surrogate one. "I love your wife's cooking and I'd be twice as fat as you want me to be if I ate it as often as I'd like to. And three times as fat if I ate it as often as you'd like me to. Things have been a little strange since I got hurt and I've been busy. And Phoebe's mad at me."

"Oh, she don't be so mad as dat."

A plate of steaming food was shoved onto the table in front of me.

"I am too as mad as 'dat.' "

I looked up into Phoebe's scowl. Or rather, her attempt at a scowl that broke up into a smile as I watched. She put down her own plate and sat across from me. One of the family slid some glasses of water onto the table for us as they passed. Another dropped off rolls of utensils and napkins, never missing a beat on the cleaning and prepping for drinks, dinner, and dancing that took over the place on Fridays and Saturdays.

Noises came from the bar area and the front of the dining room as the tables were rearranged to make a dance floor and stage for the band. Shouts and laughter gusted out of the kitchen with every swing of the doors. Phoebe and I had to lean toward each other to speak at a normal volume.

"Hey, girl," she said.

"Hey, yourself. Thanks for seeing me."

"Oh, like I'm goin' t'hold a grudge. I was mad. But I understand." She had picked up her father's accent again.

I'd already explained myself and resisted any impulse to do so again. "How are you doing?"

"Fine. I'm goin' back to the shop tonight. How's it lookin'?"

"Fine. Your cousin told me I could get Amanda's home address from you. I need to talk to her."

"Oh, that Germaine! When Hugh told me he sent that good-for-nothing to my store I thought I'd have to strangle him!"

"Which one? Hugh or Germaine?"

"Both of them! How could he do that to me?"

"He's just trying to help."

Poppy laughed, breaking into the conversation. "He's trying t'make you stop feeling sorry for your own self, girl! You come in here all long-faced a week ago and crying f'your friend. That's OK. That's right. But now you jus' being stubborn-sorry f'yourself. You're like your ma, Phoebe—ya got t'be busy."

"I am busy, Poppy."

"You is busy with everything but you. I love you, girl, but it's time you go home." He fixed his sparkling eyes on me. "You goin' t'make her go back t'her own place, ain't you, Harper?"

"I don't know, Poppy... She's pretty muleheaded."

"That d'truth!"

"You two! Worse than Hugh and Mamma."

Poppy cackled.

"Phoebe, you know you should."

She made a face. "Yes. 'Specially since everyone be bossin' me about it!"

Hugh came by with a tray full of glasses for the bar and bent down to kiss Phoebe on the head as he passed. "You get back what you dish out, big sister."

One of the glasses did a backflip out of the stack and darted toward me, trailing a familiar yellow strand. I snatched it. Phoebe put it back onto Hugh's tray with care, keeping one eye on me.

"You got you a duppy now, too?" Phoebe asked.

"Just the garden-variety poltergeist," I replied. "Nothing so nasty as a duppy—they are nasty, right?"

"They be the nastiest ol' things ever," Poppy answered for his daughter.

"What makes them so bad?" I asked him, picking at my plate of food—it was delicious, but I couldn't concentrate on eating, my brain

going in so many directions: the poltergeist, my dad, psychic walls
…

Poppy leaned back in his seat, gesturing with his water glass. "Duppies, they're the spirits what don' make it to heaven. They got lost somehow on the nine nights and they settle back to earth. But they got no heart t'feel with, no brain t'think with—their soul, it be broke in two. Half here, half the other place. They don' feel the rightness or wrongness o' somethin'. They don' think what happen. They just do what they want. They come slap you or pinch you or make f'break things."

"How do you know it's a duppy?"

"You see them. Like skeletons wearing fog. The—what they call it here? Willow wisp?—That's the thing they look like. Ancestor spirits, you can't see them—they as pure as air. But the duppy be tainted and evil. And they just get eviler and eviler the longer they hang round. Dogs be howlin' when they about and you feel the spiderweb on your face. That's the duppy sign."

I didn't know if I would call the yellow thread spiderweb, but I recalled the sensation on my face the first time I fell into it, when I investigated the room; I had thought of the feel of it as cobwebs then, myself. The idea of a ghost that grew more and more evil from a lack of conscience seemed to match the behavior of Celia—and its psychopathic master—to a T.

"Why you keep askin' 'bout duppies?" Phoebe demanded. "Maybe that's why they're botherin' you now."

I tried to calculate the response to any possible answer, but I'd never been very good at the elusive math of relationships. I stuck to the easier side of truth.

"Mark's project was about ghosts and I think there's a connection to his death. This duppy thing seems a lot like the ghost they made and maybe—"

"They made a ghost? That's crazy."

I shrugged. "Maybe it is. But I thought I'd better talk to Amanda about the night Mark got hurt."

Phoebe stared at me. "You think some ghost-thing hurt Mark. For real?"

"I don't know. But you don't get answers unless you ask questions. I need Amanda's address."

Phoebe pushed her lips together and frowned. "OK, but you be nice t'her!"

"I will."

Poppy wouldn't let Phoebe go to get Amanda's address until she finished eating and he wouldn't let me go with her to get it once she was done, either. As soon as Phoebe had disappeared through the kitchen door, he turned a searching gaze on me.

"What you really think, Harper? You think some duppy killed Mark?"

I turned my eyes toward the tabletop. "I don't know."

"You can' go lyin' t'me, girl. You know somethin' that you wish you don' never know."

"You don't need to know it, too, Poppy," I said, shaking my head.

He put his free hand over mine. He waited a minute, but I didn't confide in him or look up. He patted my hand and sighed, sounding very old and tired. "Dem sure give you a basket f'carry water," he said, shaking his head.

I made excuses to leave as soon as Phoebe returned with Amanda's information. Phoebe and her father both watched me go through narrowed, thoughtful eyes.

TWENTY-THREE

It turned out that Amanda had been staying with her parents in Shoreline. Once I had the address from Phoebe—and had been fed enough food to fatten up most of Ethiopia—I drove to the Leamans'. Although Mark and Amanda hadn't dated in months, his death had thrown a veil of misery over her that tinted her eyelids a perpetual pink and her skin ashen. She had the house to herself at the moment, but preferred to sit on the porch swing nestled under the wide overhang of the front porch and watch the intermittent drizzle.

"The house gets too stuffy," she said, pulling her feet up onto the seat and huddling over them with her arms wrapped tight around herself and a depressed olive green cloud clinging to her in the Grey.

I sat on the other end of the swing, listening to it creak in time with the slight swaying we made.

"Manda," I started, keeping my voice low, "do you remember the day Mark got hurt in the shop?"

She kept her eyes on the mist. "Yeah. The detective asked me. I remember, but I'm not sure I told him everything right. I was still pretty freaked." Her voice was too bland.

"Do you mind telling me, too?"

She shrugged, setting the swing rocking aslant. "It was kind of late. Monday. A couple weeks ago, now. Mark was stacking some books in Biography and there was this guy talking to him. Arguing, I think. I couldn't hear what they were saying, but they sounded mad. You know—kind of snapping at each other and their voices going up and down. And then the guy kind of ... threw out his fists. Like this. You know—like a cross." She spread her arms out straight from the shoulder and almost caught my cheek with the back of one closed hand. She didn't notice and dropped her hands back around her knees again. "And I saw something black flying through the air in the mirror. And it smacked into the bookshelf by Mark's head.

"Then Mark started to turn his head and look at the guy he'd been looking at the books—and this big book fell down off the shelf over his head and hit him. He sort of ... um ... shied away from it like maybe he saw it falling. And I heard him shout. I don't know what he said, just some noise like he was surprised or angry. And then the book hit him and he fell off the stool. And the guy ran away." She slapped her hands against her shins. "That was it."

"Did you know what the object was that flew through the air?"

"Oh, yeah. It was one of the gargoyles from the fireplace."

"How do you know that?"

"I went back to help Mark pick up the books. He dropped the whole pile he was stacking. So I saw him pick it up and put it away."

"What about the book that hit him? Do you know what it was?"

"Umm ... a biography of Schopenhauer, I think. Not sure. Mark didn't make a big deal about it."

"Can you describe the person he was talking to?"

"Not too well. The mirror makes people look kind of short and funny—you're always looking at the tops of their heads. Anyhow, I don't know how tall he was, but not very short or very tall, I think. Dark hair, wearing a dark jacket and jeans—I think it was jeans."

"Did you get a better look at him when he ran out?"

"No. I was going back to help Mark. I shouldn't have left the cash desk, but I didn't think of that, then."

It wasn't much of a description, and the only people it let out of the suspect list were the Stahlqvists and Wayne Hopke. Even distracted, Manda would have noticed their pale hair.

"Are you certain the person was male? Could it have been female?"

"A woman?" She thought about it, rocking in the seat. "I guess. She couldn't have been very … curvy, though."

"What about the hair? Was it long, short, black, brown?"

She thought, then shook her head with her brows drawn down in an unhappy scowl. "I don't know. I can't remember. It was just … hair. Dark hair. I wasn't paying much attention."

"Could you see a part in it?"

She kept shaking her head. "I just can't remember."

I tried to bring back any other details, but the longer we went on, the less Amanda knew. She wouldn't agree to anything she wasn't certain of or try to describe something she had to guess at. Finally I gave up, thanked her, and started to go.

"Oh," she said. "Are you coming tomorrow?"

"Coming? To what?"

"The funeral. It's at Lake View Cemetery at two. I'm sure it would be OK if you want to come."

"Oh. Thank you, Amanda. I may come. I liked Mark very much."

"Yeah. He was a great guy." She bit her lower lip and stood up. "I think I'd better go inside." She let the door swing closed on its own and I heard the first quavering breath of a sob before the lock clicked shut between us.

I went back to my truck and started south, toward Seattle.

Unlike Solis, I didn't care about motive. I only needed to know who controlled Celia. If the incident in the bookshop had been the precipitating event, then the person Amanda had seen in the mirror was Mark's killer. That person couldn't have been either of the Stahlqvists or Wayne, and Patricia wouldn't have passed for a man even in a badly foreshortened mirror. I was back to Ian, Ana, and Ken, again. Or not. Carlos had left room for error in his guess. The business at the bookstore might not have been the precipitating event or had anything to do with Mark's death. And Amanda might not remember as well as she thought.

If I assumed that I was right so far, then I might need to figure out a motive. All three of my suspects had demonstrated some control of Celia—the last séance had convinced me of that, though the evidence wasn't clear enough to determine who had done what. I could imagine some sort of motive for Ken or Ian—anger over the fakery, jealousy over the women—but not for Ana. Although she had said that it would be up to Celia to take revenge ...

I pulled into a parking lot and looked for her phone number.

Ana wasn't enthusiastic about meeting me again and this time she insisted it not be at her parents' place. She was working downtown and reluctantly agreed to meet me in the building lobby after work, but she had an appointment and could only spare a few minutes.

The west lobby of the City Centre building poured light down from the two-story windows and focused track fixtures onto collections of glass objects housed in display cases on both levels. The light ran over the glass escalator and the brass trim, turning golden and breaking into sudden bright sparks that pierced the greenery pressing against the cluster of food kiosks at the street level.

I ascended the escalator to the mezzanine. Ana came around the corner from the elevators. I walked to meet her in front of the massive installation of Chihuly disks, floating like striped and spined jellyfish and Jackson Pollock splatters that flowered in the rich colors of Persia.

"Hi," I said.

She raised her hand. The back was scored with cuts that matched a set of marks around the edge of her face and neck. Her hair had been cut to chin length, but still looked a little ragged where it had been clipped to remove glass shards from her scalp. "Hi," she replied. She sounded tired and nervous.

Glass rattled. We both turned our heads to look at the display. The swirling colors of the "Persians" quivered, jittering and chiming as the glass shapes strained toward us.

With one mind, we moved away from the display, heading for the exit and casting quick glances up to the streaming, icy shapes of the chandelier that hung from the ceiling sixty feet above the escalator.

"I'm so jumpy," Ana started. "Things like that keep happening. Some much worse."

"What would be worse than having a million dollars worth of art glass fall on you?"

She shivered. "Don't ask. I don't have a lot of time to talk to you— I'm meeting someone for drinks. Can we walk?"

"Sure."

She scrabbled around in her purse as we headed out the revolving doors. Just under the portico, she paused to light a cigarette. She stood for a moment, smoking and staring around as if she expected something to swoop down the streets and attack her. She hunched her shoulders and hugged her coat tighter. She looked at the cigarette and threw it on the ground with disgust, making a face and sticking out her tongue. "Ugh. I don't know why I do that. I stop smoking long time ago." She cocked an inquiring look at me. "You have any gum? I want that taste out of my mouth."

I shook my head. "No. Sorry." Her English, as well as her healthy habits, was breaking down a little from stress.

She shrugged. "Oh, well. Come on." She walked up to the corner and waited for the light to change in our favor. "So, what did you want?"

"I wanted to ask you if you'd ever had any kind of relationship with Mark."

Ana's face pulled down into a questioning frown. "No. I met him in January. I don't know him before then. You mean, like, did we ever go out? No."

The signal changed and she stepped out into the street. I stayed beside her. "Not at all?"

"Not alone. I go out with Mark, sure, but with the others along, too. Ian and Ken and Wayne and Patricia. Sometimes just me and Ian and Ken. But not alone. I like Mark, but that's all." Her expression grew stormy as we paused on the next corner. "You think because I go out with one man, but I'm attracted to another, I'm a slut? I have a lot of boyfriends in the past, but most of them are not nice men. I just want to find a nice man. Someone fun, someone good for me. I don't sleep around. OK?"

We crossed the next street together, heading south down Union.

"I'm sorry Mark died," she continued. "I am. He was nice. He was good, but he's not for me. I already said this to the detective from the police. Why anyone thinks I had anything to do with this?" she demanded, her English syntax shattering. Something rattled nearby.

"There's a woman involved in this. There was a woman at Mark's before he died."

"Not me!"

We walked past a hat shop, our faces reflected for chopped instants under the fedoras and sun hats. A haze of yellow floated behind us like an impression of toxic fog.

"Do you think Celia would be capable of killing Mark?"

"What?" She stopped under the awning of a shoe repair shop and turned to stare at me. "Our ghost?"

I nodded.

"No." Then she paused. "No ... maybe. But it's just us doing it. Why would any of us want to hurt Mark?"

"Why would any of you throw a table through a window or crack Ian's ribs? Why would anyone do any of the things that happened on Wednesday? Why would they hurt any of you?" She'd been one of the least hurt and that raised my suspicions as much as anything. That we were being trailed by Celia only heightened them.

Her eyes got hard. "Because he faked Celia! He lied to us!" she spat.

"And Celia took revenge like you said she would?"

"Yeah! Maybe she did!"

"How do you know Mark faked the phenomena?"

She caught her angry breath and held it, huddling herself in her coat and gnawing lipstick from her bottom lip. Then she let her breath out slowly. She turned and started to walk toward the corner. "Ken told me."

That brought my eyebrows up. I caught up to her. "How did Ken know?"

She shrugged, looking down the steeper incline on the other side of the street, toward First Avenue and Puget Sound beyond. "He used to do acting when he was a kid. He and Mark used to talk about it. I think he always knew Mark faked it."

"When did he tell you?"

The light changed. "Wednesday. Wednesday night. I saw him at the hospital when I was waiting for Ian. Everyone was upset. We talked a lot."

I stopped her again on the other side of Third in the clouds of fragrant steam that escaped from Wild Ginger's kitchen vents. The light from the huge readerboard on the side of Benaroya Symphony Hall sent shadows scurrying around the intersection with the smell of garlic and ginger. "Did you ever go to Old Possum's?" I asked.

Ana looked blank. "Huh? What's that?"

"It's in Fremont."

She was about to shake her head when she got it. "Oh! Right,

right! Mark's bookstore. No, I never go there. Fremont's hard to get to without taking two or three buses. We have the Kinokuniya and Elliott Bay near my house."

She didn't seem to know Old Possum's was a used bookstore.

She cast a look over her shoulder. "I need to go," she pled. Paranormal ribbons of yellow and blue wove around her and a slow flush pinked her cheeks. "I don't have anything else to tell you. I have to go."

I put my hands in my pockets. She gave me a strained smile and turned away. I stepped back into the shadow at the corner of the building and watched her scamper down the steep sidewalk to the Triple Door—the jazz club underneath Wild Ginger. The hazy smear of Celia's sliced energy followed her, benign as a pet. Another thread twined and writhed toward the shape of Celia like an inquisitive snake. The thread was the same color, but was disconnected from Celia and moved like a blind thing seeking something.

I wanted a better look at that wandering thread. In the dark and the bustle of rush hour I took a risk and sank back into the shadow, into the Grey, feeling the slight jolt and nauseating slip of the worlds in transit.

The mist-world of the Grey was bright silver and knotted with tangled embroideries of energy moving and darting through the cloudscape. I looked for the seeking thread and found it broken by the heavy bulk of a building and the cold blackness of a rail that guarded the edge of a pit. I sidled around, but couldn't find a door through it to pick up the other side of the thread. Frustrated, I stepped back into the normal.

I got a stare from a panhandler and a squeak from a woman who had nearly trodden on my foot. I was still next to the Wild Ginger, but I'd moved out a bit onto the edge of the sidewalk that led down to the Triple Door. I put my hand on the wrought iron rail that rimmed the air shaft around the club's frontage. Glancing down the street, I saw

Ana, distinctive in her fluffy white coat, standing in front of the club and looking down the road when she wasn't checking her watch.

I spotted the curious yellow snake of energy I'd seen before uncoiling around the Second Avenue corner. Ana didn't see it, but I did, and watched it coming. Limping a little, his jaw tight with each step, Ken George came around the corner at the other end of the questing yellow thread. Ana spotted him and bounded down the hill to meet him and put her arm around his waist. His blank planes of Grey fell away, the energy threads braided up together, mingling around the couple and the gleam-shot mass of Celia that hung close beside them. Sparks of pink, white, and blue fizzed like firecrackers around the couple, and red bolts shot across the reflective blades that thrust through the entity following Ken and Ana into the club and out of my sight.

The diminished size and the passivity of Celia left me scowling. The fake ghost had rattled the glass at us in City Centre, but took no other actions as Ana and I had walked down the street. And now it had floated behind them brilliant-colored, but passive. I wished I knew what the display meant, but I was still learning—I had avoided deeper knowledge of the Grey at times and now wished I hadn't. Every time I thought I had eliminated something, or gained information, I came up against contradiction as dense as the sudden wall in the Grey.

I toyed with the idea of following the couple into the club and hanging out in the lounge to see what happened next, but I knew they would spot me. Sight lines in the Musiquarium lounge were short and broken, and if the two had gone into the main showroom, I'd have to take potluck on a seat—if the show wasn't sold out already. I'd have to let it go and turn my energy to something more productive.

I called Mara Danziger.

TWENTY-FOUR

When I called, Mara was stuffing food into Brian and had to relay her answers to me through Ben. She made some guesses, but said she could only confirm them in my presence, so I was heading for another evening with the Danzigers. I hoped Brian would be in a calm mood, as I was already tired.

Mara let me through the door to wonderful quiet. I stood in the entry hall and blinked, looking around for signs of rhino. Mara grinned at me, her green eyes sparking with mischief.

I cast her a wary glance. "You've put him in a barrel in the basement," I stated.

"No," she replied, laughing, "though I'm sure he'll be as hungover in the mornin' as if we had done. His Irish nature is showin' through—I'm afraid he snatched a whiskey glass and helped himself before we could stop him. He was as fluthered as a fiddler at a wedding, then out like the proverbial light." She fairly skipped ahead of me to the living room.

"Brian didn't have any help getting at that whiskey glass, did he?" I asked.

"Not a bit," she replied, plumping down on one of the pale green sofas with a whoosh of breath. "The horrors'll probably cure him of ever drinking another drop again. If the Children's Services ever get wind, they'll call me an unfit parent for letting him at the booze the once and I'll never hear the end of what damage I've done my poor child. But it's blessed quiet for once. Ben just took him up to bed."

"How much did he get?"

"Oh … not much—less than half an ounce, and that watered. He just grabbed the glass and took a drink, then made the most awful face! You'd have thought he'd swallowed fire. Then he dropped a perfectly good glass of Jamey on the floor and ten minutes later he was passed out on the rug. I finally understand why my aunt used to slip a tot into my cousin's bedtime milk. He was a right monster." She caught her breath, then blew it back out in a cheek-bulging gust. "My, I am blathering on. Now, let's see what's on with you. Oh."

I stopped on the verge of sitting down as Mara stared at me with surprise. "What?"

"There's somethin' tangled on ya. Some magical thing."

I looked down at myself. "It must be the damned poltergeist, though I don't see anything."

"Well, you wouldn't, would you? It's rather like tryin' to see the back of your own head without a mirror. Every time you look it moves around. I suppose I could snip it off…"

I had an idea and I put up my hands to keep her back. "No. If I'm connected to it, it's connected to me, and I can follow this line to it—if I can find the thread to follow."

"Would you want to?"

I thought about it. "I might. Can you remove it later?"

"Well … yes. I don't see why not. It's not the same as that knot or whatever it is that monster stuck in you—though that might be why it's caught on you. Attracted like to like. Grey things sticking together like Velcro."

"I hope that won't be happening a lot in the future."

"Not likely. It's never happened before this. Just a moment, let me get the mirror so you can see it."

"A mirror—"

But she'd already jumped up and run out of the room. I shrugged and sat on the sofa in the comfortable creaking of the old house muttering to itself. Albert wafted in and circled around the room before fading away again, and as I relaxed and let the Grey flood in on me as it wished, I could see the curling, golden vines of Mara's protective charms that lay over the house. Without the charge of the rhino-boy, the Danzigers' home was serene and more restful than my own. The poltergeist didn't seem to be able to penetrate it any more than most other Grey things.

Mara returned with Ben and a small silver hand mirror. She told Ben to sit down a moment and brought the mirror to me.

"Let me just get this charm back in place," she said, muttering and fingering the edges of the mirror. She made a shape on the surface that glittered a moment in blue and gold before it sank into the mirror and vanished. "There now. It's a silly trick, but it shows you the back of yourself." She glanced into it. "Hm. My hair wants brushing. Here, you take a look and see if you can spot the thread."

She handed me the mirror and I took it, looking into the surface and seeing only a patch of straight brown hair. "You may need to move it about a bit to see more of yourself. Hold it out farther," Mara suggested.

I stretched my arms out and moved the mirror around slowly. It was strange seeing my own back from such an angle, like a weird camera. The reflection in the mirror moved like a regular mirror: in the opposite direction of my perceived motion. The small, weird view made me feel a little dizzy, but I spotted the thin yellow thread. It circled my head and neck, then spun away into the deepness of the Grey the same way I'd seen similar strands on the séance members. Now that I knew what to look for, I could catch a hint of it out of the corner of my eye.

"That's going to be a real pain to try and follow," I said.

"Why would you want to follow it?" Ben asked.

"To find the poltergeist and the person on the other end—the one who has control of the thing. I don't know how I'll follow something that's behind me, though."

"Just twist it around to the front," Mara suggested.

I looked askance at her.

"Here, I'll give it a go," she said. She put her hands up on either side of my head and hummed a bit as she tried to get ahold of it. "Stiffer than I thought," she muttered. "There's something awfully strong on the other end, but it doesn't actually care if it's behind or before, so ..." She gave a grunt, concentrating hard, and made a sudden twist with her hands. "There," she crowed.

I gasped as something wrenched across the back of my eyes. A ripping sensation like a hank of hair being yanked from the back of my head flooded my skull with a flash of pain that vanished as fast as it came. "Ow."

"Oh. I'm sorry. It shouldn't have hurt."

"It did. Not much, but ..." I rubbed the back of my head but felt nothing unusual. Another look in the backward mirror showed my head as it usually was, the yellow thread twisted now to leave its tail in front, though the loop around my head remained as it had been. I looked down my chest and saw a weak yellow gleam near my left arm.

"It's a bit off to the left..." I observed.

"I could give it another shove," Mara suggested.

I was quick to nip that idea in the bud. "No. I can work with this. How am I supposed to chase after this thing, though? When I tried to take a look at it once earlier tonight, it was cut off by a building. Or I think it was a building."

"Probably. You're not a superhero, you know. Can't see through walls."

"You can't?" Ben asked.

I frowned at him. "No." Then I realized he was chuckling in his beard. The unexpected respite from their offspring seemed to have made the Danzigers goofy.

I had never discussed the deep Grey with them, the blaze of energy defining the shapes of the world like intelligent fire in a pit of cold blackness. It had been all I could do at the time to say that it was not what any of us had thought it was. I didn't want to discuss it now, either, even if I thought I could have. I'd never had any luck before.

I gave them both a quelling glare. Ben looked a little sheepish, but Mara just made a face at me.

"I imagine once you're in the Grey, some things remain as hard and opaque as they are out here," Mara said. "But I suspect that getting around it's a matter of finding a bit of a hole to go through. Once you've got a path you can follow the strand—or at least get a look at it."

I groaned. "Are you expecting me to dive in there and chase this thing around right now?"

"Why not?" she said, getting comfortable on the sofa again. "Let's see what we can do about this. I'll have Albert spot you, just in case."

"I think I can manage without a spotter by now," I said.

"Still," said Mara. "I think what you'll need to be doing is bending the Grey a little while you're inside."

"Like I do with the shield edge? But that seems to isolate me from the Grey, not help me move around in it. Why am I supposed to be bending this stuff anyway?"

"So you can push the layers around until you find a hole to go through and follow that strand. You've said there seem to be layers to the Grey and it must be easier to bend a single layer just a bit than to pull the whole edge around. You should be able to pull on the layers of it the same way you pull on the shield. That's what I want you to try. Go in and look around. If you can see layers, try pushing and pulling on them and see if you can move them aside a little."

It sounded crazy, but then the whole thing always did. I shrugged. I breathed slowly, let go of normal, and slid the rest of the way into the mist.

The Danzigers' living room, old as the house was, was not thick with the memories of furniture and other people's lives. Mara had cleared much of that away when they'd bought the house, but some still remained as shades over shades. The humpbacked shape of an old sofa wavered a few feet from me. In the Grey, its form had the substance of memory. I moved toward it and peered sideways, then straight, through thick and thin veils of mist and cold steam. The sofa flickered a little and I could see that it seemed to flatten a little when viewed from the right angle. I put out my hand at the same angle and pushed.

The ghost sofa warped and bent. I grabbed at it and tugged. It slid. I could do it, but I didn't see what purpose it had, except rearranging the Grey furniture that littered my office and condo.

I pushed myself back from the Grey, breathing a little harder than I'd expected.

"I can do it," I puffed. "Not sure what the point is, but I can shove the furniture around, at least. It's tiring, though."

Mara shook her head. "I think that's the poltergeist strand dragging on your energy. Pushin' around in the Grey takes some work, but it shouldn't take that much or you'd be exhausted all the time."

"I used to be."

"Not anymore. Not in a long time, eh?"

"True. I'm getting used to this stuff and it doesn't seem to be trying to kill me anymore."

Ben was looking at me oddly.

"What?" I asked.

"I've never seen you do that before. It's rather fascinating."

"I can't begin to imagine why."

"You sort of ... fade out. I mean, you're here, but it would be easy to miss seeing you. In fact, you look a bit like most people think a ghost looks."

I rolled my eyes. "Goody."

Ben just looked intrigued.

I turned back to Mara. "I'm still not sure I see the point."

"Well, if it's true that the Grey has layers, then it must have layers of time as well."

"Yes," Ben chimed in. "We've been discussing it and it seems to me that since memory loops exist in the Grey—that's what the most common ghosts are, after all—these memories must be isolated capsules of time. So the Grey must be stacked up with layers of time, like fragments of pages. Like an archeological dig into time itself. Layers and layers emerging as fragments here and there. Time isn't strictly contiguous in the Grey."

"Then that explains why it sometimes seems too much or too little time has elapsed when I'm in the Grey."

"Yes, it would," Mara answered. "It would also give you another way to move through the Grey—by digging into the layers of time."

"I'm not following you," I said, shaking my head in confusion.

"Neither time nor space are exactly the same in the Grey as they are out here—they simply can't be," she explained. "If a bit of time past can stick up through the present time and show itself as a ghost memory, then it seems likely you could dig down to some other fragment of time, if you can find one nearby."

"I believe that's how ghosts seem to move through walls," Ben put in.

"How?" I asked.

"Moving along the plane of time fragments in the Grey. The ghost exists on his own time plane. When he seems to walk through the wall, what he's really doing is moving through an open space that existed there in his time. The building has changed, or the space has shifted in the Grey, but on his time plane or fragment, there's no impediment, so he just walks on through. You move like a ghost when you're in the Grey. So if you can get to a layer of time where a barrier doesn't exist, you can move through it, too."

"But I'm not from that time plane."

"I don't think it matters in your case."

"So I could dig down to the days of the Duwamish and walk around on the historic mudflats, if I wanted to?"

"Not quite," Mara interjected. "You can only reach what's there. It's not a solid plane. It's fragments and slices all jumbled up. It's memories. If there's no memory or event strong enough to survive in a spot, there'll be no bit for you to access and you might have to move along in space to find the right bit of time. You might even have to emerge from the Grey to move to another location if the Grey is forgetful."

I rubbed my hands over my face. "I'm having a hard time sorting this out."

"Why don't you try again, in the Grey," Mara suggested.

I did try. I immersed myself in the shifting world, studying it and looking for the bits of time that they mentioned, catching occasional flashes like the sun on glass, but pushing the Grey around made me dizzy and tired. Every time I emerged, Albert was somewhere nearby, but never too close, and regarding me through his tiny spectacles as if I were doing something rather shocking. By the end of twenty minutes—or that's what the clock said—I was cranky and had managed to move about as far as the living room doorway. It felt like I'd spent hours at it.

I put my hands up in resignation. "I quit."

"Oh, you can't!" the Danzigers objected.

"Not forever, just for now. My brain aches trying to bend around this and the rest of me feels like I've just danced back-to-back performances of *Swan Lake* in combat boots. This must be what you guys feel like after a day with Brian in full rhino mode."

"Oh," said Ben, running a hand through his curly black hair in sympathy until it stood up in crackling peaks.

Mara laughed, but whether at me or her husband wasn't clear. "Don't vex yourself over it. My own poor brain's a bit soggy with it right now. Think on it and it'll come," she added with a sudden yawn. "Oh, my. Surely it's not so late as that?"

"It's almost nine," Ben said.

"Cha! It can't be." She looked at the clock on the mantel. "Oh, it is. I've still got papers to grade!" She jumped up and flung affectionate arms around me. "Forgive the rush, Harper. Must retire to sling stones at my students' essays on sedimentary structures. Most of them can't seem to tell sandstone from cement, much less describe it."

Mara rushed off, leaving me with Ben.

"You're welcome to stay as long as you like," he offered.

"I should get back."

"Home, I hope."

I nodded. "Soon."

But once I was back in my truck, I sat and let my head droop. I knew I had earned my fatigue that day, but the drag had started before Wednesday's séance. I'd said nothing to the Danzigers, since I knew they would insist my own safety should come first, but unpleasant implications had come through to me. I'd caught the strand of the poltergeist early on, but the connection seemed to have become stronger on Sunday when I floundered through it in full flood. I'd been feeding it energy ever since without knowing—and in spite of Carlos's statement, I wasn't sure I hadn't contributed more than a coincidental strand to the power that had killed Mark. I couldn't let this feeding go on, but I couldn't pinch off the only handle I had on the thing.

I needed to gain the ability to stalk the poltergeist, but Mara's technique hadn't worked for me; it was too difficult, tiring, and slow to use in tracking—or evading—Celia's nimble movements through the Grey. The entity had shown enough speed and power to intimidate me. There had to be something I wasn't quite getting and it must have been something simple, since the poltergeist's master had learned it with no prior understanding of the Grey or the power in hand. It seemed to me that whatever that skill was, it was probably related to Greywalking and I'd never learned it. I'd been using so little of what was possible, because there were no other Greywalkers to ask—and I hadn't wanted to know. I was learning everything the hardest, slowest way. I'd overindulged in being stubborn.

Without another Greywalker to ask, the only other source of information was Carlos—whose skills as a necromancer glanced across mine in some obscure way I didn't understand. I wasn't sure he did, either, and the last thing I needed was a vampire mentoring me—and he had a more appropriate protégé already. But I needed help. Any kind of kick in the perspective might be useful.

I drove down to Adult Fantasies and was lucky to find Carlos in the tiny office on the ground floor.

The space was really a storeroom with a desk and chair shoved into a corner. Carlos let me in with a pointed glare that sent icicles tumbling down my spine as my stomach pitched.

I was reluctant to speak under that cloud of disapproval, but I forced the words out. "I have a quandary."

He growled, keeping his attention directed to some papers on the desk, for which I was grateful. His full attention tended to visit the colder levels of hell on me.

I closed my eyes and started, "I know I've already asked you to help me once, but I need to know more about moving through the Grey. The layers of time—or that's what—" I stopped myself before saying "we." Although Carlos was acquainted with the Danzigers, I didn't want them involved any deeper with Seattle's vampires than they had already been. "Tell me about time."

He put down his pen and clasped his hands in the pool of light on the blotter. His assessment lay over me like a weight of snow.

"What I know may not help you."

"It's more than I know." He'd realize soon enough how little information I had, so there was no point in being coy about it.

"Time takes many shapes. You'll have to learn them for yourself. It may be a river or a window, a plain or an impenetrable tor that rises from it."

"But how do I recognize the shapes? What do I do about them?"

"Past time is hard. It has no wish to bend aside. I don't move in the power. You do. You walk in it, breathe it, swim in it." His eyes blazed and flickered. "For you, I imagine time is like rocks in water and you the fish. Like a fish, you will learn the smell of it, the feel of it in the current."

My breath was a little fast, as if I'd been jogging, and there was a prickling sensation crawling up my limbs against the chill of his presence. His sudden silence brought a jolt of ice as he studied me from beneath his lowering brows.

"Time is ... just shapes. In water," I repeated, turning the thought over and over. A strange inversion of Einstein's ideas about time being a river.

"To you. Yes."

I got up and left without another word between us.

Now I was puzzled, but no less frustrated. Maybe there was something in what he'd said, but it didn't help me with the immediate problem of Celia. Thinking in dismaying circles, I found myself parking the truck outside my office. Shaking my head, I considered that if my subconscious wanted to wander, I would take the rest of me out for a drink in the thronging weirdness of Pioneer Square. But I wasn't going to do it alone. The historic district was too ghost-riddled for comfort in my current state. I picked up my phone and made a call.

Quinton met me with a hug outside the Owl and Thistle—a noisy Irish pub tucked under a pretentiously Irish stepsister in what used to be a bank on First. How often does a bank go out of business to become a bar? At ten on a Friday night, the little pub was roaring. A "Celtic metal" band—they weren't quite metal, but you couldn't call it folk in spite of the fiddler—contributed to the general clash and thunder of a crowd already drunk on beer and rugby.

Quinton wangled a table in the back near the dartboard and far enough from the band to avoid having any of the people who insisted on dancing in the tiny space land in our drinks. Our conversation was underscored by the thunk of darts and the thock of pool balls as we leaned toward each other to be heard over the wailing of the band covering the Pogues' "Bottle of Smoke."

I was half down the first pint before it occurred to me I'd had no dinner and we'd just missed the last of the pub grub. "Oh, damn," I muttered.

"What's wrong?" Quinton asked.

"Missed dinner. Oh, well. 'Guinness is good for you,' I guess," I added, pointing at a tin sign nearby that featured a comic toucan eyeing the pair of pints balanced on its prodigious beak.

Quinton laughed, then peered at me. "Hey. Really. What's wrong? You never just call and say 'Buy me a drink.' "

"Are you saying we never just have a drink?"

"No. I'm saying you never insist. It's always 'Hey, let's shoot pool,' or 'Hey, you wanna get a beer?' And I noticed that you don't want to shoot pool tonight and I don't think it's because you stink at it—which you do, but that's never stopped you."

"You started it," I countered, suddenly awkward about how to continue this conversation. "I never shot pool until I met you."

"Some people would say you still don't shoot pool. And you don't usually evade questions, either. So ... what's the matter? That case for the ego-hound?"

I found myself rolling my eyes without meaning to. "That case ... It's not even a case anymore. It's done. I'm paid. I'm out—and I owe you money, I know. But I cannot let this damned thing go. It won't let me go.

"That thing—the ghost they made—it's a serious problem. I've gotten tangled up with it, somehow, and now it's causing me trouble. It's vicious. I believe it killed one of the project members."

Quinton choked on his stout. "How does a ghost kill someone?"

"The ghost was just the weapon. One of the remaining subjects controls it."

I backed up and gave him a fast overview of how the poltergeist functioned and what seemed to have caused its jump to a different level of power and autonomy, how it had become cruel and vindictive as one disturbed individual gained control of it, growing even worse since Mark Lupoldi's death.

Quinton grimaced, shaking his head. "That's freaky."

"It's deadly. Whichever of them controls it killed Mark. I don't think he or she is going to be content to stop now that they know what they can do—and I'm sure the killer knows by now."

Quinton nodded and rested his elbows on the table as I went on. "The poltergeist's been raising havoc with everyone connected to it, but it doesn't have endless power. I've been thinking about the activity pattern and it appears that the poltergeist burns energy every time it does anything. If it's been doing a lot—like flinging tables around and breaking people's ribs—it seems to deplete its energy and have to wait for it to recharge a little. That's what it's doing right now. Once the power is at peak, someone else is going to die and this thing will pull on the energy of everyone that feeds it when it goes after that victim. It draws off me, too, and I almost feel complicit in the harm that's already been done. I feel like I ought to stop it, but it's not my job—

it's up to Solis to arrest the killer. But Solis is not going to arrest a ghost. He doesn't think in those terms, but there's no evidence linking the method to the murderer. No clues that he'll accept or that a court would, either. Well, there's Mark's keys, but no one knows where they are. The killer must have them, but how do I or Solis get to them?"

Quinton finished his beer and signaled for another round. "Why do you have to?" he asked, digging in his ever-present backpack for his wallet.

I let the waitress take my glass, then leaned forward again, pushing his wallet back into the bag. "You are not paying to listen to me talk this out. Look, this ghost is not going to fade away. It may get weaker if its collective stops believing in it—or if they're killed—but it has plenty of other power to draw on and its master is a psycho who's already done a lot of harm. This thing is not going to stop. And I don't know anyone else who can go after it but me.

"But I don't know how. I've tried to learn some way to follow it, but I can't figure it out. I don't know what to do when I catch it, or how to catch it in the first place. I seem to be stuck with the job of figuring out who controls the thing—which is the same as solving the crime I'm not even supposed to be investigating—and of convincing Solis of the murderer's identity. The real murderer, not the ghost."

Quinton made a scoffing noise. "Why? Why are you stuck with doing this job for them? They can't understand that a ghost did it, but why does it matter? So long as it stops."

"The family of the dead guy might not agree."

"I'm not callous, but they're not going to buy this story and it's not up to you to sell it. You have to consider your own position first—'cause you can't help anyone if you're dead. It's already taken potshots at you—those bookends you told me about could have knocked your head off. Whoever controls it is crazy and isn't too good at sharing his toys. Since the thing has another power source, at some point—even if it means weakening the thing a little—the killer is going to start picking off the competition—everyone who has a connection to the poltergeist and everyone who's a threat. When it does, you'll be on that list, and the more trouble you make for the guy, the closer you'll be to the top. So your sense of duty is a little backward here. You need to be free of this ghost and that needs to be done before it does any more harm to anyone. That's the important thing." He paused for more beer, then went on.

"You're fixated on a path to a possible solution, not on solving the problem. You're thinking of saving other people from the monster, not of getting rid of the monster for everyone's sake, including yours. That's what you need to be working for. It seems to me that you'll be able to find this ghost-thing hanging around its controller or its next victims. If you're going to keep it from being used, you need to separate the killer from control of the ghost. Once you've got the controller removed, it'll be easier to break the ghost. It's like unplugging the power before you start messing with the machinery. It may not be perfectly safe, but the other way is a lot worse.

"It's pretty obvious from what we saw on those early recordings that the ghost isn't very clever on its own and doesn't make decisions for itself. It gets a lot of its smarts from the group that contributes to it. If it's cut off from that, it'll get pretty dumb and be a lot easier to take out. If you can keep the controller distracted from the ghost, the ghost won't have that source of smarts or viciousness."

I stopped him, studying him a moment in amazement. "How do you know this?"

"Just compiling the information and following the logic thread to the end. I don't usually do it out loud, though, so I probably sound like a moron."

"You sound brilliant."

He grinned. "I like that. Tell me that again sometime."

"OK. Now, go on being brilliant a little longer. I think I'm getting this part."

"All right." Another sip of beer was required before he could continue. "If you can approach the ghost while the killer is busy, you can isolate it from the rest of the system—the others aren't going to be much trouble, since they don't use it for anything most of the time."

"They don't use it at all and they're being encouraged to forget."

"Good. Once it's isolated, I think the system will just fall apart. It may take a while, but it will. It shows all the signs of being an inherently unstable system and the laws of physics say that unstable systems degrade once the feedback that keeps them artificially stable is removed. So you isolate the entity—scoop it up like in a Leyden jar—and take away the input. The charge just sits in the jar until it is discharged or dissipates on its own."

For some reason I had a sudden vision of Chaos chasing her toys in the mayonnaise jar at home.

"Wait," I said. "A Leyden jar's a kind of ... battery, right?"

"More like a capacitor. Stores the electricity in coupled plates as an electrostatic charge. There's no current flow in a capacitor, which is why the dissipation is slow but the discharge is fast. Batteries store the electricity in a chemical bond that requires a current and is constantly discharging. Doesn't matter, though—it's just an allusion. You wouldn't really use a Leyden jar to catch a ghost."

But I was thinking maybe I could. I was thinking about silvered mirrors stopping the flow of Grey energy and the slowing property of glass, and I wondered if I could find a bottle to put this particular genie into until its controller was brought to heel.

"Excuse me, Quinton—I have to make a phone call. I'll be right back."

I rushed outside, forgetting the lateness of the hour, and called the Danzigers. Mara answered, sounding out of sorts.

"It's rotten late, so this had best be good."

"Mara, it's Harper. I'm sorry for the hour."

"Oh," she answered, yawning, "I thought you were the dean—the man's useless as a chocolate teapot and an insomniac to boot. What's come up?"

I told her my idea. She made interested noises in between yawns.

"Brilliant! Come for breakfast in the morning and I'll see what Ben and I can turn up." She punctuated her good-byes with another yawn.

I returned to the table caught between the pleasure of Quinton's company mixed with the possibility of a problem solved and the sense of another still hanging like a sword. And I didn't remember that I should have called Will that night until the opportunity was past.

TWENTY-FIVE

Saturday began with a jerk and the clarity of knowledge that bursts to the forefront of the mind like a bubble. There was another source of information about interacting with the poltergeist. As soon as I had completed my morning routine, I made a phone call and arranged another meeting. Then I drove to the Danzigers' for breakfast.

I met Ben on the sidewalk. He was loping toward the little rose-covered arch that marked his front steps and waved to me, jogging to catch up.

"Hi," he panted. "Look what I got." He held up a large glass container that looked like a giant, old-fashioned lightbulb with a bit more neck. In his other hand he had a manila envelope.

"What is that?" I asked.

"It's an alembic. It's a distilling flask, effectively. Heatproof glass. One of the chemistry professors lives nearby and he gave it to me. It's got a chip in the top, so it's not any good to him anymore—once they're chipped they tend to break or become unsterile. So I'm going to try an experiment with it and see if we can't make a genie-bottle for you."

Enlightenment at last. "Ah. Mara told you."

"Yeah," he replied, starting up the steps to the porch. I followed him. "She woke me up when she came to bed and I was thinking about it, so I called this guy and asked if he had anything like what you needed. Well, he didn't exactly, but he had this and he told me how to get a reflective coating on it—you want the reflective side pointing in, right?" he added, opening the front door.

I started to answer, but was interrupted by a squeal of laughter. While it was an improvement on some of the recent greetings from Brian, I still looked around the door with care before entering. There was no sign of the boy in the hall.

Ben took his prize into the kitchen.

Mara was lifting a waffle onto Brian's plate and waggling it on the fork so it flapped like a butterfly. Her son squealed again and raised his hands to snatch the waffle. Mara kept it just out of reach.

"Greedy. And what should you be sayin'?"

"Puh-leeeese?"

"That's better." She put the waffle on the plate with a scoop of chunky applesauce and a strip of bacon. Brian snarfed the bacon in three quick bites and washed it down with gulps of milk.

Mara noticed Ben and me in the doorway.

"Ah, is that it, then?"

Ben waved the alembic. "Yup." He held up the envelope. "John gave me some reflective coating film to put on the outside, too." He looked at me. "It won't be a beautiful job, but it should do the trick."

"Are you sure?" I asked.

"Well, the theory's sound."

Mara huffed. "Oh, sit yourselves down before you start going on and have some brekkie, or we'll be eatin' burned waffles with our soft-boiled theory."

Ben sat at the end of the table farthest from Brian and set the alembic's neck upside down in his milk glass, so it looked like a giant glass dandelion puff.

"Sarnies?" Mara asked.

"What?" I asked.

"Sandwiches," Ben answered. "In this case, bacon in waffles so you can eat the whole thing with one hand. Yes, please," he added to his wife. Receiving his sarnie, he tinkered with the flask with one hand and talked between bites.

"See," he said, "this container should work if I can get this tint material on flat. The glass could be thicker, but this should do for a while. The material is more like ceramic, really, even though it's clear, so it's very dense. The Grey energy moves through it pretty slowly and the reflective surface should stop the ghost from getting out once it's in."

"How does it get in in the first place?" I asked, managing bacon and waffle between sips of coffee.

"This is the good part. The reflective tint takes advantage of the reflective nature and density of the glass surface, so it's highly reflective in one direction and only a bit dark in the other. It's the same kind of thing they use on car windows. A form of Mylar, but very thin with some sticky stuff on the reflective side. Once it's in place, you can look in but whatever's in the flask will just see reflection and shadow. Um … what was I saying?"

"How the genie gets in the bottle," I reminded him.

"Oh, yeah. Well, it has two options—it can enter through the material itself, though that would be very slow, or it can go in through the opening at the neck. You just sort of scoop it up. If you face the opening toward the poltergeist and get part of it to go in, the whole thing should be drawn into the container by the conductivity of the reflective surface. Once inside, it'll be momentarily confused by the reflection. Then you stopper the bottle with something nice and dense, like rubber—which I happen to have in the envelope, thanks to John Burke—and the ghost is stuck in the vessel, since it can't disperse through the reflective surface or through the density of the material itself. If you can corner it in some dense place—somewhere there is no history, no time fragments for it to slip away on—then it will have no option but to head for you and the ghost trap. The tricky thing is going to be getting it cornered in such a place."

"Yeah, that's going to be the tricky part," I agreed with no small irony. First I'd have to stalk the wretched thing.

Mara snorted a laugh and went back to her own food. I watched Ben lay strips of reflective tint as thin as spider silk onto the glass and smooth them into place with a tongue depressor.

Brian crowed for more food and bounced in his seat.

"Oh ... blast," Ben swore, wrinkling a strip of the tint. He removed it with a single-edged razor blade and for a moment I wondered where it had come from, since I couldn't imagine anyone actually shaving with one.

I turned my attention to Mara and Brian—who wore more of his breakfast than he ate, since he insisted on raising his spoon as high as possible before pouring its load of waffles and applesauce toward his mouth. I counted us all lucky his arms weren't longer.

As we observed the spectacle, I asked, "Do kids have some kind of touch with the Grey that adults don't?"

They both paused before answering. Ben looked a bit curious, while Mara seemed mildly surprised.

"But of course they do," Mara said. She glanced at Ben.

He nodded, looking back to the flask. "Definitely. Children's perceptions of the world are different than those of adults. We know that they don't have certain types of brain structures, hormones, physical and mental developments, and so on before certain ages."

"Babies don't develop depth perception until five months and more, and who knows what's going on while they learn to coordinate their eyes with their minds?" Mara added, trying to wipe her offspring down a bit. "Stop wigglin'! Are you a boy or a worm?"

"Worm!"

She raised her eyebrows. "Are ya now? Shall I put you out in the garden? Would you like a nice bit of dirt for lunch? We've some lovely fish guts for ya. Da and I shall have the fish."

"Blech!" Brian shouted.

"All right, then, boy. Sit you still while I find your face under here…" Brian squinched his eyes and pursed his mouth while his mother wiped his face clean. She took advantage of the momentary lull to talk. "Yes, children seem to see the Grey things a bit more easily than most adults."

"The theory," Ben said, "is that perception of the Grey is caused by the lack of a certain filter in the brain. The filter is something you develop partially by nature and partially by enculturation. Most people could see more if they weren't so thoroughly enculturated to ignore certain things. We learn to focus and to tune things out because our modern society offers too many stimuli for the human brain to sort efficiently otherwise. One of the first things we learn to stop seeing is the things others tell us we can't see. It takes a pretty stubborn mind— or one with a faulty filter—to persist in seeing things the rest of the world says aren't there. Now, my personal theory is that there's some other brain structure as yet unrecognized that determines the 'depth'— so to speak—of the Grey filter or if you have it at all. You see, that would explain why someone like me still can't see the Grey, even though I've been dismantling the culturally emplaced filters for years. Most people are literally Grey-blind, just as some are color-blind."

Finishing with her son, Mara offered him a bit of plain waffle. "But there are as many theories as there are stars," she warned. "Some'll say it's an early contact with the Grey that keeps your mind open to it. Others that it's passed down by heredity or teaching. Or it's something you catch, like a dose of measles, or build up from contact, like fluoride in the water. You could be after arguing for any of them or all of them. But children do seem to have an affinity for it that adults often lack. And why are you askin'?"

I sipped coffee for a moment. "I couldn't get the hang of moving around to track the thread in the Grey. The whole layers-of-time thing didn't make sense to me," I explained. "I tried asking Carlos about it."

Mara looked startled and stared at me, for a moment distracted from Brian. "Carlos? Why would you be going to him?"

"Because he has retrocognition—he can look at the past—and I thought he might see the Grey more like I do and know something more about time."

"Did he?" she asked.

"A little, though he made it clear I was wrong about any similarity in our perceptions of the Grey. He kind of gave me the creeps about it."

"More than usual?"

I remembered his hungry look and shivered. "Yeah." I shook it off. "Anyhow. I was thinking that I must just be doing it wrong and I needed some idea how. The children of one of the séance members play with the poltergeist. Like Brian seems to play with Albert. So it has to be easier than what I was doing. Or at least it has to be something a child can do. I'm going to talk to the kids' mother."

"Right now?"

"As soon as we're done here. But that brings us back to genies in bottles."

"Oh, yes. The ghost-catcher," Mara replied. "How is it?" A glob of sticky apple splattered onto her shoulder. "Oh, Brian!"

Brian's eyes got very large. "Uh-oh." He wriggled down to the floor and bolted for the hall.

Mara growled and closed her eyes. "Do you suppose he's a changeling? Because if so, I'd like a try at having him changed back. I'd walk through Galway and broken glass mother-naked if it would buy me a quiet week."

"You could just give him more whiskey," I suggested.

"Never again," she moaned, getting up to chase after him.

"You can't just … cast a spell on him to be quiet and come back?"

" 'Twouldn't be a good idea. Abuse of power and all—not to mention the side effects. I'll catch him the old-fashioned way. With guile and cunning."

She laughed, then snuck out of the room on silent feet. I turned to look at Ben. He was grinning.

"I suspect she does use a little magic," Ben said. "She's so much better with him than I am."

"You're not too bad."

He laughed. "Praising with faint damns. Anyhow. How do you like it?"

He held up the glass vessel. Most of the lower bulb was now covered in a thin, dark blue coating that raised a rainbow sheen. If I peered at it through the Grey, the covered part looked black and solid. In the normal world, I could just see through it if I squinted a bit and got my head at the right angle.

"It's great," I said, a little surprised at how good it was.

Ben smiled. "Thanks. I'm not much good at arts and crafts, so I hope I've done it right. I'll finish up the neck and you can have it."

I raised my coffee cup. "I hope it works."

Ben's laugh was a bit rueful this time. "You're not the only one." He concentrated on his work as he continued, keeping his eyes down. "I hope this is a better guess than the last time."

My heart sank at the memory of how badly I'd misjudged things on my first Grey outing, and I could almost smell the reek of burning again. I was still carrying reminders in the knot of Grey implanted in my chest and the magical resistance that kept me from speaking of certain things.

"There is no fault on your part," I said. "What went wrong at the museum was my fault—just mine. How many times have I said so?

Do I need to speak another language to make you believe that? Quick crash course in Russian—teach me how to say 'mea culpa' and we can stop there."

He frowned at me. "Why?"

I couldn't say. The words would not come out, corked up with guilt and magical compulsion. I just shook my head and felt heavy. "It's not you," I muttered.

Ben finished the bottle in silence, slipped the black rubber stopper into the neck, and handed the whole thing to me. We could hear Mara and Brian coming back along the hall, the floorboards singing with their steps.

"Be careful with it."

I took it with both hands. "I will." Then I smiled at him—a big, fat, footlights-to-second-balcony grin. "It'll be fine. Thanks."

I made my good-byes to Mara in the hall, thanking her for breakfast and avoiding another shin-ramming by Brian with a quick slide to the door.

"Bye-bye, rhino-boy!" I called as I slipped out.

"Graah!" roared Brian. Then I heard him laughing as the door closed between us.

Brian was starting to grow on me and I wondered if I would start to like children by the end of the day, since I was spending so much time with them.

Patricia wasn't thrilled to see me again. I kept intruding on her Saturdays—which she was quick to inform me were the only time she saw her husband.

"I'm sorry, Mrs. Railsback," I said as she let me into the play yard once again. "You do understand, though, that the poltergeist will continue to hurt you and others until it's broken down. Dr. Tuckman called you about that, right?"

She nodded.

"I'm trying to help and I need your kids' help to do that. I'm only asking for a few minutes of their time."

"I still don't understand how my babies can help you," she whined.

"They play with Celia. They know how to interact with it in ways we don't."

"I still think it's Mark's ghost—"

"That may be, but it's Celia that killed Mark and it's Celia we have to get rid of."

She gaped. "Celia killed Mark?"

I looked her in the eye and let the worst moments of this investigation well back up through me, every instant of understanding regarding Celia and what it was. Something of knowledge and horror arced across our shared glance and she recoiled, murmuring, "Oh, no. Did she really?"

"I believe it did."

She backed away a step. "That's terrible. Terrible." She shook her head, but she seemed to be trying to shake the monstrous images her mind conjured, not to deny their possibility. "All right. You can talk to the kids, but only for a while—they have to get ready for lunch with their daddy."

"Thank you."

She called them over.

"OK, you guys, this is Harper and she wants to talk to you for a bit. Are you OK with that?"

They looked at her, squirming with impatience, and nodded. "Uh-huh," they chorused.

"Okeydokey. Harper, this is Ethan, Hannah, and Dylan," she explained, pointing to each in turn. They looked at me with varying emotion. Ethan was suspicious, Hannah bored, and Dylan confused.

"Hi," I started, bending down to their level. I felt like an awkward giant in their presence, since none of them was even five feet tall yet.

They seemed like miniatures to me—I was sure they'd seem bigger up close. "Umm ... I know you have a friend—a special friend—that other people can't see, and I wanted to ask you about her."

"Him!" Ethan insisted.

"Is not!" Hannah hissed back. She looked at me with clear, earnest eyes. "Our ghost is a girl."

"Is not!" Ethan fired back. "He's a boy."

"Oh, boy," I sighed. "Hey, can we go sit down on the swings? I feel like a frog bent over like this."

Dylan laughed. "You don't look like a froggy. You look like a monkey."

"Well, then ... maybe we should sit on the monkey bars," I suggested.

"Not monkey bars. It's a jungle gym," Ethan corrected. The pontificator of the family.

I straightened up. "Jungle's a good place for a monkey, too, I guess. How 'bout we go there?"

I glanced at Patricia for approval. She shrugged and made a bitter smile. "All yours, lady."

Hannah and Dylan grabbed my hands and dragged me to the jungle gym. I saw only the thinnest collection of yellow energy hanging about and wondered if this was a wild-goose chase.

Once we were at the jungle gym things changed fast.

Hannah told me to sit on a swing while Dylan and Ethan climbed up to the top of the slide.

"Celia is so a girl," she whispered to me. "Stupid Ethan."

"How do you know?"

"I can see her. She's right over there, right now." She pointed to the shadowed end of the yard where a cataract of greenery hung down near the ground. As I tracked her finger, the haze of threads firmed and grew into a column of pale yellow, pierced with bright shards of time. It had come to her call, though it was only a very small version

of the thing that had stormed through room twelve on Wednesday. I'd
guessed right: it was diminished by use and probably recharging, since
it made no move against me.

"OK, I see her, but she just looks like a blob to me," I admitted.

"It's hard to tell. She's kind of shy." Hannah shrugged.

The boys came down the slide with a ruckus and tumbled into the
bark chips at our feet.

"Hey," I said. "Can you see your friend and show her—him—to
me?"

Both the boys pointed to the same yellow haze. "There," said
Ethan.

"OK. When you play with your friend, do you have to do anything special?" I prayed they were articulate children and could explain
their games.

Ethan snorted. "Duh! You have to open the doors. Then you can
go in the ghost land."

I felt dizzy and was glad I was sitting. The ghost land. They didn't
really … go into the Grey, did they? "Oh. I'm sorry. I don't understand. I don't see any doors. Can you show me how to open the doors?
I'd like to talk to your friend, too." It was hard not to sound like a
moron and talk down to them. I was sure I wasn't doing this right, but
I was trying. And hating it.

Ethan made a dramatic shrug of disgust and turned toward Celia.

"Come on," I urged the other kids, "you guys, too. Hannah.
Dylan. Show me how. I'm a stupid monkey, remember?"

Dylan giggled. Hannah and Dylan joined their older brother and
I faded down into the Grey. I could hear Patricia's slight gasp behind
us and I prayed she'd stay out of it. I was doing this far too often, but
it appeared I would have to do it a few more times. I'd have to break
the habit when this miserable case was over.

The shifting cloud-world of the Grey was uncannily empty—the
building rested in a hole dug from the cliff edge and little history

existed here. The kids didn't have a presence so much as an impression; they made odd child-shaped holes in the fabric of the mist, limned in bright energy that fluttered through the spectrum as I watched. As I stared at them, the kids shifted and turned a bit sideways, moving their hands vertically up and then horizontally across. Where their hands disturbed the mist, a bright line appeared that resolved into a door shape. I felt sick. It was a doorway, just like the doors of dragon smoke and light I'd seen when I first came in contact with the Grey. The kids had called up a door. They'd turned sideways to it first ... looking at it from the corners of their eyes, just as I'd had to do, in the beginning. Were they all little Greywalkers? Was it possible? They stepped through their door. But they still didn't have a presence in the Grey. What the hell was going on?

I sank down lower, to where the hot grid of the Grey became visible through the mist. The children looked like dark blotches now, standing on a tilting floor of mist.

As I stared at the structures around them, I saw that the Grey was full of layers just as the Danzigers had said, fluid things, like thermoclines in the ocean, yet cutting through one another like rock strata. The kids were standing on one and Celia's weird yellow tangle on another. They moved toward the poltergeist, edging sideways, pushing with their hands and shoulders, slipping in between the layers and sliding on to new ones. I was dismayed at their approach—not much different than what I'd tried to do with Mara. But it didn't seem so hard for them. What were they doing that was different than what I'd done at the Danzigers'? They seemed to slip right onto the layers...

Slipping. Moving sideways. It was always easier to see the Grey sideways. Mara had always referred to my sudden unexpected jolts into the Grey as "slipping"—a sort of sideways movement. That's what I'd done wrong: I'd tried to go at it forward, straight on. And the time layers had been there, but they'd been stiff and heavy. But I didn't need to move them. I just needed to slide onto them. Sideways!

Carlos had said that time would feel to me like rocks in a stream—eddies in a current. I put out my hand, into the Grey, toward the stacked and tilted layers of time … and felt ripples, corrugations and fluttering edges. Standing sideways to them, I ran my hand along the stacks of ripples and they fanned like cards, flashing snapshots of time. I put my hand on one and pushed a little, just like tilting the table with Ben.

And I was in, sliding into time. I found the right layer—the one with a pale yellow edge the same color as Celia—and slid onto it, stalking toward the poltergeist and the children across the ghostly playground. Strange prickling sensations grated against my skin when I got close to Celia.

The bright, gleaming shards that hung in the structure of the entity shivered and rang like wind chimes. Looking at them was disorienting—the surfaces seemed solid, yet contained a baffling twist that came back on itself without end. I could see the children playing near those fragments, darting through Celia's web of energy like those fish that swim unharmed through the stinging tentacles of sea anemones. The thin yellow strands that fed the entity spun out for a distance until they broke off in sudden dark slabs of immovable space—the walls of the towers that were sunk around us into the timeless cliff. I could follow one thread with my eyes back to Patricia, who stood looking anxious beyond the heavy mist between herself and me. I could also see my own thin thread running into the mess that was Celia.

I moved a little closer and the entity recoiled from me, as if it knew I meant it harm. With a sudden rush of red and a blast of heat, it vanished. We all tumbled back, landing hard in the bark of the play yard by the jungle gym. I just lay on my back for a moment while the kids giggled and picked themselves up.

Patricia rushed toward us. "Are you guys all right? Did you fall?"

"We're fine, Mommy," Hannah said. The boys were gruffer in their reassurance.

Patricia couldn't seem to decide what tone to take with me. She scowled, but didn't say anything.

I picked myself up, dusting off wood chips and shaking them out of my hair.

"Well?" Patricia demanded. "Did you get what you wanted?"

"Yes," I answered. I was a little out of breath and felt a touch shaky.

"Is it Mark?"

"Huh?" It took a moment for me to put the comment into context. "No, I'm sure it's not, but I'm not a medium, so—"

"You're not? But you—" She cut herself off and her expression grew a bit alarmed.

"I what?" I asked.

"You … I don't know. I thought you were the ghost for a minute."

Well, that answered a question, of sorts.

"No, I'm no ghost," I said, smiling at the idea. I looked down at the kids who had lined up by their mother. "Thanks, you guys. That was really helpful."

Hannah and Dylan smiled. Ethan frowned. "You made him go away."

"Maybe. Sometimes they just go away on their own," I replied. I wasn't sure how I knew that. Guessing? Or dredging something up from memories I'd buried a long time ago?

Ethan would have said something more if his mother hadn't given him a swat on the backside. "Don't be rude. Now head upstairs. Go see Daddy!"

The kids scampered toward the elevator.

Patricia looked at me with a spooked expression.

"Do you need a lift to the funeral?" I asked.

She took a step back from me. "No. I'm not going. I can't get a babysitter and I can't just leave them with their father." She shook her head and kept backing. "And I don't want to see you here again. I don't want you near my kids again." Then she turned and bolted after her children, catching up to them and pushing them toward the elevator, fear boiling off her in anxious orange clouds.

As she ran away, I could see her strand of yellow energy turn a dull ash color, knotting on itself and vanishing through the buildings toward wherever Celia had fled. Before the elevator doors closed between us, it snapped and fell away like a burned branch collapsing into broken coals and cinders.

I let myself out, heading back for my office, and found myself laughing, aching gusts of amusement that brought tears to my eyes. If Patricia could have seen me, I imagined it would have confirmed her apparent opinion of my threat level.

Now I knew how this Grey time thing worked, but I needed an area with more history and mess to practice in. I could think of no place better suited than the messy historic district. And no one would be too surprised by a person acting a bit odd there; I'd have plenty of company.

Back in Pioneer Square, I saw what I'd expected to see: the Grey, streaked with glimmering layers of history, sheet-thin sections of time riven with sudden cracks and upheavals like sedimentary rocks pitched to the surface by a massive earthquake. Knowing what to look for and how deep into the Grey, I could spot tracks, shards, and loops of time scattered and strewn over the broken landscape of the Grey, each disordered slice or spire spinning out a ghost image or a pall of sensation. When I moved near them I felt the same prickling on my skin I'd felt near Celia, rather like the feeling of shaving with a dulled razor.

It was noon on a Saturday and Pioneer Square was moderately busy with locals. I was destined to look like a freak of some kind with this experiment, so I didn't worry about which kind. I turned in at the alley near my office building. Sinking into the Grey, I moved near one of the zones of heavy time striation and ran my hand along what seemed to be the edge. I felt it prickle and riffle a cold flutter against my palm.

Back when I first met the Danzigers, Albert had led me through a tunnel open only in another time. I had done it by accident then. I could do it again on purpose. I didn't try to push them this time; I just nudged the layers of time sideways, letting them tip and looking at them as they slid over each other, flickering silver images of history in the cold mist and hot neon of the Grey. When I found one that looked empty and different, I concentrated on holding it and let myself slip.

The sickening pitch of sudden movement through the Grey made me retch. I hadn't experienced that sensation in quite a while and I didn't like the reminder. With an abrupt jerk, I staggered to a stop—though I hadn't moved in space. Swallowing back a rush of bile, I looked around. The soft orange of my office building's terra-cotta walls was gone and a building of wood and shingle stood in its place. Across the brick street another wooden building bustled with business where my parking garage normally stood. I stepped to the door that led to the nearest building and tried to open it. It resisted my efforts and I had to concentrate very hard on moving it. At last, it swung aside and I went through.

It was difficult to do anything in this shadow of the past. Everything resisted my attempts to move it—Carlos had said the past resisted bending. I found it easier to wait for someone else to open a door and slide through behind the oblivious memory of the person than to try and wrestle the doors myself. The shades demonstrated a wide range of consciousness. Some saw me and treated me as if I were like them; others didn't see me at all. A very small handful saw me, but seemed aloof or upset by my presence, and some of those tried to talk to me or touch me. I shook them off and looked for a way out of this plane of time—this temporacline?

It was much harder to spot the layers and shards of time from inside one but I caught the cold eddy of one's edge and tilted it, sliding again toward something. I felt several forces tugging at me, like currents, and headed for the strongest, jolting back to the alley behind my building and out of the Grey. That wasn't quite what I'd wanted, so I tried again, sinking into the Grey, searching for the corrugated ripples of time planes. Again I found them, but I studied them more this time, looking for something specific.

I finally found one with no building in front of me and pushed it aside, then slid with the same sickening sensation of vertigo. This time, mudflats dropped away beneath me and for a moment I hung in the air at the street level of my own time. A sense of panic rescued me and I scrambled back to a more built-up time. I didn't want to risk falling to the original mudflats and then trying to reemerge in a building that sat twelve feet higher. But I stayed in the Grey this time. No sudden dump back into the normal.

At last I pushed it back and leaned against the alley wall, catching my breath. I felt as if I'd just completed a heavy workout. Glancing at my watch, I cursed. I had twenty minutes to get to Lake View Cemetery.

TWENTY-SIX

The cloud cover was solid and lowering but still not a drop of rain had fallen. The expectant chill was perfect for a funeral. When I arrived, the service had already started. The crowd was large and I spotted a lot of familiar faces: Phoebe and the staff from Old Possum's; most of the poltergeist crew; Amanda; and a cluster of people so blank and worn with grief and shock that they had to be Mark's family. I also saw a large hot spot of yellow energy hovering over the crowd like a poisonous storm waiting to break.

Following the threads of yellow from the mass, I spotted each of the séance members: Ken and Ana; Ian several feet behind them, bleak-faced; Wayne with his arm around Frankie's shoulders as she sniffled; Tuckman near Mark's parents; Terry alone. No sign of the Stahlqvists or Patricia Railsback. As I picked them all out, I noted one more face: Detective Solis. He was staying to the back where the rolling ground rose a little. I worked my way around toward him, thinking that the presence of Celia at the funeral further ruled out either of the Stahlqvists as the killer—I expected to find the entity cleaving to its master.

I stopped next to Solis. He didn't look directly at me, but cut me a glance from the corner of his eye and inclined his head a little. "Still working?"

"I knew Mark," I replied in a quiet voice.

"Yes. Not, I assume, so well as Cara Stahlqvist knew him."

"No. And I noticed she's not here, so you don't think she's the murderer."

"She's an interesting piece of the puzzle."

"In what way?"

"This case turns on a woman and her lovers—those she accepted and those she rejected. We confirmed Mrs. Stahlqvist's affair with Lupoldi and the information you gave us about the brooch—very dramatic. She preferred to make the advances—to choose rather than be chosen—she rebuffed others even though her relationship with Lupoldi was stormy."

"Others?" I asked.

He jerked his head toward the cluster of Tuckman's youngest subjects. "The usual sexual stupidity."

I wondered which of them he meant—if not all three. Cara's interests didn't seem to lie with women, so that let Ana out. But I recalled Ian's attention to her bustline and Ken's sudden bitter tone at her name. All three had been hurt in the séance, but Ana least. Was the woman at the center the killer or the cause?

I wasn't convinced of the Stahlqvist-Lupoldi scenario, though it might look good to Solis. If Cara had grown tired of Mark, their stormy relationship might have gotten lethal—or been cut short by her husband.

Maybe Ana had lied to me when she denied close contact with Mark. I stared at the members of the rotten triangle and wondered which of them might have taken "no" as a mortal insult. The yellow strands of Celia gleamed against the leaden sky above them.

I looked at Solis, trying to catch his eye, but he avoided me. "You suspect one of them."

"I've already told you that suspicion is nothing without proof."

"What about those keys? Would that be enough evidence?"

"To make an arrest, perhaps, but not to convict. I don't want this case to fail by insufficient evidence."

"Then you're no longer looking for motive?"

"I have the motive."

The clergyman at the graveside finished his final prayer and a couple old before their time stepped forward to the edge of the pit as the rest of the crowd began to loosen. Solis shot me a warning look and turned away.

I stared out over the crowd, watching Celia. The yellow haze grew thick and agitated as the crowd moved, three ropelike strands extending down. I followed them with my eyes to Ken, Ana, and Ian. Ken's Grey shield of blankness flickered as if under stress from something.

Ian had stepped next to Ana and was speaking in a low, furious voice, close to her face. She stepped back and he followed her. The knot of energy above them roiled and brightened with a flaring strand of red. I moved closer through the crowd. I could see all three of them again pulling on Celia, but they stood so close together I couldn't make out which of them the angry red line touched.

Ana swung a hand and Celia flexed and expanded, sending a sharp shaft down into the center of the three. Ian stumbled back a step or two. I couldn't see if Ana had hit him or if Celia had.

As I got close I heard Ian spitting insults, of which the nicest was "slut." He lurched closer to Ana, his right hand raised. Ken's shutters vanished and he pushed between them, exposed in a red wash, also with a hand poised to strike, and put his face close to Ian's, growling something low and venomous. Ian's seething gaze moved to Ken. The cloud of Grey around them throbbed red shot with black, boiling and distorting the air nearby. Then Ian's glare flicked over Ken's shoulder and Ian dropped back a step. Ken stepped back, putting a hand out to Ana without taking his eyes off his rival. The men's faces were studies in leashed rage. Ana's was blank and cold.

Ian straightened and looked daggers at them both. He cut his eyes away from Ana and gave Ken a cool, dismissive glance. "I'm done with the little tramp," Ian said. "Have fun, buddy."

He turned and stalked off. Ken took half a step after him, then drew up short as Ana kept his hand without yielding an inch. He looked at her.

Something bright shot down from above Ian, caroming off his shoulder and arcing toward Ana. She flinched and Ian turned his head and spat on the ground without letting his gaze touch either of them. Ana snatched the shiny object, clutching it in an unsteady fist.

The thick red storm unknotted and drifted into a thin yellow haze over the lovers' heads. Ken tried to put his arms around Ana, but she wrenched away, pulling the object against her chest.

"No," she choked. She turned and ran. Ken's Grey wall slammed up and he pursued her, but every time she glanced back and saw him, she ran faster. I saw Solis break into a run parallel to them, falling in a bit behind to follow. Over it all, the shape of Celia regathered and began to move.

I ducked into the Grey and followed the entity. It was a hard yellow gleam in the cold mist, its thread to me spun out like spiderweb between us. I lost direct sight of it, my thread seeming to cut off without warning in the wall of a building. I eased back, glancing around, and saw I was now in Volunteer Park, the Asian Art Museum building intruding its bulk between me and Celia's course. I ran around the building to the driveway and threw myself back into the Grey.

Jolting into the slippery world, I found the thread spun ahead of me, out of the ghostly shapes of the park and down the nearest street. I followed it past the impressions of the mansions of Millionaire's Row, then lost it again in the side of a large house thronged with the ghosts of some long-ago party. I paused and stared at my own strand of Celia, thinking that it would point directly—like a compass needle—toward the poltergeist. Moving around a bit, I figured out the direction and set off through the flickering ghost-world, dodging the more solid things that rose up and trying to stay out of the way of anything too interested in me. The harsh jaws of things I didn't like to think about snapped at me several times and a swarm of hungry, mindless presences dragged on my limbs, gaping mouths and cries of want tearing at me as I ran after Celia, my living brightness like a beacon—a flame to vampire moths.

I was stumbling a little, panting, when I came out again at another wall. The silken strand of Celia pointed ahead and upward. I wrenched myself back to normal, pounding to a halt in front of the Harvard Exit Theatre.

Ian worked there, but Ana or Ken might have followed him. I saw no sign of Solis, but everyone was ahead of me. Even if Solis was inside ready to arrest one of them, my capturing the poltergeist could only help. I turned back toward the cemetery, hoping I had enough time to retrieve the ghost-bottle before Celia moved.

TWENTY-SEVEN

I got lucky and caught a bus up to the cemetery to pick up my truck and retrieve the trap for Celia. I left the Rover questionably parked near the theater and bought myself inside. The lobby was busy with a moving crowd of filmgoers—a few faces seemed almost familiar, but none of them was part of Tuckman's group. I peered through the Grey for Celia, my eyes skipping over mist-shrouded faces.

Flashes of jagged time and paranormal streamers of yellow and red tangled over the crowd, vanishing through the ceiling. Whoever I wanted was upstairs. I shoved my way through the crowd and up the steps. I bolted around several normal people on the landing and pelted on to the top floor and through the STAFF ONLY door to the attic, following the thickening thread of energy and feeling it pulling on my bones.

There were voices above me and I slowed down, quieting my steps along the edges of the treads. So long as they were talking, no one was killing anyone—I hoped. I swapped the silvered glass jar into my left hand and let my right drift to my back. Pistol still snug in its holster under my jacket, I continued up the stair.

At the top lay a low corridor with two doors—one an inch or so ajar. I didn't have to duck, but I could feel the rough ceiling catching my hair as I sidled along the wall toward that door. I drew close and squinted through the opening.

The room was a storage area full of old equipment. Small, half-height doors on each end probably led to smaller attic spaces full of wiring and pipes. Dust-choked slices of light fell through a louvered ventilator just above Ian's head, leaving pale stripes on the floor in front of Ana's feet. Celia's threads were festooned like thick ropes around the room, clothing Ian in spectral illumination, but I couldn't see the entity itself from my position.

"—stupid little slant-eyed bitch," Ian hissed.

"Shut up! Just shut up, Ian!" Ana yelled. "You tell me where you got these!"

She flung a shiny object at him. It jangled to the floor in a sprawl of bright brass, steel, and black plastic.

"Those are Mark's keys. Where did you get them?" Ana demanded, her voice rising in hysteria.

In the mote of light I could just pick out the tubular shape of the bike lock key.

"You want to know?" Ian asked, his face going feral and calculating. "Then come real, real close and I'll whisper in your ear. We'll cuddle up like we used to and I'll tell you everything you want to hear."

Ana clamped her jaw tight, starting to lean forward.

I could feel the pressure of Celia's presence crush against me and the room flickered red to my eyes.

I shoved through the door.

Airless, sweltering, the room blazed in hot colors and thick coils of Grey energy. Ian and Ana both jerked their heads toward me. I could see a red line, flaring and thick as an ancient python, pulsing from Ian's body. Ana's own yellow thread was spindling away, drawing her, helpless, toward him.

I rushed to her and shoved her out of the room. "Run," I ordered, slamming the door. Then I turned back to Ian. It would be useless, but I drew the gun anyway, hoping Ian would choose to concentrate on the apparent and immediate threat, rather than on his ex-girlfriend. The press of Celia's power pulled back as if the entity were surprised. I knew it was Ian's surprise, but the feeling was eerie nonetheless.

"How 'bout you tell *me* where you got those keys," I invited. "But I think I'll stay right here—you don't look so cuddly to me."

His eyes locked on the gun for a moment, then shifted back up to me. There was a quiver of tense uncertainty in the air between us. "You ... you stupid, stupid bitch."

"You're awfully fond of that phrase. Tell me about the keys."

"Fuck you."

I laughed. "Heck of a vocabulary you have, Ian. With that sort of charm, I guess you figured Ana'd come crawling back to you."

"She did!"

"Didn't look that way to me."

"I'd have gotten her back. Her and that half-breed bastard."

"Wrong kind of Indian," I needled.

"Shut up! You don't know what you're messing with. I can hurt you without even touching you! I can take them out the same way." I could almost see him calculating his chance of launching Celia against me versus the risk of a bullet.

"Like you took out Mark?" I asked, drawing on his vanity—hoping his desire to brag would hold him back a moment.

Viciousness dripped from his voice. "He deserved it! I didn't even know I could do it, but it was easy. How could Cara want him when he was faking things I could do for real? He didn't deserve her!"

"And you killed him because Mark had what you couldn't get. What, did you see him with Cara? Or did you follow her to his place?" I heard something moving with stealth toward the door. I had to draw Celia away from whoever gathered their strength there.

Ian ranted on. "She acted like a whore," he spat. "She told me off, but I followed her. When I saw her come out, I was angry and it was so easy! He was a liar and a cheat and it was easy to crush him. And it felt so good—like breaking something you've always hated. I just wanted him dead and he was dead. And it'll be the same with that slut and her fuck toy!"

Ragged instants of memory flared as he screamed at me: wrenching impressions of creatures suffering; the green snap of bone; the powdery smash of plaster and a wash of blood; unholy thrill reflected in a dying eye.

My hand tensed around the pistol grips and I felt the HK's cocking lever compress the spring to the limit. A desire to squeeze the trigger and wipe out the source of those images fought with my urge to puke. But I only looked at Ian and raised a cynical eyebrow.

He glared at me, his stare blazing, his whole form seeming engulfed in flames and fury. The presence of the entity bloomed and expanded at my back, grinding against my spine, teetering on the brink of eruption. I felt flayed and sick with the sudden stink of it—dead things vomited up by the sea to rot on the shore in the reek of half-burned gunpowder.

I laughed at him again. I decocked the pistol and tucked it back into the holster.

"You sad, ridiculous boy. You think you can hurt them with that?" I demanded, jerking my head toward the mass of Celia gathering behind me. "You'll have to come through me first, freak."

Celia exploded against me as I dove into the Grey. I scrambled through the history of the building, finding an open door and dodging through it as heavy boots pounded into the room. Shouts, shots, noise faded into the mist of the Grey as I ran from the unnatural thing behind me.

It howled like Nemesis descending. I stumbled, tumbled, plummeted into void space … and landed with a jarring thump in something that stank of sewer and boiled with eldritch things. I was somewhere deep in the underlay of Seattle's history. Keeping a hand tight around the ghost-bottle, I clambered back to my feet and ran as fast as the clutching, ravenous mist would let me. I hurtled down a long tunnel of reek and screams.

Celia caught me and buffeted me into an incorporeal wall. My head rang against stone and I slid down into cold. I wondered for an instant what would happen if I died here, but I didn't want to find out and scrabbled away as the entity regathered its force.

Its action was sporadic as it stabbed and grabbed at me. I assumed other things distracted Ian's attention or the poltergeist's assault would have been relentless, but Celia was stupid enough to be single-minded even without his direction. It drew back after each attack, then pressed in again. I searched for exits and grabbed the first upward route I spotted, pulling myself without looking through a hole that felt like a mouth lined with raking teeth.

Icy fluid rushed over me and I found myself standing in a culvert of filthy water. An old storm drain. I'd come back up into a more recent time shard. I jumped for the rungs of an access ladder as Celia smashed against my flailing legs, tossing me back down into the water. I rolled to cushion the glass and came up panting and dizzy.

The bloodshot yellow whirlwind of energy and knife-blade time pulled back, a little dimmer and smaller than before. I realized it was losing energy with each sally. But it was still powerful enough to kill me if it got a good chance and until then, it would drain my energy with every assault. I held the flask out and ran at it, hoping to catch it, but it slewed up and vanished into a fold of history.

I took the opportunity to climb to the surface and out a manhole.

I tumbled into the path of a beer wagon. I dodged out of its way, skidding onto the sidewalk to be cut through by the heedless ghosts of long-dead pedestrians. I shuddered as they passed through me and my legs went weak. Celia hadn't reappeared yet and I was grateful for that.

I kept my feet and caught my breath, staring around, looking for a sign of the time or the place. I couldn't recognize the location. A massive building rose to my right and below me was a steep hill cut with streets of narrow, Victorian row houses, more like something from San Francisco than Seattle. I stared at the large building beside me on the crown of the hill. It was a massive structure, five or six stories with gabled roofs and corner turrets. There was a bell tower sort of thing in the middle of the main wall and a sign—

Celia smashed into me from behind, but with nothing to crush me against, I flew forward, curling myself into a ball around the precious ghost-bottle and somersaulting into the base of the building—which felt as solid and hard as anything I'd ever fallen against in the normal world. I peeled my eyes open, feeling the container still whole against my chest and belly.

Now I could read the sign. Washington Hotel. I'd never heard of a Washington Hotel, and this corner, towering over the Sound, wasn't familiar at all. The cornerstone near my head had a list of names, among them Arthur Denny.

I shook myself and got to my feet, rubber-legged. This was the old Denny Hotel. On Denny Hill. The hill washed away by R. H. Thomson during the Denny Regrade.

Now I knew where I was, the Pacific Place Mall somewhere deep in the historyless soil beneath me, and knew how I might trap the entity and force it into the flask. I began staggering down the ghost hill, feeling for a slot in the sediment of time. I could hear Celia shrieking and buzzing as it came on.

The edge of history fluttered under my groping right hand. I riffled through the knife-sharp edges of memory, pushing and scrambling for the harsh light of my own time. When it canted up like a whale broaching, I heaved myself onto it, careening through the Grey to be spit out into the normal.

I fell a few feet onto hard cement steps, keeping the bottle intact at the expense of my own limbs. Something wrenched in my left knee and shoulder as I landed on the upper steps of the Convention Center transit station. A scruffy kid with a long skateboard and two days' worth of unshaven barbed-wire beard grabbed my right elbow and helped me back to my feet.

"Oh, man, that was a real header! You OK, lady?"

"Yeah, yeah," I panted.

I took off before he could say more, feeling a hot stab in my left knee with every jolting, pounding step. I made for the corner of Seventh and Pine, just a couple of blocks west.

Four on a Saturday afternoon. Traffic was heavy, but slow enough for me to barge through. I could feel Celia's pressure against my back the whole time, but the entity was growing as tired as I, and I managed to stay ahead—I had more to lose.

A clerk in the upper lobby of the Barnes & Noble yelled at me to slow down as I rocketed through the doors and down the escalator. I didn't have the breath to tell him I'd only be a minute or I'd be dead. I slalomed through the crowd and back to the deep cell-signal death zone where science fiction shared space with romance novels.

A whey-faced teenager with long, lank hair squatted on the floor reading English-translation manga when I skittered to a halt at the end of the freestanding shelves that faced the book-lined basement walls. I backed myself up against the romance novels, facing the hard corner of SF. The shelf shuddered and rocked against my spine. My chest heaved and my throat felt raw and lined with corroded brass. There was no history to cut through here. Celia would have to play on my turf and come down the aisle just like a human.

The hot yellow knot of energy whipped around the corner and slammed down hard enough to shake the stacks. I didn't have the energy to taunt it. I pointed the open neck of the silvered vessel at it and braced.

It rushed. I tipped the bottle. One edge of the mass caught on the silvered glass and the thing smacked me hard on the side as it was whipped around like a leaf caught in a vortex and sucked into the trap. I snatched the stopper from my pocket and slammed it home.

I slumped to the floor against the corner of the shelf, a small cascade of novels pattering to the floor around me. The kid with the manga stared at me, gaping.

"What?" I asked.

She shook her head.

From my other side a voice said, "Miss. I'm going to have to ask you to leave now."

I looked up into the clean-shaven face of a security guard.

"OK," I replied. "I'm ready to go now. Can you give me a hand?"

He seemed a little confused, but put out a hand and helped me back to my feet. He appraised me, his eyebrows in a quizzical W. "What ... what happened to you?" he asked, leading me toward the downstairs doors.

I limped forward, my knee and shoulder throbbing. "I was hit by a car," I lied. I wasn't going to say I'd been smacked with a fake poltergeist.

His expression escalated to terrified. "Oh, no! Do you want to sit down?"

"No. No, I'll be all right. Just get me out of here."

He escorted me all the way onto the street, leaving me under the mall's Pine Street portico. A dirt-crusted man with a hand-lettered sign harangued the automotive traffic against trusting the police or a certain apartment manager while a combo of electric violin and ordinary sax played jazz to a grinning bulldog.

TWENTY-EIGHT

I was bruised and disarrayed and I smelled of sewers. I was surprised the cabby had allowed me into his car at all and I felt obliged to give him a very large tip when he dropped me off. I should have been paying more attention—I'd have noticed the pandemonium around the Harvard Exit. Crowds, cops, an aid car, and a press of onlookers surrounded the building.

Holding the flask in one hand, I got out of the cab around the corner from the theater and turned to find a cop by my elbow. The cab had already darted off and I was in no shape to run.

"Miss Blaine. Will you come with me, please."

I shrugged, grimacing, and limped along with the policeman.

He made an opening in the cordon and led me into the lobby. Solis stood in front of the fireplace with his back to me. Ana was in a chair with her shoulders in a defensive hunch. Ken stood behind the chair with his hands on her shoulders, glowering at Solis with an expression that flickered between defiance and panic, his cold Grey shield against the world in shreds. Another plainclothes officer loomed a few feet beyond them.

My escort stopped me a couple of yards off, but not quite out of hearing range. He nodded at the plainclothesman facing us, who gave a curt nod back. I could just hear Solis's intense, quiet voice saying, "... very dangerous. You will make every effort to cooperate with us this time, Mr. George, and there will be no repeat of your previous mistakes. Or of ours."

Ken bit his lip and nodded.

"Good. Detective McBride will escort Miss Choi home. Now, you can all go."

They trooped past me. Ken, with his arm around Ana's shoulders, shot me a puzzled look. A deep crease pinched between his brows and he started to say something, then turned his attention back to Ana, pulling her tight against his side. Ana kept her head down, exhausted and miserable.

I watched them go, then turned back to Solis, who had turned to stare at me. He was seething.

"What happened to you?" he asked.

"I fell into a sewer."

"How?"

"I don't know." Which was the truth, and a more detailed explanation would just piss him off further. "How did you happen to get here so fast?"

He narrowed his eyes and turned his head a little, appraising me.

"Let me guess," I hazarded. "You sent Ana here with a wire and those keys to see if you could trip Ian Markine up."

The tiniest trace of a satisfied-cat smile pulled at his mouth. "Miss Leaman identified the keys." His expression darkened again. "But you surprised me—you and Mr. George. We weren't ready to make the arrest. You fouled us. What did you come for?"

Now I knew why so many faces in the lobby crowd had looked familiar—they were cops. "I had some questions for Ian. I didn't get a chance to ask him at the funeral."

"About what?"

I needed to fabricate something fast. I remembered the equipment in the loft. "About faking effects in the experiments and getting caught by Mark. That storage room is full of old equipment for rigging stage effects. He knew how, but he lied about it."

"That's not what you asked him about upstairs," Solis reminded me.

"No. I overheard his argument with Ana and things made sense. You told me Cara had rejected him and he already had a complaint against Mark. The guy has an ego the size of a Metro bus and it's fairly obvious he's unstable and violent—he has a history of cruelty to animals and that's just the start, I imagine." I remembered with a shudder the pleased memory fragments of pain and death Ian had projected and his parents' distress about the poisoning of their dog.

Solis was still glaring at me. "So you barged in," he stated.

I took a risk and said, "He had something in his hand and he was trying to get Ana close enough to strike her."

"What was it?"

"It looked like a pipe." A lie, but one impossible to disprove. There were dozens of bits of pipe in the storage room.

"How did you leave the room? When we came in you were gone and Markine escaped."

"What? You didn't arrest him?"

"No!" Solis shouted. His habitual calm shattered. He was furious enough to talk.

"Markine is a very dangerous man and I do not have him in custody. I do not know how he killed Lupoldi or how he disposed of you down whatever rabbit hole you fell through. He is not of right mind. His confession to you and Choi will not stand up alone. I have evidence, I have witnesses, and I have warrants. We will search and find what we can, but I do not have the man himself!" He rammed his hands through his hair. "And he will try. He will try to harm those two—Choi and George. He tried to harm you—some kind of explosion, some kind of smoke ... What was it?" he shouted.

I gaped at him. The bright flare of orange frustration was back. My knee twinged and I insisted on sitting down, buying time before responding to that sudden burst of passion.

With the silvered alembic in my lap, I reached down to rub my aching knee. Solis pulled another chair around in front of mine and sat down, leaning forward, intent, with his forearms on his thighs.

"What happened?" he demanded.

"I don't know, exactly," I replied. I used his terms. "There was that explosion or whatever, smoke … It was confusing. I tried to follow Markine, to go out a door, but I didn't know which door I was going through. I fell through a trapdoor or a bit of rotten floor. I think I got into the basement, somehow. I thought I saw Markine and I chased after him. We ended up in the utility vaults, then the sewers. I lost him. Then I came back here."

"And what's that?" Solis asked, nodding at Celia's prison.

I looked at it. The alembic had acquired a patina of gunk and dirt, but I could still see the Grey mist and energy roiling around inside through the mirror tint. The truth was so bizarre no one would believe it. So why not?

"It's a ghost in a bottle," I said.

Solis narrowed his eyes, closing back down to his usual shuttered expression. His aggravated aurora dimmed to a thin orange line.

"Where did you find it?"

"In the sewer."

"While you were pursuing Mr. Markine. I'd like to have it, please."

"No."

"If it's connected to this investigation—"

"It's not anything you want."

"It is." He put out his open hands for it.

I stood up with the flask in my grip. His chair was blocking my way, but I'm slim enough and quick enough and doubted I'd have trouble slipping out, even with a dicey knee and a body covered in bruises.

"If you want it, you'll have to get a warrant."

He gave me a sharp look. I stared back, vacillating. I couldn't give him the bottle. Maybe I could put him on another track. "Ask Amanda Leaman to identify the person who argued with Mark the Monday before his death," I said. "I'll be surprised if she gives a positive ID on anyone other than Ian Markine."

Speculation flickered on his face. He hadn't forgotten the bottle, but he had other things to chase and he couldn't force me to give it to him without arresting me or getting a warrant. He couldn't intimidate me into giving it up, either.

"May I go now?" I asked.

"Where?"

"I need a change of clothes."

Solis gave a tight, annoyed nod. "I expect a more detailed statement from you, Ms. Blaine."

"Monday. If I can get the stink out of my hair by then."

TWENTY-NINE

The swirling, agitated thing in the flask drew my eye and I found it difficult not to stare at it as I drove to the Danzigers'. I wanted to get rid of the whole package—container and contents—but even this was a temporary measure. I wasn't quite sure how to be shut of it in a more permanent fashion. I hoped Ben and Mara would have some ideas.

I hadn't looked as bad as I expected after a shower. Quite a lot of my battered appearance turned out to be filth. I had to throw most of the clothes in the garbage—what was crusted on them smelled like sun-rotten salmon and didn't bear closer scrutiny—and I hoped my boots and jacket would be salvageable. I was amazed to note I hadn't cut myself beyond a few scrapes through my jeans. At least I didn't have to find out if I could develop some freaky infection from the ghosts of germs. It would have been my kind of luck to resurrect the 1918 flu or some extinct form of native-killing smallpox. Small mercies and all that platitude jazz. I'd popped a couple of anti-inflammatories, wound a light pressure bandage around my knee, and decided the shoulder would be fine on its own. I felt a bit stiff and sore, but figured I'd do.

When I started up the steps, Albert appeared beside me so fast he fizzed. He stared at the ghost-vessel, which reflected weirdly in his tiny glasses. I wondered how the bottle could have an image in the memory of a lens, but I supposed ghost-things might reflect other ghost-things just fine and maybe it was only what was inside the container that I saw in his specs. Mara opened the door and he rushed into the house, hovering behind her as if he expected me to pass him the jar like a basketball. I gave him a dirty look.

"Albert is acting very weird," I said.

"Well, then, I imagine it's that thing, isn't it," Mara answered, pointing to the bottle. "Bit intriguing, that."

"I almost lost it to a police detective," I continued, coming inside. "He thought it was evidence in this murder case."

Some kind of random thumping came from overhead. Mara didn't seem to notice.

"And isn't it?" she asked.

"Yes, but the first thing he'd do is turn it over to forensics and they'd pull the cork and let the nasty thing out again. And I didn't enjoy getting it in there in the first place."

"The poltergeist's in there? Then it worked. Glad to see we're not entirely barking at the moon. Come in to the living room. Ben's got Brian upstairs for a few minutes. We can put that up where little fingers can't get at it."

Mara put the alembic on top of a low bookshelf and wedged it in place with a pair of small, sand-filled geckos she pulled from a basket of toys nearby.

"There," she said, stepping back to admire it. "Looks rather dramatically alchemical, doesn't it?" Albert drifted up to look into the flask some more.

"It looks like a bottle full of trouble," I replied.

"So it is. How did you manage to keep the policeman's paws off it?"

We could hear Ben coming down the stairs with a heavy tread.

"I told him that if he wanted it, he'd need a warrant," I explained.

"He didn't like it, but by the time he's got the paperwork in order, it may be moot."

"We can only hope."

Ben entered, carrying a giggling Brian upside down by the legs. "Are you ready to turn over?" Ben asked.

"Nooooo!" Brian laughed. Then he stuck his tongue out and flapped it up and down, yammering, "Lalalalalalala ..." and waving his hands.

"What have you caught now?" Mara asked.

"This is the rare ebon-headed rhino-bat of the Pacific Northwest. Or we hope they're rare, because this one weighs about forty pounds and eats cheese sandwiches—which are now extinct in the wild."

Mara went to tickle her son on his exposed belly. "Shall we domesticate it, then?"

Brian shrieked with laughter.

"Fat chance," I muttered.

Mara shot me a sly look. "Quite right. It may be past hope. We'll be havin' to tickle it—"

Brian yowled, laughed, wiggled, and squirmed mightily, then shouted, "Down, down!"

"All right," Ben said, setting him gently on his head on the rug. Brian did a slow somersault and scrambled away from his mother's waving fingers to hide behind a Morris chair.

Free of the rhino-bat for a moment, Ben walked over and perused the container full of ghost.

"Wow. It worked. I can almost see something in there..."

"Just so long as it stays in there," I said.

"What are you going to do with it now?"

"I'm not sure. But it has to be kept away from—from the person who controls it." I didn't want to use his name. I was convinced of his guilt, but he was still, technically, only a suspect to the police. "We need to keep it safe until it falls apart. I thought of Carlos—"

"Oh, no!" Mara interjected. "I don't like to imagine what he might do with it."

I nodded. "Exactly why I'm here and not at his place. But I have no idea how long this thing may last."

Brian growled behind the chair. Albert flitted away from studying the thing in the jar to conspire with his playmate. Giggles bubbled up from behind the chair over a scrabbling sound.

My knee throbbed a little. I sat down on the sofa farthest from the child-infested chair. I didn't have the energy to withstand even a hug if it came at leg level.

Ben, still looking at Celia's temporary prison, said, "It should fall apart on its own, eventually. But as you say, we don't know when. The sooner the group stops giving it any energy or thought, the sooner that will happen."

"I've already put pressure on Tuckman to break the group's interest in it," I said. "I think two or three may have already cut themselves off from it, for their own reasons. It seemed smaller than the last time I saw it—though it was big enough to hurt."

"Hmm. The sooner they all do the same, the better."

"Perhaps we can speed it on the way," Mara suggested. "You might help the situation by removing that loop it's got on you."

I shook my head. "I'd rather do that last—even if it's a risk. If it does get loose, I'll have a way to find it again. Its master will snatch it back and use it if he can and I can't let that happen. He's threatened to kill two more people and he's serious."

"Oh," Mara said, raising her eyebrows in surprise. "Yes. But what else can we be at?" she continued, thinking aloud. "We can't exorcise it, but we might be able to break it down faster, I suppose."

"Maybe the group could unmake it … ," Ben started.

I shook my head and slumped deeper into the sofa. "They've already broken up and since two of them are on the hit list, getting them all together again is out of the question. Can we do anything to break it ourselves?"

Ben perked up. "It's not a regular ghost, but energy dissipation is energy dissipation no matter why you do it. Let me see what I have..."

He darted out of the room and we heard him rocketing up the attic stairs.

I blew out a long breath. Mara looked me over.

"You look all in."

"It's been a long day. And I don't think it's over yet."

"Most likely not."

Brian emerged from behind the chair, crouched over in a strange, brachiating posture.

"Oh, what are you up to now, little boy?" Mara asked.

"I's a rhino-bat!"

"So I hear. What do rhino-bats do?"

"Fly, fly, fly!" Brian yelled, jumping up and flapping his arms; then he ran off around the room with his "wings" spread wide, unusually quiet as he soared around the furniture without a single "graah."

As Brian was running in and out of the living room, Ben came back with a thick book.

"OK. I found it. There's kind of a standard for dissipating energy entities—which is what this is. It's not specific and it might not do the job completely so long as anyone's feeding it, but it should break the thing down a lot."

I sat up straighter. "What's the routine?"

Ben flipped the tome open as Albert swooped by him with Brian charging after. Boy and phantom dove back into the bat cave behind the Morris chair as Ben started to paraphrase.

"According to this—and this is the third reference to this process—you can disperse a ghost of this type by scattering its property and destroying its image. It draws strength from those reminders of its existence and once they are no longer there, or moved far apart from one another, the ghost has no center to cling to. It can't hold itself together without a core and it will dissipate."

"There's a power line feeding this thing," I reminded them.

"True," Mara replied, her face pinched in thought. "But it was pulled from its proper place. It will want to move back to its original alignment. If you break down as much of the 'home' environment as you can, the power line should start to move back."

"OK, maybe it will work. What's the process, exactly?" I knew things like this were never as simple as they sounded.

Ben looked back into his book. "Oh." He paused. "It doesn't say. Just 'disperse the property and burn the image with proper ceremony.' But no word on the ceremony. Mara ... ?"

She shook her head. "Not the slightest idea."

They both looked at me. My stomach dropped. "Not Carlos," I sighed.

"Afraid so. He's the expert," Mara said.

"I think he's running out of charity for me. And he may want to take the entity himself."

"I'll go with you," Mara offered.

Brian flapped past again.

"Oh, no, you won't. Not this time," I said. "If he's willing it won't be because you came and held my hand and called in favors. And I don't want to hear the argument between you and Ben over it, either."

I stood up. "I'll leave the ghost-bottle with you while I talk to Carlos. That way he can't get it from me. And I'll see what I can do about dismantling the séance room. That's the closest thing there is to Celia's 'home and possessions.' I'll call you when I'm done with Carlos and we can go on from there. OK?"

Mara nodded, a satisfied smile on her face.

Ben closed his book on his finger. "All right. We'll be up."

I nodded and headed back out, poking my cell phone.

Tuckman was not interested in helping me. He refused flat out to dismantle the séance room or to help me do it, in spite of the best arguments I could muster.

When the boss stonewalls, go for the secretary. I sat in the Rover by the side of the road and dialed.

Denise Francisco sounded like she had a cold when she answered her cell phone.

"What?"

"Hi, Frankie, it's Harper Blaine."

"Oh. You were at the funeral, weren't you?"

"Yeah."

"Were you, like, close enough to hear it?"

"Hear what?"

She snuffled before answering. "Mr. Gorgeous—you know, Ian, the looker?—he threatened his girlfriend, the Chinese girl, Ana. She dumped him for the Indian guy."

I sighed. Some people regress under stress. Frankie had bounced back to fifteen. "I don't know anything about it," I said. "But I do know you're the one to call to get anything important done and that's why I'm calling."

"Oh?" She made a noise like a goose stuck in a mangle—blowing her nose, I guessed. When she spoke again, her voice was clearer. "What needs doing?"

"We have to break up the séance room."

She paused. "Does Tuck know this?"

"He knows, but he won't do it. The project's shut down, right?"

"Yup. So … you want to break up the room so they won't get back together again?"

"That's it."

"Why?"

"Do you want the truth or a plausible lie?"

"I love it when they lie to me—but tell me the truth, 'cause you're not my type."

"Celia needs to go away. Tuck agrees, but the way to make Celia go is to break up her things and Tuck doesn't want to do it. So, since Tuck won't do the right thing, I'm asking you to help me do it. Before someone else gets hurt."

"You mean 'hurt' like that thing with Ice Queen Stahlqvist, or 'hurt' like ... dead?"

"They're both bad."

I could hear her draw her next breath. "OK. When do you want to do it?"

"Tomorrow. Can you do that? Can you get the key?"

"I'm entirely sweatless. How 'bout ten o'clock? It's a Christian school, so chapel service is from ten to ten forty-five every Sunday and no one will be in the other buildings. Good?"

"Good. I'll meet you at St. John."

"Done deal. See ya."

THIRTY

There was a different clerk at the counter of Adult Fantasies that night: a slim young guy with curly blond hair cut so close to the scalp it had become a riot of cowlicks. As I walked toward him, the chilly reek of vampire hit me. I stopped and squinted at him, seeing a cloud of red-swirled smoke dancing around him through the Grey. His black T-shirt read, "Don't make me send my flying monkeys after you." His violet eyes sparked when he caught me reading the words and he smiled with an expanse of sharp white teeth.

"Hey, Harper."

I hadn't recognized him until I saw the unusual eyes; he'd changed a lot from the crippled newbie vampire I'd found in a parking garage. "Cameron. How's it going?"

"Mostly it's going good—except for the occasional dead guy. Carlos is a demanding teacher, and I ... I miscalculated on that one. I really owe you for checking him out."

A big, ugly pause swelled between us.

He tilted his head side to side with a wry expression. "It freaks you out that I killed someone, doesn't it?"

"Yeah. I remember when it would have freaked you out, too."

He nodded, eyebrows rising. "Yeah. Sometimes I forget you're not like me. We went through so much together it feels like you ought to know everything I know."

"I don't want to."

"I get that. But this you should know—I didn't kill him, or he'd have sat up again the next night. It's kind of a complicated thing—"

I put up my hand to stop him. "Please don't explain it right now."

He looked surprised, blinking, then shrugged. "OK."

"I just need to see Carlos."

"He's out, but he said you can wait in the office, if you want." Cam pointed, a thick scar flashing white on the underside of his wrist. He noticed my gaze, but said nothing about it, just dropping his hand and giving me a vague smile that kept his paranormal presence in check. "He should be back soon."

I nodded and headed for the storeroom door, banishing speculation about the weal on Cameron's forearm. What Carlos was teaching him, and how, was none of my business and nothing I wanted to know.

I could hear the thumping of sexually suggestive music from above as I wedged myself into the chair in the stockroom office. It was a few minutes past eight o'clock on a Saturday night and the peep show upstairs was just hitting its stride. I considered propping my foot on one of the boxes to relieve my irritated knee, but thought I'd rather not display such obvious disability to a vampire, whenever Carlos got down to me. Cameron had made no comment on it, though he must have seen it, just as I'd seen his wrist.

I forced my mind from that and wondered what level of trust was implied in being allowed to lurk in the gloom with a safe full of quarters and small used bills, in a room filled with boxes packed with thousands of dollars worth of sex toys and bondage gear. Of course, it could always mean that Carlos had put some sort of necromantic curse on the goods that would reduce a thief to a lump of rotting flesh.

I shivered at the thought and dropped a hand onto my knee to check for heat. If rot was imminent I'd expect it there first.

I closed my eyes a moment, acknowledging the day's exertions. I'd been in and out of the Grey three times since morning, brushed it again just minutes ago in Cam's presence, and felt close to exhaustion now. My knee and shoulder ached, though not much worse than a lot of nights when I'd still been dancing for a living. The mild headache and vague nausea were more upsetting, since I associated those with Grey things, for which there was no pill. The nausea worsened and a chill pressed upon me just before the door opened.

I opened my eyes to see Carlos glowering down at me in speculation. His gaze rested on my knee a moment.

"Your quarry plays rough."

"You could say that." I paused as he moved inside and closed the door. "Cameron seems well..."

He waved that aside as he stepped back to the desk but didn't sit. "I have very little time for you tonight." He kept his eyes on me, but without the ire he'd displayed last time. Now he was merely impatient.

"I don't need much. I've found the master of the poltergeist and trapped the thing itself in a bottle. I don't believe that's much of a solution—"

His eyes gleamed. "A respite only."

I nodded and went on. "In theory, lack of input from the group will weaken it enough to dissipate, but I don't think I can wait that long. It has been suggested that dispersing its property and burning its image will break it down faster, but that's a guess. I have to get rid of this thing as fast as possible and you're the expert. Will you tell me what to do?"

He rumbled, thinking, no doubt sizing the situation up for his advantage. "Dismantling the setting where it was made—its place— will weaken it only."

"Better than nothing."

He inclined his head in acknowledgement. "This entity is no true ghost, so I can't help you in this directly. So long as the thing's master continues to feed it, it will maintain its cohesion. Even while it is in your bottle. So long as he finds it useful, it will remain, even if the others withdraw from it. It will be weaker without them, but to get rid of it requires an act of destruction. Its true existence lies in the Grey, so it must be dismantled there. That falls to you."

I gave him a tight, insincere smile. "I didn't want to hear that."

He shrugged, rolling black clouds of cold from his shoulders.

"The guy who controls this thing is a psycho and he's loose in the city somewhere, gorging himself on the thought of revenge as soon as he can get this thing back. I don't know if he realizes it's gone yet…"

"It isn't gone. Only blocked. But he knows that, the same way you would know if all of this"—he swept his hand around my head, gathering up strands and shreds of ghost and Grey—"were gone from your sight."

He caught my sour expression and looked amused at it. I shook it off. "Then I hope he's waiting for it to come back and not deciding to go ahead without it. I'm guessing that he's stalking his ex-girlfriend and lying in wait near her home. As soon as he has an opportunity, he'll try to kill her."

"All the better reason to dismantle this entity soon," Carlos replied. "He gains skill every time he uses it and draws more power, through its connection to the ley line. Here's what you will do."

He sat down at the desk and dashed notes on a sheet of loose paper, talking as he did. "You control the entity for now and it won't interfere. First, destroy the artifacts—all that pertains to it, everything its contributors have branded as its own. Smash them, break them, burn them. If they cannot be destroyed, they must be separated. Take everything from the room and spread it far and wide."

"I've got someone to help me with that tomorrow."

He nodded without looking up. An itching urgency rippled through the Grey to me. "You will have to isolate the weakened entity in the Grey to dismantle it. Talk to your witch friend. Request a charm from her that traps time—she'll know how to make one. With it, you will create a trap for the entity and decant it from the container into the trap. While it is held there, you can dismantle it. This instruction will help you. The charm won't last long. You will have to open the creature and step into its center—this construct appears chaotic but it is not, and only when you are in the center will you be able to see the structure. You must sort through the entity's structure to find the control strand that holds and gathers it. Without its control strand in place, it will have no cohesion."

He looked up suddenly and caught my gaze with his own. Knives and arctic wind cut me and my stomach heaved. "You should recognize the control—it's like your own connection to power. While the structure is open, the construct will drain more than simple energy if it can. Be very careful of your own connection to this creature—it will attempt to feed on whatever is at hand and it will fight you. There will be limited time. The charm can only hold the creature for a while, so be swift. If you're still inside when the charm expires, the structure will try to return to its original shape, trapping you within. I don't know what will happen to you if it does. It may cripple you. It may drive you insane."

He paused, thinking again.

"I suppose the worst-case scenario is that I'd be dead," I muttered.

Carlos grinned a wolf's smile of white daggers. "Merely and simply dead might be preferable. But this course is the only chance you have. You can step out of the structure at any time while the charm still works, but once it burns out, the entity will close and return to its master. It will be much wilier the next time you meet—unless you can break its master's control. Then it will be ignorant and easily tricked. But I doubt you'll have another opportunity to take it. Better to attack it now, while it's stupid."

He finished scribbling and handed me the sheets he'd filled with long, spiked script.

"How am I supposed to dismantle it? I don't see anything about tools here," I said, glancing through his instructions.

He scowled. "With your hands."

"Grab onto those power strands and just ... pull them apart?" I didn't like that idea. "I'm not even sure I can."

"You can do more than you realize," Carlos stated.

But did I want to? I had a bad feeling that touching the power lines of the Grey—let alone manhandling them—would effect yet more changes, and I'd never been happy with any change the Grey served up to me. A dozen other thoughts occurred to me about the possible repercussions of trailing through the Grey, looking for a place to trap Celia long enough to break it down to its constituent parts.

"I've been ducking in and out of the Grey all week and it's not entirely inconspicuous," I objected. "This may draw a little attention, even if I can find a quiet place with the right kind of Grey landscape to do it in."

He looked amused. "Tomorrow is All Hallows Eve. No one will find your actions so strange on that date."

"All right," I acknowledged. "But there is one more problem. Even if I dismantle this one, what's to stop this young psychopath from building up another, or co-opting some loose entity if he runs across one? The Grey's a free-for-all of monstrosities for anyone who knows how to reach in and grab one. And if he doesn't know now, he'll figure it out damned quick."

Carlos inclined his head and the desk lamp's sickly glow unveiled the monster's mask. And then he smiled one of his ice-light-on-steel smiles. "He'll have to be broken of the habit."

I shuddered at the sound of that. I might have no choice but to let Carlos at Ian, but I had to try to maintain control. Starting now. "He'll have to be distracted first," I reminded. "Once the genie is out of the bottle, he'll know and he'll try to use it."

Carlos had narrowed his eyes and acquired an unpleasant Mona Lisa quality. "I'd like to meet this young man…"

"That doesn't surprise me. If you can get to him, you're welcome to try."

He chuckled and the room rolled. "Show me where he is." He stood up, expectant and looming over me like a storm.

I kept my seat. "I don't know that yet. And I am too tired to fight this thing again tonight. You may have just crawled out of the crypt at sundown, but I've been up to my ass in alligators for twelve hours. Besides, there are other things to do first."

He lowered his unpleasant gaze. "True. Tomorrow will be … strange."

I couldn't—and didn't wish to—imagine what Carlos considered strange. "No doubt. Give me a direct number to call you when things are ready—telephone tag through Cameron is annoying."

Another seismic chuckle moved the room and he handed me a card from the pocket of his leather jacket. I refused his offered hand and got out of the chair myself. I had no wish to visit hell, and touching his hand would have been the express route for me. He found that amusing, too, but he walked me to the door and let me out.

"I look forward to tomorrow."

"I'll bet," I replied.

His mouth quirked, and he plucked the bright strand of Grey that linked me to Celia. "Take care, Blaine." Then he turned away and returned to the home of live girls and undead clerks.

THIRTY-ONE

The PNU campus had an eerie quiet on a Sunday morning, a wrong sort of emptiness, as if even the ghosts had gone to chapel and the buildings held their breath. Frankie was more punctual for subterfuge than work and we were in room twelve of St. John Hall on the dot of ten with an equipment cart standing in the corridor. We disturbed the breathless stillness with directed intensity.

Frankie—almost unrecognizable without makeup and wearing plain brown jeans—stood in the room and surveyed it with expert speed. "OK. Table first. It doesn't fit through the door, so we'll have to take off the legs. Luckily, I have tools."

She darted to the cart and snatched a pair of large screwdrivers that she stuffed into her back pockets. Then we flipped the table onto its back on the rug, crushing a thin, pulsing wad of energy lingering there. For a while, we struggled with the legs until Frankie lost her temper.

"You are a very bad table," she muttered, standing up. Then she heel-kicked the nearest leg with a blow that knocked the wooden piece right off its bracket. Wires and bits of twisted metal bracket trailed from the break like entrails. "Ha! So much for you, table!" she crowed. She proceeded to kick the rest of the legs off with vicious glee. We carted the parts down to the back door and loaded them into the bed of a borrowed pickup truck.

Back upstairs, Frankie unloaded the bookshelves and sorted the contents into two piles. PNU property went on the cart; the rest went into Dumpsters in the parking lot or into either the pickup or my Rover. The end tables by the sofa met the same fate as the table legs—kicked to splinters and carried away.

"You're enjoying this a lot," I observed as we puffed back upstairs again. My knee was still a bit out of sorts and I was noticing the exertion more than usual.

"You bet! I feel like I'm finally freeing myself of Tuck. It feels great, tearing up this stuff."

"How's Tuckman going to take it when he finds out?"

"Oh, he can French-kiss a whale for all I care. I'll tell him the dean ordered it and he can go argue with old baggy-pants himself. That'll win him all kinds of points." She cackled. "He is so on thin ice since his last evaluation. He said something snippy to the dean's wife at the psych association dinner the other night, too, I hear. I am reveling in his imminent downfall."

A prime example of a woman scorned. Frankie had never said what Tuckman had done to lose her respect, but it sounded like he was going to regret it.

We tore the electronics out of the rug, hauled away the couch, and redistributed the chairs to needy rooms. Frankie hauled the monitors and machines out of the observation room and stacked them on the cart. At last we were down to the photos and posters on the wall and Ken's portrait of Celia. I collected them and put them into a metal trash can.

"Do you have a cigarette lighter?" I asked.

"No," she replied. "That's a bad habit I don't have. Besides, you don't want to burn those here. It'll set off the smoke alarm. There's probably some matches in the kitchen, though."

We carried the rug and the trash can downstairs to the parking lot.

While Frankie wrestled the partially shredded rug into the truck bed, I snooped through the kitchen.

I returned with a couple of strike-anywhere wooden matches. I picked up the portrait and gave it one last look. It was remarkable how much life Ken had put into the picture. Celia looked vibrant. I set the corner of the portrait on fire, muttering a few words Carlos had written down for me.

The paper wouldn't catch fire at first; then flame leapt bright onto the inks and smoked, sending tendrils into the air that were not entirely normal, glimmering with sparks of uncanny light.

I dropped the page into the can and the fire flared higher, catching on the other papers with a gasping sound. Then something wailed, a high-pitched keening that spiraled upward into pain. A shaft of yellow shot from the burning pages, smoky and tortured, writhing. I recoiled in unpleasant surprise. A figure flickered in the burst of eldritch illumination, screaming in horror and pain, twisted in panic as the flames ate at it—a young blond woman, dressed in a uniform, her hair rolled back off her face. The fire roared and burned red, then subsided, taking the terrible vision with it.

Frankie gaped at me over the thin curls of subsiding smoke. I thought I looked the same. We both turned away from the trash can. Frankie returned to the building to fetch the equipment cart. I picked up the can and walked to the far side of the parking lot to empty the ashes into a different Dumpster. I carried the can back up to the room.

Frankie had just picked up the potted plant from the windowsill when I walked in. She brushed past me awkwardly, avoiding my gaze, and went into the hall. I looked around the empty room. Only dust and a faint, fading trail of yellow energy remained. Deeper, I could just glimpse the regular blue and yellow power lines of the grid, subsiding at Nature's pace into their normal shapes, pulling back from their unwonted displacement.

Frankie preceded me downstairs with the keys and the potted plant in her hands. Once back in the lot, she started loading the equipment from the cart into the cab of the truck.

"OK," she said at last. "I'm going to take the equipment to Tuck's office and stack it there so he can't say his data was destroyed. Then I'm going to dump this stuff in a couple different places, right?"

"Right. At least two, as far apart as possible, more if you can."

"Got it." She started to get up into the truck, then swung back down. "Hey, what was that thing in the fire?"

I felt an involuntary shiver. "I … guess it was Celia."

She looked young. "Is she gone, then?"

"I think she will be soon," I answered.

Frankie nodded. "Good. I definitely don't approve of Stygian nightmares. And hey—I'll call you and let you know what happens with Tuck, OK?"

"OK. Be careful, Frankie."

"I'm the invincible queen of the coffeepot," she said, climbing behind the wheel of the borrowed pickup. "I can't be routed by a ham-fisted Narcissus of a psychologist—or his fakey poltergeist. Sterner men than Gartner Tuckman tremble at the thought of my wrath—or they ought to." She slammed the door and started up the engine. A wave, a manic grin, and she was gone.

I drove the Rover to two different transfer stations to get rid of the detritus of the séance room. Then I went home and put some ice on my knee and let the ferret out for a romp. Satisfied tiredness settled on me—a pleasant change from the slightly drained and weighted feeling I'd been having since I'd gotten tangled up in Celia.

It seemed as if the first half of Carlos's instructions had worked as described. Now I only had to find Ian so Carlos could distract him while I tore apart the remains of the entity.

I was cozily snuggled into one of the sofas in the Danzigers' living room a few hours later while Ben lay on the floor in front of the mantel with his feet up in the air. Brian was "flying" by lying on his father's upraised soles and making whooshing noises, interspersed with giggles.

Mara came into the room with the stoppered flask in her hands. "I'm sorry. We had to stash it. Brian and Albert have been fascinated with the thing and they've been at all sorts of pains to get it. Can't imagine what they want it for, but I thought it best to move it somewhere secure. It's been in the old dry sink on the back porch since bedtime with a wallopin' great spell over the top. Someone"—she cut a glare toward Albert, who was flickering nearby—"was tryin' to levitate it until I put a stop to that. It's a good thing we'll be seein' the last of it soon. I'm done in by keepin' these two away from it."

"If this goes right, you'll never see it again," I said, putting the flask down on the table next to me. The grim substance inside seemed smaller already, simmering with less violence than the day before.

With the stopper in place, I couldn't see the connecting threads and count them; I was sure there would be fewer now than a few days ago. I had seen Patricia's thread crumble away, and the absence of the Stahlqvists at the funeral made me think they, too, had broken their connection to the entity. I had entertained the small hope that the construct would have broken down with the destruction of the séance room, but it hadn't. It had always been able to operate with as few as four participants and the way it had harassed the individuals the past few days convinced me it no longer needed that critical mass to hold together. Even though the original power line was drifting back to its proper place, the entity was still connected to the grid and to Ian's control.

"What are you planning to do about it?" Ben asked.

"I assume you concocted some plan with Carlos, then," Mara added.

"Yeah," I replied. "It's already started. I got one of the assistants to help me break down the séance room and spread everything around. When I burned Celia's portrait, we saw a face in the flames."

"That would be the artificial personality—the sort of soul the art-ist put into it—going. That's good and bad, though, as it now has no personality of its own, but only what its master lends it."

"Which will be as smart and as crazy as he is—and there's no doubt the guy is smart," I said. "I'm hoping that he's getting arrogant, though. He certainly seemed to be. He makes mistakes when he's feel-ing cocky."

"So it's definitely one of the young men?" Ben asked.

"Yeah. Solis said the whole thing revolved around a woman and for a moment I thought that might mean it was one of the women who controlled it, but the person who threw it at me was one of the guys."

"So what are you going to do about it? Do the cops know?" Ben grunted as Brian squirmed around.

"Solis knows who and I'm pretty sure he's keeping a close eye on the next potential targets—he didn't say so, but he'd be stupid not to, and Solis is far from stupid. But he's not going to be looking for the entity and I'm not sure how close the controller has to be to use it the way he did on Mark. It's possible he'd be outside any surveillance area. I think I can track him down, though—he still has a connection to the entity that will tend to point to it, like a compass. Mine does, so I assume his does, too," I explained. "He's got to be in one of two places—he likes to be near the victim. He gets a kick out of seeing what he can do. If I take the bottle with Celia in it to both those areas, I should be able to spot his control thread trying to hook up to the entity even through the container—it's not a perfect trap, after all."

"Then what?" Mara asked.

Albert drifted over to Brian, and the little boy laughed too loudly to speak over.

"Down now," he demanded.

As Ben was settling him back on his feet, I started to answer Mara.

"Once I've found him, Carlos will help me distract Celia's controller while I dismantle the entity."

"Carlos is going to help you? I can't say I'd fancy another round of workin' with him myself."

Brian took off, chasing after Albert and making his rhino roar.

"I'm not expecting to enjoy it, either," I replied, "but he can't take out the entity—it's never been alive, so it's never died. That means he can't get a handle on it, unless someone else attached to it dies or we kill something, and I think that would be a bad idea. Mark didn't hang around to leave a convenient connection. According to Carlos, his life was snuffed out so fast there was very little residue. He's told me how to take the thing apart in the Grey. I seem to be the only person with the right skills for the job. What I need from you is a charm that will stick the ghost in one spot for a while."

Ben followed his son out into the hall.

"A tangle," said Mara.

"What?"

"There are several ways to bind something, but most are spells you cast on the person or thing. A tangle's a portable sort of charm—rather like flypaper. Where you drop it becomes sticky for a while."

"That's it," I said. "How do I get it to work?"

"In this case, you'll want to create a time loop with the tangle, to hold the ghost a while, so you'll have to be dropping the tangle on a repeater ghost to create the trap and then pouring your poltergeist onto that time loop. That loop's like a bear trap—as soon as your poltergeist enters the loop, it'll grab on to it and hold it still in time until the energy of the ghost is dissipated, or burns through the loop."

"How long is that?"

"Usually an hour or so—depends on the strength of the ghost and the tangle. I'll make a good one, though."

"How long will it take to make it?"

"A few minutes. I'll have to go fetch some cuttings from the garden. I'll nip out. You keep your feet up—that knee still looks a mite tetchy."

I snorted. "I'll stay put—I'm conserving my pain threshold for later."

She laughed a single whoop and left me alone in the living room.

For a few minutes, all was calm, wrapped in the protective spells of the house. I took several long, slow breaths, letting tension flow away on the exhale. I closed my eyes for a moment. Which was a mistake.

Shouting a "Graaaaahh!" the rhino-boy galloped into the room with Albert right behind. Ben was several feet farther back.

Albert circled Brian, who tucked his head down and charged.

Albert wafted backward into the end table by my elbow.

Brian rammed his head against the polished blond oak.

The table rocked.

I swung my arm to grab …

the bottle …

fell …

crashed …

smashed.

A storm of mirrored glass whirled into the air with a shriek that shook the house. Hot yellow and bloodred, the entity gathered itself and sped toward the door.

Brian dropped to the floor with a yowl.

Mara rushed in holding a small circle of greenery in her hand and stopped, wide-eyed, in the doorway, looking back and forth between the shattered glass in which her son had plopped himself and the blazing shape that roared past her.

I jumped up and started after the entity, my knee throbbing in protest of the sudden movement. I made it to the sidewalk before I lost all sight of the entity.

"Goddamn it!" I spat.

The thin yellow strand of energy that linked me to the entity sprang taut, pointing southeast. Toward Chinatown.

I dashed back into the house, grabbing for my bag and jacket.

"I have to follow it!"

Mara shoved the little circlet of plant material into my hands. "It's not as good as I'd like—it'll only last about half an hour—but it'll do. Be careful of the thorns."

But it was too late; they'd already pierced into my palm. I shoved the ring of blackberry vine into my coat pocket and whirled to pursue the ghost that wasn't a ghost to Chinatown.

THIRTY-TWO

I had parked the Rover on Jackson and started on foot into the real heart of Chinatown. The thin yellow strand in front of me pointed mostly south and a bit east. I came down Maynard, past the red-and-yellow painted front of the Wing Luke Asian Museum, to Hing Hay Park on the corner of King Street.

This short stretch of King, from the railroad terminals at Fourth to the current freeway overpass that soared over the remains of Ninth, was the place the Chinese had resettled after the Seattle Fire and the end of the Exclusion Act. The whole stretch of buildings ahead and to the east had been built by Chinese businessmen between 1890 and 1930. I paused a moment to get my bearings and watched a troupe of kids—black, brown, and yellow, wearing Halloween masks—playing on the wet, rust-colored bricks of the park, ducking in and out of the red-pillared pavilion, to the annoyance of a couple of old men playing checkers on the stone tables inside. I heard the kids whoop and chatter, skipping away as the men waved impatient hands at them. Teenagers and young men grown too old too fast gathered in clutches around the benches and stone tables at the edge of the park, talking trash in half a dozen languages.

The stores and restaurants—shabby, but proud—were busy with

the Sunday dim sum crowd. Visiting Caucasians goggled along the streets, standing out, pale in the mixed throng, to the China Gate, Four Seas, Sun Ya; ducked into Pink Godzilla for Japanese video games; carried tinted bakery boxes or bags from Uwajimaya and the Kinokuniya bookstore bulging with imported food and manga, or clever bribes for the evening's invasion of trick-or-treaters. The odor of food and fortune cookies, garbage and wet asphalt mingled with the sounds of Sunday chatter and random music in snatches from every opening door.

I checked the compasslike thread of Grey.

Ana and her parents lived a block to the southwest, as the crow flies, but the thin strand of yellow pointed southeast. I went east along King and stopped again on the next corner.

Now the strand looped around and pointed back toward Maynard. I turned, looking up and down the street. I spotted a narrow alley behind an apartment building. A sign at the mouth of the alley on the south side of King directed traffic to an aquarium and pet store. CHILDREN WELCOME it declared.

I started to stroll across the street against the light and drew up short as a blue and white SPD patrol car rolled around the corner from Maynard. I watched the car come toward me, then turn south again onto Seventh, its occupants looking intense and stern.

I crossed the street and strolled back toward the alley, pausing again at the door to an import store beside the pet store sign. I pretended to read the sign on the door as I checked the yellow strand again.

Due south. Ian was down the alley somewhere. I poked my head around the corner. The alley was only half the length of the block on the west side, the far end being a parking lot for one of the restaurants. Only a few back doors opened on the rest. It seemed an unlikely place for a pet store.

I started down the alley. It was just wide enough for a delivery truck to get down and I could see a gouge high up in the green-painted tile on my left from where one hadn't been careful enough. A gold carp wind sock fluttered over the door to the pet shop, flicking a desultory tail over the alley with each gust of food-scented breeze. Silvery shades of Grey flickered in the shadows of padlocked doorways as I walked toward the fish.

From the green wall on my left, a deep doorway with once-impressive double doors—secured with a rusty chain and aging padlock—and a rank of glass brick gave up an unpleasant gleam in shadow. I walked past and entered the pet store.

Pretending interest in a tank of goldfish, I looked down at the Grey tether around my neck. It pointed back toward whatever lay behind those chained doors. I started to sink toward it and felt a ghastly wash of emotions and deadly cold.

"Can I help you?"

I jerked back from the repulsive sensation and turned to face the man behind me. He was slender, about fifty-five to sixty, and wore a faded green bib apron over his clothes. Thick, unfashionable glasses magnified his eyes so he seemed to stare through me.

"I'm just looking," I said.

He inclined his head. "Well, we have lots of fish, lots of aquarium equipment, if you like. I have some new goldfish in the back, some little birds, too. Do you keep fish?"

"No. I have a ferret. I'm afraid she'd eat them."

"Oh, yes. Curious and hungry. That's the ferret." He started to walk deeper into the narrow little shop, into a half-gloom lit by the glow of the fish tank lights.

I followed him.

"How long has this shop been here?" I asked. "Looks like it's been here forever."

"Oh … almost thirty years. Fish and birds are good pets for apartments. Fish are very beautiful." He stopped beside a tank full of brilliantly spotted fish with bulbous bodies and bulging eyes, trailing long fins that floated in the water like the garments of drowned women.

I stopped to admire them. Or try to. They floated, serene, then swam in sudden, wiggling bursts: startled fishy geishas flouncing their kimonos. The sign beside them read VEILTAIL DEMEKIN. They were very expensive.

I looked up and caught the man studying me.

I smiled. "What's in the shop next door?"

His eyes narrowed and his expression went cold. "Nothing."

"What used to be there, then?"

He drew back from me, stiff and disapproving. "That was the Wah Mee. A very bad thing happened there."

"I'm sorry. I didn't know. What bad thing?"

He sighed, shaking his head. "You should let it alone—people here still hurt over it. You should go now—go on. Get out of my shop." He advanced on me, picking up a mop from a nearby bucket.

I hurried out and stopped against the wall farther down the alley. The shopkeeper stood in his doorway and glared at me for a while, then went back inside, closing the door. Now I really wanted to know what had happened behind those padlocked doors. The entity was in there, which meant Ian was in there. I didn't dare walk past the row of glass brick again. If Ian could see out of the scratched, pitted glass, he might recognize me and bolt before I could return with Carlos. I studied the indentation in the wall that formed the recessed doorway. There was another narrow door between it and the aquarium shop—perhaps the back door to the import shop or to the mysterious space itself. I drifted away down the alley to Weller, thinking how I could find out more about the padlocked shop.

I headed toward Sixth on Weller, thinking. The mysterious doors were almost in a straight line with the back of Ana's building, a mere block and a half from the front door. The shop, Ana's home, and my truck's parking spot to the north on Jackson made a near-perfect equilateral triangle. As I walked, distracted with geometry, something crept into my mind.

I'd seen two more patrol cars pass by—one on Maynard, another on Sixth—and been passed by a duo of foot patrolmen. I went into a tea shop on the corner of Sixth and Weller and ordered a cup of bubble tea. Sitting at the bar, facing Sixth, I lingered over the thick, sweet concoction and gazed out the window.

I could see the front of Ana's building from my seat. Another customer—a Filipino man with neatly trimmed hair—read a newspaper and nursed a pot of tea. I took my cup and slipped back outside.

I strolled, looking in shopwindows, gazing around like a tourist. I didn't spot Solis, but I guessed he or his partner was nearby. Halloween and Sunday shoppers notwithstanding, there were too many cops and too many people with time to kill loitering near the Fujisaka condominiums. I kept walking and checking for another hour. I stopped in a bakery called Cake House My Favorite and glanced out the floor-to-ceiling windows before I moved on to the hobby shop next to Pink Godzilla to watch the street through the displays of Japanese collectible toys and video game posters. Then I looped back down past Union Station, the Metro stop, and the Asian Antique Emporium on Fifth, back across through the new Uwajimaya Village, and past the Nisei apartments.

The patrols were loose, but the clutches of loiterers were concentrated within a block of the Fujisaka. I suspected there were cameras and telescopes trained on the front door from one of the empty shop spaces in the old Uwajimaya building and from one of the buildings on Maynard. That's what I would have done if I'd been Solis—guard the doors at front and back, put patrols on the street and outlying watchers on the corners, if I could get them. If there had been no other major crimes this week, the detective pool would be available to assist him for a while. Ian's threats against Ana and Ken were only twenty-four hours old and serious enough to warrant attention for a few days. At some point Solis would have to drop the assistants and maintain the surveillance himself, but not yet.

And Ian wasn't likely to wait very long. He had the entity back now, and his fury was still hot enough to make him impetuous. I only hoped he'd wait until after dark to attack. It seemed likely, since the entity was weakened and it made sense to let it recharge a bit. Also, the confusion of costumed children and party-seeking teens would cover any sally Ian might make to view the results. He could sneak out into the open end of the alley and see the back of the Fujisaka building, hear the sirens on Sixth, watch the confounded police emerge from their useless ambush. No one would look his way for a few minutes and he could slip away into one of the half-empty buildings or under the freeway to Little Saigon, a few blocks farther to Rainier Valley or up to First Hill by routes no car could take. If the cops didn't spot him at once, he'd ease into the mess of Seattle's jumbled downtown neighborhoods and vanish.

My knee ached with a low throb, demanding rest and ice. I headed back to my truck.

I looked up the Wah Mee when I got back to my office—I had several hours to kill until dark—and recoiled from the information.

There was a lot of history to the Wah Mee. It had started out as a speakeasy, then been a swanky nightspot when the International District swung all night and hosted some of the biggest names in jazz. By 1983 it had become a little seedier, and was then a private gambling club for local Chinese business owners. The night of February 18, 1983, three young Chinese men had taken fourteen of their neighbors prisoner in the club and robbed and shot them all. Only one survived. "The Wah Mee Massacre" remained the worst mass murder in Washington history. But most people didn't remember it had happened and some, like the pet shop owner, didn't want to be reminded of the community's betrayal by three of its own.

*   *   *

"The bottle is broken and the genie is loosed," Carlos rumbled. His disquiet was infectious, hitting me in cold, black waves. "Unfortunate." I'd brought him up to speed as I drove toward Chinatown.

"Yes, it is," I agreed, refusing to apologize. "We'll have to adapt. The good news is that I found Ian—or at least where he's holed up. He's just outside the police surveillance zone, but there are patrols both on foot and in cars. We'll have to move in from the east with care and get through the door fast. There are two doors on the alley. Both are padlocked, but Ian must have gotten through one of them. There used to be a door on King Street, but that area's an import shop now and cut off from the old club. I think I could make my way in, but it's not a route you can take and I'd rather stick together, if we can."

He continued to growl in the back of his throat for a few moments. "All right. Since you cannot simply decant the entity onto your trap, you'll have to lay the trap and lure it in."

"This isn't going to be easy, is it?"

"It never was. But this will be riskier initially and our time will be shorter. The police will be curious if we give them cause."

"Yeah. And the detective in charge knows me on sight."

"Complicated."

"We'll just stay out of his sight until we're done. Then you leave and I'll take the fall for the break-in."

Carlos fell silent for the rest of the drive.

I parked the Rover under the freeway and stopped Carlos before he got out. I handed him a package I'd picked up.

"It's a cape," I said.

He raised an eyebrow at me.

"We have about three blocks to go down a major street with cops patrolling it," I explained. "It's Halloween, so we're going in costume—no one will notice—so I figured, why not dress the part?" I was going out on a rickety limb, but it had seemed like good camouflage at the time.

"I see. And what are you?"

I held up the fluffy ears on their headband. "I'm a cat burglar." I already had the all-black outfit on. I got out of the Rover and put the ears on, then clipped the tail to my belt. I hoped it wouldn't foul my pistol if I needed it. I stowed the spare clip and my cell phone in my jacket pockets and locked the truck.

Carlos's natural menace was not diminished by the cheap polyester cape. Six feet plus of Iberian glower and a palpable badass aura went a long way. I pulled on gloves as we strode down the street toward Ian's hiding place.

Small monsters were parading on the streets amid an upwelling of the unseen. The wet air boiled with ghosts and the world felt slippery beneath my feet. We came to the corner and I stopped, glancing down to be sure the thin yellow strand still pointed into the alley.

"It hasn't moved yet," I muttered to Carlos.

"It will soon. Something is shifting toward death."

Maybe it was the suggestion, or maybe I caught it, too, but a frisson ran up my spine and the street seemed to ripple. My bones itched. I cast my gaze around, looking for cops, and led the way down the alley when I saw none. Their attention was in front of them, not behind.

We drifted down the darkness to the chained doors. Carlos started to reach for the lock, then drew back. "This is the Wah Mee."

"Yes," I answered. "You know about it?"

"It drew me here. I can feel them still. The thirteen."

"And Ian?"

His brows drew down. "Yes. Beyond this wall. He revels in it. He doesn't know what drew him here, but he feels the bloody carnage. He is feeding the entity on the death within."

His frown became a black storm of anger. I pulled a small fold of the Grey between us, pushing the horror of him back.

"Carlos," I begged in a whisper. "We have to move."

He touched the chain, sliding his hands down to the crusted pad-lock. His fingers found a broken link and he lifted the lock away. The defaced and weathered mahogany door pulled open with a thin sigh, as if relieved by our presence.

We eased into the vestibule. The door swung shut. Before us was another pair of doors. Red doors and a sea of heaving Grey. I saw the phantom portal swing open and three shapes rushed out into the night, laughing. Carlos pulled open the real door and we walked into the empty bar, into a maelstrom of unhealed pain and memory.

The curving question-mark bar and dining area were thronged with ghosts. They packed the space, layer upon layer, moving through each other, coming and going up the stairs at the back, through the door behind us. Laughing, talking, the calling of a dealer from the other room, the TV behind the bar flickering images of ancient shows and forgotten news. Then shouting, the sudden screams of a woman. The ghosts thinned, some going on, oblivious, as a confusion of rob-bery and death played out in front of us through their heedless, vapor-ous bodies.

"What the hell—?"

I backed away from the consuming images in which I'd been lost and felt a padded rail at my back. I'd wandered into the bar without knowing I'd moved. Through the boil of Grey I saw Ian in the gam-bling room a step below, through an arch of lucky-red pillars, the floor still stained with twenty-year-old blood where fourteen people had been shot in the head and left to die.

Carlos grinned at him, shedding his cape. "I want to speak to you, boy."

"Miss Clever Dick and her cop friend," Ian said. "Fuck you."

Carlos laughed and the world shuddered as he started toward Ian.

The sudden reek of rot and the whirling knives and hot light of the phantasm shot down toward Carlos. He batted it aside and continued, grinning, fangs bared, the whirl of his own bleak darkness spreading like ink in water.

Ian jumped back in the face of the impossible, implacable thing bearing down on him.

I brushed off the cat ears and started in, tripping over a spectral corpse that stared with horrified eyes from a spreading pool of silver blood.

The thing that had been Celia dashed me into one of the pillars. I rolled to the floor, feeling the hot flow of phantom gore over me. I pulled the tangle from my pocket, its thorns prickling into my still-sore hand through my glove.

The entity dove again, blazing bloodred: pure fury and hate now. I slid across the dust-thick floor and tumbled to my feet through an oblivious pair of dancing ghosts, swaying together in incongruous romance among the bleeding images of the dead.

I dropped the tangle onto the dancing ghosts, who swirled into sudden stillness—a faded photograph superimposed on the memory of the night three young men robbed and shot fourteen of their neighbors.

I heard Ian scream and started to look, catching a movement of black out of the corner of my eye.

Then the dervish of hate swept down on me again, howling. And froze in the shade of the dancers buried knee-deep in the horror of murdered bodies.

I wavered.

Carlos roared. "Now, Blaine!"

I dove into the entity, into the knives of time and the barbed wire of Ian's fury woven into it. I slipped and twisted my way through the tesseract of what had been Celia, just as I had run through time and space to elude and capture it, feeling blood in the palm of my glove where the thorns of the tangle had ripped my hand. I slid over frozen lakes of memory and crashed deeper into the structure of power and madness, seeking the center, where the control must lie.

Something was muttering, crooning images of terror. "... in the fire, limbs crisped and split ... own living eyes ..."

The entity's tectonic plates of memory shifted, sliding and buckling under me, throwing me against the agony of a shred of Mark's death, hanging in the frozen storm like a drop of crystal. The dancers had stopped but the other ghosts had not and they brushed through the suspended entity, disturbing chimes of memory and pain that rang on my own bones.

"... implacable. They crawl beneath your skin ..."

That voice; part Ian, part Carlos, speaking nightmares. I shook the sound from my ears, staggering back into the depth of the thing I hoped to destroy.

"... dolls of flesh ..."

I buried my hands in the tangle of energy and memory, wrenched at the structure that resisted me, fought as if alive, pulsing in my grip and burning over my nerves. Nausea swamped me as I felt I was tearing some live thing to shreds. I gagged and clutched for support, reeling in the swamp of remembered blood rising from the floor on the tide of unwholesome light. I was lost in the maze of knotted rage that had been Celia, unable to find the core and open it up to be destroyed.

"... drinks your soul and will ..."

Desperate, I clutched at my own thin thread and followed it down into the clenched bud of the monster's core. Coiled tight, the heart of the entity looked like a pulsing spiral-rose of blood and fire. Wincing with fear, I clutched the thing and twisted it backward, unwinding the spiral through a writhing curtain of time.

"... eternal ..." No, not Ian. Carlos, turning Ian's horrors back on him!

Then the core opened and I stared down into the web of human desire that had formed it. Four broken threads, one more frayed almost through, my own a pale golden color against the yellow and blue weave, shot with ashen gray and warped with Pyrrhic red. The red lines pulsed like arteries, feeding on something, swelling toward an overload of corrupted power as something else fed on the brightness of the life that bound the entity together. White flashes of memory seared my eyes and I tried to turn away.

Images and sensations erupted in my mind: a book tumbled from on high and struck my chest; a whirling brooch sliced into my cheek; a wooden slab rammed into my thigh; a shocked instant—

I tried to rip myself out of the fully flowered heart of the thing—out of the boomerang memories of Ian's cruelty pouring from the collective memory of the entity. I struggled in the net of flooding madness.

A tide of specters washed around the room, crashing against the corner where Carlos stood, muttering over Ian. Nightmares and memories, every eternal terror that ever crawled or clawed through the thoughts of men, he poured into the gaping mind of the young man who shuddered and dwindled at his feet.

"What are you doing?" I gasped. "Stop it!"

Carlos turned a vicious face to mine. "Is he worth your life? Look to the charm!"

I shot a glance down and saw below the shape of murder that the tangle was burning to a circle of ash. Only a small fragment of thorn and vine remained. I threw myself back into the construct's core.

My heart racking, trepid, against my ribs, I grabbed for the blazing center of the vile red core, for Ian's control line. My bleeding hand closed on the power line and the agony of the inferno roared up my arm, spreading through my body. A sad sigh of smoke coiled up and the splayed layers of the entity shrieked as they rushed inward.

I bit down, tasting blood, yanking with all my might as the dancers lurched. Time and memory crashed in and I yelled, plummeting backward, shredded by the flying knives of history whirling outward.

The stained floor slammed into my back, ramming my pistol into my kidney, my shoulder making a grinding sound as I hit. Reality swam in the mist of Grey and near-unconsciousness.

Carlos bent over me. "You're not done." He hauled me to my feet, his touch stabbing me with horrors, and set me before a tangled skein of yellow and blue threads that hung pathetically in the air, wafting in an unfelt breeze as the shooting played out again around us. "Finish the job," he added. "Pluck it out."

My left arm hung limp from a misshapen shoulder. With my right hand, I pulled the frayed strand of Celia's tether from around my own head and tore it from me. It felt like some horrible weed was drawn from my flesh, its spreading, spidery roots gone deep into my limbs. I stumbled and shied from another touch of Carlos's hands.

I panted and blinked, finding the last pathetic shred of the entity turning in the air as from a gallows. I stuck my good hand into it, pushed, and it fell to pieces. The shower of yellow and blue threads glittered and vanished.

I sank to my knees, looking toward Ian. He was huddled in the corner against a broken table, staring, cloaked in a strange, black haze. His lips moved, but he didn't see anything normal people would see and the words were a gabble of broken thoughts. I hadn't pulled the plug fast enough to save him from the memories of his own actions, the torments he had inflicted on the helpless filtered through Carlos's necromancy and poured back into his mind like poison. He seemed smaller, burned hollow, and I knew I hadn't imagined that Carlos had somehow drawn the living power of the entity through Ian into himself as he drove him mad.

"You bastard," I muttered. My shoulder and knee were throbbing and I had no more energy to express my fury, revulsion, and despair.

He chuckled, the burn scars on his face fading as I watched. "I am. He was not so very hard to break—his mind already teetered on the edge. I only made sure he would fall into chaos, not into power. It's best."

"When I believe you, I'll let you know," I whispered, swaying. My back blazed pain, my tongue was clumsy in my mouth and I tasted blood from biting it. The world swam in blazing colors and restless silver ghosts.

"Even in victory, you spit like a cat." I felt the rolling disturbance of his amusement. "Formidable creature. Assure yourself this was necessary. It was what had to be for everyone's sake."

There was some noise from outside. Carlos glanced over his shoulder. "Do you wish to leave here?"

"No," I gasped, falling against the wall and sliding down. "The cops—"

"Are coming." He stood and melted into the darkness.

I was alone with the ghosts. The twenty-year-old memory of robbery and murder played again before my eyes. I waited for the police as I watched the shade of the lone survivor of that bloody night crawl from the room.

Solis found only me and Ian.

EPILOGUE

N o one would have been believed and judged competent to stand trial when they raved about ghosts and vampires, sex and death, and women who danced in curtains of blood and fire. During his hearing, Ian's sudden fits of screaming, swearing, and sobbing did nothing to advance a finding for sanity, even though the things he said were true. I would not have called what I had done in the dread light of the entity dancing, however.

Ian had been quiet at first, sitting still and calm beside his lawyer. His demeanor and responses had been almost childlike in simplicity and lack of focus. Then he had burst into profanity and screaming. Guards removed him from the room after the second rage of hysteria, when he had raised his hands to his face, shrieking and gouging at his own eyes. He was committed to Western State Hospital, confessing to Mark's murder over and over in gruesome detail. I knew he'd never be coming out; Carlos had deranged his mind too far for hope of recovery.

While he wasn't sane enough to stand trial after the fact, the summary hearing found Ian sane at the time of Mark's murder. Ian had been a diarist. In the office of the Wah Mee, Solis discovered a notebook in which Ian had written everything he'd thought, felt, and planned. His intended actions through Celia, coldly detailed, were perverse and violent, written in a neat draftsmanly hand, between precise margins.

My name was included in his list of those he'd meant to have Celia "remove," just below Ana's, Ken's, and Cara's. The testifying psychologist believed that Celia was Ian's own disassociated personality and that everything he attributed to Celia was something he had done—or wished to do—himself, deluded that he had some kind of magical powers. I wouldn't have argued with that concept. With his increasing skill, Ian might have been able to do what he'd written. I was glad not to have tested the hypothesis, though.

Solis was never happy with my story of being spotted by Ian and of a phone call that had brought me to the Wah Mee, but I refused to change it and there was nothing he could do. My office was six blocks from Uwajimaya and my claim to have been shopping in the neighborhood was attested by his own observers.

The Lupoldi family accepted the official finding and Amanda Leaman confirmed that it was Ian who'd argued with Mark the Monday before the murder. No mechanism for Mark's death was ever found, since no one but Ian and I accepted the notion of killer ghosts.

The lack of a weapon made the case quite unsatisfactory to Solis, but the rest of the evidence was strong enough to close the file. His colleagues consoled him that his clearance record remained unblotted by the mystery, but he turned a chilling silence on them and further discussion died.

Frankie called to tell me Gartner Tuckman hadn't dodged the grant review or the specter of having unleashed a psychopathic killer, and his credibility fell apart. He was dismissed and a fraud investigation was initiated. Terry was left scrambling to find a new thesis reviewer. I figured he'd do better without Tuck.

Frankie also informed me that Ken and Ana had both changed their address cards and were cohabiting. "I wouldn't call it an engagement," she said, "but they look like they're headed that way." I guessed family objections meant less when life seemed shorter.

Of the Stahlqvists, only the business news had word and that mostly bland. Patricia Railsback and Wayne Hopke dropped from my radar like stones in water. I tried to settle back into normal cases—or as normal as they get when some of the clients start out dead—but grasping the burning lines of energy in dismantling Celia had seared the Grey deeper into me and it was harder than ever to shake it off. Most of the time, I no longer bothered.

The knee and shoulder I'd landed on were injured worse than I'd imagined, and I replaced my morning jog with time at the gym, working them back into shape.

On the Monday before Thanksgiving, with no phone call to warn me, Will Novak came through my office doorway. Tall—almost gangly—with prematurely silver hair glinting from the hall light, he leaned on the doorpost and smiled at me, glimmering pink sparks like I'd seen around Ken and Ana.

"Hi, Harper."

"Hi, yourself, stranger."

"Got any plans for the national holiday?"

"Yeah."

"Oh?"

I nodded. "I thought I'd rent a pile of DVDs and gorge on old black-and-white movies and turkey potpie. Want to join me?"

"Are you coming apart?"

"Yup. Wanna try to stick me back together?" Well, I hoped he could, but I wasn't sure we'd still get pink sparks.

He came in and kissed me and grinned and said, "Think we can find *Suspicion*?"

Cary Grant as a man who might be a psychopathic killer ... My stomach pitched and I felt cold. "I'd rather not," I said. "Maybe we could find something a little lighter."

In quiet moments, guilt, anger, and regret found me and I didn't want to see a film that would remind me of Ian and of what I hadn't stopped Carlos from doing to him. Ian wouldn't kill anyone else, but he lived in endless nightmares. I didn't know that I could have changed that; I only knew that I hadn't.

The Wah Mee massacre really did happen. I discovered it through the HistoryLink.org project online (www.historylink.org/essays/output.cfm?file_id=382) and did some additional research before incorporating the site of the then-forgotten crime into my story. By an unsettling coincidence, I was a week away from submitting the first draft when the story returned to the front page of the local papers due to the parole hearing of one of the men involved. It felt pretty weird to walk down the streets of Chinatown and hear people discuss it, when they had said nothing of it for years.

In doing the research, I found that Seattle's International District is a font of intriguing tales, many of them tragic, bizarre, or touching. The fertile soil of history offers great material for a series like this, and I hope to continue bringing forgotten bits into the light.

I also dug into the history of the Women's Auxiliary Army Corps and the women's Auxiliary Ferrying Squadron, from which eventually came the WASPs (WASP, to be more correct) to generate Celia's backstory. Celia's story is intentionally flawed, but the actual evolution of the WASP and the tales of the women who flew military planes are fascinating and worth a look, and I regret having had to warp them. If you care to look into them, I suggest starting with the US Centennial of Flight Commission's website about women in the military in World War II (www.centennialofflight.gov/essay/Air_Power/Women/AP31.htm) and the Texas Woman's University WASP History website (www.twu.edu/wasp/history.htm).

In concocting this story, I did, of course, spend quite a bit of time looking into the real Philip project, and had a lot of difficulty finding a copy of Owen and Sparrow's book *Conjuring Up Philip*—it's been out of print for quite a while and even used copies can be hard to find. Ben's statements about the experiments are true—amateurs continue to attempt to re-create the experiments, and there is evidence of broadcast and film documentaries being aired in Canada in the 1970s, but the actual recordings seem to have vanished. After reading the book and being in fact rather skeptical myself, I'm not convinced that the experiments were more than hopeful self-delusion, but it makes a wonderful premise and I'm not the only one to think so. Since the book was first published, many other authors and scriptwriters have mined the Philip experiments and their copycats for supernatural thrills.

Being skeptical, I felt it was only reasonable to look at the other side of the issue and include some of the faking techniques. I got some excellent help on this score from Richard Kaufman, professional magician and owner of the Genii forums for magicians, and from James Randi's Web site at randi.org. I also read Randi's book *Flim-Flam* and parts of Harry Houdini's book *A Magician Among the Spirits,* as well as the biographical work *The Secrets of Houdini* by J. C. Cannell.

Further interesting ideas on death came from *Spook* by Mary Roach. I also picked up a ton of interesting info that I wasn't able to include here from Sandra Haarsager's excellent biography of Seattle's lady mayor, *Bertha Knight-Landes of Seattle.*

Not long ago, a reader sent me a note asking why Harper didn't have a cell phone in *Greywalker*—it seemed anachronistic to him, and it is. This got me thinking that there are some odd things about the first book and this current one that I should probably explain.

Greywalker was written (and therefore happens) in 2000, and when it was ready for publication, I chose to leave it as it was rather than update the locations, since so many were important to the way the plot unfolded. Many of the businesses I mentioned went out of business in the years between writing and publication—the original Fenix Underground building that housed the fictional Dominic's fell down in the Mardi Gras earthquake of 2001; the Wizards of the Coast Game Center closed and the building now houses a Tower Records, also on the verge of closure as I write this. Several of the restaurants are no more, and several others had to be fictionalized a little or moved to avoid upsetting owners—most notably the former rumrunner's house on Magnolia bluff. There is no restaurant in the location given in the book, but a similar restaurant does exist on the other side of the canal.

Carlos's shop also exists under a different name, but I figured the owners wouldn't be too pleased to know I'd turned their manager into a vampire necromancer and made their staff totally weird, so small changes had to be made. There is, however, no Radio Freeform, although there are radio towers on top of Queen Anne Hill.

In this book I was able to use existing places most of the time. The parks, monuments, restaurants, and businesses do exist where I said they do, except for the restaurant owned by Phoebe Mason's family—that's based on an actual place called Ida's Jamaican Kitchen that went under in 2002—and Phoebe's bookstore, which is an amalgam of three great used-book stores in the Seattle area. Yes, there really is a troll under the bridge, and Lenin does, indeed, stride into the future of fast food. Pacific Northwest University is entirely fictional.

And because of a question about cell phones, I ended up with the scenes in the downtown Barnes & Noble bookstore—which truly is the cell phone death zone.

So, having warped and twisted and willfully ignored bits of intervening time, I've brought Harper's world back in sync with our own timeline, but the past will continue to play a big part in these books—not just because it's part of the structure, but because I always seem to find something interesting there.

—KR

Greywalker

Harper Blaine is a small-time private investigator trying to earn a living when a low-life savagely assaults her, leaving her for dead. For two minutes, to be precise.

When Harper comes to in the hospital, she begins to feel a bit ... strange. She sees things that can only be described as weird-shapes emerging from a foggy grey mist, snarling teeth, creatures roaring.

But Harper's not crazy. Her 'death' has made her a Greywalker – able to move between our world and the mysterious, cross-over zone where things that go bump in the night exist. And her new gift – or curse – is about to drag her into that world of vampires and ghosts, magic and witches, necromancers and sinister artifacts. Whether she likes it or not.

Sara Paretsky meets *The Sixth Sense* in the first novel in the Harper Blaine *Greywalker* series. A perfect blend of supernatural thriller and hard-boiled P.I., Kat Richardson's debut urban fantasy novel has earned comparisons to Jim Butcher, Tanya Huff and Charlaine Harris.

Praise for Greywalker:

'Nonstop action with an intriguing premise, a great heroine, and enough paranormal complications to keep you on the edge of your seat. Richardson's characters are multidimensional and engaging, and I enjoyed this book all the way through' Charlaine Harris

'a creepy and original addition to the Urban Fantasy landscape' Tanya Huff

'Fast-paced fun, this first novel will captivate fans of *Charmed*, *Buffy* and Charlaine Harris' *Publishers Weekly*

'An appealing debut, *Greywalker* has an opinionated, stubborn, and likable heroine, and a plot that clicks along with nary a hitch' *Romantic Times*